FLAMES OF CHANGE

DANI LOUGHARY

Fox Haven LLC

Book Cover by Gabriella Regina

Map by Brushtoblades

Editing by Ana Hansen

Chapter Header Illustrations by vecteezy.com and canva.com

Author's Note

Flames of Change is the sequel to Embers of Fate. If you haven't read that one, you will need to go back to it first. Contained in this book are the following content warnings. Please be mindful of them, your mental health matters!

- Grief/Anxiety

- Chronic Illness

- Gendered Language/Bigotry (Though the book itself is LGBTQ+ friendly!)

- Adult Language

- Explicit Sexual Scenes, including spanking and restraints.

- Violence/Blood in fight scenes

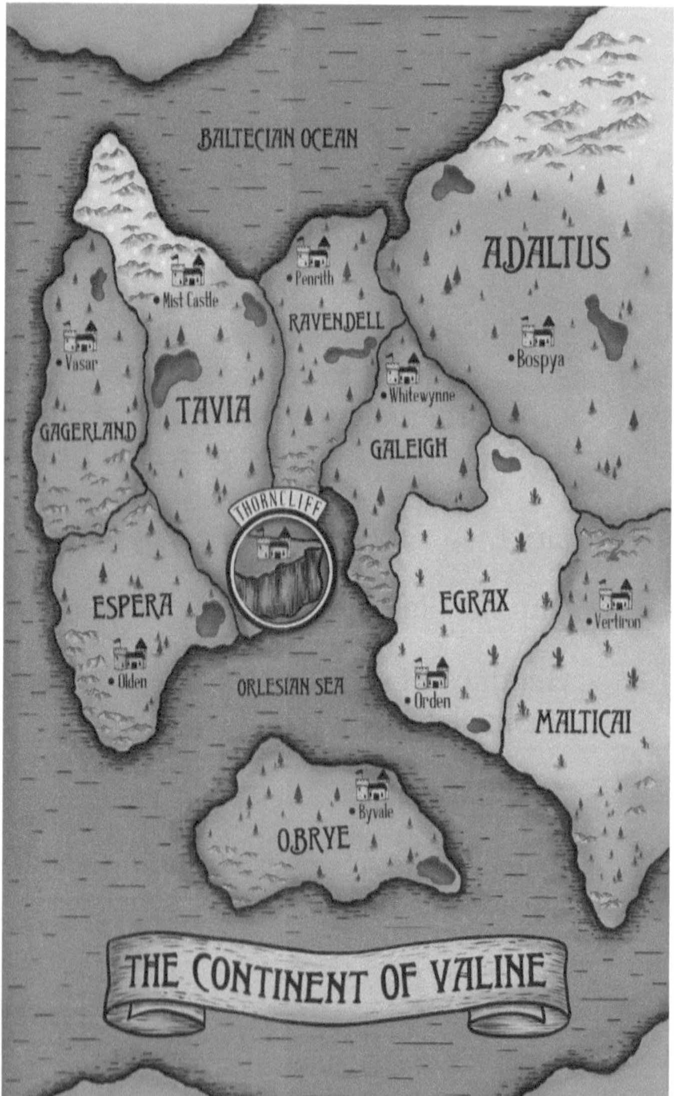

BALTECIAN OCEAN
ADALTUS
Penrith
Mist Castle
RAVENDELL
Bospya
Vasar
Whitewynne
TAVIA
GALEIGH
GAGERLAND
THORNCLIFF
ESPERA
EGRAX
Vertiron
Olden
ORLESIAN SEA
Orden
MALTICAI
Byvale
OBRYE
THE CONTINENT OF VALINE

PRONUNCIATION GUIDE

Tyreal- Teer-ee-al
Hedontas- Huh-don-tis
Andais- Ann-day-is
Anya- Ah-n-ya
Viamar- V-eye-ah-mar
Drakon- Dr-a-ken
Isolde- Eye-soul-day
Samyad- Sah-my-ahd
Damaris- Duh-mar-is
Thalion- Th-al-yon

CHAPTER ONE

Chaos.

There was no other word to describe the scene that greeted Gwen and her friends as they emerged from the catacombs into the chapel courtyard. Everywhere she looked, sisters and servants huddled in clusters, many injured or weeping in fear. What had happened? Seraphina and the others were already in the catacombs when the spell released. Surely that was why they'd regained power. Had the spell that the High Sister cast below somehow rippled up here as well?

Screams erupted from the stables, pulling her attention. The young girl who'd first greeted them at Mist Castle staggered out, slapping at smoking spots on her robes. Sparks emitted from her hands, igniting new ones as quickly as she could get the others out. Behind her, flames licked hungrily at the wooden stalls, black smoke twisting into the sky, the acrid scent of burning hay and wood thick in the air.

"Fire!" Tyreal shouted. "Get to the horses!"

Several sisters sprinted forward, conjuring balls of water from their canteens. Gwen's heart pounded as they pushed through the stable doors. Akasha reared in her stall, neighing in terror as tendrils crawled along the edges of her stall. The smoke nearly choked her, and it was becoming difficult to see. Her magic sprung upwards within her, easier than it ever had before. She knew with certainty that she no longer needed a source to conjure the water. With less than a moment's thought, the water sprung from her hands, dousing the fire.

"Easy, girl," Gwen said, stroking the horse's flank. "It's over. You're safe." Akasha nickered and huffed, bumping her head into Gwen's shoulder.

Across the stables, Anya and the others battled the blaze, their shouts barely cutting through the crackling pops and panicked whinnies. Tyreal fought to keep hold of Braken, but the massive stallion reared back in a frenzy, slamming his hooves against the wooden door with enough force to rattle the entire stall. His muscles bunched, nostrils flared wide, and his dark eyes rolled wildly. The scent of smoke sent him straight into blind terror.

Tyreal approached slowly, hands raised, voice low and steady, "Easy, Braken. Easy, boy."

The horse threw his head back, teeth flashing as he snapped, forcing Tyreal to pull away. Another kick sent splinters flying, and Gwen flinched at the sharp crack of hooves against the wood. If he broke through the stall, there'd be no stopping him from bolting straight into the chaos outside. Not to mention all the people he would hurt along the way.

Gwen's pulse pounded. They needed to get things under control, and quickly.

"Tyreal," she said, reaching for him. He stepped back with her, keeping a wary eye on Braken. The horse was still wild, his powerful body slick with sweat. "Do you think the spell affected you?" she asked, voice tight. "It's changed people here. What if you can use your power now?"

Tyreal grimaced as Braken struck the door again. "I don't even know what my power is," he said. "I can feel something, but I don't know how to use it."

He let out a frustrated breath, shaking his head. "I tried with Alric, and it got me nowhere." His jaw tightened. "If this damned horse would just listen to me—"

Braken reared again, and Tyreal swore under his breath, pushing Gwen further back. The other horses had caught the fear—Akasha neighed sharply, hooves scraping against the stall floor, and the others shifted uneasily. If they lost control of the stable, it wouldn't just be Braken running wild.

Another brutal kick. Another splintering crack.

"Bloody crows," Tyreal snapped. "There's no time to mess around with magic! Mark my words, if I get killed calming this big bastard, I'm dragging him into Ganderly with me." Braken's next rear would have sent him crashing into the door, but Tyreal lunged first, grabbing hold of the horse's bridle. Braken fought him, hooves slamming, but Tyreal held firm, forcing the stallion's head down.

"Enough," he growled.

Gwen feared Braken would strike out, but the sheer, unrelenting wall of Tyreal's stubbornness and authority stopped the horse in his tracks. His sides still heaved, but the panic in his eyes dulled to wary distrust. His ears twitched, no longer pinned flat, and his breath, while ragged, slowed. He didn't relax entirely—wouldn't with the fire so close—but he had stopped trying to break free.

Gwen exhaled sharply. Hesitantly, she stepped closer, brushing her fingers over Braken's sweat-damp muzzle. The stallion exhaled, flaring his nostrils against her palm, his skin twitching beneath her touch. Not calm, but no longer frantic.

Tyreal let go with a muttered curse, rubbing the back of his neck. The tension didn't leave his frame, and Gwen almost swore she caught the faintest flush creeping above his beard. "Sorry about not trying—"

Without thinking, she wrapped her arms around him, pressing a quick kiss to his lips to cut off his words. "Don't apologize. It was wrong of me to ask you to try under that sort of pressure."

He gave her a half smile and stepped back to survey the damage, leaving Gwen to look back out in the courtyard. The immediate danger had passed, but nothing she saw eased her anxiety. The High Sister's spell clearly reached beyond the catacombs—but how far? When Myaessa cast her spell, it wiped out magic across the entire continent of Valine, except for the handful of royal women and their descendants.

Had the High Sister done the opposite?

"We need to get back to Thorncliff immediately. If this spell is causing all of this," she gestured around them, "everywhere, Pip won't be able to handle it alone."

"Looks like he'll have magic too, if it has," Tyreal added, his expression grim. "I'm not sure about mine exactly, but I wasn't the only man affected." He motioned for her to look across the courtyard to where Anya guided Max into shaping rocks into makeshift crutches for two injured women. "I hope for everyone's sake, it was just contained to Mist Castle. Hardly anyone outside these walls even knew magic existed," he said, and then scoffed. "Not that we typically have that sort of luck of late."

Sister Seraphina's commanding voice interrupted them. "Tend to the wounded! If they can walk, send them to the Great Hall!"

The older woman took charge of the courtyard, and it was already far less chaotic. Her steadfast calm cut through the panic, and she organized everyone like a commander on a battlefield. Tyreal appeared to respond to her like one as well, quickly asking, "What injuries are we dealing with, Sister?"

"The explosion in the kitchens caused many burns and broken bones, and one girl is severely injured. We need more healers, but your mother is the closest, and she is three days ride from here." Seraphina motioned for them to follow her towards the Great Hall.

Gwen fell in step beside her. "Tyreal may be able to help with the injured, but we haven't had time to work with any awakened powers. Though it looks like others are getting it under control fairly quickly." Gwen pointed with her chin towards Max and Anya.

Seraphina nodded. "Aye, it seems everyone here has some magic at their disposal, but only the trained sisters can control it. May the Gods favor us, and it is only here at the castle. I cannot imagine what will happen if it is not."

Inside the hall, the air was thick with the scent of smoke and sweat. Injured sisters lay on hastily arranged cots, their groans filling the cavernous space. Gwen kneeled beside one of them, tearing strips from a pile of clean fabric to use for bandages. The simple, repetitive task somewhat steadied her frayed nerves.

Soon, the wounded would be cared for, and the Great Hall would empty. The thought of facing the stain Alric's blood had surely left behind made her nauseous. At least Sister Seraphina had sent someone to collect him and prepare him for his eventual pyre. She didn't know if she could handle looking at his body after everything else that had happened. The weight of his death, the brutal truth about her father's murder, and the High Sister's death piled themselves upon Gwen, each one heavier than the last. She'd have to face it eventually, the yawning chasm of grief waiting to swallow her whole. But not now. Not yet. She couldn't afford to break.

A sudden wave of anxiety slammed into Gwen, making her heart race and her breath hitch in her chest. It didn't feel like it normally did, though. Anxiety was an unwelcome but familiar visitor. She glanced around, trying to make sense of it. There had been tension before, but now it was considerably worse. Everyone seemed on edge, their unease mirroring her own with furrowed brows, wide eyes, and tight lips.

Her gaze fell on Tyreal, kneeling beside the badly burned kitchen worker that Sister Seraphina had mentioned. The woman's eyes locked onto Gwen's, wide and glassy, more panicked now than pained. As if it wasn't bad enough that the poor woman was injured.

Gwen crossed the room quickly and placed a hand on Tyreal's shoulder. "Are you alright? I feel... strange. Like everything is closing in. I think everyone else is feeling it too."

"I'm trying to help her, heal her like I did with Max, but it isn't working. I don't know what the hell I am doing." He shoved his hand through his hair, breathing sharply through his nose.

Realization swept over her. "I think you're projecting," she said softly. "Your feelings are spilling out and overwhelming everyone."

"Well, that's perfect. Got any idea how to stop it?" he snapped.

Gwen didn't flinch at his sharp tone, though a flicker of her own temper rose before she smothered it. She knew him too well—helplessness wasn't a feeling he often encountered, and he always handled it poorly. "Let me help you," she said, her voice calm despite the anxious wave crashing over her. Years of grappling with that same emotion had honed her ability to manage it, though she'd never seen it as a gift until now. She tightened her grip on his shoulder. "Focus on me. Not her pain, not your doubt. Just me."

Tyreal clenched his jaw, his eyes darting from Gwen to the wounded woman. Her breathing quickened, her fingers trembling as they grasped for something, anything, to hold on to. Gwen reached out, taking the woman's uninjured hand, keeping her voice steady. "It's alright. You're safe."

Gwen captured Tyreal's attention, forcing him to look at her. She inhaled slowly, holding his gaze. "Breathe with me. Block everything else out."

He hesitated, letting out a shaky breath before closing his eyes. Gwen followed his lead, slowing her breathing to steady him. Slowly, the tension in the room eased. The woman's frantic gasps evened out, her breaths shallow but steady. The air felt less heavy, the panic fading.

Tyreal's eyes snapped open, his expression hardening. "Better?" he asked, his voice still rough around the edges.

"Better," Gwen confirmed, though a lingering tightness in her chest remained. "When we have more time, I'll teach you how to shield properly and keep your power under control."

Tyreal rubbed at his temple. His eyes darted to the woman lying before them, much of her skin blistered and charred from the flames. Her shallow breaths rasped in her throat, each one looking more and more painful.

"I don't know if I can help you," Tyreal said, kneeling again beside the burned woman. "I don't know if this power works like that. I'm so sorry."

Gwen continued holding the woman's hand as she tried to give Tyreal an encouraging smile. "You healed Max, remember? You didn't know how to help him then either, but you still did it."

Tyreal's brow furrowed. "That was different. I didn't even realize what I was doing with Max. I just... I just wished I could help, and suddenly my hands were glowing." Uncertainty laced his voice, desperate to be of service. "This feels different."

"You don't have to know how," Gwen replied softly. "If Lila is right, it's more about the intention. You *wanted* to help Max, and you did. You want to help her, so just focus on that. The rest will follow."

Tyreal closed his eyes and hovered his hands over the woman's burns. He exhaled slowly, obviously trying to push away his doubt. Gwen watched closely as a faint golden light shimmered from his palms—the same light she had seen when he healed Max.

Time slowed, as if she could see every moment slipping through the hourglass.

Then the glow intensified, enveloping the woman's ravaged skin. Her breaths deepened, steadied, and the blackened flesh paled beneath Tyreal's hands, transforming from seared tissue to pink, healing scars. It wasn't perfect, but it was enough.

Tyreal's eyes fluttered open as the golden light faded from his hands. He stared at the woman, his expression caught between disbelief and exhaustion. "It worked?" he asked, his voice barely above a whisper.

"Yes," Gwen said, a smile tugging at her lips. "Just like before, with Max. You have the ability—you just need to trust it."

Tyreal stood, gripping the hilt of his sword in a way that was so familiar that it pulled at something in Gwen's chest. "This is all a damned mess." His voice dropped. "Lovell, the High Sister, Alric, and now magic." He shook his head. Now that the immediate danger was past, exhaustion was clearly catching up to him, and admittedly, Gwen could feel it too.

Max and Anya approached, and Max visibly swallowed. "I don't think I can go back up to that room. I want to do Alric's funeral pyre as soon as we can, and then I very much want to start the journey back. I need to be home." He exchanged a heavy glance with Gwen, the weight of everything they'd lost and everything they still had to face pressing in on them. She gave him a sad smile.

"We all need to get back to our homes," Gwen said quietly. "I'm worried magic may not only be in Mist Castle." The more she thought about it, the less likely it seemed. Myaessa's spell hadn't been, so neither would its reversal.

Anya sucked in a sharp breath, her bright blue eyes widening. Her hands curled into fists in her skirts, and she bit her bottom lip with her teeth. "I suppose it makes sense, but surely the Gods wouldn't be so cruel?"

Tyreal shook his head. "The Gods had nothing to do with this," his said, voice rough and edged with fury. "This was one madwoman and a prince so desperate for power that he didn't care what it cost." The stormy gray of his eyes looked darker, as a hardness settled over his features that Gwen rarely saw. "Diplomacy is over. When I find Lovell, my sword will remind him of what desperation truly feels like."

Gwen nodded, though it made her stomach churn to think of what lay ahead. "I agree, but that too must wait. If magic has spread, we have to deal with the immediate crisis."

Anya shuddered, looking between them. "Can you imagine what..." Her words dried up mid-sentence, and she pressed her fingertips against her lips.

Gwen didn't need to imagine it. The destruction, the panic, the towns falling apart as people grappled with this new reality. It would only take one mistake—a misplaced spell, a burst of uncontrolled power—to tear lives apart. The more she thought about it, the more urgently she felt their need to return to Thorncliff.

"We need to get home," Max said, cutting through the silence. "Now."

Gwen nodded, but before she could respond, another voice broke through the tension.

"I might know a way to get you there faster." Lila stepped forward, her lips curving into a faint smile. "There's something in the woods you should see."

CHAPTER TWO

The forested slopes of the mountains stretched wide before them, sunlight filtering through the canopy of towering pines. The air was so crisp and cold that it almost burned in Gwen's lungs. The breeze carried the earthy scent of pine needles and damp soil. Shafts of light illuminated patches of moss and fallen leaves on the forest floor.

Lila stepped confidently through the undergrowth, boots crunching the leaves along the way, obviously familiar with the path through the rugged terrain. Gwen followed closely behind, confusion warring with anticipation inside her. What could her cousin possibly have to show her out here in the woods that could help them get home?

"We're almost there," Lila said, looking over her shoulder at the group. "It's just past this ridge."

The incline grew steeper, the forest growing denser as they ascended. Branches tangled overhead, casting dappled shadows that shifted with the breeze. When they finally reached the crest, the woods gave way to a sunlit clearing nestled against the rugged mountainside. Gwen came to a halt. Though the vista was lovely, it was the heart of the clearing that stole her breath.

In the clearing stood a circle of towering stones, their weathered surfaces etched with carvings. They glowed faintly even in the daylight, and as she moved closer, she realized the etchings were runes. The air near the stones felt different, charged with some kind of energy that made the hairs on Gwen's arms rise.

"What is this place?" Gwen mustered enough air to speak.

"Well, based upon my research, it's a portal," Lila replied, stepping near the stones, but not inside the circle. "I've been coming here to think for years. The records say Myaessa stepped through one near Thorncliff to arrive here, where she built Mist Castle."

Tyreal stepped closer, weaving a hand around Gwen's arm. She glanced at him in annoyance, well aware that he was keeping her from stepping into the circle. His face was tight with concern. "I've seen stones like these before," he said, his voice low. "There is a set near the spring and the fairydew tree, though it's deep in the woods, almost hidden by moss. And I've seen others in my travels, scattered across Tavia. Always in the woods, and they've always given me the creeps. It's almost like they are... watching." He shuddered and coughed to cover it up.

"I'm surprised we've never heard of them. Surely people have stories about them." Anya hovered her fingers over the runes on the stone closest to her. She leaned forward to inspect them, but only with the top half of her body, as if reluctant to enter the circle.

"The common folk did. The stories just might not have ever made their way up to the royals." Tyreal smiled, but it didn't reach his eyes. He shifted uncomfortably, his grip nearly painfully tight on Gwen's arm. "I've heard it tell that creatures made them before the royal families came, and they've been forgotten by time."

He eyed the stones, tugging on Gwen to pull her a step away from them. "And I've heard parents use them to warn children from wandering off into the woods. They said the stones were cursed, and anyone who touched them would disappear forever."

Gwen tried to step forward, tugging against Tyreal's grasp and cutting her eyes at him sharply. She felt drawn to the faint hum of magic she could hear emanating from the stones.

"Don't give me that look. What kind of High Captain would I be if I let you just wander into that?" He cocked an eyebrow at her before turning to look at Lila. "I'm assuming you think this one works again?"

"I believe there's a chance. That's why I brought you all up here to look at them. I wanted to see if something was different, and now I know. I've been here a million times, and I've never felt what I do now." Lila looked at Gwen. "But if I'm right, I imagine you're feeling a pull towards them, aren't you? I think these portals are keyed specifically to the Thorncrest line."

Gwen nodded. Tyreal's frown deepened at her response. "Why would you think that?" he asked, posture tense. The hand not gripping Gwen's arm moved to rest on his sword hilt.

"The archives suggest it," Lila explained. "I think Myaessa built these portals during the war. They only exist in Tavia, as far as I can tell. If they could be used by anyone, they'd have been more of a threat than an asset. Keying them to the Thorncrest bloodline would have ensured control."

"She would have been a terrible leader if she hadn't," Tyreal said dryly. He didn't sound convinced.

Gwen frowned, knowing he was going to dig in his heels. She understood the risks, but she wanted to move closer to the stones to inspect them. The urge to touch them was now nigh overwhelming. She shrugged off his hand and tugged away from him.

He cast her a warning look. His lips pressed into a tight, straight line and he crossed his arms across his chest before he continued. "What if you're wrong, though? What if anyone can use them?" It was obvious he was already going through a million different worst-case scenarios in his mind and developing defense strategies against them.

Lila's confidence wavered for the first time. "I... I can't be certain. The records are incomplete."

Tyreal's dark gaze moved across the towering stones. "These things are a security nightmare. If anyone else figures out how to activate them, they could move entire armies."

Anya cocked her head at him. "So we're just supposed to take the long way home and leave everyone to deal with this on their own for nearly a moon? Not even try? Don't be ridiculous."

"I'm saying we don't know enough," Tyreal shot back. "Do you expect me to just let Gwen step through blindly into something that might not even lead to Thorncliff?"

Gwen turned to face him, hands on her hips. "Tyreal, I'm the queen. I can't stay here while my kingdom unravels."

His jaw clenched, frustration flashing in his eyes. "And what if I can't follow you? If these portals are tied to Thorncrests, I might not be able to go through. You'd be alone for nearly a month while I ride back, with Lovell already on his way to Tavia. Absolutely not. This isn't happening."

"My place is with my people," Gwen said softly, holding his furious gaze. She understood what he was feeling, but she didn't see a choice.

"And my place is at your side, protecting you!" Tyreal growled angrily. "How am I supposed to do that when you're jumping through magical portals that could lead anywhere?"

Gwen's hands clenched into fists as she fought to contain the rising heat of her anger. Pip needed her. Her people needed her. Tyreal's obsessive need to shield her from every danger felt in that moment more like an obstacle—exactly what she didn't need right now.

Her jaw tightened as they stared each other down. The tension crackled between them. She thought briefly about what Cook had said about their stubbornness before they'd left Thorncliff. This was the worst kind of argument, one where neither of them were wrong. He was correct about the danger. She was correct about needing to return home.

Max stepped forward, resting his hands on both of their shoulders. "Perhaps there is a third option," he said calmly.

"What do you mean?" Tyreal asked sharply.

"Test it first," Max said simply. "If Gwen can use the portal, she can return just as quickly. That way, we know where we stand."

"Or," Tyreal snapped, his voice rough, "I test it first. If these portals are keyed to the Thorncrests, I need to know that before Gwen steps through. I'll go first."

Gwen opened her mouth to argue, but Tyreal was already moving into the circle. His hand hovered over the runes, their faint glow casting an eerie light across his features. He turned back to face her, his expression still taut and more than a little angry. "If this is a danger to anyone, better it falls on me than on you."

Anxiety coiled tight in her chest, her breath hitching. His earlier fear made more sense now. If he stepped through, anything could happen. Her voice wavered slightly as she asked, "And if it doesn't respond to you?"

Tyreal's jaw tightened, his gaze lingering on her for a heartbeat too long. The muscle in his jaw ticked, his lips pressing into a thin line as though he held back a storm of words. His hand flexed at his side, tension rolling from him. When he finally spoke, his voice was low, clipped, each word laced with reluctant resignation. "Then you will try."

The group fell silent as Tyreal pressed his palm against one of the stones. For an instant, the carvings flared with light, the hum of magic thrumming faintly in the air. Then, just as quickly, the glow dimmed, the energy dissipating as though rejecting him entirely.

Tyreal stepped back, his frown deepening. "Damn it," he muttered, shaking his head. "It won't work for me."

"Then we stop wasting time," she said, brushing past him. "It's my turn."

She laid her palm flat on the weathered stone. The runes flared brilliantly, their glow spilling across the clearing like sunlight breaking through a storm. The hum returned, a deep resonance that thrummed through her chest and down to her fingertips. She hoped this worked, even if it meant she would *never* hear the end of Tyreal's lectures. With a deep breath, she closed her eyes and thought of Thorncliff, and of Pip.

The pull of the stones was all-consuming. Gwen's vision blurred as the world around her dissolved into a kaleidoscope of color and sound. She was unraveled and remade all at once, her body no longer tethered to the earth. The air pressed against her, heavy, as if trying to mold her into something new.

Then, the world snapped back into place with a dizzying jolt as Gwen stumbled on soft grass. Her knees buckled, and she caught herself with trembling hands, her breath coming in shallow, uneven gasps. The air of Thorncliff's woods filled her lungs, carrying the familiar scents of home—earthy pine, damp moss, and the faint tang of a sea breeze in the distance. The spring flowed near her, and she could just make out the purple leaves of her fairydew tree.

She wanted to move. Every fiber of her being screamed for her to run to the castle, to see Pip, to make sure her brother was safe. But as she pushed herself upright, the world swayed, and a wave of exhaustion slammed into her. The portal's magic had drained her, leaving her muscles weak and her limbs sluggish. She wouldn't make it on foot, not in this state. And more than that, she had to test the portal with Tyreal. He was right. She couldn't risk facing Lovell without him, not if there was another option.

She ground her teeth and forced herself to focus. She was queen—she didn't have the luxury of acting on impulse. Gathering the last reserves of her strength, she closed her eyes and thought of the clearing, Tyreal's stormy eyes, and Anya's laugh.

The journey back was harder. The pull of the portal was stronger, more painful. She wanted to scream, but she had no control over her body to do so. By the time she stumbled back into the clearing, her body felt like lead, and her vision blurred at the edges.

"Gwen!" Tyreal's voice rang out as she collapsed to her knees. Strong arms wrapped around her before she hit the ground, pulling her close. His worry was palpable as he cradled her against his chest. "Are you hurt? What happened?"

"I'm fine," she mumbled. Words felt nearly impossible. "The portal works. It takes me to

Thorncliff, but I can't... I can't test if you can come through. Not now."

Tyreal lifted her effortlessly, as if she weighed nothing. She thought he might lecture her about the risk she had just taken, but he simply said, "We'll try again tomorrow."

They began the trek back to Mist Castle, Tyreal cradling her in his arms. The steady rhythm of his steps was soothing, and Gwen let her head rest on his shoulder, allowing the exhaustion to pull her under. But despite her fatigue, her mind refused to quiet.

Tyreal's voice broke through her spiraling thoughts, quiet but firm. He stroked her hair tenderly. "I can *feel* you overthinking," he said. "Rest, sweet girl. We'll face it all together."

CHAPTER THREE

B reakfast was a subdued affair. The events of the previous day hung over them all, chilling the air despite the fire crackling in the hearth. Gwen pushed her food around her plate, her appetite nowhere to be found. If it had been up to her, they would have skipped the meal entirely. There was too much to do, and the urgency made her restless, tapping her foot rapidly under the table.

But Tyreal had insisted. "You still look pale." His tone had left no room for argument. "You won't be of any use to anyone if you collapse again."

He was annoyingly correct. The exhaustion from the portal's magic lingered, making her body feel heavier than normal. So, she dutiful-ly chewed the bread and sipped her tea, tast-ing none of it, while her mind raced ahead. The need to get back to Thorncliff, and to Pip, pricked under her skin, sharp as needles. She couldn't stop thinking about him. Did he have powers? Was he terribly afraid? What if he was hurt?

However, the Sisters of the Mist were her people too. They were frightened. And even if they wouldn't admit it aloud, she saw it in their faces—the High Sister's death and those of her cronies had created a power vacuum. More than half of the council was gone, and the remaining sisters were no longer certain of their place in the world, their purpose.

After breakfast, Gwen held a brief meeting with Sister Seraphina. The Chambers of Coun-cils felt like a bigger room now, without the High Sister's commanding presence.

"I'll do what I can," Seraphina said, when Gwen asked her to take over as temporary High Sister. "But I'm uncertain the other sisters will accept me."

"They will," Gwen said firmly. "Mostly because you have kept the High Sister from destroying everything we were supposed to stand for. I know the royal families don't interfere with the Sisters normally, but this is not a normal cir-cumstance. For now, since Mist Castle is in my land, I am giving an order."

Seraphina nodded, but there was an obvious strain on her normally open, cheerful face. It wasn't fair to leave all this on her. None of it was fair.

As was so often the case since she'd become queen, Gwen had no choice. She needed to return to Thorncliff, and if magic had indeed spread, the Sisters would be needed to help people understand and control their powers. Someone had to remain at Mist Castle in the meantime to lead them while Gwen consulted with the other royal families.

"The Sisters are not a Tavian institution," Gwen admitted, more to herself than to Seraphina. "I can't decree what their future should be without consulting the other royals. But..." She paused, weighing her words. The Sisters could not continue without oversight, not after what had happened. Their unchecked power had led to corruption, and while Gwen wanted to believe that Seraphina would not fall into the same trap, the stakes were too high to leave it to chance. "The time of the Sisters' independence has passed. The world is changing. We all must change too."

Seraphina's face softened. "Quite right, Your Majesty. I'm not sure that I'm the one to help lead them through the change, but I trust your judgement."

Gwen smiled at Seraphina and gave her hand a gentle squeeze. "We will find a way forward," she said with a confidence she hoped sounded convincing.

Down in the stables, she found Tyreal, Max, and Anya waiting. Tyreal double-checked the straps on the horses, his shoulders tense. Max stood nearby, his expression distant as he cradled Alric's sword in his hands. Anya hovered just behind him, her gaze flitting between Max and the small cart holding Alric's shrouded body.

Gwen hesitated a moment before stepping fully into the space, her presence drawing all their attention. She knew she couldn't avoid it, and hated herself on some level for feeling as she did, but it was so hard to be near them when their grief was so palpable. She hadn't even processed her father's death, and now she knew he'd been murdered. It all threatened to be too much.

"We're ready." Tyreal's eyes raked over her frame, scrutinizing her in a way that had nothing to do with attraction. She knew he was looking for any sign that she couldn't handle this, an excuse to call the whole thing off.

He had reluctantly admitted the night before that he knew she was right. He said that magic still made him terribly uneasy. He couldn't make plans around it. It was simply too unpredictable.

He must not have found an excuse, because he turned away from her with a sigh. She glanced at Max, who had set the sword aside and now anxiously checked the cloth over Alric's form, making sure it was tightly tucked around him. "Are you certain about this?" she asked gently, though she already knew the answer.

Max's shoulders straightened, and he met her gaze with tear-filled eyes. Dark circles stained the skin beneath them like bruises. Guilt from her earlier hesitation washed over her. She wasn't the only one reaching a breaking point. Max had faced his own near death, being ill, and now this? Everyone had their limits.

"Alric loved the sea," he said, his voice thick with emotion. Her friend struggled to continue, and Gwen stayed silent, letting him take whatever time he needed to find the words. "He would hate for his ashes to be left here, in the cold mountains. He deserves to rest where the waves can carry him."

Gwen's chest tightened. She understood the need to honor the dead. It would have been unthinkable to have her father's pyre anywhere other than by the sea at Thorncliff. However, she wasn't entirely sure the portal would allow all of them through. She'd barely made it through the second time, and she'd been alone. Yet, how could she ignore her friend's pain? If it was within her power to give him this, she would. She chewed at her bottom lip, but finally gave a gentle nod.

"We'll try," she said softly. "I don't know if the portal will handle the strain. If I can handle the strain. It took so much out of me last time." She glanced at Tyreal, whose lips pressed into a thin line. She almost hated to admit it out loud, not wanting to give him his excuse. He said nothing, his face an unreadable mask.

"All we can do is try," Anya interjected hopefully. "Maybe with all of us having magic, the strain will be shared by all of us as well. You are merely the key to unlocking the portal. It could be easier with more people." She grabbed Max's hand. "If it doesn't work, though, we'll head back to Tyreal's mother's and hold his pyre there. We can take his ashes with us if we must, or at least scatter them at that beautiful pond."

The corner of Gwen's mouth tipped up into a sad smile, grateful as always for her best friend's unwavering optimism. "I think Akasha should pull the cart. We have the best chance of bringing Alric through if he is attached to me in some way," Gwen said quietly to Tyreal. He gave a sharp nod and gripped the long wooden shafts, guiding them carefully along Akasha's flanks. He aligned the shafts with the harness traces attached to her breastplate, securing the straps that dangled from the leather loops on either side of her collar. Akasha gave a soft nicker and lifted her head high, as if she understood the importance of what she was being asked to do.

The sharp, discordant cawing of birds filled the air. Gwen shielded her eyes from the bright sun with her hand. A large murder of messenger crows swooped down into the courtyard and stables, the rhythmic beating of their wings filling the air. They landed haphazardly—on rooftops, railings, and even the edges of the cart, fluttering and jostling for space. Overhead, more crows spiraled down from the sky, their numbers darkening the clouds as they veered toward the rookery.

The noise was nearly deafening, and so many birds suddenly landing made the horses snort and pull against their reins. Gwen stepped closer to Akasha, running a hand down her mane and whispering soothing words to her. Max and Anya both stood open-mouthed, staring at the crows.

"Well, that's unsettling," Tyreal muttered.

Three crows hopped toward Gwen, their sleek black feathers glinting as each waited for her to whistle and identify herself. Five birds did the same for Tyreal, cawing loudly at him, as though the weight of the messages they carried demanded urgency. More birds approached Anya and Max. The rest of the flock scattered, flapping noisily as they sought their intended recipients elsewhere in the castle.

Gwen's stomach clenched, an icy knot forming as dread coursed through her. She didn't need to open the scrolls tied to the crows' legs to know what they almost certainly said. Magic had indeed spread past Mist Castle, and Valine was descending into chaos. She closed her eyes, gathering her strength for what was to come before whistling and retrieving the messages.

The birds responded instantly, hopping closer to her and cawing back three times. She knelt, her fingers trembling slightly as she untied the first message. It was from Andais and straight to the point: *You need to return.* No explanation, no details. The unspoken words carried all the weight they needed to.

The second scroll bore Cora's mark, and Gwen felt her pulse quicken as she unraveled it. Cora's handwriting was usually elegant, but now it was hurried and uneven. *Unexplainable happenings in Hanover. Tensha had to intervene to stop a riot. Need to speak with you.*

Then came the last scroll, smaller and more hastily tied than the others. As soon as Gwen saw the scrawl of a child on the parchment, her heart sank. Pip. His message was painfully short, but it hit her like a physical blow. *I need help. Please come home.*

The parchment shook in her hands as she read it again, as though repeating the words might make them easier to bear. But they didn't. She pressed the note to her chest, willing herself to stay calm even as the ache in her chest spread. She could almost see Pip's frightened face, and the thought made her breath catch.

It didn't appear that the messages anyone else got were any better. Everyone looked upset by the contents. "We need to leave. Now," Gwen commanded, leaving no room for any more concerns or lectures. Tyreal nodded in eager agreement, and she thought that somehow made everything worse.

Before long, the stones loomed before them, stark against the gray sky. Akasha shifted beneath Gwen, ears flicking back and forth as they got closer. Gwen tightened her grip on the reins, murmuring softly to Akasha, though she wasn't sure if she was reassuring the horse or herself.

The others weren't faring much better. Braken stamped his hooves and tossed his head beneath Tyreal, clearly displeased by the strange energy radiating from the stones. Anya's pale gray gelding danced sideways. Even Max, who always seemed so at ease on horseback, struggled to keep his bay stallion in check as the animal snorted and resisted moving closer to the circle.

"Are you sure this is going to work?" Max asked, his voice tight as he glanced between the stones and Gwen. He gripped the reins, his knuckles pale, as he fought to keep control of his mount.

"No," Gwen admitted, because lying felt pointless. "But we don't have another option."

She urged Akasha forward, the mare's hooves crunching over frostbitten grass as they approached the circle. "Come on, girl," Gwen whispered, leaning forward to stroke Akasha's neck. She pulled Akasha to a stop at the center of the circle and dismounted. Her heart pounded as she stood there, her mind racing. There weren't exactly instructions on how to activate the portal for a group. What if it didn't work? What if it still only let her through? Or worse, what if it tore her apart for trying?

She closed her eyes, taking a deep breath to steady herself. The cold air stung her throat as she pushed back the knot of anxiety in her chest, reaching deep within to find the well that contained her magic. What previously had seemed so familiar, now held an unknown depth like the ocean. It was so much more than the faint embers she had known all her life. It surged beneath her skin, wild and untamed, and a new fear unlocked. Could she control her magic now? *Please, Myaessa,* she thought, *if you can hear me, guide me. I don't know how to do this, but I need to.*

Gwen reached out and laid her hand on a stone. The runes pulsed, faint at first, then brighter as she focused. A low vibration rippled through the ground, and the horses grew even more agitated. Akasha stamped and whinnied, the sound sharp and frightened. Behind her, Tyreal cursed under his breath as Braken reared, and Anya struggled to keep her gelding from bolting.

The air inside the circle shimmered, the energy building like a gathering storm. The runes glowed brighter, and the low vibration grew into a hum, resonating deep in Gwen's chest. She closed her eyes, focusing all her energy on holding the magic steady, willing it to work. A portal opened in the middle of the circle, blues and silver shimmering lights swirling into each other.

"Now or never," she called, the words barely audible over the rising hum of the portal. "Quickly!" She threw her leg over Akasha's saddle, settling herself and gripping her reins.

Anya eased forward, but then fell back. "I think we should all go together. See if we can share the load," she said, the colors of the swirling portal casting strange lights across her face.

Max hesitated, his gaze flicking to Alric's body on the cart. "If it doesn't work—"

"It will," Gwen interrupted. "Let's go! Everyone think of Thorncliff as we go through."

Max nodded and moved forward to line his stallion up with Anya's gelding, reaching out to hold her hand, as Tyreal and Gwen also moved into place.

Tyreal glanced quickly at Gwen before straightening on his saddle. "On my count! We go in on three!" he proclaimed loudly. She was proud of him in that moment, the way he led even when she knew his fear must be practically eating him alive.

"One!" Tyreal counted, shouting over the sound of the portal.

Gwen's heart pounded as she felt the portal pulling at them, a magnetic force tugging her toward the swirling light.

"Two!" The hum of the portal grew sharper, the colors swirling faster, frenzied.

"Three!" Tyreal shouted, spurring Braken forward as the others followed in unison.

The world seemed to tilt as they plunged into the portal, the light swallowing them whole. Gwen clenched the reins tightly, her knuckles white, as Akasha surged forward beneath her. The world around her blurred into a swirl of color and sound, though the sensation wasn't as painful as before. Instead of feeling like she was being unraveled and remade, the magic seemed steadier, as though the others were indeed helping to carry the weight of the journey.

Landing on the grass back home was no less disorienting. Akasha's hooves hit the ground with a heavy *thud*, and the mare neighed loudly, breaking into a fast gallop to distance herself from the portal. The cart behind them jolted and bounced wildly, threatening to spill Alric's body.

"Akasha! Easy!" Gwen shouted, pulling sharply on the reins to steady the panicked horse. With a few firm tugs, she brought the mare down to a trot, her breath coming in quick puffs of white mist in the cool air. She cast a glance over her party, scanning each of them to ensure they were accounted for and unharmed. Tyreal, Max, Anya, and even the cart carrying Alric's body all seemed intact, though their mounts were still restless.

Satisfied, Gwen clicked her heels gently, urging Akasha forward. The group fell in line behind her, moving through the familiar woods where the dense canopy above shimmered in hues of deep green, tinged with the darker colors of autumn. The path twisted and wound toward her spring and the fairydew tree she always sought refuge under.

"Gwennie. Look," Anya said softly, her head tilted upward as she stared at something off ahead. A look of wonder had settled on her friend's face, her mouth falling open.

Gwen followed Anya's gaze to the tree, and her heart skipped. The fairydew leaves, usually a rich, velvety purple, were alive with motion. Hundreds of golden lights shimmered and danced amongst the branches. Each moved independently, some even looking like they were chasing after the others. One would suddenly veer off in a different direction, like children playing tag. Their glow illuminated the bark with a warm, ethereal light.

Gwen slowed Akasha to a stop, almost scared to make a sound for fear of ending what was happening in the tree. The entire party did the same, even the horses seeming to barely breathe. Silence settled around them, save for the soft rustling of leaves in the breeze. And something else, something faint but high-pitched and melodic, like the chime of distant bells. Gwen strained to listen.

"What do you think it means?" Tyreal asked from beside her.

"I don't know," Gwen admitted, her voice hushed. She couldn't tear her eyes away from the golden lights. "But it's... beautiful." For one moment, she could forget everything pressing in on her and just sit in the wonder of watching something magical.

Too soon, other sounds broke the stillness, and the lights froze and dimmed. Gwen had a feeling that they still remained in the tree, and she couldn't shake the feeling that hundreds of eyes were suddenly on her.

She sighed sadly and clicked her tongue to get them moving again. Someday she would have time to investigate whatever was in the tree. Today was not that day, though. Thorncliff loomed in the distance, and she needed to get home.

CHAPTER FOUR

"The queen approaches! Open the gates!"

The cry echoed from the towers along the outer wall.

The gates creaked open to a village in turmoil, as bad as the scene they had entered when they emerged from the catacombs the day before. Had it really only been a day?

Crowds of people filled the cobblestone streets, voices raised. Vendors' carts lay overturned, their wares scattered and trampled. Tavian guards were attempting to maintain order, their shields raised as they circled a large wagon near the village square. The guards' formation was tight, but it was clear they were struggling. The panicked crowd pressed inward, shouting angrily and jostling to get closer.

Tyreal's heart sank. This was exactly what he had feared. He gave a sharp, high-pitched whistle that cut through the noise like a blade. Heads snapped toward them, and the crowd slowly settled, but only to a point. One small spark would catch the group ablaze again.

Tyreal pressed himself and Braken closer to Gwen and Akasha, his hands tightening on the reins as he surveyed the restless mob. The need to protect her was visceral, even if he knew she could handle herself just fine with her magic. Old habits died hard.

A man near the wagon stepped forward, face bright red and puckered in anger. "Your Majesty! High Captain!" he called. "They're cursed—dangerous! They're going to burn us all down!"

Gwen dismounted smoothly, her boots hitting the cobblestones with a soft *thud*. Tyreal repressed the urge to sigh and possibly strangle her. She just had to barrel into danger. Couldn't just stay on her horse, where she could easily make an exit if she needed to. Oh no, not his Gwen. Sometimes he was convinced the gods had made him fall in love with her specifically to drive him insane. He dismounted as well, standing close to her.

She faced the angry man, posture relaxed. Tyreal knew she was trying to force the man to mirror her. He just wasn't sure if it would work.

"Who are you speaking of?" she asked.

The man gestured wildly toward the wagon. "Them! The ones who've been touched by this... this curse. Look what they've done!" He pointed to a nearby wall, where black scorch marks marred the stone. "Fires, tiny storms that flooded the streets—people have been hurt! They shouldn't be here. They shouldn't be anywhere near us."

Murmurs of agreement rippled through the crowd, and several villagers nodded emphatically. Gwen raised a hand, silencing the crowd. "I understand your fear," she said, her voice carrying over the square. "However, it isn't a curse. I have returned from Mist Castle, and this is happening all over Tavia. Something we thought was lost to history has returned. Magic has manifested in anyone who has any drop of royal blood in them."

A ripple of unease moved through the crowd, punctuated by sharp whispers. "Magic?" a man closest to the guards and the wagon scoffed. "Magic isn't real."

Gwen's eyes narrowed and her head cocked slightly. Her gaze was icy and unyielding, and Tyreal braced himself.

"Do you have a better explanation for any of what has occurred? Or perhaps, this?" With a twirl of her hand, she conjured a fireball and made it dance over her fingers.

A vein in Tyreal's temple throbbed. If they made it into the castle, he was going to put her over his knee and lecture her for an hour about rash decisions.

The crowd gasped loudly, a collective intake of breath. Some stumbled back, clutching each other as their wide eyes fixated on Gwen. A few muttered prayers to the Gods. She let the flames dissipate from her hands and raised them slowly, palms open. "I know you are all afraid," she began. "And I know this is all very confusing. But these people are your neighbors and friends. They are not suddenly monsters. We are Tavians. We are better than this."

Her words were met with skeptical stares. "They merely need to learn how to control their powers," she continued, her voice growing louder and more firm to stress her point. "I am working with the Sisters of the Mist to create a plan, one that will help those who have been affected and ensure the safety of all the people of Tavia and Valine."

A voice from the back of the crowd shouted, "And if they can't control it? People could be hurt! Or killed!"

Gwen's jaw tightened, and Tyreal recognized her trying to stay calm and not lash out. She still had a pinched look of exhaustion around the corners of her eyes, and he knew she was desperate to get to Pip. "You have my word," she said resolutely. "We will figure this out, and you will be safe. I will not abandon you, but I will not allow you to turn on each other either. All of you are my subjects and my responsibility."

He could tell there were some lingering doubts, and a few of the villagers still had a bloodthirsty look to them. Sometimes just the slightest hint of a justified reason was all someone who craved violence needed. He stepped forward, resting his hand on his hilt. "You heard the queen," he said sharply, letting his voice carry across the square. "Any harm done to these people—or to anyone—will be met with the full force of the law. This kingdom doesn't stand for mob justice."

The man who had spoken before paled and stepped back, muttering under his breath. The crowd dispersed, though they cast wary glances back over their shoulders.

"To ensure your safety, we will take these people to the castle and out of the village while they learn to control their powers," Gwen said, which seemed to help slightly.

Gwen and Tyreal moved forward to the wagon, the guards stepping aside to allow them access. Six people huddled inside shifted uncomfortably, their gazes darting between him and Gwen. One of them, an older man with soot-streaked clothes and hands blistered from burns, looked up at Tyreal. His eyes were hollow with grief and exhaustion.

Recognition made Tyreal's stomach clench. He knew this man. He frequented Rosegate, the tavern in town, and they would often play dice together. "Mason..." Tyreal trailed off, unsure of what to say.

Mason flexed his injured hands, taking a shuddering breath. "My boy should have been in here with us." The man's voice was raw with anguish.

Tyreal's throat tightened, and he glanced at Gwen. "What happened to him?"

Mason swallowed hard. "My boy, he... he burned our house down." His voice broke, and he choked back a sob before continuing. "He didn't mean to. He couldn't control it. But the flames—they spread too fast."

Gwen's eyes filled with tears, and she climbed into the wagon, placing her hand on the man's shoulder. Mason looked up at her gratefully, gently resting one of his injured hands on hers. "Do you know what the worst part is, Your Majesty? The neighbors just watched. A few tried to help, Gods bless them, but most—" He looked away, his jaw clenched tightly. "They just stood there. People who'd known him, who'd known me, our whole lives. And they stood there."

Gwen's face crumpled. "I am so sorry," she said. "This should never have happened. No one should ever have to deal with that kind of horror. They were so very wrong."

Mason shook his head, his haunted eyes brimming with a desperate anger. "How could they do that? How could they stand there, watching my boy scream, and do nothing?"

The question hung in the air, heavy and unanswerable. Tyreal clenched his fists at his sides, struggling with his own frustration. He thought of the villagers pressing against the wagon earlier, their fear making them rabid. He'd seen men turn cold and unthinking when confronted with something they didn't understand.

Mason fell silent, looking away from them and staring off into the distance, lost in his grief. Tyreal glanced around at the other people in the cart. "How did they round you all up, if you have magic now?"

A young girl, slightly younger than Pip, spoke up. She looked terribly frightened, but her chin jutted out in a determined way that reminded him of Gwen at that age. It would have brought a rueful smile to his face under different circumstances. The girl clasped her hands in front of her, as if trying to hide their tremble.

"The guards said they were taking us up to the castle," she began softly. "One was nice. He said Prince Pippen and the Lower Captain would figure out a way to help us. I think that was mostly true." Her gaze dropped to her hands, and her next words came out faster, as if she needed to get them out before fear stopped her. "Once we got in the cart, the villagers got closer. They were shouting things. And a different guard got a scary look on his face and started trying to convince the others..." She trailed off.

Gwen turned to face her, asking gently, "Convince them to do what?"

The girl hesitated, her eyes darting to Tyreal as if afraid he would be mad at her for speaking ill of his guards. He nodded softly, keeping his expression as encouraging and neutral as he could.

"That maybe they should just get rid of us," she whispered. Her voice wavered, but she pressed on. "The friendly guard told him to shut up, but I heard it. We all did."

Tyreal squeezed his hilt, but didn't want to frighten the girl any more. "Do you know which one said that?"

She bit her lip and looked at Gwen. Gwen smiled softly. "Go ahead. This is Captain Blackbane's job. He needs to know these kinds of things to make sure our guard runs like it should."

"It... It was the man with the scar on his chin. He hurt me when he put me into the wagon. So I told my brother to stay hidden."

Gwen reached for the girl's hand. "You're very brave, and you did the right thing protecting your brother. I would have done the same thing."

The girl's eyes darted to her left, but there was nothing beside her. Tyreal frowned. She was obviously hiding him, but he wasn't sure where. The cart wasn't that big. "Sweetie, what's your name?" he asked quietly.

"My name is Elle. His name is Finn. But he's scared. He's younger than me."

"And where is Finn right now?" Tyreal asked.

Elle hesitated again, eyes darting around the wagon as she fidgeted with the hem of her tunic. "He's... here," she whispered. "You just can't see him." She trailed off, obviously afraid that she had said too much. Gwen and Tyreal exchanged a glance. "After the villagers started chasing us after I made the flood, he got scared. And then he just... disappeared. Like, he's invisible. So I told him to just stay hidden and stay quiet."

"Elle, I want to tell you a secret," Gwen said with a soft smile. "I've only ever told one other person it out loud before, and that is Captain Blackbane here. I have had magic since I was a little girl, pretty close to how old you are right now. I was very lucky, because my mama had it too, and I could train with the Sisters of the Mist to understand it. But if I was like you, and it happened in this very scary way, I would want to hide Prince Pippen away from everyone too. I promise you, as your queen, that I won't let anything happen to him. And neither will Captain Blackbane."

Her face was so full of kindness and empathy as she spoke that it made Tyreal's throat tighten. For every ounce of darkness in his soul, he was convinced the gods had put light in Gwen's. The little girl's eyes lit up, and he could see her relax. To begin to trust.

Elle looked at Tyreal, seeking his assurance as well. He leaned his arms on the rail of the wagon and looked at her seriously. "I give you my oath as High Captain that if anyone tries to hurt you or your little brother, they will have to fight me first. Have you heard stories of how much I like to fight? Because... it's a lot." He smiled at her and gave her a little wink.

Elle giggled and then took a deep breath. She reached out tentatively to the empty air beside her and whispered, "It's okay, you can come out now."

For a moment, nothing happened. Then, with a faint shimmer, the outline of a boy appeared, his form solidifying slowly as if he were stepping out of a mist. He clung tightly to his sister's arm, his wide eyes darting nervously between Gwen and Tyreal.

Gwen smiled softly. "Hello, Finn. You're very brave for coming out. I know this has all been very frightening, but you're safe now."

Tyreal straightened. He scanned the group in the wagon again, a nagging question tugging at him again. "Why didn't any of you use your powers to protect yourselves when the crowd pressed in?" he asked.

Mason frowned, glancing at his fingers as if they betrayed him. "I tried," he said. "When they started shouting and shoving, I thought I could scare them off. But nothing happened. I couldn't make it work." He nodded towards the younger man beside him. "Mathias tried too, but it was the same for him."

Mathias nodded grimly. "I was so scared, and I wanted to stop them, but it was like whatever made me take flight just disappeared."

The others murmured similar accounts, their confusion and frustration palpable. Gwen tilted her head slightly, her brows knitting together. "You think it was because you don't have control over your abilities yet?" she asked.

The group nodded almost in unison, their expressions downcast. "It has to be that," Mason said. "We don't know how to use this... magic. It comes and goes when it wants."

Tyreal could tell that Gwen was not satisfied with this answer. Honestly, it made little sense to him, either. It didn't add up. So far, everything he had seen suggested that magic surged when tied to raw emotion. Fear should have made it stronger, not made it disappear. He gave Gwen a faint shake of his head, though. They would have to press that mystery later.

Tyreal stepped back from the wagon, his jaw tightening as he looked around them for the guard with the scarred chin. Villagers were still lingering at a distance. "We need to move," he said to Gwen quietly. "I'll take care of this guard and then meet you at the castle."

Gwen hesitated, her gaze flicking over the wagon's occupants. She gave a slight nod, though her eyes lingered on Tyreal. "Be careful," she said softly. He nodded and helped her out of the wagon so she could get back on Akasha.

He motioned towards one of the younger guards nearby, a man named Rykan, barely nineteen summers gone. "Elle, is this the guard that was kind to you?" he asked. When she nodded, he addressed Rykan directly. "Take the wagon straight to the castle gates. No stops, no delays. Understood?"

"Yes, High Captain," the guard replied, snapping to attention and pressing a fist to his heart.

Tyreal found Max and Anya, mounting their horses beside Gwen. "Keep her safe. Watch for anything else unusual. We do not know how many people may have had their magic awakened." He jutted his chin outwards towards Anya. "Especially you. You have the sharpest eyes out of all of us."

Gwen scoffed. "Excuse you. Of the two of us, I am the expert archer, and I have impeccable eyesight."

Anya grinned. "I've been watching her for nearly as long as you have, High Captain. We'll be fine. Just make sure that guard knows not to cross you again."

Tyreal's lips twitched into a smirk. "Oh, I will."

Gwen pressed into Akasha's flanks, and they all took off. Tyreal scanned the crowd, finally spotting the guard with a long scar over his chin. Tyreal approached and stood directly in the guard's view, arms crossed tightly across his chest. Tyreal walked to him, finally coming to a stop in front of him. "I believe you and I need to talk."

The guard hesitated, then shrugged. "Of course, High Captain. What do you need?"

Tyreal motioned for the man to follow him, leading him to a quieter corner of the square, away from the lingering villagers and other guards. As soon as they were out of earshot, Tyreal leaned towards the man. "Tell me, has any part of the training that you've received in my guard made you think I would be okay with you threatening to get rid of children?"

The guard flinched, though he quickly masked it with a dismissive scoff. "I don't know what you're talking about. I was just helping get them into the wagon and away from the villagers before a riot broke out." Tyreal stared at him flatly, silent, and the man started stammering. "I was just talking," he said. "The townsfolk were spooked, and I was trying to keep things under control."

"Under control?" Tyreal repeated, his voice dangerous. "By threatening innocent people? By breaking the trust you're sworn to uphold?"

The guard shifted uneasily, but he held his ground. "I didn't mean it, captain. It was just words. You know how people get when tensions are high."

Tyreal stepped closer, his voice dropping further. "You terrified a child. You betrayed the very people you're supposed to protect. You've brought shame to this uniform." Anger was swelling and churning within him, desperate for a release. All they had experienced of late, all the fear and pain, fueled the monster that threatened to consume him.

That was the problem, wasn't it? He understood bloodlust well. The desire to take out all
those feelings on this man was intoxicating. No
one would even question him. He could just sink
his blade into the guard's belly and leave him
on the ground with his entrails hanging out.
He was Tavia's High Captain and could do as
he pleased. He gripped the front of the man's
uniform, dragging him closer.

He had always lived with this kind of darkness.
There was blood on his hands over the years.
A memory bubbled to the surface of his mind.
Tyreal, about fifteen summers gone, hands and
voice shaking as he admitted his darkest secret
to his father after tangling up with a fellow
young guard. How sometimes he thoroughly
enjoyed the violence. Craved it, almost. Tommen had sat beside him on the ground and
cleared his throat.

"Me too," he had said. The simple honesty of
the words had shocked Tyreal. Tommen continued, ignoring his sons, gaping mouth. "It's what
you do after the feelings though that matters. A
man is weighed by his actions."

The guard inhaled in shock and opened his
mouth to respond, bringing Tyreal back to the
present. He must have seen something in Tyreal's face, a glimpse of the monster that lurked
beneath. He blanched, the pupils in his eyes
blowing wide.

Tyreal swallowed and shoved the guard away
from him. "You're dismissed," he said coldly.

"Pack your things and get out of here. Your service in the Tavian guard is over."

Relief washed over his face, quickly followed by panic. "Captain, please—"

"This isn't a discussion," Tyreal snapped. "You will leave Thorncliff by nightfall. If I hear of you anywhere near this village again, you'll answer to me. And I will not be merciful a second time. Do I make myself clear?"

"Yes, captain," he said quietly, shoulders drooping.

"Go," Tyreal ordered, stepping back but keeping his eyes locked on the man until he slunk away.

As the guard disappeared into the crowd, Tyreal exhaled slowly, the tension in his shoulders lingering. He rolled his head, popping his neck, and trying to shake some of it out.

He doubted there was any real reprieve from the stress and chaos coming anytime soon. He wanted to rage at the sky, at the gods themselves, but he remembered how he'd begged them the day before to help him get to Gwen in time. His gaze shifted to the wagon in the distance, where Max and Anya flanked Gwen, keeping the group moving steadily toward the castle. Her mop of unruly curls caught the sunlight.

"I don't mean to be impertinent," he whispered to the gods. "I thank you for granting my wish yesterday, and I am grateful she is safe. Could we maybe just have a moment to breathe before the next challenge? Please?" He sent up his prayer and then he sighed, turning to return to his horse and catch up to Gwen.

CHAPTER FIVE

Gwen dismounted quickly, just barely managing to toss her reins toward Micah. The castle guards, already alerted to her approach, cleared a path for her as she strode into the courtyard. Andais was waiting near the door of the kitchen. As usual, he wore a white tunic beneath his training leathers, tailored to fit his broad shoulders. He liked to joke that the contrast of the light fabric against his dark skin was so visually striking that women were just naturally drawn to him and away from Tyreal.

A joke she'd never found funny, honestly, mainly just because it reminded her how many women were attracted to the man she loved. Jealousy was a personal flaw she needed to spend more time working to improve.

He had taken out his braids during her absence, his black, coiled hair cropped short, tapering into a tight line where the hair was shaved down to the skin around his ears. He looked stressed, unlike his normally friendly expression—but at the sight of her, relief crossed his face.

"I am so glad to see you, Your Majesty."

"Please get these people somewhere safe and away from anyone but trusted staff," Gwen said quickly as she approached. She didn't pause, trusting Andais to fall into step beside her. "Have Klause see to any wounds and ensure they are given food, water, and anything else they may need. If anyone treats them poorly, they answer directly to me or Captain Blackbane. Is that understood?"

"Yes, Your Majesty," Andais replied immediately.

Gwen continued, barely slowing as she walked through the kitchen, nodding briefly at Cook but not taking the time to stop. "Where is the prince?"

Andais lengthened his stride to keep up. "The prince is with Hedontas in his chambers," he said. "There's been—"

"Yes, I know," Gwen interrupted, then softened her voice, realizing she was snapping at him when he didn't deserve it. "The same thing as with the people in the wagon. I will explain everything as soon as I can, or Captain Blackbane will. For now, I need to see Pippen."

She glanced over her shoulder, not slowing. "Make sure the prince and princess are seen to their rooms. It's been a hard journey."

Andais gave her a tight nod, breaking off to carry out her orders. Gwen didn't watch him go. She trusted him to handle the details without question. Right now, her focus was entirely on Pip.

The hallway to Pip's room was eerily quiet, though there were more guards than normal. As Gwen hurried past, each guard saluted her with a clenched fist over their chest. She nodded curtly in return, sweeping past them to the room.

Jameson stood outside Pip's door, his back stiff but shoulders slumped. The hem of his uniform was untucked and the fabric was rumpled, as if it had gotten soaking wet and dried on his body. One hand gripped the hilt of his sword while the other scrubbed at his face. At the sound of her approach, he straightened abruptly. Dark smudges marked the hollows beneath his eyes, making it clear he hadn't slept the night before.

"Your Majesty, the prince might be resting—" He cut himself off as Gwen fixed him with a sharp stare.

"Jameson, move. And go get some rest. That's an order. Captain Blackbane and I will handle things from here."

"Aye, Your Majesty." The young guard's shoulders sagged with relief, and if Gwen wasn't so focused on Pip, she would have felt sorry for him. What a way to start your new promotion—having your charge suddenly develop some kind of magical powers. She didn't envy him. Jameson pushed the door open for her, and Gwen rushed inside.

The interior was stifling, the air thick with the heat of a roaring fire. Hedontas sat slumped in a chair near the hearth. The room itself was in complete upheaval—furniture overturned, growing puddles on the floor from the dripping ice stalactites and thick, jagged frost creeping along one wall.

Pip sat curled on the floor in front of the fire, a large blanket wrapped around his small frame. He had his knees pulled tightly to his chest, his face partially hidden by the blanket's folds. At the sound of the door opening, his head shot up, and his wide, tear-streaked eyes locked onto Gwen.

A spectrum of emotions flickered across his face—relief, fear, shame—before settling into something sharper. Pain. A soft gasp escaped his lips, and suddenly his skin shifted. It shimmered briefly before hardening into a rigid sheet of pale, frosty ice that spread from his neck to his fingertips.

"Pip!" Gwen exclaimed, rushing toward him.

He flinched back, his voice trembling as he cried out, "Don't touch me! I don't know how to stop it!"

Gwen stilled mid-step, her heart twisting at the raw terror in his voice. "Pip, it's me," she said gently, crouching to meet his eyes. "You're safe now. I promise."

Hedontas spoke up from his chair. "This has been happening on and off since yesterday. We don't know what it is, but Andais said you might." He was cradling his hand against his chest, and it was wrapped in thick bandages. The tips of his fingers that were visible were black and the older man's face was pinched in pain and exhaustion. Her heart ached for him and Pip.

Pip's icy hands clenched into fists, his shoulders trembling. "I didn't mean to!" he choked out, his voice cracking. "Hedontas tried to help, but it just happened! Everything I touch—it freezes!"

Gwen dropped to her knees in front of him, lowering herself to his level. "Shhhh, Pip." Her voice was soft, like she'd soothed him after nightmares long ago. "I'm so sorry this happened, and I'm so sorry I wasn't here to explain. But you're not alone. I'm here now, and I know how to help."

His tear-filled eyes met hers, the fear in them so raw it almost broke her. She reached out a hand, letting the faintest flicker of fire ignite in her palm. His eyes widened in fear, but she smiled reassuringly at him. "First," she said gently, "I need you to take a deep breath with me. Can you do that?"

Pip's breath hitched, but he nodded shakily, his small shoulders heaving as he tried to match her slow, steady breathing. Gwen let her own breaths come in a deliberate rhythm, showing him the calm he couldn't yet feel. "Good," she said, her tone still soft. She edged the flame closer to him, holding it near but not quite touching. "Now, feel the warmth from my fire. It won't hurt you. Just feel it. Focus on it."

He hesitated, his body rigid, but his gaze stayed locked on hers. She could see the frost creeping down his fingers recede, little by little.

"When you're ready," she continued, her voice as steady as her flame, "I'm going to touch your hand. It won't freeze me, Pip. I promise. Don't be scared. Just tell me when you're ready."

For a moment, he didn't move, his breaths coming in uneven gasps. Then finally, he whispered, "Okay."

"You're so brave," she whispered proudly. Gwen leaned forward, her heart pounding as she closed the space between them. Carefully, she reached out and wrapped her warm fingers around his icy ones. The chill bit into her skin, but she concentrated, summoning her fire to just the right warmth—not enough to burn, but enough to hold the frost at bay.

It took effort, her magic straining to balance the delicate push and pull, but she managed. She never would have been able to hold it like this before. Closing her eyes, she let her power brush against Pip's, slipping past the frozen edges of his magic and searching for the source, just as she and Anya had always done at Mist Castle all those years ago.

The connection grew stronger, and in her mind's eye, she saw it. Pip's magic was wild and untamed, an empty field pummeled with merciless snow and frozen rain. A small figure sat huddled at the center of the field, barely visible through the biting wind and frost.

"Pip," she whispered, "close your eyes and go into yourself, where you can feel me right now. Can you do that for me?"

It took a moment. His fingers twitched against hers, but then his shoulders relaxed. The huddled form in the field stirred, turning toward her. Gwen's heart swelled as the small figure lifted its head.

"Good job," she said proudly. "You're doing so well. Now, I want you to imagine the biggest, strongest wall you can think of. Something that can hold back all this cold. It doesn't have to be perfect, just strong enough to keep it safe and contained."

She paused, giving him a moment to think. "Mine looks like the cliffs at the edge of the castle," she continued gently. "Solid, unbreakable stone. Anya's is like silver gossamer, wrapped in thorny flowers made of iron. You can build yours however you want. It can be anything—something that makes you feel safe."

The icy wind in the vision began to still. Pip's form tilted its head slightly, considering, and Gwen could feel the frost recede. It wasn't much, just the smallest retreat, but it was enough.

"That's it," she murmured. "You're in control, Pip. You decide what your wall looks like. Take your time."

It started with a sound—a deep, low rumble that reverberated through the icy silence. Gwen could almost feel the ground beneath them shake, even though it was in their minds. The dragon rose from the snow like it had been lying in wait, its body shimmering with countless crystalline scales that caught the faint light and scattered it like tiny rainbows. Its wings stretched outward, vast and unyielding, forming a protective canopy over the frozen field.

"Can you see it, Pip?" Gwen asked gently.

"Yes," he whispered, his voice tinged with wonder. "It's... a dragon. A big one. Bigger than anything."

"Good," she encouraged, her heart swelling at the strength replacing the fear in his words. "What's it doing?"

"It's... wrapping itself around me," Pip whispered, his voice steadier now. In her mind's eye, Gwen could see it—the dragon curling protectively around the figure at the center of the field. Its tail encircled the core of Pip's magic, and its head lowered, its glowing eyes watching Gwen as if gauging if she was friend or foe.

"The dragon is strong," Gwen whispered, "and it's yours. It'll protect you, but it listens to you. You're the one in control."

Pip nodded, his lips moving silently as he shaped the image further, and the dragon grew clearer in Gwen's mind too. "It's not just sitting there," he said after a moment, his voice stronger now. "It's breathing fire... but not like your fire. It's blue and cold, and it keeps everything bad away." The blue flames spread outward from the dragon, creating a fiery circle around both it and Pip.

"Perfect," Gwen said, her voice thick with pride. "That's exactly what it should do. Nothing can get through that dragon unless you let it."

She couldn't see the blizzard or the figure anymore. Just the dragon coiled tightly around the core of Pip's magic, a warm, protective glow forming where the huddled figure had been.

In the real world, the frost on Pip melted away, warmth seeping back into his small hands. Gwen smiled, tears filling her eyes, but she didn't let them fall. "Your dragon is incredible. He's strong, and he's keeping you safe."

Pip nodded faintly, his breaths steadier now. "He feels real," he whispered. "Like he's... alive."

"That's because he is, in a way. He's part of you," Gwen said. "He's yours. He listens to you."

She hesitated, gauging his calm before continuing. "Now, one last thing," she said carefully. "It might not work yet, and that's okay. Sometimes it takes practice, but it's important that you try."

Pip's brow furrowed, the faintest hint of doubt creeping back into his gaze. "What is it?" he asked hesitantly.

Gwen moved to sit cross-legged in front of him with his hands in hers. "Have your dragon make me leave," she said. "He won't hurt me, not unless you tell him to. But I want you to tell him to push me out. You're in control, Pip, and that means you decide who stays and who goes."

Pip stared at her, doubtful. "But what if he doesn't listen?" he asked. "What if I can't make him?"

"Then we'll try again another time," Gwen said simply. "I think you can, though. Just focus, like you did before. Imagine him turning toward me, his wings spreading, his breath pushing me out of the field."

Pip swallowed hard, but after a moment, he closed his eyes again. Gwen followed suit, allowing the connection between their magic to strengthen once more. In her mind, she could see the dragon stir, its glowing eyes flicking toward her. The snow on the ground around its massive body shifted as its tail unwound, lifting from the field.

"That's it. You're doing it." The dragon's wings spread wide, the gust from their movement sending a swirl of snow cascading toward Gwen. "Good," she said. "Keep going."

The dragon's head lowered, and its breath rushed toward her, icy cold and howling. Gwen felt the connection between their magic weaken, her presence firmly pushed away from both it and Pip.

Then the field faded entirely, and Gwen opened her eyes to find him staring at her, wide-eyed but triumphant. "I did it," he said proudly. "He made you leave."

Gwen smiled. "You did," she said softly. "Which means you're in control now, Pip. Not the magic. You." A large yawn overtook him, and he blinked sleepily at her. "Yeah, magic is really draining, especially in the beginning. Hop into bed and get some rest. We'll talk more about it when you wake up, okay?"

After Pip had safely settled into bed, she turned to Hedontas. "Tyreal should be here any minute. He should be able to heal your hand, and then we can explain everything."

CHAPTER SIX

After Tyreal and Gwen finished briefing Andais and Hedontas, heavy silence hung over the room. The crackle and pops of the hearth fire were the only sound besides the scratching of Gwen's quill.

While they spoke, Gwen had worked at her desk, drafting a decree to send out to all the towns and districts in Tavia. As she wrote, Tyreal could see her biting her bottom lip, her hand hesitating before each sentence. He knew her well enough to guess the reason. She wasn't worried about clarity or diplomacy—she was blaming herself, shouldering the weight of all the pain as if she had been the one to perform the spell. Tyreal could feel the questions that were undoubtedly racing through her mind right now: *How many have been hurt or killed because of fear and ignorance? How could I have prevented this?*

There was little to be done to stop those thoughts. Some of it was just Gwen, stubborn and unyielding, but more than that, it was just part of being a good leader. The best ones always seemed to struggle with the burden of command. Even when they shouldn't. Even when it broke them. He knew that better than most. The gods knew he had certainly blamed himself for the lives he'd lost, even when there was little to be done differently.

She handed it to him to read over. Tyreal scanned the words. Gwen kept the message brief—an explanation that the High Sister had cast a spell that reawakened an ancient, forgotten magic in anyone with any trace of royal blood. She explained it had caused the High Sister's death. Gwen warned against harming anyone affected and promised that representatives from the castle or Sisters of the Mist would be dispatched to assist and guide them. Affected people were also welcome to come to Thorncliff if they needed a place to stay.

He nodded. "It's the best you can do for now," he said quietly, though he knew the words brought little comfort.

She gave him a grim half smile and took the parchment back. She gnawed at her lip again, this time staring at the large stack of parchment on her desk. She drummed her fingers on the desk before looking up at him. "Getting someone to copy these and then attaching my seal would take valuable time we don't have. If only I could…" She trailed off.

Tyreal cocked his head. "What are you thinking?"

"My magic is much more suited for fire, and, well… I guess light, since that's how I killed the High Sister. I *can* do things with water, earth, and air, but not easily or even necessarily well. I wonder if I could copy this decree. I've seen magic replicate itself before. I can mirror flames, so could I mirror my writing?"

Hedontas shifted uncomfortably in his chair. With Gwen's help, Tyreal had healed the frostbite on his hand, and it now rested on his leg, the skin pink and new. The older man said little of anything as they explained, his face remaining carefully neutral. Andais had been calmer and more focused on the logistical applications and problems the magic posed, which wasn't unexpected. Andais had harbored suspicions ever since Gwen's confrontation with Skensington. Hedontas had been blindsided.

"If your magic has never worked like that before, is it safe to try?" Hedontas asked quietly and with a not insignificant amount of fear in his voice.

Gwen offered him a reassuring smile, though Tyreal noticed the faint tension in her shoulders. "It will either not work at all, or it will," she said simply. "I've been doing magic for over half my life. I promise, no one will get hurt from me trying to copy these papers."

Hedontas made a low, noncommittal grunt and looked away. Tyreal caught Andais's eye, and the other man shrugged lightly, as if to say, *He'll come around.*

Gwen closed her eyes, taking a deep breath to help her focus. She hovered one hand over the written decree and the other over the stack of papers. Her nose scrunched up in concentration, and Tyreal felt a surge of affection bloom in his chest. Chaos now swallowed their lives whole, but watching her, it struck him that this woman would soon be his wife. For years, he'd never let himself hope for that. Yet here they were.

For a moment, nothing happened.

Without warning, a golden light flared, cascading over the parchments in a rippling wave. All of them held their breath as the light dimmed, retreating into Gwen's fingertips. She opened her eyes and gasped, startled laughter spilling from her lips. "It worked!" she exclaimed, picking up one sheet and turning it toward Tyreal. The decree had been perfectly replicated, each word and flourish identical.

Hedontas let out another low grunt, though Tyreal could hear a faint note of surprise—and perhaps grudging respect. "Pretty neat trick," the older man admitted.

Gwen grinned widely. "I'll admit, I had my doubts. I was really just hoping, I guess." She turned to Tyreal, her eyes shining with excitement. "I wonder what else my magic can do."

Tyreal's smile softened. Unable to help himself, he cautioned, "Don't push yourself too far."

She rolled her eyes, giving him that annoyed Gwen look Tyreal had come to both expect and secretly enjoy. Andais chuckled, leaning forward and resting his arms on his knees. "Good to see not everything has changed," he said wryly.

The moment of levity faded quickly, though. Andais' face sobered, the faint lines around his mouth deepening as he frowned and he clasped his hands in front of him. "However," he continued seriously, "I'm afraid I have to ruin the mood. We have serious matters to discuss."

Hedontas snorted. "As if we've just been sitting around telling jokes until now."

Andais gave a bemused smile, but his gaze lifted to meet Tyreal's, dark eyes narrowed. The tension in his posture was unmistakable. The firelight flickered across his rich brown skin, accentuating the shadow of stubble from the long night spent with Pip. "I was worried about Lovell's arrival even before you told me about his plans with the High Sister. But now..." Andais paused, exhaling heavily as he rubbed a hand across his jaw. "Now that he has magic, that adds a whole additional layer of shit I don't know how to prepare for. Pardon my language, Your Majesty."

Gwen waved a hand dismissively, the other pinching the bridge of her nose as if trying to hold back a growing headache. Tyreal frowned. She was pushing herself too hard. She'd been exhausted when they left Mist Castle, and that was before everything that had occurred since they got to Thorncliff. "Trust me, Andais, I've heard worse. And honestly? I hadn't even had time to consider the possibility of Lovell also having magic," she said.

Hedontas leaned forward, face grave. "Is there any way to guess what kind of magic he might have?"

"No," Gwen replied, her voice flat, though she let out a humorless laugh. "It could be anything. This new magic is wild and unpredictable. Before, the remnants left behind were mostly elemental. But now?" She shook her head. "That doesn't seem to be the case. One sister at Mist Castle could transport herself across distances, and another could shapeshift. One of the children from this village this morning was able to disappear completely. Elemental magic seems to make up most of what we've seen, but it's such a small sample compared to the bigger picture."

Andais snorted darkly, leaning back in his chair. "Maybe we'll get lucky, and he set his own ship on fire and got lost at sea."

Tyreal couldn't help the small, bitter smile that tugged at his lips. "If only we were ever that fortunate," he sighed.

"The one thing working in our favor," Gwen said with a deep breath, "is that Lovell won't have any more control over his magic than anyone else has shown so far. No one on his ship will help him gain it, either." She turned to Tyreal, rubbing her temple as she gave orders. "See if you can get reports from any of our sailors or anglers who might have spotted his ship or heard rumors of what's happening on board. I'll call an emergency meeting of the council to fill them in on everything—and prepare them for what's coming."

Hedontas cleared his throat and asked quietly, "Will you be telling them about Tyreal? And your intent to wed?"

Tyreal stiffened at the question, unable to place the strange note in Hedontas' voice—was it concern? Doubt? Something else entirely?

Gwen's fingers drummed lightly on the desktop, considering the question. "I had planned on it," she said finally, meeting Hedontas' eyes. "Hiding truths now when so many secrets were just revealed feels disingenuous. Also, we already announced it at Mist Castle. I don't know how long it will take for those crows to fly with the news, but I have to assume they will."

Hedontas shook his head. "Suppose it doesn't matter then."

They all fell silent again. Gwen's expression remained composed, but Tyreal could see the flicker of uncertainty in her eyes. "Why?" she finally asked.

Hedontas leaned forward, resting his forearms on his knees, mirroring Andais. "If we're on the brink of war, this isn't the time for the men to doubt Tyreal. They may think of him as a royal and *not one of us.*"

Andais scoffed. "Why would they? They've fought under Tyreal's leadership for years. He's earned their respect a hundred times over. And let's not act like this is a secret—everyone knows he's been in love with the queen forever. This changes nothing."

Hedontas spread his hands in a shrug. "Normally, I'd agree with you, but people are scared right now. We've seen how fear twists minds, Andais. The world is shifting—magic, royals, the way everything works. It's too much, too fast. To suddenly be told there's another royal family, that there are royal bastards with magic? People will have feelings about that." His gaze flicked to Tyreal before returning to Gwen. "Tyreal becoming Consort might bring some of that to the surface."

Tyreal felt a faint tightening in his chest at Hedontas' words. He didn't flinch, but he could feel the tension creeping into his jaw. "I don't give a damn what people think of me," he said firmly. "My place is at Gwen's side, whether as High Captain or as Consort." He believed the words, but hearing someone he held such respect for voice doubts did something inside his chest that he wasn't sure how to process.

Hedontas raised a brow. "We all know that. I'm just asking, how many of your men will feel the same way? You've earned their loyalty, Tyreal, but fear makes even the best soldiers forget."

Gwen straightened, her gaze sharp as she addressed Hedontas. "So, what do you suggest, then? That we keep it a secret until we're out of this crisis? Until Lovell is defeated?"

Hedontas shook his head. "I'm not saying keep it a secret. As you said the cat is already out of the bag, people know. Just... be prepared. People may find this as an excuse to doubt his place—or yours."

Andais leaned back in his chair, arms crossed over his chest. "The men aren't as fragile as you think, Hedontas. They've seen Tyreal fight, bled beside him. If someone whines about him being too royal, we can sort it out the hard way."

Hedontas snorted darkly. "You forget already, they were my men until just a moon or so ago. I'm not saying they're fragile. I'm saying change frightens people. Hell, *I'm* frightened. And pissed off." He paused, his gaze sweeping across the room before resting on Gwen. "The difference is, I'm old enough to recognize why I'm feeling this way and not take it out on anyone. Not everyone can say the same."

He shook his head. "You lot brought me on as an advisor, so there's my advice. Take it or leave it," he spat, with more venom than Tyreal had ever heard the man use in front of Gwen before.

Without waiting for a response, Hedontas stood, his chair scraping softly against the floor. He paused for the briefest moment near the door, his back to them, then added in a softer tone, "Just be careful and watch your back. I don't want to see anyone else get hurt."

The need to check on Gwen pulsed in the back of his mind, unrelenting. It wasn't the sharp, panicked fear that had gripped him when she was in danger at Mist Castle—this was quieter, but no less consuming. Duty had dragged him away from her after Hedontas' departure. The countless demands of leadership while on the brink of war had filled his hours, meetings with his men, dispatching crows to sailors. Still, the urge lingered, gnawing at him. Even now, as he visited the villagers they'd rescued, his thoughts strayed to Gwen.

The villagers with magic had been set up in a building far past the stables, on the furthest edge of the castle grounds, towards the wall that led to the beach. It had been originally intended as housing for guards when Thorncliff was first built. Back then, the guard force had been small, but as the village and country grew, they had outgrown the space, requiring a full barracks. It wasn't an ideal solution for their visitors, but the staff had cleaned it thoroughly. For now, the villagers were warm, fed, and safe.

Tyreal pressed two fingertips into the center of his forehead, massaging slightly as the weight of so many unknowns weighed down on him. What would they do when more arrived? The simplest solution was to send them to Mist Castle through the portals, but that would mean Gwen or Pip would have to lead the way, and he didn't like how exhausted Gwen still looked from the trips she had already made.

The portals were a headache. He was grateful for Myaessa's foresight in keying their use exclusively to her bloodline—that was the only thing stopping him from having them torn down immediately. Still, it would be far easier if he could use the damn things himself.

A stray thought crept in, tugging at his focus. Tradition dictated that anyone marrying into a royal family adopted their surname. When he and Gwen married, he would technically become a Thorncrest. Would that be enough for the portal to accept him? The possibility gnawed at him, and he bit his lip in thought. He'd need to send a letter to Lila to see if the archives contained any record of Myaessa's husband accessing the portals on his own.

Hedontas' words floated back through his mind. There was truth there, even if Andais didn't want to admit it. Fear made people act in irrational ways. Too often had he seen men forget every bit of their training when staring down death.

Hell, it was hard enough for *him* to accept that he was technically a royal now. He could easily see where everyone else would struggle as well. Tyreal sighed to himself, wishing not for the first time that his father was still alive. What he would give to sit down with him over a mug of ale and talk about all of this. He knew his father would dole out some helpful advice after having a lengthy chuckle over the fact that Marie was a long-lost royal.

He acknowledged the guards in front of the villagers' building. He found himself scanning their faces for hesitation or judgement, even though he knew it was unlikely word had spread this soon. Hedontas' words had gotten to him more than he liked.

"You just missed the queen, High Captain," one of them stated as they opened the door for him. The guard looked as he always did. Neutral. Respectful.

He buried the urge to sigh again, choosing instead to give a sharp nod. Of course he had. She wouldn't have been able to resist coming down and helping the villagers get some semblance of control over their powers, no matter how exhausted she was feeling. Gods, she vexed him, no matter how much he respected her leadership.

Most of the villagers were asleep, finally able to get some rest after Gwen had helped them.

All except Mason, who sat in a chair, staring into the fire in the hearth. Tyreal took the chair near him, staying quiet, but trying to show the older man that he wasn't alone. Sometimes, that was all a person needed. All they could bear.

"She's a fine queen," Mason said quietly, almost detached, as if he wasn't actually speaking to Tyreal. "I appreciate what she's done. But... I'm so damn angry. Angry at my neighbors. At whatever royal cursed my bloodline with this. At her—and the rest of them—for keeping it a secret. Is that treasonous?"

He never looked away from the fire as he spoke.

Tyreal let the words settle before answering. "Are you planning to act on that anger? Against her?"

Mason exhaled, slow and deliberate. "I'd be lying if I said a part of me didn't want to. Maybe just to end it all, because I know what you'd do to me." His eyes flicked to Tyreal, as if testing him, but Tyreal didn't move. Mason turned back to the fire. "But no. I won't be the reason another good person gets hurt. I can't imagine what it takes to hold a kingdom together, to keep people calm. I think I understand why they kept it from us."

Tyreal nodded. "That's not treason. That's being human. You just lost your son in the worst way imaginable, and your world turned upside down. You're allowed to be angry." A pause. "There are better ways to handle your pain than trying to bait me into killing you, though. I'm kind of busy, if you haven't noticed. It would be rather inconvenient."

A bitter laugh scraped from Mason's throat. "Fair enough, I suppose." He shook his head, shoulders slumping forward. "I can't stay here, not after this. As soon as I know I have full control of myself and the villagers won't immediately attack, I'll be gone. I don't think I can ever look at these people the same way." His voice threatened to crack.

Tyreal stood, resting a hand briefly on the back of Mason's chair. "I wouldn't stay either." He nodded toward Elle and Finn, curled together on a cot. "But maybe take them with you. Not to replace your boy—never that. But they need someone too. Someone who understands."

Mason didn't respond, but his eyes moved towards the sleeping children.

Tyreal wasn't sure if the man would take his advice or not. Hell, maybe it wasn't even good advice. He didn't know what sort of father Mason had been. It felt right, though, somewhere deep in his gut, in a place that had never steered him wrong before.

Like that pressing instinct to check on Gwen. Tyreal squeezed the older man's shoulders and left him there with his thoughts.

CHAPTER SEVEN

As Tyreal strode through the kitchens, a firm hand snagged his arm. He barely had time to turn before Cook shoved a tray into his hands, containing tea, an assortment of cookies, pickled vegetables, and cured meats. He lifted a brow.

"She didn't look well when she came through here," Cook said, keeping her voice low. "I've seen that look on her, always right before one of those nasty headaches. With everything going on, she'll try to push through it. But you—" She leveled a knowing look at him. "You're the only one who might get her to stop."

Tyreal exhaled sharply, glancing at the tea. "Klause put something in it?"

Cook gave a quick nod. "And the sweets and salty foods usually help. It won't fix it, but it might take the edge off."

He ground his teeth and sighed. Gwen had always suffered from headaches, but some were worse than others. The truly bad ones left her curled in darkness, unable to stand the barest flicker of candlelight. Sometimes, they even made her physically ill. They didn't happen often—but right now, at the worst possible time, they could take her down for hours. Maybe longer. And Cook was right, she'd try to fight through it. She always did.

"Where is she?"

"I think she went to the chapel to speak with the Arbiter," Cook responded.

That made sense. Gwen frequently sought refuge there. Cook had already dismissed him, turning back to a mound of dough, but her words followed him as he left the warmth of the kitchen.

Tyreal swept through the halls, careful to hold the tray steady, but unease gnawed at him as he walked. The medicine and food would help—but was there something else he could do? Something *only* he could do?

It was exhilarating and nerve-wracking at the same time. On the one hand, being able to ease Gwen's pain would be a damn fine use of this power he still wasn't sure about. There was always the chance that he would make it worse, though.

Tyreal exhaled sharply, forcing the thought aside. He could simply ask her and see what she thought. There was no harm in asking.

Outside the chapel stood the young guard who had been kind to the villagers, Rykan, helmet tucked under one arm, shifting his weight like he wasn't used to standing still for quite this long.

"You're not usually in castle rotation," Tyreal said, "especially not guarding the queen."

Rykan's spine snapped straight. "No, High Captain," he said quickly, clearing his throat. "Captain Andais reassigned me after the village incident. All the guards who there were reassigned—well, other than Thane, who you dismissed. Captain Andais thought it best the villagers not see the same faces again, in case tempers were still high."

"Fair enough," Tyreal said. "But you're posted to guard the queen alone. Why? You're competent, and I've had no complaints, but you're green. This is the most important post in the whole damn castle."

"I—I'm not alone. Not really, High Captain," Rykan said, flushing red. "Merren ate something at lunch that turned on him. He's just stepped to the privy, should be back any second. The Arbiter's inside with the queen. She's not unguarded."

Heavy footsteps echoed down the corridor. A moment later, Merren appeared at a jog, looking pale and sheepish, sweat beading at his brow.

"High Captain, I was just in the—"

"Privy. Yeah, I know," Tyreal snapped. "You don't leave a royal post with a trainee. I don't care if your stomach's turned inside out and your bowels are hanging out of your ass. You send a runner or you hold the line."

"Yes, High Captain. Understood."

"Never let me catch you abandoning your post again. I'm with her now. Merren, you can go see Klause if you need to. Rykan, resume position."

Satisfied that he'd properly scared the piss out of them, Tyreal turned for the chapel doors and pushed them open.

As he expected, Gwen sat beneath her favorite tapestry, depicting Myaessa riding into battle on the back of a dragon. Knowing the truth about magic and their history, the tapestries held more meaning now. How long had it taken for magic to fade into legend? Had it been gradual, or had someone ensured its erasure?

He shook his head and eased onto the bench beside her, setting the tray down between them. The porcelain clinked softly as he poured the tea, then held out the cup without a word.

She hesitated. He saw it in the slight tensing of her fingers, the flicker of stubborn denial in her eyes. But he also saw how she angled her head away from the light filtering through the stained glass, how tight the muscles in her jaw were, the fine tremor in her hand when she finally reached for the cup.

She was in more pain than she would admit. Anger bubbled in Tyreal's chest at her stubbornness. Why must she always push herself to a breaking point? Gods, she frustrated him. She took a careful sip, her shoulders dropping ever-so-slightly. "I know it's a bad one. And you know you should be in bed." His voice was quiet, careful not to be too loud or press too hard.

"How could I possibly sleep right now?" she snapped. "There's too much to do. I shouldn't even be in here, I just..."

"Needed somewhere quiet to try to gather the energy to push through the pain," he finished for her.

She didn't argue, which told him everything he needed to know.

"There's nothing that needs handling this very minute," he continued. "The crows are carrying your missive. Pip is safe and well. The villagers are adapting to their magic. You were already exhausted when we got here, and now you're hurting." He nudged the tea closer. "Come on, Gwennie. Drink your tea and let me take you to your room."

She shook her head, reaching for a cookie and breaking off a small piece to nibble on.

Their time away from the castle—everything that had shifted between them since—made it impossible to keep his distance as he once would have. So he didn't—wrapped an arm around her shoulders and drew her against him with a sigh. She leaned into him without hesitation, resting her head against his chest.

He knew she'd give in, eventually. She just had to fight him a little first, to prove something to herself. They sat like that for a moment, the only sound the faint patter of rain against the tall windows. The chapel was cool and quiet, the scent of incense and candle wax lingering in the air. He shifted on the wooden pew, easing her into a more comfortable position.

"I wanted to try..." He hesitated, his fingers flexing slightly against her arm. "I mean, if you think it isn't a terrible idea..." He cleared his throat, irritated with himself for stumbling over his words. He felt like a boy again, fumbling through his first attempt at bravery.

Gwen let out a quiet breath, amusement threading through her still-pained voice. "You going to spit it out, big guy, or make me guess?"

His lips twitched, but the nerves didn't fade. "I wanted to try to heal your headache. Or at least see if I could." He exhaled slowly, staring at the opposite wall. "I don't want to foul it up and hurt you, though."

He was grateful he wasn't looking at her—his face felt too warm, his uncertainty too exposed. He hated that he *felt* uncertain. Thus far, using magic had been reactive. This was different. A headache wasn't a gaping wound or frostbitten flesh. He couldn't *see* the damage, couldn't tell what needed fixing. And what if he failed?

The thought sat heavy in his chest, unfamiliar and unwelcome.

He'd always been the one in control, the one who knew what to do. Gwen had never seen him hesitate, never seen him unsure. Suddenly, he realized how much that mattered to him.

He wasn't afraid of failing. He was afraid of failing *her*.

Gwen shifted, lifting her head to look at him. "I don't think you'd hurt me," she said softly. "You'd have to *want* to. Intention matters with magic. And while I know that is a feeling you frequently have, I don't think it would apply in this instance." A small smirk played at her lips, though exhaustion dulled its usual sharpness. "We can certainly try. And if you *can* heal these headaches, I'm keeping you chained to my side forever."

He chuckled. "Thought you were already planning on that."

"Mm, yes. You are rather good in bed," she said with a throaty laugh.

Tyreal snorted, but he had to admit, there was a certain warmth that spread through him at her easy confidence in him—even now, when he wasn't sure of himself.

She gathered his hands in hers, guiding them gently to her temples. Her skin was warm beneath his palms, her pulse fluttering just beneath the surface. "Just focus like you have every other time," she said. "I know you don't get headaches like these, but you *know* what a headache feels like. Try to picture that—and picture it easing off."

He arched a brow. "You say that like you actually know how healing magic works."

"Oh, I have *no* idea," she admitted breezily. "So much of my magic is just figuring it out as I go."

"So just making shit up?"

"Pretty much." She shot him a pointed look. "You're stalling because you're nervous. Get at it, High Captain."

Tyreal took a deep breath and closed his eyes. He tried to summon the memory of every headache he'd ever had after too many ales the night before—the dull throb behind his eyes, the relentless pressure squeezing from either side. But there was nothing. He couldn't even sense his magic. It was as if it didn't exist.

Frustration burned through him. He clenched his jaw, his grip on Gwen tightening slightly before he forced it to relax.

Fine. If remembering the pain wouldn't work, then he'd try something else.

When he had healed Max, he hadn't focused on the injury itself. He'd focused on how much he needed to help, how he refused to let Gwen's friend suffer. And gods, he hated seeing Gwen in pain. That sharp twist in his chest whenever she winced, the helplessness clawing at him—it was unbearable.

He poured all of that into his intent. The desperate want, the bone-deep need to take her pain away.

But no warmth bloomed in his palms. No golden glow flickered at his fingertips. Just silence.

"Dammit," he growled, pulling his hands away.

Gwen caught them before he could retreat completely. Her smile was soft and understanding, and that was almost worse than if she had been upset. "What happened?"

"I just... couldn't feel my magic within me at all," he admitted. "I guess I couldn't hold on to what a headache feels like."

She hummed in understanding. "That's how air has always been for me. Other than the catacombs the other day, I've never really been able to use it by myself." She gave his hands a reassuring squeeze. "Maybe this is just something you can't do yet. Like anything else, it takes practice before you're truly skilled."

Tyreal let out a noncommittal grunt. "I'm sorry, Gwennie. I wish I could have eased your pain." Frustration still bit at him, but he pushed it aside. "Now, let's get you to bed. Do you want me to have someone draw a hot bath first, or do you just want to sleep?"

She sighed, rubbing her temple. "I think I just want to sleep. I'll need a bath in the morning before I call the council." A shadow crossed her face. "Gods, I wish Cora were here. I hope she and Tensha return soon, for a multitude of reasons."

"I sent a crow directly to Tensha, urging them to return as soon as possible. They should have already been making their way back to Thorncliff by now from visiting the larders." He helped her stand, nodding toward her half-empty teacup. "Finish that. Did you talk to Malcolum?"

She took another sip as they walked down the aisle between the benches. "Yes. I told him everything. It was a relief to be completely honest with him at last." She exhaled, her steps slowing slightly. "He wants to pray and meditate on how to guide us through the upheaval of everything to come. I'm not sure if I'll tell the council tomorrow or not. I appreciate Hedontas' opinion, but I also don't want to risk everyone finding out from someone other than me and it feel like another lie by omission."

Tyreal studied her, weighing his words. "I spent most of my life pining for you, never thinking I could have you. A little more waiting won't kill me if you think it's best." He gave her a soft smile and leaned in to brush his lips softly against hers before they opened the doors of the chapel, in public again. "I can see both Hedontas' and Andais' points. But we have the corridor between our rooms—we can manage. At least we don't have to sneak around *forever*, or worry about you being married off to someone else."

He opened the door for her and nodded at Rykan as they exited. "You may go see if the Lower Captain needs you for anything else."

The hallway outside the chapel was brightly lit with torches, their glow flickering against the stone walls. Gwen winced and swayed slightly, shading her eyes with her hand. Before she could protest, Tyreal scooped her up into his arms, bridal style. She made an exasperated sound as she tried to prevent the cup from sloshing the contents onto his tunic.

"Finish your tea. Now." His voice left no room for argument.

She huffed. "Assuming you don't make me spill it first!" After a moment, she settled against him. "This is the second time you've carried me like this in two days," she murmured, her voice smaller than he liked. "I'm going to get spoiled."

He looked down at her with a teasing grin. "You've been spoiled your whole life."

She squirmed. "The staff—"

"Know all about your headaches. This isn't new." His arms tightened around her. "So lay your head on my shoulder and hush. *After* you finish that tea."

With a quiet sigh of annoyance, she tilted the cup back and drained it in a single gulp.

As he carried her through the corridors, the servants and guards they passed gave knowing, sympathetic glances. By the time they reached the royal suites, Tyreal was already issuing orders. "The queen is not to be disturbed for the rest of the night, except in an emergency. If anyone needs something, they can find me."

"Yes, Captain Blackbane," the guard at Gwen's door replied, standing at attention. "Shall I have one of her ladies draw a bath?"

"No, she wants to sleep." Tyreal adjusted his grip on her as she tucked her face further into his shoulder. "But let them know she wants one first thing in the morning, and someone will need to tend to her hair since Cora isn't here. I'm going to stay here until she's asleep. You're dismissed for now."

The guard nodded and slipped away as Tyreal carried Gwen inside, nudging the door shut behind them. He eased her onto the bed, kneeling at her feet to pull off her riding boots.

"Thank you." Her voice was barely above a whisper. "For taking care of me. I know I'm terrible at taking care of myself."

He chuckled. "You are. We've been doing this dance for most of your life. I doubt either of us would know how to do anything else." He gave her calf a gentle squeeze before straightening. "Arms up."

She obeyed without argument, exhaustion keeping her from making a joke as he tugged her tunic free and stripped away the rest of her clothing. She untied her braids, fingers sluggish.

"Where are your shifts?"

"Wardrobe by the window." She shivered. "It's chilly without a fire, but the light will hurt."

"Luckily, you have enough blankets and furs to keep warm." He reached for a soft linen shift, helping her into it as if he'd been doing it for years. There was no urge to ogle her nude body, not when she was in this kind of pain. He just wanted to take care of her. "I'll build a fire once you're asleep."

She wrinkled her nose. "Klause put something in the tea, didn't he?"

"He did." He smirked as he tucked the covers around her. "And given how much you're whining, it's already working."

She huffed, but didn't argue.

Tyreal brushed a few stray curls from her face, his hand lingering as he pressed a kiss to her forehead. "Get settled, sweet girl. You've done all you can for today, and everyone is safe."

Her breath evened out beneath his touch, and he stayed there, fingers threading gently through her hair, until she slipped into sleep.

Satisfied that he wouldn't wake her, he moved to the hearth. In a way, he was grateful he could not control fire. There was something familiar and soothing about stacking the kindling into the perfect shape. Striking flint with his blade, he carefully fanned the sparks into a flame, and then added the tinder.

He eased into a sitting position on the floor in front of the hearth. In the stillness of Gwen's chambers, he had a moment to catch his breath from the events of the prior days. He stared down at his hands, and it was impossible to not feel resentful towards his power. If he could even call it that.

The image of Alric on the floor flashed in his mind, blood pouring from him as Tyreal tried and failed to save him. All the fear and anger he'd felt in that moment swelled again in his chest. He couldn't save Alric. He couldn't help Gwen with the headaches that sometimes debilitated her. What good was any of it?

Tyreal rubbed his hand on the back of his neck, struggling to get his breathing back under control.

Gwen shifted on the bed, drawing his attention. Her lips pursed and her nose scrunched, and it dragged a smile onto his lips. All the negative emotions dulled. Being around her was always the best soothing balm. He wished he could see what she was dreaming.

He stripped down to his sleeping attire and slid under the blankets beside her. He knew it would be the wiser choice to go back to his own chambers, lest a stray servant find him asleep with the queen. He just couldn't bring himself to care. He needed rest, true rest. And the best place to find it was curled up beside the woman he considered home.

CHAPTER EIGHT

Gwen heard the crunch of sand and stone beneath her bare feet, the rhythmic crash of waves against the jagged shoreline. The wind should have been sharp with autumn's chill, her thin shift no barrier against the cold as the fabric wrapped around her legs. Yet she felt nothing.

A dream, then. It had to be. She'd just never experienced one this vivid, this tangible.

A strange pull urged her forward as she picked her way across the uneven rocks. When she glanced over her shoulder, Thorncliff Castle loomed in the distance, its dark silhouette barely visible against the night sky. She'd never wandered this stretch of coastline before—not that there was much shore at all. Just treacherous, towering rocks broken up by narrow slivers of sand.

She glanced downward to judge her next step and frowned. Blood welled from fresh cuts on her feet, smearing the stone beneath her.

Good thing this is a dream, or I'd be in a world of pain. Not to mention what Tyreal would do if he saw me climbing around like this.

A wave surged against the rock she balanced on, water rushing over her ankles. She slipped. Instinct took over and she twisted mid-fall, narrowly avoiding smashing her temple against the unforgiving stone. The sea swallowed her whole for a breathless moment before spitting her back out, her soaked shift clinging to her skin. She was grateful the dream wasn't letting her feel anything, because she'd be freezing if she could.

She staggered upright, her pulse thrumming. The sensation dragging her forward was stronger now, a command thrumming in her bones.

The rocky stretch ended at a sheer wall, a narrow gap barely visible in its craggy surface. A cave entrance, though calling it that was generous—it was hardly wide enough for her to squeeze through. Tyreal would never fit.

Gwen hesitated, shuddering at the tightness of the space. In any other situation, she'd never force herself into such a confined passage—she *hated* tight spaces. The pull in her chest didn't care though, and it wouldn't let her turn back. Gritting her teeth, she summoned a flickering orb of flame to light the way, and she stepped inside.

The tunnel was little more than rough-hewn stone, pressing in on all sides. Then, just as the walls threatened to close in completely, the passage opened into a small cavern.

Empty.

Frowning, Gwen swept her gaze over the smooth rock walls. Nothing but stone met her searching eyes.

Confusion twisted in her gut. What had led her here?

She turned to leave—

A voice echoed through her mind.

Heir of Thorncrest. Stay.

Gwen stilled, scanning the cavern again. Nothing. Just smooth stone and eerie silence. "Alright," she said, voice steady despite the unease curling in her gut. "Though this would be much easier if I could actually *see* you."

You can see me. You simply do not yet understand what you see. But you will soon enough. You reawakened magic, and thus, me.

A frown tugged at her brow as she picked apart the words. "Not entirely sure what that means. I assume you're behind this strange dream?" The steady drip of water from her hem formed a dark pool around her feet. With an irritated sigh, she focused her energy, drying herself if only to stop the annoying drip sound.

Are you certain it is a dream? the voice asked, a hint of a laugh threading through its tone. *Humans have such limited understanding. But no matter—I will answer your question. I brought you here because you must see. You've awoken us, and for that, I am grateful. I told Myaessa I did not agree with her plan, though none of us foresaw the consequences.*

Gwen slowly sank to the ground, pulling her knees up, resting her arms across them. "You knew Myaessa?"

Yes. And the ones before her. I existed in this land long before your kind called it Tavia.

Gwen exhaled sharply. *This land.* Not this kingdom. *This land.* Whoever—or *whatever*—this was, it was ancient. She chewed the inside of her cheek, considering. "If you won't let me see you, can I at least have a name? Feels like I should know the thing currently inside my mind."

As she spoke, she tested her mental shields. The rocky walls in her mind remained intact, her magic untouched. No intruders lingered in the private space where her power resided.

And yet— *You cannot trespass on something you* **created**. The voice turned almost indulgent, edged with amusement. *Your magic stems from* **me**.

For the first time since this strange dream had begun, unease prickled down her spine. How had it known she was checking her shields? And what did it mean, *her* magic coming from it?

The more she thought about it, the less certain she was that this *was* a dream.

Gwen stayed silent, choosing to wait, to listen. The voice would offer more in time, she was sure of that. Instead, she focused on its earlier words. That she could *see*, but did not yet *understand.*

Shifting her weight, she swept another critical look around the cavern. It still appeared empty, but something felt off in the stillness—something just beyond her perception. She conjured a larger fireball, tossing it into the air. The warm glow stretched across the stone, deepening the shadows. And that was when she saw it.

The far wall was a different color than the surrounding rock. Subtle, but unmistakable.

She tilted her head, curiosity stirring. Rising to her feet, she moved toward it.

Not going to ask what I mean, little Thorncrest? The voice curled through her mind, reminding her of parents questioning their toddlers, leading them towards the answer so they could find it on their own.

Gwen shrugged. "I assumed you'd tell me when you were ready. You're the one who dragged me here, after all. Clearly, you want to explain—I'm just indulging whatever game you're playing."

She reached out, pressing her palm to the surface. But instead of cool, rough stone, warmth met her skin.

Leathery. *Alive.*

Her breath hitched. Before she could react, movement flickered to her left.

And then—an eye. Massive, golden, slit-pupiled.

A sharp gasp tore from her throat as she stumbled backward, loose rocks scattering beneath her feet.

A deep, rumbling sound reminiscent of laughter echoed through her mind. *Ah, I'd forgotten how delightful it is to reveal myself to humans. It has been so very long.*

Gwen's pulse pounded. "What... What are you?"

In your tongue, you call us dragons. But that is not our name.

She barely registered the cold rock beneath her palms as she pushed herself upright, still trying to process what stood before her. A dragon. A real dragon.

The massive golden eye blinked slowly. *I am Viamar.*

Unsure of how one should greet a dragon, Gwen inclined her head and gave a slight bow. "Hello, Viamar. I am Gwendolyn Thorncrest, Queen of Tavia. But I suppose you knew that already, since you brought me here."

I did not know your name. Only that you were the heir. I must tell you a story. When your ancestors first arrived, we watched. Humans had never set foot here before, and you struggled to survive. We are tied to the land, and the land is tied to us. It was rich with our magic, brimming with life. And so, we shared it with you.

Gwen frowned. "So that's what you meant about creating our magic? You gave it to us?"

Those among us that wanted your people to thrive. At first, your people flourished. His eye closed, less of a blink and more in remembrance. *You built kingdoms, forged alliances. But humans are... impatient. Restless.*

He huffed as if disgusted. *The magic we shared became a tool in your wars, twisted by greed, by the hunger for power. Disputes over land, over crowns, over who deserved to wield magic led to devastation. The war that followed nearly tore this continent apart.*

Gwen nodded. "I know the history. The Great War. Why not take it back when things went wrong?"

When he answered, the words were clipped and sent a cold shiver down her spine. *What is gifted cannot be taken back.*

She didn't know how to respond.

"Could you have stopped the war?" Gwen finally quietly asked, her mind reeling as she tried to piece what he was telling her into the history she knew.

Viamar's pupil narrowed. *We chose to stay out of human affairs. It was not our place to rule you. It pained us to watch, and some wished to intervene. I argued your people were still young, that in time, you would find balance. But things only worsened. The land began to suffer. Magic* became *a weapon of destruction instead of cre-ation.*

He took his time answering—the cave growing nearly silent other than the air rushing out around her feet. Viamar's exhaled breaths came from the nostril she had mistaken for a rock formation upon entry. They were hot and smelled vaguely stale. Like she'd expect in a space that hadn't been used in quite some time.

He finally spoke, pained. *And then Myaessa lost everything.*

Gwen stiffened. "Myaessa..."

Her husband and child were slain. When she came to me, she was... different. Hardened. She told me she had found a way to end the war—by ending most humans' abilities to access our magic.

Gwen nodded. "Yes, the spell she enacted with the other families up in the Mist Mountains. It wiped out magic for almost everyone, save for a few women from each line. What we kept were mere embers of actual magic. Just enough that she hoped we could prevent war if it happened again."

I should have cautioned her harder against it. I didn't believe it could be done. That she, or any of the other humans, would sacrifice themselves. Even I did not expect what followed, though. As the magic faded, so did we. The dragons fell into slumber. I suspect the other magical beings did as well.

Gwen stared at him. "And now that magic has returned?"

Viamar's golden eye gleamed. *I am awake, aren't I? And I can only imagine the others are as well. Which is why I brought you here—to warn you.*

She exhaled. "What exactly are you warning me against?"

Keep the peace, he said, the threat obvious in his tone in her mind. *The only good thing that came from us being forced into slumber is that Myaessa was right and it ended the fighting. The royal families must be united. If war begins again, I cannot promise the other dragons will be as forgiving.*

A knot formed in her chest. "It might already be too late. Someone is coming for me with intentions that aren't peaceful. And now, he has magic. He's half the reason magic has returned. The woman who performed the spell meant to restore it only to their family, to rewrite what Myaessa did. The spell didn't do what she thought it would, though. It restored it to everyone."

Viamar was silent for a long moment. Then his voice came, deep and final.

Then you must stop him. Or this time, the drag- ons will not stand aside.

Gwen shot upright with a loud gasp, heart hammering.

The dim light of her bedchamber came into focus—the stone walls, the fire crackling in the hearth, the heavy drapes that shielded the night beyond. Tyreal was already moving, yanking his sword from where it rested beside the bed.

"What is it? What's wrong?" He had obviously been sleeping beside her, and the light from the fire glinted off his rumpled hair, illuminating the musculature on his bare chest and the loose linen pants slung low on his hips. His eyes darted around frantically, trying to locate the source of her fear.

"I..." Her breath came in quick bursts. "I had a dream. It was so real." She pressed a shaking hand to her face, trying to steady herself. As her fingers brushed her skin, she froze. A sticky residue clung to her fingertips. It was one she knew well, having grown up where she did. Dried saltwater.

Dread coiled low in her stomach.

Frantic now, she threw the blankets aside and looked down. Dried blood streaked her feet and calves, the jagged cuts aching now that she was fully awake. A deep throb pulsed in her shoulder, as if she'd struck something hard.

Tyreal swore as he caught sight of her injuries. "Gwen, what the hell—"

"It wasn't a dream." The words barely left her lips before the full weight of them crashed over her.

She had been there. She had spoken to him.

Gwen tried to slow her racing heart by pressing her fist to her chest, but the orange and red flickering glow from the hearth on the ceiling made it impossible. An unbidden image appeared in her mind—the castle banners and flags on fire, smoke swirling above the spires, screams rising from her people down below.

She shuddered as bile rose in her throat, the image so vivid she could practically smell the burning fabric. The stakes had seemed high before, now they felt mountainous.

CHAPTER NINE

"Captain Blackbane?"

The young woman's voice rang out over the sounds of grunts and clashing steel in the training yard. Tyreal glanced up from where he stood, arms crossed, watching his men push through another brutal drill. If war was coming, they needed to be at their best. Though with dragons in the equation now, it wouldn't matter much against fire and talons. Still, he supposed he controlled what he could.

He turned, recognizing her as one of Gwen's maids. With a sharp whistle, he signaled the men to take a break. "Aye, lass, what can I do for you?"

She hesitated, shifting on her feet. "Jameson—uh, Captain of the Heir—he sent me." She stumbled over her words, a flush staining across her cheeks. Tyreal arched a brow at her slip-up and smirked. Ah, so Jameson had himself a lady friend. Good for him.

"Um, he sent me to find you. Things are getting... heated in the council meeting. He thinks you should be there," she finished lamely. A flush spread over her full cheeks, staining the skin to the roots of her dark blonde hair.

Tyreal's humor quickly faded. Jameson might not always be the most tactful, but he was perfectly capable of handling some noble squabbling. If he was calling for backup, it meant things were getting heated to a point that he was worried about his ability to protect Pip *and* Gwen. He gave her a curt nod and strode off, taking the steps to the library two at a time.

The raised voices reached him well before he pushed open the heavy doors. He stepped inside and a hush fell over most of the room. A couple of men continued talking, though their volume dropped considerably until they eventually stopped.

Tyreal caught Jameson's eye in silent thanks and moved to stand behind Gwen. Jameson inclined his head in response, but his eyes quickly darted away in a move very unlike the younger guard. Tyreal pushed the thought away, choosing to focus on what was happening in the room more than any possible strange actions from his men.

Strange how different things were since the last time he'd stood in this place for a similar reason. Had it really been less than two moons since she first sat on the throne and he'd threatened Skensington?

"Well," Gwen said icily, "I'm glad to see that fear of Captain Blackbane can silence you like rational adults, since respect for your queen apparently isn't enough."

She inhaled deeply, visibly reining herself in. "I understand why you're upset. You feel lied to—because you were. That was a decision made by all the rulers of our land over five hundred years ago. The Sisters of the Mist required a blood oath to keep magic a secret. No one could have foreseen what happened."

"We would just like to know if there are any other life-altering secrets you're keeping from us, Your Majesty," Willem Kirken, an advisor from one of the western districts of Tavia said, with a hint of a sneer leaking through his words. While Tyreal could agree with the man's overall message, if he didn't watch his tone, Tyreal would be happy to remove his ability to speak. He stepped nearer Gwen, a deliberate movement for Willem to see, his hand going to the hilt of his sword. Willem's eyes widened, and he cleared his throat before settling back in his chair, looking properly chastised. Tyreal fought the urge to smirk.

Gwen's eyes flashed. "If there are, they will be revealed in time. You are my advisors—not my arbiters, not my father, and certainly not the gods above. I do not answer to you." Her fingers tightened on the arms of her chair until her knuckles shone white. Around her feet, the hem of her gown swirled in unnatural currents around her feet, and the parchments on the table in front of her slid away as if caught in a leisurely breeze. He frowned. It would be an interesting development if other powers were beginning to respond to her heightened emotions, particularly air, since she had the least control over it. She would need more training, and quickly.

"I think," Sir Jonah interjected smoothly, "what Lord Kirken was trying to say, Your Majesty, is that we can't properly advise you if we don't know what else may be coming towards us. You have to admit, we are scrambling to catch up. And now, with your impending nuptials to a commoner—" He coughed, eyes wide and cheeks red as he glanced at Tyreal. "Well, it's just a lot of change in a very small amount of time."

Tyreal felt his back stiffen in surprise, but he didn't allow it to show on his face. Gwen hadn't been sure she would tell the council, but clearly she had decided and plowed ahead without consulting him. She was queen, that shouldn't bother him, and yet, it did somewhat. Suddenly, Jameson's glance away made more sense, and unease churned in his belly.

Gwen pinched the bridge of her nose and took a deep breath with her eyes closed before fixing the council with a steely gaze. "I am trying to be patient. Truly, I am. I understand the last few days have been unsettling—frightening, even. But we have far greater concerns. Prince Grigor is sailing toward us with unknown magic and a clear intent to overthrow our country. The return of magic has sent shockwaves through every kingdom, and the Sisters of the Mist need oversight before this spirals further out of control."

She straightened in her chair, loosening her grip on the armrests. Her jaw tipped upwards, and she pushed her shoulders back. Her pose was regal, and the words that left her mouth next were delivered accordingly. "I do not have time to hold your hands like frightened children while you struggle to accept reality. Either rise to meet these challenges, or leave this council. Furthermore, I distinctly remember telling you before I left for the Mist Mountains that I wanted to expand this council. Where are my fresh faces?"

A heavy silence settled over the room. The men avoided her gaze, a few of them clearing their throat and shuffling papers.

Gwen's fingers curled into fists against the tabletop, her voice dropping to a quiet, lethal register. "All of you are dismissed."

Luca Fitzsimmon swallowed hard. "F—From the meeting, Your Majesty?"

"No." Her eyes locked onto his, unflinching. "All of you are dismissed from this council. I made myself clear before my father's funeral pyre—if I did not feel well-advised, there would be consequences. And yet, here we are."

The stunned silence was broken only by the creak of chairs as men shifted uneasily.

"Luca, you will remain as Keeper of the Castle Coin, unless you give me reason to believe you aren't capable of the position. And let me remind you," her voice turned razor-sharp, "you are already on thin ice, given the forged donation records regarding the larders. Since of course, you claim to have no knowledge of how that happened."

She let the accusation hang in the air for a moment before leaning back in her chair. All around the space, tapestries began fluttering, their edges slapping against the walls. Gwen's hair lifted away from her shoulders, the curls floating outwards.

"Everyone else, get out." She didn't raise her voice. She didn't have to. The finality of the words were clear enough.

They stared at her, mouths agape in shock and a touch of fear.

Tyreal cleared his throat. "I believe you've been given your orders, gentlemen."

Muttering under their breath, the council members shuffled toward the door. As the last of them exited, Gwen let out a sharp, frustrated cry, throwing her hands outward. Flames roared to life in the library's hearths, the sudden heat licking at the walls, feeding from the air she was also slinging outward.

Jameson flinched, but kept his composure.

"I tell them we are on the brink of war, and all they care about is how they could have used magic to their advantage if they'd known sooner." Gwen clenched her fists, closing her eyes as she forced a deep breath through her nose. "Which is exactly why we were oath-bound not to tell them in the first place."

She exhaled sharply and sank into her chair, seeming to fold inward on herself. Gone was the self-assured queen, replaced by a woman suffering from a bone-deep exhaustion brought on by too much grief and stress in too short of a time span. Tyreal's heart constricted at the sight. He so badly wanted to scoop her up and hold her. "Maybe I shouldn't have done that. It'll only fuel their narrative that I'm just an emotional woman, unfit for my position."

Pip hesitated, then stepped closer. "If you hadn't, they still wouldn't have respected you. You warned them what would happen. Papa always said a leader has to stand by their word." He shifted his weight, running his hand along the underside of the table. He wrinkled his nose and bit the corner of his lip before speaking. "I lost control a little, too. There's ice all over the bottom."

They followed his gaze. Meltwater dripped onto the floor, forming a small puddle.

Gwen gave him a small smile and took his hand. "You kept it mostly under control, though. No one saw, and you didn't hurt anyone. That's more than I could say at your age." Her smile turned wry. "Once, after an argument with Tyreal, I set an entire row of tapestries on fire. Papa never believed that was an accident."

"I knew that was you. I just never could figure out how," Tyreal grumbled with annoyance.

Gwen smirked. "You never were the brightest."

He shot her a look before turning toward Jameson. "Have someone bring a training dummy down to the dungeon. We will meet you there."

Gwen raised an eyebrow. "You're taking us to the dungeon? Should I be concerned about a coup, High Captain?"

"Always, but not from me, not today at least," he said with a brief grin. "It's the safest place for you and Pip to train. You haven't tested your magic since it fully returned, ice responding to your emotions is proof of that, and the prince hasn't trained at all. That needs to change. Besides, it'll help both of you work off some frustration."

Pip let out an excited yelp and took off, nearly knocking into Jameson on his way out the door. Tyreal was glad to see it. Though Pip showed bouts of maturity far above his age, he was still a boy. It brought a grin to his face, and from the corner of his eye, he saw one on Gwen's too.

Jameson sighed, muttering a curse before hurrying after him, calling for him to slow down.

Tyreal reached for Gwen's arm and pulled her close. She tensed, but in anticipation, not fright. He leaned in, his lips brushing the shell of her ear. "I know everything is a mess, but I have to tell you—I love watching you dress down those incompetent, self-serving jackasses with all of them aware that you are *my* terrifying and brave woman. Almost as much as I love the idea of helping you vent your frustrations." His voice dropped, and he delighted in the way goosebumps broke out across her skin from his breath against it. "Underneath me. On top of me. Whatever you prefer. You don't scare me, Your Majesty."

She caught his mouth with hers. As always, the instant they touched, it was like striking flint to steel—heat, hunger, an unrelenting spark. Tyreal growled low in his throat and backed her against the wall behind the nearest bookshelf, one hand tangling in her hair, the other gripping her waist, as though anchoring himself.

She pressed into him, deepening the kiss, her fingers twisting in his hair. She gave as good as she got, sucking his bottom lip between her teeth until he nearly saw stars with the wanting. He broke away only to trace his lips along her jaw, down her throat, leaving a trail of fire in his wake. Her breath hitched.

She whined prettily, pulling his hips tighter against hers. "Tyreal, please, I need—"

"I know what you need, sweet girl." His voice was rough, aching with restraint.

And gods, he wanted to give it to her—right here, right now, propriety be damned. "Do you think you can be very, very quiet? If I hear a sound, I'll stop." As he questioned her, his hand was lifting the heavy skirts of her dress, exposing an expanse of creamy thigh adorned with a garter holding up her stockings. His mouth went dry, and when his eyes met hers, he knew pure hunger showed on his face.

She nodded eagerly, though they both knew it was probably a lie. Tyreal smirked and kneeled in front of her, lifting her thigh over his shoulder. He got to work, pressing his mouth to her, parting her with his tongue. He avoided her clit at first, knowing she needed to be worked up before she could handle direct stimulation. Instead, he sucked and teased along the outside, working a finger into her. Gods above, he could spend eternity right here, her flavor exploding on his tongue and her wetness soaking his beard.

He looked up at her, positively delighted to see her beautiful face scrunched up into a look of near-agony as she tried to contain her sounds. He'd grin if his mouth wasn't otherwise occupied. He wondered if she'd make it over the edge before she made a sound. His instincts told him she was ready for him, and he eased another finger in, curling them in the way she liked as his lips wrapped around her clit, tugging and sucking gently.

Gwen inhaled sharply, grinding her teeth together. The thigh over his shoulder shook, and he knew she was close. A wicked thought came to him, and he doubled his efforts, getting her right to the very edge, till he could feel her fluttering around his fingers—and then he slowed down. As he knew she would, she let out a sound of frustration.

He eased her thigh down, lifting his mouth away from her before standing. She gaped at him, completely shocked that he would actually stop. "What are you doing? I was—"

"Oh, I know. That was the rule, though. No noise. You've got no one to blame but yourself." He lovingly flicked the tip of her nose and smoothed her skirts back into place.

"You bastard! You did that on purpose."

"I wanted to take you over the edge. You're the one who couldn't be quiet like a good girl. You'll just have to take out your frustrations some other way." He gave her a wicked grin.

Gwen shot him a dark look, a flush staining her decolletage, and straightened herself up. She pushed past him, back rigid and looking every inch an angry queen. "Compose yourself, captain, your pants look a bit... *ill-fitting.*"

A knock sounded at Gwen's chamber door. She set down the wide-tooth comb she'd been working through her damp curls and called for entry, silently hoping whoever it was wouldn't bring more bad news. Between the throbbing headache the night before, the dream-walking, and an afternoon spent training with Tyreal, exhaustion weighed her down.

The door opened, and when Gwen saw who it was, she let out a relieved cry and jumped to her feet.

"Cora!" She rushed forward, throwing her arms around her friend. "Thank the gods. I've missed you. I was so worried about you and Tensha."

Cora hugged her back just as tightly. "I'm very glad to be back. It was certainly a memorable trip." She pulled back, studying Gwen with warm brown eyes. "Though it sounds like yours was even more eventful than ours. Captain Blackbane filled us in on most of the details. How are you holding up?"

Gwen sighed, sinking back into her chair. "I'm... struggling. It feels like I never have time to process anything before something worse happens," she admitted quietly, looking down at her feet. Tyreal had healed the cuts from her dream the night before, but tiny sliver scars now lined the edges of them.

Cora nodded knowingly and moved behind her, picking up a towel and gently drying Gwen's hair as she spoke. "You haven't had a moment to breathe, that's for sure. But at least you and the captain can finally be open about your feelings. That's something good, right?" She smiled softly at Gwen in the looking glass. "When should I tell the seamstresses to start on a wedding gown?"

Gwen couldn't stop a happy grin from surfacing. "I already instructed them to do so. It's going to be stunning and unlike anything anyone has ever worn before." They giggled together, and for the briefest of moments, Gwen felt light and normal.

Like it always did, reality reared its ugly head, and Gwen frowned. "Hedontas thought telling everyone was a mistake. He wanted us to wait. I had already announced it to the Sisters of the Mist, though, so it was just a matter of time before it got out. I thought it was better for me to be the one to tell people than for them to hear rumors, but given how my advisors responded..." Gwen trailed off and scrunched her nose.

Cora reached for the oil for Gwen's tresses, but Gwen stopped her with a hand on her arm. "You don't have to fix my hair, Cora. You've just returned."

Cora snorted. "Somebody needs to. This looks a bit of a mess, even wet. Though I suppose we knew it would after being on horseback for so long." Her fingers worked the oil into the curls. As she worked, she hummed thoughtfully before speaking. "I understand why Hedontas thought that. I would argue though, with everything already in upheaval, now is the perfect time. People are already reeling from the return of magic. Revealing that Tyreal descends from another royal family feels like part of that same revelation. If you'd waited, it might have felt like another secret you'd kept from them. And you know how much they love feeling betrayed."

Gwen closed her eyes, letting the silence stretch between them as she savored the feel of Cora's fingers in her hair. There was something steadying about the simple act, in a way so little had been lately.

Cora's argument echoed Gwen's opinion, and in her heart, it felt *right*. Still, she hadn't missed the disgust the nobles had barely disguised after she'd made her announcement, even ones that had known and liked Tyreal his entire life. After her encounter with Viamar, the weight of making the wrong decision felt heavier than ever.

"We're waiting for word from the anglers." She exhaled slowly, tilting her head back into Cora's hands. "Any sign of Prince Grigor's fleet. And I've called for the ruling families to come to Thorncliff. We need a plan."

"Do you think they'll all come? With their own countries struggling with magic's return?"

Gwen sighed. "I hope so. Or at the very least, I hope each will send a representative. I want us to all stand united against Lovell and prevent a war before it happens. Also, we must come to an agreement about the Sisters of the Mist."

Cora stepped back, admiring her work as Gwen's curls settled into soft, bouncing ringlets. "I'm afraid I don't have much advice for politics," she admitted. "But at least you'll look presentable for royal visitors." She squeezed Gwen's shoulder and offered a reassuring smile in the looking glass. "Captain Blackbane mentioned that you'll be attending a funeral for Prince Maximilien's guard tomorrow. After that, we can make a plan for the parts I can help with."

With a quick curtsy, Cora slipped out, leaving Gwen alone with her thoughts. They spun in a thousand directions at once. Grigor. The Sisters. Announcing Tyreal's claim as Consort. Preventing war. Preventing destruction at the hands of dragons. It was too much. She needed a reprieve, just for a little while.

As if summoned by her desperation, the hidden door in the wall swung open, revealing Tyreal. His damp hair clung to his forehead, the scent of soap and clean linen drifting toward her. She said nothing, but the hunger that had smoldered in her since their stolen moment in the library roared back to life. Judging by the way his gaze darkened as he took her in, she wasn't the only one.

Without a word, he reached for the hem of his tunic and pulled it over his head, dropping it carelessly to the side. "Stand up," he commanded, voice low and sure. "Tell Andais you're going to bed and that you're not to be disturbed."

A shiver ran down her spine at the rough edge in his tone, but she wasn't about to give in so easily—not after what he'd pulled in the library. Lifting her chin, she met his gaze with stubborn defiance. "Who said I'm ready to go to bed?"

Tyreal set his sword down by what had already become his side of the bed, then turned to her, his posture relaxed but resolute. Confident.

"No," he said simply, closing the space between them. "You need this as badly as I do. Right now, you aren't the queen. The weight of the world isn't on your shoulders." His fingers traced her jaw before skimming down to her lips, his thumb pressing lightly against the soft curve of her lower one. "You're going to listen. You're going to do as you're told."

His voice dropped to a dangerous whisper. "In here, you belong to *me*. Tomorrow we will face the rest of it, and I will follow your every command, but not tonight."

She stared up into his stormy eyes, a battle warring within her. Her pulse raced so fast, she wondered if he could hear it. He waited for a moment, letting her decide. He was right.

She needed a reprieve. Maybe in the morning, things would be clearer.

She stood and went to her door, cracking it open and informing Andais that she was retiring for the evening and didn't want to be disturbed.

Andais smirked. "Yes, Your Majesty." He almost certainly knew Tyreal was in her room. She rarely announced to him when she was going to sleep. Her cheeks flamed, and she suspected it was part of the game.

She closed the door and came back to Tyreal, who remained in his spot by the bed.

"Good girl."

CHAPTER TEN

"That night at the inn, you admitted something to me, and I haven't stopped thinking about it. Do you remember what it was?" Tyreal's voice was thick with desire as he watched her come back to him from the door.

She swallowed, anticipation, desire, and a bit of nerves filling the space within her chest. "Yes. I told you that..." She bit her bottom lip. The look on his face made her belly feel like it did when Akasha jumped over a large ravine with Gwen on her back. Like the bottom of it would drop out. "I told you that the day you spanked me when I was younger, that I liked it. And that I've thought about it several times since then."

"Did you touch yourself when you thought about it?"

"Yes."

"Sneaky girl. Take your clothes off."

The sudden change from his questions to the order was disorienting. Her brows furrowed. "What?"

He stepped closer, his hands sliding into her hair and lightly tugging on a curl. He stretched it out until it was almost straight, and then let it bounce back up into its normal shape. A hint of a smile played on his lips, but his eyes were impossibly dark. "I said, Take. Off. Your. Clothes."

He trailed his fingers along her jaw before turning and sitting on the edge of the bed. His legs were spread out in front of him, arms casually crossed in a relaxed pose, like he was waiting to be entertained by a jester or musician.

Gwen could feel her cheeks flame with embarrassment again, but the heat in her belly only intensified. She took a deep breath and chastised herself mentally. She'd been nude in front of him several times. Why did it suddenly feel different? She untied the knot on the belt of her robe, moving to slide the material off her shoulders quickly to get this part over with.

Tyreal clicked his tongue and made a *tsk* sound as he shook his head. "No. No. Slowly. I want to watch you."

Her mouth fell open, and she almost complained or challenged him again. Something in his gaze, though, stopped her. He *wanted* her to resist. Just a little. Just enough to give him a reason to come up with some elaborate way to punish her, like his game in the library earlier.

Her chin raised and her shoulders straightened. If he wanted to have a reason for denying her release, she certainly would not give it to him. She did as he bid, slowly releasing the ends of the belt and sliding each side of her robe off until it pooled on the ground at her feet.

She ran her hands along the front of her shift, letting the fabric conform to her curves. A look crossed his face, but it was so quick, she couldn't quite put a finger on what it was. It almost looked like humor, but not mockery

Gwen toyed with the ribbon along her neckline that held the fabric together. She untied it slowly, her eyes locked with his.

Tyreal reached down and palmed himself, his enjoyment of her show obvious. He didn't move to take his breeches off, which confused her. She had no idea exactly what his next move would be, and it terrified her. No, *terrified* wasn't the right word. It exhilarated her specifically because there was an edge of fear over it. Not of him, never that. Just the unknown of it all. She was very much out of her depth, and he was her only guide through it.

The ribbons slithered from her grasp. The shift joined the robe on the floor, and she stood in front of him, now completely nude.

His eyes roved over her, slowly, as if taking in every inch of her body. She could feel the blush moving down her neck and décolletage, the skin heating as if it had been in the sun too long.

"You act as if you haven't seen me before," she said, trying to mask her sudden nervousness.

"My sweet girl, I've never been able to look away from you, whether in court regalia or riding clothes. Why would you possibly think the sight of you like this would be less enticing?"

She smiled softly, her eyes fluttering closed, and she tried not to be overwhelmed by his words. Gods, how she loved this man.

"Come over here and lay yourself across my knees facing the floor," he said. His voice was firm and commanding now, where just a moment before it had been heartbreakingly tender.

"What?"

He arched a brow at her and waited silently. Apparently, he didn't intend to repeat himself again.

She walked to him and the bed, every step feeling heavier and hotter than the last. Given his earlier question about the night at the inn and the position he wanted her in, she now had a pretty solid idea of what his next action would be.

Tyreal took her hand and helped ease her into position. It wasn't overly comfortable, but it wasn't unbearable either. She rested her forehead against her crossed arms, the urge to hide her face nearly overwhelming as the embarrassment washed over.

He brushed her hair back, hooking a finger under her chin and forcing her to look at him.

"I need to explain a couple of things, since you are new to this. I'm in control, yes. Not nearly as much as you are, though. One word, and everything stops. No questions asked. Do you understand that?"

She nodded. "What word?"

"Three words, actually. It's best to have them be things that you probably wouldn't normally say in the heat of passion, but things that are easily familiar. I've been thinking for awhile about what would work best for you. Seems to me that riding terms would probably work well."

"Riding terms?"

"Mm-hmm. I'm thinking *halt* if you want to stop, obviously, and *trot* if you want to slow down." His voice was sweet again, and his fingers kept caressing over her face and arms.

"Why couldn't I just say *stop*?"

"Well, because sometimes it's fun to pretend you want to stop. That I'm doing these horribly dirty things against your innocent maiden will, but you don't *actually* want me to stop. This way, with *halt*, I know you mean it and everything stops. Instantly," he said.

She thought about that for a moment, and the heat in her belly pooled again. Yes, she could very much see how that sort of game could be quite enjoyable. She cleared her throat. "So just the two words?" She could hear how husky and needy her voice already sounded, and it just heightened everything further.

"No. One more. Occasionally, I'm going to check in with you. Make sure you are enjoying yourself and want to continue. I think we will go with *gallop* for that."

"Alright," she nodded.

"Repeat it back to me."

"If I want to stop, I say halt. And everything stops. If I want to slow down, I say trot. And if I want to keep running, I say gallop."

"Good girl. Now, if I tell you I'm going to make this round beautiful ass of yours a lovely shade of pink with my hand, where would you say you are at?"

She bit her lip and turned her head back away from him, but he wouldn't let her. Finally, she swallowed, and said, "gallop," so quietly she wasn't sure he could hear her.

He must have, because a moment later, his hand came down on her ass cheek, hard. She gasped in surprise, nearly leaping off his lap. His other arm locked down across her back, holding her in place, and he rapidly brought down several more swats, alternating sides. She tried to squirm away, but he was simply too strong, and that fact alone had the tension coiling within her.

The pain was a lot to take in, but just as she was about to say *trot*, he slowed, caressing her flesh tenderly. He cupped each side with a gentle squeeze and rubbed his hand in circles until she settled on him again.

"You have no idea how absolutely perfect it is, Gwendolyn Thorncrest, to put you exactly where I've wanted you for so many years. You're stunning draped across me." She could practically hear the devilish grin in the timbre of his words.

Then the swats resumed. She kicked her legs and made needy whimpering sounds as her head swished back and forth against the bed.

"Tell me where you are at, Gwennie," he said roughly, his hand pausing from the swats to slide between her thighs and tease along the edges of her lips, tickling the curls there.

"G...gallop."

"Is that for me touching you like this or me spanking you?"

She took a moment, looking deep within herself for the answer. Did she like this? The spanking? Or did she just want him to touch her and finger her until she got the release she desperately needed?

The truth was that the pain was cathartic. A release from everything she had been bottling within her in a physical manifestation she could handle. She had the power to turn this on or off with one word, and it somehow made her feel more in control than she had in a long while, even though it followed her submitting to his use of her body.

"Both. I... I want both."

"Fuck yes you do," he growled.

Tyreal swatted her once on each cheek for good measure and then scooped her up back to a standing position. He guided her towards a wall, leaning down to snag the belt from her robe as they walked. He pressed her body back against the stone, and the chill against her heated and bruising flesh made her hiss.

He raised her arms above her head and held her hands around the base of a sconce. He quickly made loops around her wrists with the sash, tying it into a knot that he could quickly release if needed. Unable to resist, she tested the restraint and found it held firm.

"What are you going to do?" she whispered.

"Whatever I *want*. And there will not be any lashes on my back for it or any royal inquests into the misuse of the queen's body. You are all mine."

Gwen bit her lip and watched him look over her trussed-up form like a hungry predator. She felt incredibly vulnerable, which heightened her desire further. Underneath it though, something else churned. Anxiety swelled beneath her ribs and a hot wave of shame washed over her.

She was supposed to be *queen*.

Tyreal was, despite being the man she loved and her soon to be husband, still technically one of her subjects. What did it say about her that she was letting him tie her up and use her this way?

The High Sister's insults rang through her memory, *women who allow common filth to defile them outside their marriage bed—*

She tried to shove the thought away, to focus on what they were doing. What happened in her and Tyreal's bedroom was no one's business but their own. But the memory of the High Sister brought everything else along with it. The attack. Alric's death. The truth about her father.

Tyreal must have seen something on her face because he stopped moving towards her and tilted his head quizzically. "Where you at, Gwennie?"

Her cheeks heated, the flush and warmth spreading down over her body. "Halt. I think we need to—" she choked out.

The belt of her robe incinerated around her wrists, the ash floating down onto her shoulders as she dropped her arms. A rush of air exploded outward, knocking candles from their stands and sending loose items skittering across the floor. The heat radiating from her skin spiked, rolling off her in waves she couldn't contain.

He reached her in an instant. "Gwen," he said sharply, concern cutting through his tone.

She tried to move away, but the wall was still against her back and she was effectively pinned. "Stay back, I can't—" Her voice broke, panic threading through it.

He didn't listen.

She knew he wouldn't.

His arms closed around her, and the heat burst from her skin, searing where he touched. She smelled the bitter tang of burning hair and heard his hiss of pain. But he held firm.

"Tyreal!" she cried, struggling to reign her power back in. She mentally dove downward into the place where her magic lay and was horrified to see her normally solid circle of stone crumbling and broken in places. The magic within was too much, so much more than it had been when she first built her walls, and it swelled outward with her heightened emotions.

"Look at me," he ground out through clenched teeth. His face was contorted with the effort of holding her, but his gaze never wavered. "You're safe. I've got you. You can control this."

Her body trembled violently as the power churned and raged. The harder she tried to rein it in, the wilder it seemed to grow. Tears evaporated to steam on her cheeks. "I'm hurting you!"

"Burn me to a crisp if it's what you need. I'm not letting you go."

The words broke her, and as if surrendering to the pain was what her body had been waiting for, the power stilled as quickly as it had erupted. She collapsed against him, no longer fighting to keep him away.

"I'm... sorry," she sobbed, her voice muffled against his chest.

He pressed a kiss to her temple. "I'm the one who should be apologizing. We don't ever have to do that again, or anything more than that. The choice is always yours."

She clung to him until the storm of emotion finally passed, until the sobs eased into quiet sniffling.

"Do you want to tell me what happened? Did I do something wrong?" he asked gently.

Gwen shook her head. "No. My emotions just got the best of me. You pulled everything to the surface and it all came out. I felt ashamed for enjoying what you were doing, and then the shame reminded me of her. It twisted into fear, and then grief. I couldn't hold it in."

"Are you sure I didn't push you too hard? I'm so sorry I didn't check in on you enough." His voice caught, and when she lifted her head, her chest tightened at the tears shining in his eyes.

"No. Don't take this on yourself," she whispered, kissing his cheeks and pressing her forehead to his. "I did enjoy it. And I feel... lighter now. I think I needed to face it and let it consume me."

She drew back, her gaze falling on the burns marking his chest and palms. The skin was red and raw, but not blistered—painful, yet not lasting damage. Her throat ached at the sight of it.

"I hurt you," she murmured, brushing her fingers over the marks.

"And I'd let you again," he said simply, covering her hand with his uninjured one.

Her heart clenched at the steadiness in his voice, at the way he held her as though she was worth every wound.

"Tyreal," she said timidly, looking at him from beneath her lashes. "Will you... make love to me? Maybe gently and slowly?"

The faintest smile curved his lips. "I will never say no to that."

CHAPTER ELEVEN

G wen slipped her hand into Anya's, their fingers lacing together as they watched Alric's pyre burn. The acrid scent of smoke curled in the air, stinging Gwen's throat, but she welcomed the burn. It was nothing compared to the hollow ache in her chest.

Alric had been a good man—brave, loyal, kind, and someone she had admired greatly. He had believed in the three of them, that they could make actual change for the commoners with their ascensions to their thrones. His loss weighed deeply on her, but it was nothing compared to the grief weighing on Anya. Nothing compared to what Max was feeling. Alric had been as constant to him as Tyreal was to her.

The flames snapped and hissed, their hungry tongues licking up the wood with sharp pops. Firelight danced across Anya's face, casting her features in a soft, amber glow. It might have been beautiful, if not for the sorrow written so plainly there.

Her black gown was plain, nothing like the lavish silks and ruffled layers she once wore in Vasar. Some of that was because of Tavia's simpler fashions, Gwen knew. But there was more to it than that.

Anya was changing.

She'd thought her husband dead, then killed a man not in self-defense, and watched the High Sister—the woman she'd once revered—fall. Ever since, Gwen had noticed the shift in her voice, her choices, even her clothes. It felt like a form of quiet rebellion. Anya was dressing not to appease her court or her parents, but to reclaim something of herself.

Women's fashion had always been more than vanity. Many people overlooked that. It was armor, a language all on its own. Anya's spoke of a woman slowly stitching herself back together after being broken in places no one could see.

"I can't believe we're back here again," Anya murmured, her voice barely audible over the fire. "So much senseless loss."

Gwen exhaled slowly, thoughts of Anya's fashion and personal growth chased away by the grief that was now so familiar. "It's going to get worse if we don't bring Grigor to heel quickly.

We need the rest of the families to see reason, to agree on overseeing the Sisters and magic before more blood is spilled." She gave her friend's hand a gentle squeeze. "I'll need you and Max for that."

Anya nodded. "I don't think my family or Max's will be an issue. And I trust Eliana to convince hers. That gives us four. If the others side with Lovell, though..." She hesitated, jaw tightening. "We'll be outnumbered."

Gwen chewed on her bottom lip, her mind spinning through every possibility, every risk. She hated this kind of politics—the constant maneuvering, the need to stay two steps ahead, to weigh alliances and personalities like pieces on a game board. Why couldn't they all just simply tend to their own people and show a shred of decency?

Anya exhaled sharply, straightening her shoulders as if coming to a decision. "Come on," she said firmly. "Let's drag Max away from here. The pyre will burn all night. We can spread Alric's ashes tomorrow." She turned to Gwen, determination flickering in her cerulean eyes. "The four of us need to put our heads together. We have to figure out how to get all the families on board."

Gwen hesitated, glancing toward Max. "I hate burdening him with this right now." Cora had found him a black silk tunic, with a woven pattern that barely caught the light. It was long enough for his lanky frame, but was baggy around his shoulders. Anya had slicked his wavy hair back with an oil, and he looked like a stranger.

This wasn't the Max she knew—the cheerful diplomat, the man who could smooth over tensions with little more than a well-placed joke. This man looked hollow. Hardened. Angry.

Like he was ready to set the world ablaze just to make the pain stop.

Standing this close, Gwen could practically feel his grief rolling off him.

Anya shook her head. "You weren't given any time," she said softly. "It's been less than two moons since you stood in that same spot. But this..." Her gaze flickered to the fire, where the flames had completely engulfed Alric's shrouded body. "This is what it means to lead." She sighed. "Besides, he functions better when he's busy."

Without waiting for a response, she walked to Max and slipped her arm through his. "We'll gather his ashes tomorrow and scatter them to the sea. Tonight, we must honor his legacy the only way we can—by stopping Grigor before he drags us all into war."

Max let out a sharp, bitter laugh. "Alric wasn't afraid of war. He knew sometimes violence was the only answer. If I had just listened to him—if I'd kept my mouth shut and let them kill her when we had the chance—none of this would have happened." His voice was hard, jagged.

"You couldn't have known—" Anya started, but he cut her off.

"But he *did*." His hands curled into fists. "He and Tyreal both warned me. They saw it coming. He said she'd come for us, and she did. Now Alric is dead because I was too blinded by my own damn ideals. Too caught up in being the perfect diplomatic prince." He spat the words like they disgusted him.

Gwen met Tyreal's eyes, and he grimaced in sympathy. Alric and Tyreal *had* wanted to take out the High Sister before she struck. The guilt Max was feeling wasn't unique to him. Gwen had also hesitated, and if she thought about it too long, she'd get sucked into the void of the *what ifs*.

That didn't help move them any closer towards the goals they needed to be focused on. It was an indulgence they couldn't afford.

Gwen stepped closer, gripping his arm firmly. "Max, this isn't what he would have wanted for you. He told me your personality made him believe you could leave the world a better place. That preventing war was a good first step in doing so. That requires you to be yourself—diplomatic, charismatic, and kind."

Max scoffed, his throat working as he swallowed hard. "And what have those things gotten me? Huh?" His voice cracked, and for just a breath, the rage slipped, exposing the pain beneath. "Ran through with a sword. My best friend dead. A wife that…" His jaw clenched along with his fists as he stopped himself.

Anya stiffened beside him, her lips parting slightly. "A wife, that what?" she asked in a loaded voice, a soft tremor in her bottom lip. A heavy silence fell over them as Max just stared at her, his mouth opening and closing as if he was fighting with himself on whether to continue the sentence.

Tyreal stepped in, clasping Max's shoulder and breaking the charged eye contact between the newlyweds. "I've lost more people than anyone here," he said firmly. "Listen to me—anger is part of grief. But if you let it fester, it'll consume everything. It'll make things worse." His gaze flicked between them. "Everybody needs to take a breath and calm down before things are said that can't be taken back."

Max was silent, but after a long beat, he gave a sharp nod.

Tyreal's eyes met Gwen's. He gave her a small, knowing half-smile, the kind that said, *Be patient. Give him time.*

An idea occurred to her, and she cleared her throat. If Max couldn't pull himself from his pain, maybe she could redirect it. Shift his focus to the bigger picture. Make it tangible.

She said to Tyreal. "We need a boat."

He did not like this plan.

Since the moment Gwen had revealed the truth about magic, his life had been a relentless string of dangerous situations, each one more absurd than the last. But none—not a single one—compared to *willingly* rowing towards a cave that might house a *fucking dragon.*

The oars cut through the dark water in steady strokes, but his gaze stayed locked on Gwen, hoping his expression conveyed every unspoken thought screaming through his head. She ignored him.

Of course she did.

Tyreal exhaled through his nose, his grip tightening on the oars. He understood his role, understood that she was still his queen. His duty was to follow her commands, especially now, when she was trying to pull them all back from the brink of war.

That didn't mean he didn't long for the version of her he'd had the night before—the woman who had unraveled beneath him, who had needed him to bring everything to the surface so she could face it. That woman wouldn't be steering them straight toward a dragon if he didn't *let* her.

And yet, here they were.

Plus, the oars were hurting his burned palm. Klause's balm could only do so much, and Tyreal hadn't been able to make his magic heal himself. Adding another mark in the "healing magic is useless" column he kept in his mind.

The rocks near the cave were just as treacherous as Gwen had described in her dream. Dismounting the boat proved just as difficult. By the time they were all on solid ground, they were more than a little wet.

On the way over, Gwen had explained her encounter with the dragon to Anya and Max. He had to give them credit—they were doing a far better job of hiding their skepticism than he'd expected.

Then again, it was a lot harder to doubt when you woke up beside someone who had been beside you in bed all night, only to find them covered in bloody scratches and dried sea salt.

"I don't think you're going to fit in there, and someone has to keep the waves from taking the boat," Gwen said to him. He blinked at her in confusion. Surely, she hadn't just said what he thought he heard.

Tyreal let out a dry, humorless laugh. "I'm sorry. For a second there, it sounded like you were suggesting I let you walk into a cave where you *last saw a dragon*—alone."

"Not alone," she corrected. "Anya can come with me, and I think Max can fit. And it's a *dragon*, Tyreal. What exactly would you do if things went sideways? Besides, if he wanted to hurt me, he already had his chance."

Tyreal's jaw tightened. "Yeah, well, that was before you showed back up with *uninvited guests*. We don't exactly know much about dragon etiquette, do we?" His frustration edged into his voice, but as he eyed the narrow entrance to the cave, he knew she was right. He wouldn't fit.

"Come now, children, stop squabbling. Fortunately, we can *fix* these things, remember?" Anya flicked her hand, and the water obeyed, lifting the boat onto a nearby rock before freezing it in place. She continued speaking without turning towards Max, refusing to look at him, her tone still edged with frost for her husband. "Can you widen the opening for us? Do you remember how to reach your power?"

She hadn't forgiven his near slip earlier. That much was clear. The newlyweds would almost certainly be having words later, and Tyreal didn't envy the young prince for it. Anya frightened even him.

Max nodded and closed his eyes, scrunching them as he focused. Tyreal found himself relieved he wasn't the only one who had to *concentrate* to access magic. Anya and Gwen made it look effortless, but for him and Max, it took work. He knew, logically, that years of practice made the difference—just as Pip would struggle to wield a broadsword while Tyreal could swing one in his sleep.

Didn't mean it chafed any less.

The rocks groaned and cracked. A large chunk of stone broke free from one side of the opening, sending a cascade of smaller rocks down around their feet, and Max floated it out of the way before sending it crashing into the waves below.

Tyreal gave him a curt nod of thanks and stepped forward to lead the way. Gwen's hand landed on his arm, stopping him. "You were right," she said, "about the uninvited guests thing. I *hadn't* considered that. It's probably best if I go first... in case I need to explain."

Tyreal closed his eyes and swallowed the growl of frustration that threatened to rise. Instead, he motioned her forward.

Hopefully, this wasn't a mistake that would cost them all their lives.

They eased through the tight tunnel, following Gwen and the soft glow of her light orb. Max occasionally had to widen the passage, shifting the rock as best he could, but otherwise, their descent was uneventful.

Then the darkness began to lift.

A faint glow seeped in from ahead, growing brighter with each step. Gwen let out a confused noise. "I don't understand. There was no light before. It was completely dark." She led them further down before halting.

Tyreal barely registered what he was doing before he grabbed her shoulder and yanked her back against his chest out of instinct. His free hand dropped to the hilt of his sword, though he knew she was right—if something *was* waiting for them, steel wouldn't do much good against a dragon.

"This…" Gwen's voice wavered as she stepped forward again, leading them into a massive, open space. "This wasn't here before."

It wasn't a cave. Or at least, not anymore.

The ceiling had been ripped away, jagged boulders scattered around the edges like shattered bone. Sunlight streamed through the gaping hole above, spilling golden light onto the stone floor. And in the center of it all stood the strangest rock formation Tyreal had ever seen.

A deep, primal instinct clawed at his chest—*leave.*

He had felt this before, on battlefields soaked in blood, when his eyes saw something his mind wasn't ready to process. A delay, as if his brain refused to acknowledge the truth before it was safe to do so. The body always knew first.

And as they stepped closer, as Gwen eased them further into the space, his mind finally *registered* what his body had already understood.

The formation wasn't rock.

It was *breathing.*

Hot gusts of air puffed across the stone floor toward them, each exhale sending pebbles skittering across the floor outwards.

He meant to grab Gwen and drag her back into the tunnel.

But he was a breath too late.

The dragon's massive golden eyes snapped open, its pupils narrowing into razor-thin slits as it swung its head toward them.

Tyreal went rigid.

That shape—those slitted pupils—triggered a long-buried memory. His papa, kneeling in the dirt beside him, pointing at a dead viper, its eyes blank and unseeing. *That's how you know if a snake is venomous, boy. Though, if you're close enough to see it, you're probably already too late.*

His heart slammed against his ribs.

These eyes weren't too small to notice.

Meaning they were *definitely* too close.

CHAPTER TWELVE

S eeing glimpses of Viamar's face before had not prepared Gwen for the sheer scale of him. He lifted his massive head from where it had rested atop his front claws, jaws parting wide. To eat them? To breathe fire? To yawn? She couldn't say, but something deep inside warned her not to overreact—that he would find it *rude*.

Hello, little Thorncrest. The voice resonated through her mind, rich and wry. *Have you brought your friends to try to slay me?*

Tyreal stiffened beside her, and she felt Anya and Max do the same. She realized he was speaking to all of them. A flicker of shock rippled through her at his words, and she blinked in surprise. She hadn't even considered that the dragon might think they would do such a thing.

"What? No," she blurted. "I wanted them to meet you, to understand the severity of what we're facing. They're from two of the other ruling families." She hoped the sincerity in her voice was enough to assure him.

Viamar let out a low, amused rumble.

Your warrior thinks slaying me might be the right course of action.

Gwen's gaze flicked to Tyreal, who didn't bother to deny it. He simply shrugged, fingers still twitching near his sword. She sighed. "That's just who he is. Don't take offense. He won't try to harm you."

Viamar inhaled, making all of their clothing pull forward, as if taking in their scents. *Fire, water, earth... and healing?* His head tilted, considering. *How interesting, for a warrior, there's irony in that.* He stretched with the lazy grace of a sun-drenched great cat, spine rolling before blinking at them, his second, translucent eyelid sliding briefly over his golden eyes.

Well. You've seen me now. How else can I help you understand the severity? He scratched at a spot behind his ear with a massive claw as he yawned.

You've interrupted my nap. Some dragons would eat you for less.

Max took a half step forward. "How many other dragons are there? If we are to be good neighbors, I'd like to understand more about your kind and your ways."

Gwen felt a flicker of relief. Even through his grief, Max's diplomatic instincts still held. He hadn't let pain and rage fully consume him—not yet.

Viamar regarded them in silence, his golden eyes unreadable. He was weighing them, deciding whether they were worth his time. The longer he remained quiet, the heavier the moment became. Gwen's chest tightened. He didn't trust them. And why should he? Humans had failed him before, repeatedly.

When your kind first landed on these shores—what you call Valine—we numbered close to thirty, including our young. There was something beneath the words, a pain carefully buried but not quite hidden.

"Before Myaessa cast her spell," Gwen asked quietly, "how many remained?"

Viamar exhaled, the hot breath stirring the folds of her skirt. *I cannot be certain. We are territorial by nature and do not communicate unless we must. However, I know there were... casualties. So, fewer.*

His neck extended, bringing his face lower, and his massive head loomed close enough that Gwen could see the fine texture of his scales. He snapped lightly at the air, his voice turning sharper. *Your heartbeat betrays you, warrior. You're pleased to know of our losses.*

Gwen, Max, and Anya took a step back out of instinct.

Tyreal did not. He held firm, chin high, eyes unwavering. "I am never glad for casualties," he said evenly. "I *am* tasked with protecting this kingdom, and as a warrior yourself, you can't blame me for taking comfort in knowing I might stand a chance if something threatened my people." He let the words settle before adding, "But only in defense."

The words seemed to appease the dragon. He relaxed his stance, though another sound rumbled from his throat, something like an amused chuckle. *I do not know why you humans insist on lies to make yourselves feel better. It must be because you are so very young. You do not care about the people of this kingdom, warrior. Not really. You care about the safety of your mate above all else. You would let me burn this entire land if I promised she would live.*

Tyreal's jaw tightened, but he didn't deny it.

Gwen wasn't sure why the words struck her so hard. Tyreal had made it clear nearly her entire life that his duty was to her above all else. Yet somehow, hearing it laid out so plainly by Viamar made it feel heavier, more real.

The dragon flexed a wing, stretching it high above his back before giving it a slow, deliberate flap, as if testing its strength. He really was a magnificent creature—if one could get past the bone-deep, instinctual terror he inspired. His wingspan covered most of the pit they stood in, thick and leathery yet almost translucent in the light filtering through the broken ceiling.

*You **should** care about your mate above all else. For that, you have my respect, warrior.* His voice was quieter now. Viamar turned his head, gazing upward at the sky rather than at them.

It was Anya who finally broke the silence. Her voice was soft, filled with a kind of sweetness that made the question feel less intrusive than it might have otherwise. "Did you have a mate?"

The dragon was still for a long moment.

I did. He offered nothing more.

"I'm very sorry for your loss," Anya said gently. "And for any part our ancestors may have played in it."

Viamar snorted softly. *You have a kind heart, dragonfly. Ask whatever questions you wish, but quickly. I want to return to my nap. I've been hunting at night to regain my strength and not startle your people. You will need to tell them soon though, little Thorncrest.* His voice darkened. *Not all will do the same once they can truly take to the skies again.*

Tyreal cocked his head, brow furrowed. "Do you truly believe that if we can somehow stop this war with Lovell before it starts, the other dragons will let us live in peace?" Gwen knew that tone—the one he used when his mind was trying to make a plan and stay steps ahead of the enemy, the one she imagined he used on the battlefield. However, this was not a battle he could fight with steel alone, and she hoped he knew it.

Viamar's golden eyes lingered on Tyreal, the weight of his gaze stretching the silence until Gwen had to fight the urge to speak. Had Tyreal insulted him? Challenged him? Finally, the dragon exhaled, the gust stirring dust and loose stones at their feet. *I do not waste time on beliefs, warrior, only what I* **know***. And I know this—war breeds war. Even before Myaessa's spell, we fought to keep some of our own from wiping out humankind entirely. Another war would only remind those who sleep why they were beginning to view you as prey.*

Fear coiled deep in Gwen's belly, making her nauseous. Could humans ever truly have peace? History had never painted an optimistic picture. Myaessa had sacrificed her life, believing magic was the root of war, that greed and ambition would always twist it into destruction. And in the five centuries since, had there ever been true peace? Borders still needed defending. Tyreal had fought in skirmishes, and she still commanded an army, prepared for a war that always seemed inevitable. What would finally tip the dragons over the edge? It felt like a guillotine blade suspended above them, waiting for the moment to fall.

Max must have been sharing similar thoughts. His handsome face pinched in worry. He cleared his throat. "If and when the other dragons wake, is there a way we could speak to them? Make them see we plan on differing from our ancestors? Already I can guarantee that at a minimum, four of the original ten families you all knew will work as allies. We are all represented in this cave."

Before Viamar could answer, Tyreal spoke. "You speak of dragons being territorial, and your tone is not favorable about the others. That leads me to believe that dragons aren't pillars of peace and friendship among themselves. Surely, they cannot expect perfection from us." Gwen winced. She agreed with him, but she also didn't know that antagonizing the grumpy dragon was wise.

Viamar let out a low, rumbling chuckle, the sound reverberating through the cavern walls. *Perfection? No. But understanding? Fear? That, they expect. You are correct, warrior—dragons are not creatures of harmony. We have fought over territory, over prey, over pride. Some of us have lost more to our own kind than we ever did to yours. But the difference is, we are honest. We do not pretend at peace while sharpening blades beneath the table. Humans build their treaties upon sand, hoping the tide will not wash them away. The others do not trust you or believe you are capable of growth.*

Gwen swallowed, relief flooding through her that yet again, Viamar found Tyreal to be amusing rather than disrespectful. Perhaps the two were more alike than it would seem from their species. "Then how do we prove otherwise?"

Viamar's golden gaze settled on her, unblinking. *You show them something greater than fear. You show them something worth keeping. Now, leave me. My patience wears thin and I wish to return to my nap.* With that, the dragon burrowed his head back under his front arm and shielded his eyes with a wing. They had been dismissed.

For the first time in what felt like forever, Gwen was alone. The quiet should have been a relief, but it pressed in around her as she tried to focus on the security reports about a pirating ring from Tyreal in front of her. He'd been trying to break it up for a while, even going so far as to ban the one he thought was behind it all from Tavian waters. Kiel something or another, she couldn't remember. Viamar's words wouldn't stop running through her head. *You will need to tell them soon though, little Thorncrest.*

Magic. Tyreal. Dragons. Every decision she made lately came with another secret to keep. She tapped her fingers on the desk, the steady rhythm the only sound in the room. She let out a slow breath and looked up at the painting of her father hanging above the fireplace.

"You prepared me for a lot, Papa," she murmured. "But not this."

And why was that? Because as far as she knew, Lorne had never been told the truth about magic. Maybe her mother had shared the secret, but if she had, he'd never let on, not even after her death. Not when Gwen spent summers training with the Sisters. He'd never given her even a hint. Would things have been different if the Sisters had told people the truth back then?

Wasn't that the same thing she was doing right now, though? She had been honest about her intent to wed Tyreal, but she hadn't said a word to anyone other than Tyreal, Max, and Anya about the dragons.

Her fingers curled into fists on the desk.

What was the point of leading if she had to do it from behind a wall of lies?

Not for the first time and certainly not the last, she wished her father was here to tell her what to do.

Gwen pushed up from her chair, her muscles aching from sitting too long, and started pacing the length of the room. Her fingers twisted together as she tried to resist chewing on her thumb. However, the coppery taste of blood filled her mouth—she'd chewed her bottom lip raw without even noticing. So much for not hurting herself with her anxiety.

A soft knock broke the heavy silence. The door cracked open, and Andais peeked inside. "Your Majesty, Prince Maximilien wishes to speak with you. May he enter?"

She nodded, and Max stepped in, shutting the door behind him. He was alone, his usual polished composure replaced with exhaustion. Deep lines creased his forehead, and the tension in his shoulders made him look older than his years. Without a word, he dropped into the chair near the fireplace, his long legs stretching out in front of him like he barely had the strength to sit upright.

Gwen arched a brow and gestured toward the decanter of spirits. When he didn't refuse, she poured two glasses and handed him one before sinking into the chair across from him.

Max stared into the amber liquid for a long moment before speaking. "What would you be if we hadn't been born into these positions? If you could choose anything?" His voice was far quieter than usual.

She blinked. "Gods, what a question." Not that she had never wished for something else—she had. Many times. But she'd never considered what she would *do* beyond being able to freely marry Tyreal. Trying to lead and do what was right for all of Tavia was all she knew.

Still, she let herself consider it. "Part of me loves the idea of living with Tyreal in the mountains, raising babies, with no politics, no wars, no councils to answer to. But another part of me..." She exhaled. "I don't think I'd know how to exist without leading."

Max shook his head, taking a long sip from his glass. "I never enjoyed leading. I can negotiate, keep people from tearing each other's throats out, and make peace when it's needed. This—" He gestured vaguely, to the burden of responsibility pressing down on them both. "Deciding what's best for an entire kingdom, making choices that could get people killed—" He leaned forward, rubbing his temple. "I hate it. My brother would be a better king than I ever will be. I feel more like an emissary than a ruler."

Gwen frowned. "You don't really believe that."

He let out a humorless laugh. "I do."

"You're exactly the leader Espera needs. Diplomacy is your strength, and that will be critical in the days ahead. Besides, you're not the one making this decision. Your father is. You still have time to sharpen your leadership skills." It was true, but it still opened the ache in her chest and a tiny flare of jealousy. She did not have that luxury.

Max let out a slow breath. "Only partially true. I have to write to him about what I witnessed today, tell him what I think the right course of action should be, and I don't know what that is. My gut says people deserve the truth, but I'm not in the right headspace to make that call." He ran a hand through his hair. "Anya is still avoiding me."

Gwen winced. "Yes, well, you stepped in it earlier. What exactly were you planning to say to her, exactly?"

His throat bobbed as he swallowed hard. "That if things were different, I would worship her, but they aren't. And sometimes, it gets to me."

She held his gaze. "You mean if *she* was different?"

He sighed, the sound heavy with frustration. "Yes, but also no." He leaned back, staring at the ceiling like it might hold the answers. "I love her for who she is. I don't wish to change *her*. Two things can be true at the same time. Loving her and not wishing to change her doesn't make it any easier to be married to someone who doesn't want you. Or at least, doesn't want you physically, when you *do* want them." His grip tightened around his glass. "I won't force her to my bed just to produce an heir, ever. And I don't blame her for not wanting me. She can't control that." He let out a bitter laugh. "Our marriage is worth it. What we are building together is worth it. But gods, it isn't easy."

Gwen's heart twisted for them both. There was no simple answer, no perfect way forward. Love without passion might have worked for others, but for two people who had always craved that kind of intimacy, it was a slow agony, a quiet loss neither of them had asked for.

"You can tell her that, you know," Gwen said, watching a muscle on Max's jaw flex as he fought for control of his emotions. "She's just as aware of the realities of your marriage as you are. If you let her sit with this too long, she's going to come up with something far worse than whatever you were actually about to say."

He let out a breath that was almost a laugh, but held no humor. "I know. I'm a coward." He shook his head, rubbing his hands over his face before dragging them down to rest on his thighs. "She's probably in the kitchens by now, eating her weight in Cook's famous cookies and cursing my name. I should go talk to her, but—" He exhaled sharply. "It's just a lot today, Gwen. Losing Alric, realizing dragons might wipe us all out for something we had no say in. I feel like I'm drowning."

She hated seeing him like this. He was always so sure of himself, so calm in the face of chaos, and now he was unraveling beneath the weight of it all.

"What would Alric have told you to do?" she asked softly.

Max huffed out a bitter laugh, shaking his head. "You know exactly what he would have said. He never backed down from a fight." His voice turned rough, like the words scraped his throat on their way out. "He'd tell me that royals and nobles always think they know what's best for the people, but rarely do."

Gwen swallowed hard, the lump in her throat making it hard to breathe. That definitely sounded like something Alric would say. Blunt in his honesty, but always fighting for the people who had no voice.

"He hoped we would be different," she said, blinking against the burn behind her eyes. "Maybe we need to *be* different."

"What does that look like?" he asked her earnestly.

"I don't know yet. Hopefully, I will figure it out soon."

CHAPTER THIRTEEN

Tyreal rapped his knuckles lightly against the chamber door before pushing it open. Cora nearly collided with him on her way out, arms full of linens.

"In a rush?" he asked, catching her by the elbow before she dropped anything. A grin tugged at his mouth. "Or just eager to watch Tensha in her fighting leathers showing up the other guards?"

Cora flushed, her eyes narrowing even as her lips twitched. "I'll have you know I'm very hard at work. Some of us aren't suddenly royal and about to marry the queen." There was no bite to her words, only good-natured ribbing.

Either way, the words landed. Harder than they should have. Tyreal smoothed his expression into something easy and playful so she wouldn't notice how she'd accidentally made his guts twist. Because it wasn't just Cora. Word had spread since Gwen's meeting and dismissal of the council, faster than a wildfire.

He'd never felt so keenly aware of so many eyes on him before.

"Go on then," he said lightly, stepping back to give her room. "Don't let me keep you from your very important *work*."

"Quit annoying Cora and get in here, High Captain," Gwen's voice carried from the window seat with a hint of amusement.

He crossed the room to her, forcing himself to relax and push all thoughts of everyone else out of his mind. She was curled up with her skirts gathered around her knees, staring out the window. Her fingers twisted in the fabric, a subtle sign of tension he knew all too well.

"How are you feeling?" he asked gently.

She let out a long breath. "Max is writing a letter to his father tonight, but I don't know what I should do. Should I send letters about the dragons to the nobles now, or wait until they're here to tell them in person? It feels too big for a letter. But waiting feels like another lie, or like waiting for a blade to fall."

Tyreal leaned against the wall, studying her as she expressed her worries. She was chewing her bottom lip in addition to picking at her thumb. He frowned. That wasn't just nerves. There was something else bothering her, something more personal and important to Gwen, not Queen Gwendolyn.

He pushed off the wall and moved to the window seat. He tilted her chin up with his fingers, forcing her to meet his gaze. "It's not just the dragons, though, is it?" His eyes flicked to her lips, the skin swollen from her abuse.

Her throat bobbed as she swallowed, then shook her head. "No, not just that." A beat of silence stretched between them before she spoke again, the words tumbling out quickly as if she was afraid if she didn't get them out, she wouldn't say them at all. "I realized that I didn't really talk to you at Mist Castle before I announced my intent to wed. And then we got back here, and I just kept going. I never asked for your input."

Gwen paused, before whispering, "Are you sure about us?" She shifted, tucking her hands into her lap as if bracing for his answer.

Tyreal blinked, then let out a slow, incredulous breath. "Now and then, you say the stupidest shit."

She smacked his arm with a half-hearted scowl. "I'm serious."

"As am I." He shrugged like it was the simplest thing in the world. "I told you at the inn, sweet girl. I'm never letting you go." His voice softened as he reached for her hand, twining their fingers together. "You are mine, and I am yours."

She didn't pull away, but he felt the tension in her grip, knew she wasn't quite convinced.

"Am I worried about how people will treat me?" Tyreal exhaled, running his thumb over her knuckles. "Some. It has been an adjustment. People are acting stranger than I expected. That doesn't change my desire to have you as my wife, though." He squeezed her hand, hoping his conviction showed through his words.

Gwen's lips curved into a lopsided half-smile before she ducked her head, almost sheepish. "It's silly, I know. Max was confiding in me earlier about the harsher realities of his marriage to Anya. They love each other, but the circumstances of who they prefer to share their bed with make it hard. I guess I got it in my head that marrying me, stepping into all of this, would feel like a cage to you."

He didn't answer with words. Instead, he leaned in, capturing her mouth with his own. He understood her fear because he carried his own. Not of feeling trapped, but that the gods would realize their mistake and rip this from his hands.

She sighed, melting into his body, her fingers threading into the thick hair at the nape of his neck. He groaned as she tugged, a quiet, greedy sound. Would the wanting ever stop? Would he ever get enough of her?

Before he could think better of it, he gripped her waist and hauled her onto his lap, smirking against her lips at the startled squeak she made. Tyreal let his hands roam, fingers itching to undo the precise, controlled style Cora had arranged her hair into. She could command him without a crown—just by letting her hair tumble free, wild and loose, down her back.

He knew he'd never hear the end of it if he did, but he couldn't resist snatching a couple of pins so that a few curled tendrils bounced down around her face. She sucked in an indignant breath, mouth falling open, and he smirked. He kissed her to distract her from her ire and redirected his hand to the curve of her breast, fingertips tracing lightly over the fabric of her dress.

Gwen squirmed at the teasing touch before planting her hands on his chest and shoving him onto his back. A wicked grin crossed her face, her hazel eyes darkening to a rich, whiskey hue. She tugged his tunic free from his breeches, fingers toying with the waistband, teasing at the laces holding them up.

She slid further down his thighs, pressing warm, open-mouthed kisses against his stomach. His cock strained against the fabric, and for a moment, he debated taking back control. Which brought up memories of their brief foray into submission to him the night before and only made the dilemma worse.

She tugged harder at the laces, untying the top knot, and looked up the length of his torso, her gaze nearly undoing him—

Right before she launched an attack of tickles along his ribs.

Tyreal yelped, jerking so hard that he nearly sent her flying. Gwen was the only person on the entire continent of Valine who knew his secret—he was, embarrassingly, ticklish. A fact he'd only admitted because at the time, he never believed they'd ever touch each other enough for it to matter.

"Brat!"

Gwen laughed, triumphant, as Tyreal twisted beneath her, cursing through gritted teeth. She showed no mercy, her fingers seeking every vulnerable spot along his ribs, his sides, even daring to brush along the sensitive place just beneath his collarbone.

"You're a menace," he growled, catching her wrists and flipping them so that she was pinned beneath him now.

She squirmed, breathless with laughter. "I don't know what you're talking about."

He arched a brow. "Oh, you don't?"

She shook her head, eyes full of mischief, but her legs wrapped around his waist. And gods, he could drown in the way she looked at him.

He lowered himself just enough that his lips brushed hers when he spoke. "Then I suppose you won't mind if I return the favor."

Her eyes widened. "Tyreal—don't you dare—"

It was too late, though. He'd decided on his course. He attacked, fingers quick and merciless, and she squealed, bucking against him in a desperate attempt to escape. She was strong, but he had the advantage of weight and knowing exactly where to press to make her laugh until she was gasping.

"Okay—okay!" she managed between breathless giggles, her limbs too weak to fight him off. "I yield!"

"Mm, I don't know," he said, smirking down at her, fingers still poised threateningly. "That was a vicious attack. I think you need to be punished for it properly."

"Oh, and what would that entail?" she asked, arching a brow even as she caught her breath, biting at her bottom lip.

Before he could answer, a sharp tap echoed through the room.

Once. Twice. Then again.

His head snapped toward the window. A sleek black crow sat perched on the ledge, its beady eyes watching them with unsettling patience. A thin tube was secured to its leg.

The mood between them shifted in an instant.

Tyreal sat up, muscles tensing as he ran a hand through his already-messy hair. "I only have one report marked critical enough for the crows to find me in a bedroom."

Gwen moved with him, sliding off the bed as he crossed to the window. "The one about Grigor?"

He nodded as he whistled to the crow, unfastening the message once it accepted. As soon as he unfurled the parchment, bloodthirsty anger threatened to swallow him whole.

"What is it?" Gwen asked quietly.

He didn't answer right away. He scanned the message again, and once more for good measure, as if the words might change. Finally he spoke, his voice tight. "Lovell's ship is making record time."

"So much for our hopes of him sinking." She sighed. "I suppose he has a skilled crew, and the weather has been fair…"

"No." Tyreal's jaw clenched. "His sails are full, even when the wind isn't blowing."

"Bloody crows." Gwen sank into a chair, all traces of playfulness gone. She dragged a hand down her face, pressing her fingertips into her forehead as if she could push away the implications of what they'd just learned. "He must have the same power the High Sister did. She was always the best at controlling air."

Tyreal exhaled sharply and set the parchment down, his fingers curling around the edge of the table to steady himself. "Why the hell isn't he struggling? Everyone else has. It takes time, effort. No one on that ship should be able to help him like you, Anya, or the sisters have done for the others."

Gwen shook her head, teeth catching on the edge of her thumb before she even realized it. "I don't know." Her voice was quiet and distant, the glazed look in her eyes telling him she was mentally back in the catacombs. He'd seen that sort of look far too often with his men, and he hated seeing it on Gwen's face now. "If I had to guess, I'd say she tried to prepare him. She thought the spell would bring magic back to their bloodline alone."

"And she knew she'd almost certainly be at Mist Castle when it happened, and unable to help him," Tyreal finished for her. It made sense.

The High Sister had been intelligent and cunning. Honestly, it was a shame she had lost herself in her madness. He frowned as he noticed Gwen continuing to irritate her poor, abused thumb.

She pushed to her feet, the chair scraping softly against the stone. Tyreal tensed, too late to catch her wrist to admonish her. She stalked across the room, pacing near the hearth. "How long do we have?"

"Best guess? Three to five days, depending on how much he needs to rest." Tyreal's mouth pressed into a hard line. "And that's assuming he's alone. If any other Lovells are with him, they could have similar power."

Gwen stopped mid-stride, shoulders locking tight as she spun to face him. The worry on her face gutted him more than a blade ever could.

"Do you know for sure the king isn't with him?" Tyreal asked.

"I certainly have heard nothing to suggest that King Zendor or Prince Caldrin have left Adaltus," she bit out. "But your spies would know more than my courtiers." The sharpness in her voice cracked on the edges, unraveling into a sigh. "I'm sorry. I'm not angry with you. I just—*why* can't anything be simple?"

He crossed the space between them, cupping her shoulders in his hands and resting his forehead against hers. "Because it never is," he murmured. "The gods enjoy their little games."

Her shoulders sagged, but only for a breath. Then she straightened, spine rigid and chin tilted upwards. Her queen armor. "Go find everyone. Hedontas, Andais, Cora, Tensha... anyone whose opinion I'll actually listen to. I'll warn them about the dragons. Then we plan."

The ache for battle pulsed low in his gut. He turned before it showed too clearly on his face. He knew she was aware that he would do anything to protect her, but this part, he tried to shield her from.

Gods, how he longed to end this with a blade. No politics. No waiting. Just violence. Nothing and no one standing between Gwen and safety.

He crossed halfway to the door, then stopped. Something in him resisted moving further. He could rally their troops and help with battle planning. The problem was, he knew that wasn't what Gwen wanted to do.

This wasn't how he knew to protect her, and the wrongness itched like an old wound that hadn't healed clean.

Still, doing nothing would be worse. Without a plan, Grigor Lovell and men just like him—ruthless and hollow with ambition—would gut this kingdom from the inside. His jaw set as he turned away from her towards the door, shuttering whatever emotions might show on his face. "Yes, Your Majesty. I'll bring them."

She blinked at him in shock. He wasn't sure why the formal title left his mouth, not exactly.

Only that in this moment, anything less than responding as her High Captain felt wrong.

CHAPTER FOURTEEN

"There are fucking dragons now?" Hedontas asked, voice rough with disbelief. Gwen had never heard him sound quite so overwhelmed. He sagged back in his chair, rubbing a weathered hand down his face as if he could scrape away the absurdity of what she had just told him.

Andais didn't bother with words. He slid a heavy glass of spirits across the table towards Hedontas, then served another for himself, dark liquid sloshing as an air bubble glugged its way to the top from how quickly he poured it.

Gwen couldn't blame them. She had spent so many days now in a cycle of wanting to laugh, cry, or pour herself a drink that she had lost count of them. She cracked her knuckles, looking up towards the rafters of the library as if she could somehow find her father's soul to give her some kind of help. "It has been an eventful few days, hasn't it?" The dryness of her voice tasted bitter. "Yes, there are apparently dragons now. I am not thrilled about it either. Least of all with this ultimatum they've laid at our feet."

Her gaze swept across the table. These were her people, the ones she trusted the most—and even so, the news rattled them all in different ways.

Tensha was as unreadable as ever—arms crossed, chin tipped slightly down, she studied Gwen silently. The only outward appearance that she was truly affected by the news was that she had reached for Cora's hand. She never showed affection in public.

Beside her, Cora toyed with the fabric of her dress, twisting it tight around her fingers. Her eyes were distant and unfocused. She looked overwhelmed, her round face pinched so much that you could barely see the freckles that dusted across her nose and cheeks.

Pip nearly broke Gwen's heart. He sat stiff as a board, wide-eyed and too quiet, looking every bit the young boy everyone always tried to convince her he wasn't anymore. But right now, he was vulnerable, scared. She reached across the space between them and laced her fingers through his. She gave his hand a gentle squeeze, offering what she hoped was a reassuring smile, or at least one that didn't appear fragile as it actually felt.

Max cleared his throat, bringing everyone's attention to him. "Take your moment," he said, voice firm but not unkind. "Be shocked. Be scared. You've earned it." His gaze swept around the table. "Then set it aside. Time is not something we have in abundance, and there's too much on the table for us to waste it."

Gwen glimpsed the king in him then, albeit a reluctant one, the man who hadn't asked for his future but would shoulder it anyway. And he would do it well. She sent a silent prayer to the gods that they would figure out a way through this mess, and that Tavia and Espera could build a better future for Valine.

Hedontas snorted, setting his glass down and rubbing at his jaw. "Suppose it would be too much to hope your new dragon friend might just burn Prince Grigor's ship to the sea floor? It'd save us a hell of a lot of trouble."

Gwen shook her head. "I'm certain he won't intervene," she answered. "If we want the other dragons to believe we can coexist—humans, magic, all of it—we have to handle this ourselves."

"Did you get your crow sent off to your parents?" Tyreal asked, his question aimed at both Max and Anya. It was one of the few things he'd said since they'd all gathered. He'd left Gwen to steer the conversation, sitting quiet and unreadable at her side.

She wished she could crack open his mind, just for a second. Ever since that shift back in her chambers, when he'd started calling her by her title again, something had felt off. Like a storm churning out at sea while the sun still shone on the coast.

Maybe he just needed time to process everything. He did that sometimes, pulling inward until the pieces made sense to him. The anxious part of her worried it was something else, a knot twisting in her belly. Maybe, in the shadow of what was coming, he was building up invisible walls, preparing to push her away in the name of keeping her safe. Surely he wouldn't do that again—they had made a promise to each other. And he had just reassured her in her chambers. Still, though, that had been before this shift. She frowned, eyes raking over him, but he either didn't notice or was ignoring her.

"Yes. I sent one as well," Anya said. "We marked them as urgent, and paid the crows handsomely, so they should arrive this evening." She laid her hand gently over Max's, and Gwen caught the gesture. It distracted her from Tyreal and brought a smile to her face. It seemed the two had found some peace after Max had left her chambers. Thank the gods for small favors. She hated seeing either of them upset.

"Good," Gwen echoed. "It's better that it came from you both. It's unfortunate I can't get word out to the other royals before they arrive, but it feels too serious for a letter from a fellow sovereign. I want to tell them in person. Any word on their movements?" Her gaze shifted to Tyreal and Andais, knowing their intelligence tracked the flow of key figures across the borders.

Andais inclined his head. "Some, Your Majesty. We already knew the prince and princess' families would come. But we've just received word that King Drakon is traveling here from Galeigh. And the King and Queen of Egrax set sail this morning; they're expected within two days. No timeline yet of Princess Eliana's family, though I suspect they will come as well. I've heard the birth of their grandchild went smoothly, so it's likely the king and queen will accompany her."

"Anything from Ravendell or Malticai?"

He shook his head. "Nothing yet, Majesty. Ravendell's dowager queen is unlikely to travel, given how young their new king is, and her late husband was a longtime ally of Adaltus. Malticai remains as unpredictable as ever. They've kept to the middle ground for years, and how they respond now is anyone's guess."

"Galeigh and Egrax despise each other," Gwen said, "so we'll need to keep a careful eye on that. Diplomacy will be key—your time to shine, Max." She offered him a wry smile. "If we secure support from either country, or better yet *both*, we'll have support from most of the continent, even without Malticai."

Hedontas frowned. "Support in what, exactly? If our goal is to prevent a war, what are we asking them to stand behind?"

Gwen grimaced. "Oh, nothing too complicated," she said, voice edged with sarcasm. "Just the small matter of forming a council made up of every kingdom, one that can mediate disputes before they spill onto battlefields. And ideally, some kind of safeguard that will keep us from sliding into another war, and hopefully stop the dragons from burning us all to ash."

"That safeguard will have to have some bite to it. Not just empty words, but some kind of common interest to keep the countries talking instead of marching," Tyreal added.

"Why not just repeat what Myaessa did?" Hedontas offered with a shrug. "Wipe out magic completely this time. I'm sure plenty would prefer that."

Gwen's eyes flicked to Anya, catching the subtle unease in her friend's expression. One that mirrored her own. It was a fair question, even if it sat poorly in her gut.

"For one," Gwen replied, trying to keep her voice neutral to not reveal how much the idea bothered her. "Myaessa's spell demanded a life in return. Hers. I doubt anyone will race to volunteer for that outcome."

"The High Sister didn't die when she reversed the spell," Tyreal said quietly. "That knowledge doesn't leave this room, by the way." His gaze swept across them all, hard and deliberate, to make his point. "The people think she died from the spell. They don't know that Gwen killed her. I would prefer to keep it that way."

He shifted, a flicker of something that looked very near hope crossing his face for the briefest of moments before returning to neutrality. "Maybe it was my family's blood in her spell that made the difference. Myaessa didn't have that for hers," he reminded her. He drummed his fingers on the tabletop as he chewed on the idea. "It's not the worst idea—no more magic, no more dragons, just Adaltus left to face, and I can handle them the old-fashioned way."

Gwen arched a brow, folding her arms. She could tell that he desperately wanted this to be an option, and though she couldn't fault him for it, it irked her. "Alright, sure, maybe that could work. Just one small hitch—how exactly do you plan on getting blood from Lovell's line? And even if we somehow pulled off that miracle, would you be willing to let me test your theory? Because I'm not about to ask anyone else to sacrifice themselves on the off chance you're right."

Tyreal's frown was deep, laced with more than simple irritation at Gwen's sharp tone. She met it with a shrug, utterly unbothered. "With that idea mostly settled, what else can we do to make this work?" she asked.

"A ball." Tensha's voice startled them all.

Gwen blinked, surprised. "A ball? Like, a dance?"

Tensha nodded and leaned forward, resting her clasped hands on the table. "Yes, the gathering kind. For you and the captain's betrothal."

When no one immediately spoke, a flicker of impatience crossed Tensha's otherwise impassive face. She let out a slow sigh. "You want to control the... how do you say? The way the story is shaped," she said, casting a glance toward Cora.

"What?" Cora's brows knitted and then lit up. "Oh! Control the narrative."

"Yes." A rare, fleeting smile tugged at Tensha's mouth as she looked at the woman beside her. A warm look of love passed between them before her focus returned to Gwen. "You want to shape the narrative—that this court is a neutral ground, and that this union is the right course of action. So, act like it."

Max tapped a finger against his chin, thoughtful. "Etiquette would force them into civility. No one starts a war while they're guests under banners of celebration. Get them dancing, get the wine flowing, and the next day, maybe they'll hesitate before sharpening knives."

Gwen frowned, brows furrowed as she looked around at them all. "Is that even appropriate? With everything going on with magic..." Her voice faltered, doubt creeping in. "To throw a ball after that feels—"

"Brilliant," Anya finished confidently.

Gwen blinked at her.

"If you appear frantic, like you're grasping for help, the other nobles will circle like sharks," Anya continued, leaning forward. "They'll weigh what they stand to gain from your desperation instead of seeing the real threat—the dragons and the risk of war. But if you stand tall, presenting this new future as a foregone conclusion, you change the game. A ball isn't just a celebration, it's a statement. You're telling them that Tavia is unshaken, that you're still sovereign here. And under your roof, they will be forced to act accordingly."

Silence followed, everyone thinking through the possibilities.

Tyreal broke it with a nod. "I'll leave the details of parties to the rest of you, but the timing could give us an edge." He stood and paced near the table as he thought. "Everyone gathered and celebrating when Prince Grigor arrives would force him to play catch-up. He won't know about the betrothal. He won't know you've already taken this to the public. We might actually catch him off balance."

Hedontas grunted, arms crossed. "Or it gives him a chance to wipe out multiple rulers in one go," he warned darkly.

"Though," he continued, a grudging acknowledgement in his tone, "he'd be a fool to try. Thorncliff's walls have stood against every siege in history, and the rulers wouldn't be unarmed. They have their own magic and the Tavian guard."

Tyreal and Andais nodded in agreement.

Gwen chewed at her bottom lip, deep in thought. "I don't think Grigor is capable of a direct assault, even with other Lovells beside him. Not yet. He isn't trained enough. He might be able to conjure wind for his sails, but storming a hall full of rulers who also wield magic, many of them highly trained?" She shook her head. "No. I'm with Tyreal on this. The timing could work. It might actually force Grigor to reconsider."

She exhaled slowly. "I'm still concerned by how it will be seen beyond these walls," she admitted quietly. "The other royals will understand. They'll read the subtleties, the politics beneath the wine and music. But the common folk..." Her thumb unconsciously rose to her mouth, anxiety creeping into her voice. "To them, it might look like we're celebrating while the world teeters on the brink. The city guards have had to break up several fights already as people grapple with everything that happened after magic's return."

Her gaze dropped, shoulders tensing, as she closed her eyes. "I fear they'll see me as indifferent, a queen too busy dancing while the kingdom fractures beneath her feet."

The words tasted bitter as they left her. "If that happens," she continued, "we won't just be facing down the dragons—I'll also be staring down a rebellion. Even if we bring Grigor to heel, that would still show the dragons that we are incapable of peace."

Tensha again broke the silence. "Then show them the truth before they can assume the worst."

"Meaning?" Gwen asked, opening her eyes to look at the dark and stoic woman across from her.

Tensha shrugged, appearing somewhat uncomfortable with the amount of attention she had already received by speaking up. "Don't throw the ball behind the castle walls. Do like you did for the funeral pyre. Open the gates and make the people part of it."

Max made a thoughtful sound. "It would make the people feel included, and it would feel very... you. You've already laid the groundwork of making them a part of things, of tearing down that veil between the happenings in the castle and the happenings out there. It will assure them they are a part of this new future you keep speaking of. Give them food, music, and a queen and future King Consort that walk among them."

Tyreal and Andais both groaned at the same time, forcing a laugh from Gwen that she hadn't expected. "Come now, boys, you already did half of the hard work for the funeral pyre. You have some idea of what security measures would need to be in place."

She looked at Hedontas. "What do you think? You were the most concerned about how people could react to the truth about Tyreal before. This betrothal ball is just an extension of that."

The older man took his time answering, staring into the spirits in his glass before lifting his head to meet her eyes. "It could buy you goodwill. They liked you opening up the funeral, which was an idea that most of us thought was unnecessarily risky. That risk was the right one, though. Sending Lorne off like that was perfect. I trust your judgement, Your Majesty."

She drew a breath, smiling gratefully at him. The weight in her chest eased some. "Alright. We host the ball for the royals, yes, but we also hold a celebration in the streets. The people will eat and drink with us, and Tyreal and I will walk through town. Everyone will know that we are in on this together."

Cora reached across the table and squeezed Gwen's hand. "And they will see that they have a queen who wants to hide nothing from them and include them in everything."

"Gods damn it," Tyreal growled, "Right, another security nightmare celebration it is. We have very little time, so we need to get to work on preparations." There was a flicker of pride in his eyes when he looked at her, but he quickly glanced away.

The doubt from earlier crept back in and settled beneath her breastbone.

CHAPTER FIFTEEN

Tyreal rolled onto his back, flinging an arm over his face to block the sunlight streaming through the uncovered window. He'd forgotten to draw the curtains when he'd returned to his room the night before.

He'd been up late with Andais. Deep in strategy, maps spread across the table and trying to make safety protocols for the betrothal ball, the parade through the streets, and Lovell's arrival. He told himself he hadn't gone to Gwen's room so he wouldn't wake her. A braver man would probably admit that wasn't true. Something else had kept him away, and he knew it.

He'd hoped a night alone might bring clarity. Instead, he'd tossed in the sheets, haunted by scenarios and half-formed doubts. He knew how to fight—how to outflank, outthink, survive. That part came easy, even with Lovell's magic now in play. But court politics? Diplomacy? They might as well be speaking another language. There'd been no training for this, no battle drills or sword forms to help him navigate this world, or the pressure of standing beside a queen instead of charging ahead of an army. He'd always led from the front, and if he wasn't leading, he was behind her, protecting her back. That was where he knew who he was. Where things made sense.

Word had already begun to spread across Tavia. He had already received a letter from his mother congratulating him. She was headed to Thorncliff. She likely wouldn't make it to the betrothal ball on time, but with the help of Sister Kelra, who could appear and vanish in different places at will, they were making record time.

He hadn't lied to Gwen the day prior; he had no doubts about his desire to be her husband. He loved her more than life itself. Could he be the man she needed at her side, though?

Tyreal let out a groan and shoved the blanket off. The bed felt too big without her in it. He already missed her warmth, the way she curled toward him in her sleep. He had not slept away from her side since the day their relationship had changed at the inn. He knew he owed her more than silence. She was likely already wondering why he hadn't come to her, her feelings almost certainly hurt. The last thing she needed right now was further stress because he was drowning in doubt.

He ran a hand through his hair, still tousled from sleep, and crossed the room barefoot. The stone floor was rough against his soles, starkly cold from the warmth of his bed. His gaze drifted toward the hearth, where ashes clung stubbornly to charred logs. For a moment, he considered lighting a fire—then dismissed the thought. He was stalling, and he knew it.

With a sigh, he dressed quickly, pulling on a tunic and boots with the practiced ease of a soldier who'd done it a thousand times in the dark. The halls outside were quiet, the hour too early for servants or courtiers. Still, it wasn't Andais outside Gwen's chambers this morning. Their late-night planning had required a different guard, so he wouldn't be able to go the direct route.

He eased into the hidden corridor that linked their rooms and pressed his ear to the wall at the opening to hers. Silence met him. No soft rustle of sheets, no quiet hum of her voice. Carefully, he eased the concealed painting open and peered into the room.

The space was cloaked in shadows. Only the faint, fading glow of embers in the hearth offered light, casting the room in the faintest golds and reds. Her curtains were tightly drawn, just as he knew they would be. Gwen never forgot them—his morning-averse queen clung to sleep like a cat curling deeper into a sunbeam.

A smile tugged at the corners of his mouth before he could stop it. He crossed to the bed quietly so as not to wake her just yet. She was bundled beneath the fur blanket, nearly swallowed by it. Only the tip of her freckled nose peeked out from the edge, the rest of her face buried in warmth.

His chest tightened. Just that small, familiar sight made something in him ache.

She deserved someone born for this. A polished diplomat. Someone who could glide through palace life with effortless charm and a silver tongue. Instead, she had him—a soldier with hands roughened by the hilt of his sword, a hunger for violence, and a magic that seemed ill-suited for a man of his talents. He couldn't even heal her head when it ached or himself when she burned him.

Still, she'd chosen him again and again, even when given every opportunity not to. He wasn't the King Consort she deserved, but he was the one she would have. Because he was hers. Fiercely. Helplessly. Completely.

And because he knew her well enough that walking away would be useless. She'd only follow.

He lifted the edge of the furs and slipped beneath them, careful to keep his boots off the bedding. The warmth and scent of her were immediate—comforting and familiar. He reached out and gently brushed a finger against the tip of her nose.

She wrinkled it in response, mumbling something incoherent as she burrowed deeper into the blanket. He tried again, a little more insistent this time, and finally, her eyes fluttered open.

She blinked at him, a sleepy smile curving her lips, but only for a moment. Then her expression shifted, the smile falling as something guarded flickered across her face. "You didn't come to bed," she said softly. "Why?"

He hesitated. The easy answer came first—the lie. *Didn't want to wake you.* They'd promised each other no more of that, though. No half-truths, no softening the edges. "I needed to get some things straight in my head," he said. "And I got to bed late. I didn't want to bother you. But mostly it was the first reason."

She studied him for a moment. "Did you?" she asked. "Work whatever it was out, I mean?"

"I think so," he said quietly. "I don't doubt my love or wanting to grow old with you, Gwennie. That's the one thing I've never questioned." He hesitated, his voice roughening. "I just doubt... myself. What good I am to you as King Consort. I know how to be your High Captain. I've trained for that almost my whole life. But politics?" He exhaled. "I don't know how to navigate that world. I'm scared of failing you."

Gwen blinked at him once, then twice, before narrowing her eyes. "Do I get to hit you now for saying stupid shit?"

Her hands came up to frame his face, warm palms bracketing his cheeks. She leaned her forehead against his before pressing a soft, lingering kiss to his lips. It was slow and sweet, the kind of kiss that didn't rush or grasp—just *was*, like they had the rest of their lives to get it right.

He deepened it instinctively, but she gave him a playful shove.

"No, I don't think so," she said with a grin. "I haven't even freshened my breath yet." She tossed the blanket aside and stood, stretching with an effortless grace. A flick of her fingers sent the hearth roaring back to life. Another gesture opened the curtains, though she sent them careening open a bit too forcefully. She frowned and scrunched her nose.

It settled something in him. Gwen, even after years of training, still struggled with her new air magic. It was a small reminder that not everything came naturally to everyone, not even her.

And that made him feel a little less like he was already failing.

There was something looser about her now, a sense of ease he hadn't noticed was missing until it returned. Even with the weight of the crown, the tension of the coming ball, and the politics pressing in, she sparkled in a way she hadn't before—like some dark, hidden corner of her soul had finally come into the light.

He hadn't realized how heavy it must've been, carrying the secret of her magic and her love for him for so long.

"Did you and Andais make headway on the ball's security and the march through the town?" she asked, moving through the room as she prepared for the day. She summoned water with a flick of her fingers, filling the tub and heating it with a slow swirl of her hand. Steam curled into the air, misting around her.

Tyreal watched her for a beat, warmth tugging behind his ribs. "Aye, we did," he said. "You were right. We'd already laid the groundwork with the funeral pyre. These plans are pretty similar in structure." He tilted his head, lips quirking. "That's a neat trick with the water."

"Like that, do you?" she asked, amused. "It's definitely more convenient than waiting for someone to fetch the water. Even at Mist Castle, I couldn't do anything like this before the magic unlocked."

She faced away from him as she spoke, her fingers catching the hem of her shift. "It's amazing, but terrifying, how much more I have at my disposal now." The fabric lifted, and he got a perfect view of the smooth lines of her back, the dimples just above the curve of her ass. The sight had his fingers itching to palm them, to squeeze the tender flesh until she squeaked.

She glanced over her shoulder with a knowing smile, then stepped into the steaming water and lowered herself in, slow and unhurried. "A shame you didn't come to bed last night. Perhaps I'd be more willing to share my bath with you."

He chuckled. "Ah. It's to be like that then? Punishment for my transgressions?"

She shrugged prettily. "Perhaps. You are free to leave the room and not watch me bathe, if it bothers you."

"If I ever choose to not view you nude, love, you either need to have me put to death or taken to the Arbiter for possession."

She laughed, and his own lips tipped upwards in response. He felt lighter now, having voiced the fears out loud. What couldn't they face together?

The buoyant happiness he had felt in Gwen's chambers was evaporating like morning fog under direct sunlight. The warmth of her kiss, the quiet reassurance of her touch, it all seemed like a distant memory the moment they stepped beyond her door.

Here in the marbled halls of the palace, people were already treating him differently. Staff were tripping over themselves, unsure of how to address him. They bowed too quickly, or not at all, but in a way that seemed deliberate and cold, even if they wouldn't have before. Those people still called him High Captain, but there was a stiffness in their voices he had never heard, a hesitation.

Not to say it was everyone. There were some staff members with genuinely cheerful smiles for the pair of them. Cook had practically thrown herself on them, hugging them both fiercely around their necks and dabbing at her eyes with her apron. She had declared the feast they would have for their betrothal ball would be unlike anything Tavia had ever seen. The memory soothed Tyreal's frayed nerves for a moment, until they passed a group of his men, and he saw their drawn expressions where they once would have laughed freely with him or given a mocking salute out of view of the queen.

"Just give it time. Everyone will relax soon enough. It's just a transition," Gwen murmured beside him, her voice low enough to stay between them.

He gave a terse nod, jaw tight. It *should* have comforted him, the feeling of her arm looped through his. That they could walk like this, like lovers, without the need to pretend or force distance between them. Instead, all he could seem to focus on was the way his worn training leathers, a soldier's uniform, looked next to the fine fabric of her gown.

A courtier stepped into their path. He bowed low to Gwen but barely inclined his head to Tyreal. His gaze drifted appraisingly over him.

Tyreal felt it for what it was, the judgement inherent to it. He bristled, opening his mouth to respond, but Gwen squeezed his arm once. A silent *stay calm*.

"Hello, Sir Rashir. Have you word from your king and queen about if they will join us for the meeting I've called?" Gwen's voice was slightly icy as she stared down the handsome courtier from Malticai.

Rashir smiled, all charm and polish. "I have not heard yet, Your Majesty, but I'm sure the announcement you sent out this morning about the ball may change things. I believe they will want to come in person to witness this *historic* change."

"Funny, I would have thought my original request to discuss magic and Prince Grigor would have been of more interest to your rulers." Her expression didn't flicker as her subtle barb landed. To his credit, Rashir didn't react either. The friendly, somewhat bland, look on his face never changed. These were precisely the battles Tyreal was not trained to fight.

"Of course, Your Majesty, everyone will be most eager to talk about that and magic's return," Rashir continued, voice smooth. "I don't presume to have any thoughts about such heavy matters of state. Far above my courtier station, I'm afraid, so you'll forgive me for being interested in your betrothal. It is unusual, elevating a guard to King Consort. Malticai thrives on tradition, but we admire boldness."

Tyreal met the man's gaze head-on. He may not be trained in politics, but one thing the battlefield had taught him was never to look away from a potential enemy. Never back down or let them see they are getting to you. Rashir was a smaller man, with slicked-back hair and a patterned tunic topped with a short, stiff collar.

Gwen smiled sweetly. "Which is why I am so fortunate that the man the gods chose for me is no ordinary consort and is instead gifted with royal blood, per Valine traditions. Not to mention that Tyreal earned his place at my side, more than any born to it."

Rashir inclined his head. "Yes, very fortunate indeed. In Malticai, we say the gods tested the royal families with fire before they crowned them. I look forward to seeing how yours burns." He stepped aside with a smile, but his words lingered.

They walked on. Gwen didn't speak right away, and neither did Tyreal. The self-doubt churned in his gut like soured ale.

When Gwen finally spoke, he was surprised to hear an edge of humor in her voice. "How badly did you want to punch him?"

The corners of his lip tipped up, despite his mood. "Only a little."

"You didn't though. Look, you're already adjusting to political games."

He huffed a laugh. He could hear the strain in it, but Gwen didn't call him on it. She just kept her arm looped through his, guiding him through the wide corridor like they didn't have a care in the world. Certainly not rewriting the traditions of their land, dragons, impending war, and annihilation. That was one thing he loved about her, about them. She always knew when to push and when to let him sit with what he was feeling. He tried to do the same for her.

They passed a pair of nobles who dipped into half-curtsies and quick bows. Their eyes flicked toward Tyreal, then skittered away just as fast. He repressed the urge to sigh. He knew that this was to be expected, but there was something different about experiencing it. No longer common, but not one of the nobility either. Feeling like he didn't belong anywhere was new and uncomfortable.

"Are they always like that?" He asked. "The courtiers I mean. The... smirking. The posturing. I admit, I haven't truly paid them much attention before."

"Not always." Gwen's mouth pulled into a tight line. "Just when they think they've found a weak point."

"And they think it's me."

She didn't answer right away. Which *was* an answer in itself. "I don't think it has anything to do with you or me," she said finally. "They've had to adapt to a lot of changes in a very short amount of time. Looking down their noses at the common folk comes naturally. In times of fear, I think some people revert to what is familiar, even if it's cruel."

Tyreal gave a noncommittal grunt. He agreed with her. He just wasn't sure what it said for their hopes that they could build something new.

CHAPTER SIXTEEN

"Is it terribly wrong of me to be excited about this ball when there is so much else going on?" Cora asked, pinning yet another curl in place. Gwen was quite certain that she had to have at least a hundred pins hidden amongst her hair at this point. It was hard to be upset about it, though, when the effect was so beautiful. The curls swooped and draped around her crown in a purposefully messy updo that Gwen couldn't recreate if her life depended on it.

A grin tugged at the corner of her lips. "I'll admit, I find myself rather excited too. It certainly doesn't hurt that this gown is positively stunning. How on earth did you and the seamstresses pull this off?"

Cora giggled. "Perhaps we have a bit of magic of our own, Your Majesty." She pinned a sheer black veil into the back of Gwen's hair, letting it flow down over her shoulders and the back of the gown.

Gwen stood before the looking glass, turning slowly to take in the gown from every angle. For once, the mourning elements didn't feel like a burden. The cream-colored silk rested off her shoulders, smooth against her skin, while gold embroidery tracing delicate swirls along the neckline and over the bodice. Long, billowy sheer sleeves flowed to her wrists, ending in narrow cuffs of gold lace. The overskirt flared from her waist, its hem lined with black roses outlined in gold, the design curling up along the split panels. Beneath, a black underskirt shimmered faintly with the same gold embroidery as the top. Cora had brushed a fine layer of crushed shell powder across Gwen's shoulders and collarbone, leaving behind a subtle glow that caught the light with every shift and sigh.

"Tyreal is going to simply stop breathing when he sees you." Cora said, stepping back with a proud smile. "This is quite the masterpiece we've pulled off."

"I believe Tensha might have the same reaction," Gwen replied with a warm grin. "You look beautiful, Cora. Remind me to have Luca give the seamstresses a hefty bonus. They've more than earned it lately." Gwen clasped her lady's hand, looking over the gown she wore.

It echoed Gwen's in shape, though simpler in design, a soft smoke-blue silk layered over a gray underskirt. Black rose vines were embroidered along the hem and sleeves, marking her place in Gwen's court. The corset laced up the front with black ribbon, and a thick black border lined the bottom of the skirt.

Cora blushed, and they both giggled. "I'll admit, I'm curious how they dressed Tensha," she said. "She refuses to wear a gown, and the court still doesn't know what to do with a female soldier."

Gwen nodded. "Tyreal is in the same boat. Still High Captain, but now the incoming King Consort. So many rules my court already likes to break."

"That's what makes us the best court, Your Majesty."

Gwen smiled again, and the two left her chambers, collecting Pip and Jameson as they went. Andais followed close behind, both guards dressed in the same golden ceremonial armor they'd worn at their swearing in.

She had seen little of them—or of Tyreal—in the last day and a half. With nobles arriving by the hour and staff working nonstop, the entire castle had been in a frenzy preparing for the ball.

They paused outside the great doors to the throne room, now repurposed as the ballroom. The low thrum of conversation filtered through the heavy wood. Gwen exhaled slowly, steadying herself against the ever-present wave of anxiety rising inside her.

"Go over the plan with me again," she said quietly to Andais.

"Of course, Your Majesty," he replied. "You and Prince Pippen will be announced first. You'll take your seats and welcome the guests. Then Tyreal—er, the High Captain, or King Consort...?"

Gwen cut him a sideways glance, lips twitching. "Pick one."

He cleared his throat. "Right. He'll be announced and join you. You'll validate him as a member of one of the original royal families, introducing him as Tyreal Blackbane Ardienne. Then you'll announce the betrothal. After that, we march through the city then come back to the castle and kick off the feast and the ball."

"And all the royals are here?"

"All the ones we expected, Your Majesty. The King and Queen of Malticai arrived just a short while ago. Staff got them to their guest suites with just enough time to freshen up and find their seats."

Gwen gave a small nod. "Alright then. Good. Maybe this is going to go fine." She exhaled apprehensively, trying to quiet the flutter in her chest. "That gives us nearly everyone on the continent, if they all agree. Which, of course, they rarely do. But no pressure." She took a deep breath and ran her hands over her skirts, praying to any gods that would listen that her palms weren't so sweaty they would mar the beautiful fabric. She gave a nod to Andais, and he stepped ahead to pull the heavy doors open.

She slipped her arm through Pip's and lifted her chin, fixing on a dazzling smile. This was still her betrothal ball. No matter what came next, tonight she got to stand beside the man she loved. She hadn't allowed herself to believe it was possible until now.

She looked around the room, smiling at the flags from across Valine that her staff had hung along the walls. The tables sparkled with polished silver and crystal, and every available surface bloomed with as many flowers and as much fall greenery as her people could gather. Candles filled the room, in sconces, candelabras, on tables, and more, giving the space a warm, golden glow.

As they reached the dais, her heart gave a small jolt at the sight of the third throne. One for her. One for Pip. And one for Tyreal.

Papa, if you can hear me… thank you, she thought, letting the gratitude and joy wash over her—just for this moment.

She straightened her dress, turned, and faced the crowd. "Welcome everyone, and thank you for coming on such short notice. I am grateful to see so many friendly faces on a day that I have dreamed of for most of my life. Though there are many serious conversations we will face in the coming days, I hope that you'll join us tonight in celebration with our court and with the people of Thorncliff. Soon, I will formally present the High Captain and restore his family's name to the records of Valine's royal bloodlines. A scribe from the Sisters of the Mist is here to witness and verify that restoration. Afterward, we will march through the city to celebrate with our people before returning here to begin the feast."

As her last words echoed through the hall, there was a pause, just long enough to make her stomach twist. Finally, there came applause. Polite and practiced at first, the kind nobles offered out of habit. Then it grew, carried by some of her guard and nobles she recognized, both Tavian and a few from the visiting courts. Anya and Max clapped the hardest, and Anya's mother offered her a brief smile.

Not everyone joined in. There were a few that remained still, hands folded and their expressions unreadable. Gwen wasn't surprised by this. She had known that reactions would be mixed. She just hoped that she could get them to see reason about the things that mattered. Her marriage to Tyrcal, ultimately, was none of their concern.

The soft hum of conversation eventually returned, but there was a charge beneath it now. Curiosity. Speculation. Questions waiting for answers.

And then, a shift.

The crowd turned toward the doors, as if sensing Tyreal's arrival before the crier had even spoken. Gwen's stomach flipped, her pulse skipping. In Tavia, traditions were a little different. The wedding itself would be small and private, a quiet ceremony of just the two of them, with their vows spoken before the Arbiter the next morning at first light. This was the real spectacle. The betrothal ball.

For all intents and purposes, after this public moment, they were considered wed to the general populace. She had dreamed of this day since she was a little girl.

The crier stepped forward, his voice ringing loudly and causing everyone in the room to go silent. "Presenting His High Honor, the High Captain of the Tavian Guard—Tyreal Blackbane."

The doors opened.

Tyreal stood tall in the entryway, his expression unreadable but calm. His outfit was somewhere between formal ceremony and military uniform that was uniquely his. A cream silk tunic, a perfect match to her gown, lay beneath a charcoal gray jacket fastened with rows of gold clasps. Gold embroidery traced the cuffs and sleeves in intricate patterns, and over his heart bloomed a large golden rose. The Thorncrest symbol. Now partially his.

A long black velvet cape, edged in gold and stitched with climbing roses, hung from one shoulder, trailing behind him with each step. She knew without asking that it could be removed in seconds. He'd have insisted on it, just in case he needed to fight. His sword still hung at his hip, and while he was every bit the royal figure tonight, his hair was still slightly tousled. His boots were still a little worn.

He looked like a man between two worlds. Soldier and royal.

And somehow, impossibly, hers.

She didn't realize she'd been holding her breath until his eyes found hers. In an instant, the rest of the room faded and all she could see was him. He gave her the smallest nod and a signature Tyreal smirk, and she smiled—couldn't help it.

She lifted her hand and motioned for him to come forward. "This is a moment none of us expected," she began, her voice sure and clear. "Those of us who spent our summers with the Sisters of the Mist were trained to think about the tenth family. What it would mean if they returned, a name lost to time, and a bloodline thought extinguished." She paused, letting her eyes linger on the other royal women she knew had always carried the embers of magic. "The truth always has a way of surfacing, even when we least expect it. The gods work in ways we rarely understand, but for this, I am grateful."

Her eyes found Tyreal again, letting the weight of her next words settle over the room as they stared at each other.

"I present to you Tyreal Blackbane Ardienne. High Captain of the Tavian Guard, the heir of the lost tenth royal family. His claim has been verified by the Sisters of the Mist, and I stand before you tonight to restore his name to the records of Valine's history." She took a breath, and she could not remain somber, breaking into a smile as happy tears welled in her eyes. "As Queen of Tavia, I recognize his claim. I formally state my intention to take him as my King Consort. Tomorrow, we will say our vows in front of the gods, and from that day forward, he will be known as Tyreal Thorncrest."

She wasn't sure if it was a response to her obvious happiness or something else entirely, but the applause that followed felt different—less formal, less restrained. Genuine. Or maybe she was just too wrapped up in the way Tyreal was looking at her to believe anything else.

When she finally glanced away from him, she saw people on their feet, clapping with genuine warmth. A few guests even wiped at their eyes. If anyone looked less than pleased, Gwen chose not to see it.

Tyreal walked the length of the aisle toward her. Unhurried. A swagger full of confidence. The velvet cape whispered across the stone floor, gold roses catching the light with every step. When he reached the dais, he dropped to one knee before her and looked up, meeting her gaze without hesitation.

"I formally state my intention to accept this betrothal," he said, voice strong and unwavering. "To stand beside you as King Consort as you rule our country. Forever, my queen. And my wife."

Pip stepped forward from his seat, a gold diadem cradled carefully in his hands. He glanced at Gwen, who gave him an encouraging smile. Taking a breath, he cleared his throat. "As the queen's only male relative…" His voice cracked. His cheeks flushed deep red, but thankfully, no one laughed. The audience just waited with him patiently.

He pushed through. "It is my pleasure to welcome you to our family."

With careful hands, he placed the diadem on Tyreal's head. Then he stepped back, lifting his chin with quiet pride. "Arise and face the people as the future King Consort of Tavia."

Tyreal rose smoothly to his feet and turned to face the crowd. Pip stepped away from the center and moved to the chair on Gwen's right. It left the space beside her open, the one that had been Pip's until she took a consort. Tyreal stepped up onto the dais and into that space, only the fact that his hand remained on his sword hilt hinting at his nervousness.

Gwen reached for him, laying her hand over his. Their fingers laced together, and she grinned at him. As one, they lifted their joined hands toward the crowd.

The response was instant. Cheers rose from the room, louder than before and far more confident. The sound echoed through the hall, the energy contagious. For the first time in weeks,

Gwen didn't feel the weight of grief or fear pulling her under. Just joy. And strength. And something that felt a lot like hope.

She looked out over the gathered crowd, heart pounding. "Let us go celebrate with the people of Thorncliff!" she called out loudly.

The doors were already being opened, and lanterns lit the path out through the castle courtyard and towards the gates of the inner wall. Just beyond, her city and her people waited to celebrate with them. They walked past staff and guards, and Gwen stopped briefly to hug Cook tightly. The villagers with powers stood off to one side, and Gwen winked at Elle, who she had made sure had a beautiful gown for the occasion. All of them had been shown to have enough control of their powers that Gwen had granted them all permission to leave the castle if they wished after the celebration. She wasn't sure who would or wouldn't stay, though Tyreal seemed to think that Mason would take the children with him.

The gates opened before them with a low groan, and the roar of the crowd as they realized the couple was approaching was nearly deafening. Gwen and Tyreal stepped through, their footsteps echoing across the stone bridge that arched from the castle courtyard towards the road into Thorncliff proper.

Lanterns floated above the procession route, bobbing gently in the early evening breeze, their glow casting warm gold and amber across the path. Autumn leaves swirled at their feet, the reds and burnt oranges catching in the folds of her skirt. Ahead of them, the main road had been cleared by the guard, lined on both sides by Thorncliff's citizens. Merchants, tradesmen, farmers and barkeeps all craned around each other to catch a glimpse of the happy couple. Children perched on crates and ledges for a better view, under the eyes of watchful and nervous mothers.

People cheered as they passed, and she could hear music drifting from the square ahead. It was a markedly different atmosphere than the last time she had been in town, just a few days prior. It had been stifling with fear and anger on that day. Now there was only joy. She'd have to thank Tensha a thousand times for suggesting this. It was exactly what the city—and she—had needed.

Flower petals rained from second-story balconies, tangling in her hair and catching on Tyreal's shoulders. A few children darted past the guards, giggling. Tyreal gave a small nod, signaling the guards to let them through. They ran up to her with wide eyes and outstretched hands, offering her small, clumsy bouquets of wildflowers. She smiled and accepted each one, turning to Tyreal with a grin. He was still alert, tension coiled in his shoulders, eyes scanning the crowd out of habit. But there was something softer in his face now. The cheers, the flowers, the laughter were working on him, loosening the weight he'd been carrying after she had made everything public.

Gwen caught sight of familiar faces as they continued forward—old shopkeepers who'd watched her grow up, the baker whose bread nearly rivaled Cook's, and a few barmaids who looked just disappointed enough to earn a sideways glance from her.

Tyreal caught it, and to his credit, flushed slightly. He offered her a sheepish, one-shouldered shrug that turned into a cocky grin.

She tried to scowl, and failed. It was impossible to stay annoyed with the city glowing like this around her.

Banners hung from windows—some in Thorncrest colors, others clearly painted by children, all bright and joyful. A small band stood in the square's corner, playing old folk songs saved for weddings and harvest festivals. She couldn't help but smile at the familiarity of it all.

They rounded the last bend in the procession, and the Rosegate Pub came into view. The patrons caught sight of them and erupted into cheers, rowdy and full of affection. Tankards were raised. Someone let out a whistle.

"I hope this doesn't mean a total loss of my best customer, Your Majesty!" Tish, the barkeep, called from the doorway.

Tyreal's ears turned red, but he didn't stop grinning. A teen slipped out from behind Tish, carrying a foaming mug of ale with both hands.

Gwen laughed and gave Tyreal a nod. "Go on."

He accepted the mug and downed it with enthusiasm. The crowd whooped, and Tish shouted something about always keeping a seat open, just in case.

"Perhaps not a loss," Gwen called back. "Though I suspect his time will be spent a little differently from now on." She said it with a laugh, and the good humor was legitimate, but a flicker of jealousy stirred somewhere beneath the joy.

It doesn't matter, she reminded herself. *Whatever came before, he's mine now.*

She tightened her hold on his arm as they continued the last stretch toward the square, where the feast and dancing waited. "My time *will* be spent differently from now on. I no longer need substitutes, do I?" he said, low in her ear. It made her belly tighten, and she bit her bottom lip with something far more enjoyable than the anxiety that had plagued her of late.

She gave him a grateful grin, and they made their way back towards the castle and their waiting feast.

CHAPTER SEVENTEEN

Tyreal pushed his plate away with a quiet groan. Cook hadn't exaggerated when she said their betrothal feast would be one for the history books. The table was still crowded with dishes—slow-roasted lamb glazed in honeyed wine, buttered root vegetables so rich they melted on his tongue, delicate pastries filled with spiced cream, and a citrus-glazed fish he hadn't even touched. Every bite had been better than the last, and he was pretty sure his jacket no longer fit the way it had that morning.

"I am fairly certain," he murmured against Gwen's ear, resting his arm along the back of her chair, "that if I eat one more bite of anything, I'm going to explode."

She turned just enough to meet his eyes, her mouth curling into a grin. His heart stuttered in his chest. Gods, she looked radiant. The soft curls of her hair caught the light, and if he looked closely, he could make out hints of gold and copper threaded through the dark, like the gods had been thinking of a sunset when they made her. Her skin shimmered in the candlelight, probably Cora's doing, or maybe Gwen had magic he hadn't discovered yet. Either way, he was spellbound. And the neckline of her gown wasn't doing him any favors. The way the fabric skimmed over the tops of her breasts made his mouth go dry. He'd never let himself picture her in a betrothal gown. That future had always belonged to someone else—someone noble, chosen. Not him.

"I hope you're not so full that you can't dance with me, King Consort," she said, dragging out the title with a mischievous lilt. "I'd hate to be forced to entertain myself on the dance floor with others."

"Oh, sweet girl," he whispered, leaning in again. "Look around. I think you'd be hard pressed to find anyone willing to dance with you and risk the wrath of the scary commoner."

Her eyes sparkled.

"Besides," he added, dropping his voice, "even if they did, I'd so hate to get blood on your pretty dress."

She laughed, a light and unguarded sound that could rival any chapel bells. Around them, staff were helping guide the visitors away from the dining room and back to the throne room for the ball. "I suppose I am stuck with you, then. This dress is simply too perfect to mess up."

He leaned in even closer, pressing his lips to the outer shell of her ear. It was intoxicating, the ability to be this bold in public with her now. "I very much intend on messing it up by leaving it in a heap on our chamber floor, just so you know. It's gorgeous, but I prefer what's underneath," he breathed hotly against her flesh.

He was delighted to see a shiver race through her, and goosebumps to break out down the smooth column of her throat. He hadn't even truly touched her yet, and already she was responding. Gods, he was a lucky man. A dark chuckle escaped him, and he stood, reaching his hand out towards her. "Care to join me for a dance, Your Majesty?"

She slipped her hand into his, and they walked into the converted throne room. Staff had been hard at work, moving the rows of benches out so that the floor in front of the dais was open for guests. Small round tables hugged the walls, already cluttered with half-full cups of wine and ale. Swaths of white silk and a flower chain had been draped over the backs of Gwen's and his thrones.

His throne. What a bizarre set of words that he had never expected.

The moment they entered, music swelled from the gallery above. Light, joyful notes floated through the ballroom, echoing off the stone and stained glass. It reminded him of the laughter in the village that morning—unfiltered, contagious happiness. Tyreal couldn't help the grin that broke across his face.

They stepped onto the dance floor and parted, turning to face each other. She gave him a small, encouraging smile. She knew he'd been nervous about the formal dance in front of everyone. His personal dance experience was limited to raucous bouts on bar tables, or slow, drunken spins with a pretty girl. The only reason he could even halfway pull this off was because he'd watched her when she had learned.

He pushed the nerves down deep. He could do this. He *would* do this—for her.

She stepped forward first.He mirrored her.

They closed the space between them slowly, their steps in quiet sync. At the center, they paused, still not touching. He bowed low. She didn't curtsy—she *couldn't*, not as queen—but she dipped her chin, lashes sweeping down against her cheek in a graceful nod of acceptance.

When her eyes met his again, they didn't waver.

They linked elbows, their free hands tucked behind their backs, and turned in slow, careful circles with the rhythm of the music. Tyreal nearly laughed. He was orbiting her—like the moon around their world. Fitting. But he kept his focus steady, matching her pace.

They spun outward, shoulder to shoulder, her profile catching the candlelight as she faced the crowd. He was sure everyone could see the blatant adoration on his face as he openly stared. When they turned back toward each other, he guided her into a closed hold. One hand found the small of her back, firm but gentle. She rested hers against his ribs, and their joined hands lifted above them, fingertips just brushing.

He turned her outward with a gentle twist, letting her spin away in a sweep of skirts before pulling her back in, their hands never fully parting.

A soft laugh escaped her lips. "Bet you're grateful now for all those hours you spent guarding me while I learned these dances."

"Deeply," he murmured, then added with a crooked smile, "though I'm fairly certain I still look like a fool to half the room."

She shook her head. "Not sure who you mean. There's no one else here. Just us."

Eventually—too soon—the last notes of the song drifted into silence. His hand lingered on the small of her back. Gwen kept her fingers curled against his ribs, head tipped back to look up into his eyes. Unable to resist her allure completely, he brushed his lips against her forehead before stepping back.

The next song began as Tyreal and Gwen stepped off the floor, leaving room for other couples to take their place.

"I believe one formal dance is all you're getting out of me," he said, offering her a grin as they made their way toward their thrones.

They didn't get far.

King Samyad and Queen Raveena of Malticai approached, their courtier Rashir hovering just behind. Tyreal's jaw tightened. Rashir wasn't doing anything wrong at the moment, but the sight of him still made Tyreal itch to throw a punch.

He'd never met the royal couple in person, only heard whispers over the years. Malticai kept to itself, neutral but reliable in trade. Still, they rarely sent anyone but Rashir to this part of the continent, let alone their monarchs.

Samyad was shorter than Tyreal but broad across the shoulders, standing with the confidence of someone who knew exactly how to handle himself. His skin was a rich umber, his dark hair pulled back and crowned with a gold circlet etched in fine script. The deep blue of his robe was trimmed with silver thread—refined but unassuming. A soldier-king, perhaps. Tyreal didn't sense a threat, but the man's sharp gaze made it clear he could be one if he chose.

Queen Raveena walked at his side, and Tyreal felt a flicker of admiration that would've been dangerous if he wasn't so thoroughly devoted to the woman beside him. She was stunning—poised, watchful, and radiant in a marigold and rose ensemble that Tyreal thought was called a sari, though he made a mental note to ask Gwen later to be sure he didn't make an ass out of himself.

The fabric was draped so that it moved like water when she walked. Her long braid was woven with gold beads that caught the candlelight as she inclined her head in greeting.

To Gwen, not him.

Not that he minded. He was glad to see it. He had overheard some tidbits of conversations earlier that seemed to imply that some expected Tyreal to control the throne, simply by being a man. Despite his common upbringing. He could not express how little he was interested in that.

"A beautiful dance, Your Majesty," Raveena said. "Your people must be pleased to see such unity between their queen and her... betrothed."

The pause before *betrothed* was impossible to read. Tyreal couldn't tell if she was unsure of what to call him or if it was a subtle political jab.

Gwen smiled, smooth and practiced. "Thank you. And thank you both for coming on such short notice."

"I would have thought you'd be too busy with everything going on to host a ball," Samyad said, his tone clipped. "Though I suppose it helps when you have advance knowledge others did not."

Tyreal caught the flicker of guilt on Raveena's face before she masked it. So, Samyad hadn't known about magic's return until it was already happening. That would grate on a man like him—a natural-born king left in the dark.

"Not much more advance, I'm afraid," Gwen replied. "We knew of its existence, yes. But the rest, I've been learning right alongside everyone else these past few days. How did the return of magic affect your people?"

"It was an adjustment," Samyad admitted. "Raveena and my mother were instrumental in helping the other royals acclimate to their powers."

His expression softened as he spoke, and Raveena gave him a warm smile. Whatever tensions had existed between them, it looked like they would weather it. The pair had been betrothed upon Raveena's birth, similar to Max and Anya, but Tyreal suspected there may be a genuine love between them now.

Still, Tyreal noted something in Samyad's phrasing—*other royals*. No mention of bastards. Were there none in Malticai? Or were they simply not acknowledged?

"If only we had all been so fortunate," came a sour voice from behind.

Tyreal turned to find King Korian Drakon of Galeigh looming nearby. Much like at King Lorne's funeral pyre, the man again wore a permanent scowl. He still dripped in gold and jewels, but now bandages peeked from beneath his cuffs and collar. Tyreal debated offering to heal him, but he'd wait to see where Drakon landed on the issue of Lovell first.

Gwen and Raveena exchanged a quick look. They were around the same age and almost certainly had trained together at Mist Castle. They knew each other.

"I'm sorry no one was there to guide you, Your Majesty," Gwen said evenly. "If you or your people need help learning to control your magic, I'm sure any of us would be glad to assist."

"I have my powers under control," Drakon snapped. "I don't need help."

Gwen opened her mouth to respond—

Then the doors slammed open.

"*Dragon!*" a man shouted.

The entire room froze. The man at the entrance stood gasping for breath, face red, his eyes wild.

"A dragon! It's circling over the water!"

For a single heartbeat, no one moved. Then chaos erupted.

Chairs scraped back. Voices rose in a wave of confusion. Tyreal moved to Gwen's side, hand at her elbow as people surged toward the courtyard.

"Well," Gwen muttered, "I suppose I don't have to worry about telling anyone now."

"Yeah," Tyreal said, "assuming we aren't all about to be roasted alive."

They stepped into the night.

From the courtyard, the sea was hidden by the outer wall, but the sky above was clear—just a few lingering clouds and the fading violet hues of dusk. Then a shout came from the guard tower. Tyreal's men were already flooding in, trying to push forward for a better view, but the vantage point was too low.

He caught Andais's eye and nodded toward the towers. He couldn't yet see the threat that had been named.

He didn't need to wait long.

The flap of wings cut through the air like thunder. A gust of wind swept through the courtyard as Viamar soared overhead, vast and impossible to ignore. Gasps broke out all around as people stared upward, mouths open, the dragon's massive shadow stretching across the castle stones.

Tyreal had seen him before in the cave, and he had been terrifying then. That had been nothing compared to this. He hadn't seen him in flight, in his full, terrible beauty. All around him, people were having the same reaction, complete awe mixed with a reverent fear.

Viamar banked into a wide circle above the castle, his movement smooth, unhurried. There was no aggression in it—yet.

Then a roar echoed across the water. Another dragon.

Viamar answered, and it did not sound friendly.

And just like that, everything shifted.

Tyreal knew the feel of a crowd right before it turned. That breathless, tense freeze before panic bloomed. He saw it on their faces, the awe fading, replaced with fear. Wide eyes. Stumbling steps back. People who didn't understand what they were seeing and assumed the worst.

Warrior. Little Thorncrest. I would advise you to get these people inside.

Viamar's voice echoed in Tyreal's mind.

How in the bloody crows were they supposed to accomplish that? Controlling a crowd this size was impossible at the best of times. Panic only made it more dangerous. One spark and everything would collapse.

He turned to Gwen, only to find a wall of bodies between them. A tide of nobles and guards had surged forward, drawn toward the spectacle in the sky, separating them with staggering speed.

He pushed forward, fear gripping him, though it eased when he saw Rykan and Merren flanking her, both with their hands on their swords and shields ready. It wasn't how he wanted it. It wasn't his body protecting her, but it was enough. For now.

Gwen shouted commands, trying to restore order, but the rising panic drowned out every word. Other monarchs raised their voices too, calling for calm, but the tide of fear had already pulled people under.

And then the second dragon came.

It screamed overhead, a piercing, unnatural sound that made everyone wince and try to cover their ears. This one was smaller than Viamar, more compact, its scales a deep, electric blue that shimmered with each snap of its wings. It circled tight and fast, the way a hawk might stalk its prey—sharp turns, sudden dives, movements that spoke of calculation, not curiosity.

The crowd felt it too. The awe they had shown Viamar was twisting into dread. He couldn't blame them, his instincts were screaming at him to run. The blue dragon wasn't merely circling—it was hunting.

Viamar landed. The castle spire cracked beneath his weight, and his roar tore through the air of the courtyard. The sound hit hard, slamming into Tyreal's chest. Windows shattered in the towers above. Stone cracked and fell in rolling chunks down the sides of the castle. Shards of glass rained down like knives.

Several hands lifted at once—Gwen, Anya, others—trying to cast shields over the crowd, to hold back the debris.

Nothing happened.

No shimmer of magic. No pulse. Just empty air.

A beat passed. Then the screaming started again—higher now, frantic, as people were injured. Someone shoved. Someone else threw a punch. It didn't matter who. It never did. Once panic took root, it grew fast and wild. People surged toward the castle doors, only to slam into the crush of bodies already clogging the entryway. It was a bottleneck. A trap. And it was closing.

"*Men! Get to your charges!*" Tyreal shouted fiercely. He caught Gwen's eyes, filled with confusion and panic as she kept trying to cast magic. That look nearly undid him.

He moved.

The first body in his way was shoved aside. The next, he barreled through with a shoulder. No hesitation. No diplomacy. That time was over. If magic was useless, then he'd rely on what he knew best to reach the woman he loved—brute force, grit, and sheer determination. Good, old-fashioned violence was far more familiar than spells anyway.

He drove forward through the mob, punching, ducking, shoving his way through until he reached her. There was no time to be gentle. He wrapped an arm around Gwen's waist and hauled her over his shoulder. She didn't resist, thank the gods, but she kept twisting, trying to raise her head, scanning the crowd.

"Pip!" she shouted, frantic.

"Jameson has him! Keep your damn head down!" Tyreal growled, slamming his boot into a man's chest to clear the path ahead. He didn't know if it was true. He could only hope. But he needed her calm until they were somewhere safe.

His gaze shot to the spire again. Viamar was still perched above, wings wide and watching.

Then the second dragon shrieked again and dove towards the crowd. More people screamed, and Tyreal nearly dropped Gwen as bodies roiled around them, desperate to get out of the courtyard.

Viamar launched from the spire and collided with the dragon, shoving him out of his path towards the humans. Fire burst between them. They spiraled through the air, attached to each other as they hurtled towards the cliff wall.

Waves of nausea rolled through Tyreal as he realized there was a solid chance the dragons might shatter the barrier that had defended Thorncliff for centuries.

At the last possible moment, Viamar sank his teeth into the smaller dragon's throat. It twisted back hard, screeching in pain, wings flailing for lift. It scrabbled at Viamar with its back legs, and the larger dragon finally released it.

It turned, retreating toward the sea, wings looking a little worse for wear. With any luck, maybe it would tear Grigor to pieces on the way. The beast had seemed hungry for a fight. Maybe a light appetizer would appease him for a while.

The Tavian guard were gaining control now, forcing order into the chaos. They'd broken the bottleneck at the castle doors, guiding people inside and subduing those who kept fighting. With space opening up, Tyreal pivoted toward the far edge of the courtyard, angling for the larder.

The rosebush near the corner was flattened, petals scattered across the ground.

Good.

Someone had used the tunnel. That meant he'd probably been right about Pip. Relief washed through him. He was quite fond of the prince, and he certainly didn't want to lose his brother-in-law on the first day. Not to mention what his soon-to-be wife would do to him for lying.

Standard protocol in circumstances of crowd violence was to move the royals to an alternate safe zone while the guards handled containment. Dragons weren't usually part of the equation, but when it came down to it, the steps were still the same. Isolate. Protect. Control the damage.

And pray it didn't get worse.

Clearly Gwen sensed the imminent danger was passing, because she was squirming on his shoulder. "Let me down! I need to find Pip and figure out what is going on."

"I'm taking you to Pip. And I think it's pretty clear what is going on. At least one other dragon made their decision, and Viamar just saved our asses. Now we just have to make sure he *keeps* wanting to."

"Well, yes, but my magic..." She trailed off, and he felt heat along the back of his tunic. "Appears to be back. So why the hell did it fail all of us before?"

CHAPTER EIGHTEEN

"Tell us how long you've known about the dragons and what you did to our magic!" King Drakon's fist crashed down on the table, rattling silverware and sending a half-full goblet skittering onto its side. Crimson wine spilled in a slow spread across the carved wood, pooling like blood as it made its way outwards toward Gwen.

She pushed her chair back with a scrape, more out of instinct than intent—half to keep the wine from staining her betrothal gown, half to block Tyreal, who was already rising beside her, every muscle coiled. His hand hovered at his hip. She touched his arm, giving a terse, small shake of her head. His jaw tightened, and she heard him breathe a huff of frustration out of his nostrils. Drakon's guard had moved as well, and the two of them were now attempting to stare each other down. Finally, the other guard conceded and sat.

Gwen's head was beginning to throb.

"I've told you," she said, her voice carefully measured even as frustration frayed its edges, "I just learned about the dragons, and I don't know what happened to the magic. I didn't cause this. In case you didn't notice, I lost my magic, too. There are witnesses—everyone here saw it happen."

"And everyone here could have died because of it," Drakon growled. "We were unarmed. You really expect me to believe that it was just some coincidence that you called us all here, dragons fought in the skies above us, and you somehow got away completely unharmed?"

"Is that what you think?" Gwen asked incredulously. "That I orchestrated a public brawl between two dragons at *my own betrothal ball* so I could what? Show off? Scare you into working with me to fix this damn mess?"

Gwen tried not to snap. She tried to be a queen. But she was tired. Scared. Furious. Couldn't the gods give her one night? Just *one*—to be normal? Happy and in love, and enjoying her betrothal ball?

Her voice snapped through the room like a whip before she could stop it. "As if I *want* to be here right now, arguing with all of you, rather than spending the evening with my betrothed like any sane person would."

She'd barely been able to catch her breath after confirming Pip was safe. She'd marched straight to the library, picking pieces of broken glass out of her hair along the way. Her staff had already gathered the monarchs there, and by the time she and Tyreal arrived, the room was buzzing with angry whispers and clipped questions.

Someone mentioned Tyreal had broken one of Drakon's guard's nose en route to her when the man had gotten in his way. Tyreal had offered an apology, but she doubted anyone believed it.

Now, the monarchs glanced around at each other. No one answered her. A few had the decency to look guilty. Most at least looked convinced. Drakon, though, looked like he was desperate to catch her in a lie.

"Maybe the dragons are what took away our magic," Queen Isolde of Gagerland said, a little too brightly, from her seat beside her daughter. Anya clenched her teeth, but stayed silent, tracing her finger along the new faint scar on her chin. Tyreal had healed most of it. What was left was barely visible, but it was there, marring her friend's perfect face, and Gwen wished she could ask her how she felt about it. Later. She'd check in on her later.

Anya's gown had once been a sleek, soft rose-colored silk with a dangerously low neckline unlike anything in fashion in any court. The fitted bodice and clean lines were a far cry from anything her friend had ever worn. It had been sexy, almost scandalous, and Anya had looked ravishing in it, glowing with confidence.

Now it was torn and bloodied. Glass had shredded the sleeves and ripped through the skirt, leaving behind jagged edges and dark stains.

Tyreal had tended to Anya's wound, but it was the state of the dress that had sent Queen Isolde into a fit of horrified muttering about wasted silk and tailoring, even if it *was* unfit for a princess. She was still dabbing at the ruined hem with a monogrammed handkerchief, as though her efforts might undo the damage if she just willed it hard enough.

Anya, for her part, sat rigid with silent annoyance. She didn't snap or roll her eyes; she was too well-trained for that, but Gwen didn't miss the tightness in her mouth or the way she angled her body ever so slightly away from her mother.

It might've been amusing, if the night hadn't gone to complete shit.

Gwen shook her head. "I don't think so. At least, not from Viamar. Myself, Princess Anya, and Prince Maximillen were all able to use our magic in his presence. I suppose it's possible the other dragon might hold that kind of power—but it doesn't track. Why encourage peace if they can simply take magic away and stop us from fighting magical wars?"

"I'm less concerned about the temporary lapse in the magic I've only had for a few days," King Samyad said dryly, "than I am about the two *giant fucking dragons* that were just fighting in the sky above my head."

Gwen gave a sharp nod of agreement. "Losing our magic is a mystery we'll need to solve, but I agree with King Samyad. That wasn't the reason I called you all here." Her gaze swept the room, lingering on each monarch. "Keeping this from spiraling into war is our first focus. Earning the dragons' trust—if still possible—is part of that. Everything else is secondary."

"I'm still not entirely sure what Prince Grigor hopes to gain from threatening Tavia. How do we know his intentions are truly malicious? I've heard no indication that the king has any sights on taking over." King Damaris said, leaning back in his chair, one arm draped casually along the back of his wife Marenya's. "Yes, the High Sister wanted to restore magic solely to their family line. That doesn't automatically assign guilt. Couldn't this just be a jilted suitor trying to win back your favor? I heard your rejection wasn't exactly... gentle."

Gwen didn't much care for his tone, but given the circumstances, she was loath to call him out on it just then. She needed him, or at the very least she needed him not to side with Lovell if she hoped to maintain peace.

Tyreal had no such hesitation.

He crossed his arms over his chest, jaw tight. "I'm the High Captain of the Tavian Guard. Do you honestly think I'd waste time and resources on all of this if I didn't have fucking proof?" he snapped, lip curled upward.

Gwen resisted the urge to wince. It was a fair question, and one that she also wanted to voice. But Damaris was a proud peacock of a man. He didn't take kindly to being blatantly questioned, even if he liked to do it to others.

Damaris let out a derisive snort. "I think you would, if you hoped it might validate this marriage."

Before Gwen could speak, Drakon interjected, unable to resist digging at Damaris. "I'm less concerned about this *marriage*," he drew the word out condescendingly before continuing, "than I am with these claims about Adaltus." Gwen had to breathe slowly in her nose and out her mouth to keep her anger in check. Gods, she hated this man.

"If he is power-hungry for more land, or working on behalf of his father, he won't stop at Tavia, and my country is the closest. I would think everyone here would be more concerned about that than a commoner rising above his station," Drakon continued, spreading his hands wide for emphasis. His gaze flicked to Tyreal, a small smirk playing at the corners of his mouth.

Tyreal stiffened, going silent, the rage rolling off him nearly palpable.

No one else seemed to notice. And that was the problem, wasn't it? At the ball, when the glass was raining from the sky and people were panicking, it had been Tyreal who had gotten the guards into motion and helped get everyone to safety. There had been no questions about his place then, just actions. In that moment, he had been exactly what they had needed. Proof that even in this world of new magic and dragons, good old-fashioned strength and practicality still had a place.

But now? Now, they moved around him like he was furniture, ever-present and an item to be used for their comfort. Nothing more. They bristled at each other; they argued and prodded and postured, instead of actually doing anything. They didn't ask for Tyreal's input, even though he had far more practical experience than they did with battles.

Gwen wanted to reach for him, to say something to pull him back in and show him she understood. But the moment kept shifting. There were too many moving pieces, too many consequences if she got the balance wrong.

When she didn't speak fast enough, when her silence stretched just a breath too long, she worried he noticed. That the space between them cooled in a way she wasn't used to.

Her stomach twisted. Anger flared hot through her, as it so often did these days. Gods, being this furious all the time was exhausting. She felt the heat gathering in her palms, flames licking beneath her skin, testing the boundaries of her mental shield. She tried to shove it back down, but as she gained control of it, the air power she was still learning swirled around her feet, lashing the hem of her skirt.

"I don't need your validation," she said, voice low and sharp, everyone's goblets now flying off the table and shattering against the wall. "I am queen of this land and you will respect that just as I'd do in your countries."

Everyone gaped at her and shame washed over her. There was an adage somewhere about not being in charge if you constantly had to remind people of it. She swallowed, and took a deep breath. "I called you here to address the threat Lovell poses—and thus the dragons, yes—but also to decide what we'll do about the Sisters of the Mist. Nothing more," she said quieter.

"Let's lower the temperature a bit. We've all reviewed the records the scribes brought backing up the queen's claims. Her marriage is not what we are here to discuss," Max interjected, palms spread open and voice soothing.

"Isn't it, though?" King Thalion's voice was calm, almost curious, though Gwen caught Eliana's slight wince at her father's bluntness. "I've heard some about your plans on putting commoners on your advising council. Now, with marrying Tyreal, lost royal blood or no, the argument could be made that you're taking the first steps toward dismantling monarchies altogether."

He leaned back in his chair, large fingers steepled as he studied Gwen. She didn't think his intent with the question was malicious, but she couldn't be sure. With his silver-threaded beard and storm-gray eyes, Thalion could easily look intimidating when he chose to. In fact, he looked as though he might be even harsher than Drakon if pushed.

This was a king who had stood firm beside his daughter Eliana when she claimed her true name and transitioned to a princess. Thalion had already defied tradition for the sake of what was right. Surely, he would be on her side. Right?

"I'm not trying to create conflict," he added, the corners of his mouth twitching with something softer as he glanced toward Eliana—checking, perhaps, that she wasn't upset with him. "Or even say I disagree with your marriage. But it's not separate from your politics. It sounds to me that it's central to how you plan to build peace."

Gwen took her time before answering. She hadn't considered that her message might be perceived that way, but she could see Thalion's point. *Did* she want to dismantle the monarchies? The thought gave her pause. She wasn't entirely sure. Her knee-jerk was to say no, but she couldn't deny that change was long overdue.

At last, she shook her head. "That wasn't my intention. I don't want to dismantle the monarchies, but I want to make them better. For far too long, we've all ruled based on councils of handpicked nobles who don't truly represent our people." She leaned back in her chair, crossing her arms.

"We cling to rules that no longer serve us. Why were we only allowed to marry other royals? To keep magical bloodlines pure? And yet now, there are commoners with magic—in several countries at the very least, though I'd wager it's all of them." She pointedly looked around the table, waiting to see if anyone denied it. She was met with silence. "So clearly, plenty of people broke the rules, and we all ended up in the same place, anyway."

"Perhaps we should discuss your proposal to bring us all together—the one Maximillen mentioned in his letter," Queen Solena said, her tone warm as she laid a hand over her son's with a fond smile.

"Clearly some of us were given information, but not all," Drakon snapped, eyes narrowing on Gwen before shifting to Max.

"Just because their children like them enough to keep them informed, that isn't a reason to get testy, Drakon." Damaris's tone was pleasant, but the dig was unmistakable.

Drakon bristled. "Testy? Says the king always whining about a handful of scouts crossing invisible lines on a map."

"A handful of scouts?" Damaris's voice dropped into something colder. "You've had soldiers stationed across our border for months. That isn't reconnaissance, it's occupation."

Drakon stood, chair screeching in his haste.

Damaris followed.

The hall tensed, and the pool of spilled wine began to drip on the floor from the jostling.

Max rose, hands open and voice calm. "Enough." It wasn't loud, but the command was clear.

Gwen didn't expect it to work. Max was good with diplomacy, but he was just a prince, and these two kings would likely ignore him. To her surprise, the room did quiet, and though they shot each other dirty looks, both kings returned to their seats. She was impressed with her friend's ability, but she'd be lying if she said it didn't hurt. Was it simply because he was a man? They would never have listened to her like that, not without fear of Tyreal's blade. Given how things had been going, she wasn't even entirely sure they'd listen to Tyreal unless he outright threatened them.

She felt her face flush as her anxiety and doubts rose within her.

"Let's hear the queen's proposal," Max continued, distracting Gwen from the spiral. She nodded to him, grateful. As she looked around the group, though, the anxiety returned. A simple but terrible truth was repeating itself in her mind. She did not know if she could hold them together.

CHAPTER NINETEEN

Queen Isolde's handkerchief was turning pink.

Some of Drakon's spilled wine had soaked it before the servants swept through and cleaned up the mess. He certainly had made no move to do it himself. The embroidery of her initials was bleeding into red. Isolde wrinkled her nose and tossed the cloth onto the table like it had personally offended her.

Tyreal watched the movements with far more interest than he had for the posturing happening around him. A part of him always did, studying people's hands and their energy. Staying a step ahead required it. Sometimes clenched knuckles were the only clue he got before someone struck.

Isolde's move said enough—the cloth had still been functional, but now it was tainted. So it needed to be discarded.

Anya's eyes flicked towards it. Tyreal wondered if she was thinking the same thing as he was. Would her parents throw her away too, if they saw her for who she actually was? She hadn't been subtle with the changes in her behavior since they had left Mist Castle. Maybe she didn't care anymore.

"I don't think the dragons care about who starts the war," Gwen was saying, voice tight. "They will not differentiate between sides. If we don't hold together now, we may not get another chance."

She was right.

He wanted to say something—anything—to make them see it. This was the real threat. Not Lovell. Not tradition. *Division.* That was how they'd fall. Armies didn't fail because of weapons. They failed when trust broke down between soldiers.

They wouldn't listen to him. He knew that. He was just Gwen's sword. High Captain of the Guard, yes, the commander of Tavia's army. But to these people, armies were only extensions of their command. What could he possibly say that they'd care about? They hadn't earlier when magic failed, and him and his men saved them. They didn't want a soldier. They wanted someone who could fix the world with pretty words while not threatening anything about the status quo.

When Gwen stood, Tyreal did not move.

She caught the hesitation. He saw the flicker of a frown before she smoothed it out.

Still, he stayed seated.

Not because he didn't want to rise with her—but because she hadn't looked at him. She hadn't spoken up when Drakon insulted him. And he understood why. She couldn't afford to here. But it still stung. Still further cemented his feelings of being an unnecessary burden.

"What I'm proposing is something that should've been put in place when the Sisters of the Mist were first formed," Gwen said, voice clear. "They were supposed to guide us toward peace, but the only laws they ever passed were about keeping bloodlines pure."

Tyreal watched the energy in the room shift, even from her allies. And not in a good way. He didn't think that she had as many agreeing with her as she had thought she would. The flushed spots on her cheek told him she had already figured that out. She would not back down on trying, though. She never would.

"They never had oversight," Gwen went on. "No accountability. That gave the High Sister enough power to betray us all. Though, they also had no input on us. They were mere figure-heads."

"What sort of input would you give them?" Thalion asked, frowning. "We are monarchs. We rule our countries as we see fit."

Tyreal liked Thalion. Respected him, at least. He hoped he'd listen, but it was hard to say.

Gods, he missed Alric. They would be sharing suffering eye rolls right now over the posturing of the nobles.

"We are," Gwen agreed. "I'm not proposing to change that. However, I am proposing a way for others to step in if we are making choices that put us on a path to war. War affects us all. What I'm proposing is a council, hopefully made up of nine kingdoms. Nineteen seats. Equal voices between royals and representatives *elected* from each of us, with each nation annually rotating an elected tiebreaking official."

There weren't any shouts or outrage. Not out loud, at least, but Tyreal could see it in the sets of their shoulders. *They think she's overstepping,* he thought. *They are only hearing erosion of their control.*

"You're asking us to surrender our power. How is that not dismantling the monarchy?" Drakon said quietly. Dangerously.

Gods, Tyreal hated being right, almost as much as he hated that man. His sword hand itched to run him through.

"No, I'm asking to share it," Gwen said.

Drakon snorted. "Same thing. And who will lead this council? Let me guess."

"No one," Gwen answered. "As I said, tiebreakers rotate annually. We will draw names on who gets the first year and assign from there. Every voice is equal."

"Sounds like a child trying to change the rules just because they can," Drakon objected. "Commoners rising. Nobles kneeling. A crown made meaningless."

Tyreal heard Gwen's breath catch, though her face remained impassive. He knew she felt alone against the others. He could see it in the tense posture of her shoulders, and the way she kept tucking her thumb into her palm to keep it from lifting to her mouth. Just a girl trying to hold a broken world together in her bare hands. Anya, Max, and Eliana weren't rulers yet. They couldn't carry this weight.

And neither could he.

He still didn't know what his place was in this room. What he could do. Whether speaking now would help her or make it worse.

So he stayed silent.

And every second stretched, tightening around his ribs like chain mail that didn't fit anymore.

Then Anya stood.

"Be serious," she said. "She isn't asking anyone to give up power. We will still live in our gilded halls and have the final say in what happens between our borders, up to the point that what we decide could affect everyone else. If she wanted to be a tyrant or to strip everyone of their powers, she wouldn't be asking your opinion." Her eyes didn't flick to her mother or Max as she spoke. She just said it, like the truth was simple. Because it was.

"She's offering you the path to peace. Take it, or don't, and we all die in dragon fire. But don't dress it up as anything other than the same cowardice that got us into this mess. You don't fear rebellion. You fear change. You fear losing a crumb of the power our families have held onto for eons."

Anya's parents turned to her with their mouths agape. Even Max looked mildly shocked, though it quickly disappeared behind his diplomatic façade.

Gwen met Anya's gaze with a grateful smile. She didn't look at Tyreal.

And why should she? Anya had said what he hadn't. Done what he hadn't.

He looked back down at his own hands. Unmoved. Unbloodied. Useless.

The door shut behind them with a dull *click*.

Gwen didn't speak.

Tyreal didn't either.

The silence between them stretched longer than it ever should have. She couldn't remember the last time she'd felt this uncomfortable around him. Maybe after she first revealed her magic—but even then, he'd been angry. She understood angry. This was something else.

This was distance.

Gwen crossed the room and sat at her vanity, staring into her looking glass. In it, she could see him near the wall, by the painting that hid the corridor between their rooms. For a moment, she wondered if he was thinking about running through it. It was hard to believe that just that morning, she'd been seated here with Cora, laughing and admiring her hair, her gown, her future.

She dropped her gaze. She wasn't ready to look at him yet.

She reached up and began removing the pins from her braids. Her scalp ached beneath the weight of them now, and the headache already building behind her eyes didn't need encouragement. She hated undoing the look. It had been beautiful, but right now, everything felt like it was unraveling. Certainly not what she had expected to feel the night before her wedding ceremony.

"What was I even in there for?" His voice was low, almost too quiet to catch.

She didn't turn to him. "You're the High Captain. The King Consort. Where else would you be?" Her voice came out flat, laced with exhaustion. She didn't mean for it to sound so cold. She was just tired. Bone-deep tired.

He laughed. There was no humor in it. "Neither of those titles seemed to matter to anyone in that room. You certainly didn't speak up when they reminded me of my unimportance."

"That's not fair."

"Find the lie."

She stood. "You think I don't *want* to defend you? That it doesn't tear me apart, holding my tongue while they act like you don't belong?"

He said nothing.

"I need them. I can't do any of this without their support! What do you want from me?"

"I want to not have to be defended at all!" he snapped. "If I really belonged there, they'd see me."

"Then say something!" she shot back. "You just sat there. This isn't the last time nobles will look down on you. *Speak.*"

"I *did*. And it made things worse." He stepped towards her, raking his hand through his hair in exasperation. "I opened my mouth, and Damaris used it to dismiss you. Every time I speak, I hand them another reason to doubt your judgment—because they don't believe in me. In *us*."

"That's not true."

"Then why didn't you look at me? Reach for me? Something to show you didn't feel the same way they do, that we're in this together."

Her throat closed, and she could feel the pressure of tears welling in the backs of her eyes. "Because I needed to hold the room together," she said, louder than she meant to. Was she trying to convince him or herself? "If I defended you, there was the chance that they would have walked and joined Lovell. I *need* them to see me as a leader, not some girl too in love to think clearly."

They stared at each other, the silence full of unspoken hurt. She broke eye contact first, turning and rubbing her arms like the chill in the air was something she could fix and not coming from inside herself.

"I'm trying to lead a kingdom," she said, quieter now. "And I'm trying to be a wife. I've never done either before. But I know I can't do either by choosing one over the other."

"I never asked you to choose."

She looked up at him. His face was unreadable. But his body said everything—fists clenched, shoulders tight, like he was begging the universe to give him something to fight to let out all he was feeling.

"You didn't have to," she whispered.She felt it every time they walked into a room and the air changed.Felt it when no one addressed him.When they only looked at her.And she'd let it happen.

"I've told you a million times that I need you and want you by my side. I have stood up for you every time before now. I was wrong to hesitate, but don't you see? I don't know how to fix this. How can I combat their bullshit views and get them to go along with my plan?"

"That's just it! I do see. I understand the logic and the defensive tactics. That's my point. I don't belong here. You cannot rule this country and keep this peace with me at your side!"

"Don't say that!" she said, sucking in her breath. Tears threatened at the corners of her eyes and her hands shook. "We made promises. After the inn. After the catacombs. Here in our bed. We are meant for each other."

"Maybe we're not," he said. "Maybe we just *wanted* to be. Maybe we're just as wrong as the High Sister, thinking we were chosen. That the gods were pointing us in the right direction."

His voice was bitter. It cracked something deep inside her.

Surely, he didn't believe that. He couldn't.

"This is more than that, and you know it. For you to be royal—"

"I'm *not* royal!" he shouted.

She flinched.

"If I were, I wouldn't feel like a ghost every time we walk into a council room. Like I'm allowed to stand beside you *only* if I stay silent."

"That's not what this is," she said. Then, colder than she meant: "Is this about your pride? About me being queen and you being consort? Do I emasculate you, Tyreal?"

She regretted it instantly.

He didn't explode.

But his eyes narrowed. "You know good and well the answer to that question, Gwendolyn. I don't give a godsdamn about your crown. This isn't about pride. It's about reality. I don't belong in this world."

"That's not true."

"You know it is."

A pause. Heavy. She hated how fast the silence returned.

"We've loved each other our whole lives," she said, almost a whisper.

"I know," he said. "That's the worst part." He didn't look angry anymore, just tired. Hollowed out. "I don't know if love is enough to keep me standing there, watching you carry a weight I can't help you lift."

Her pulse thudded painfully in her temple, the sign of a headache forming on the horizon.

"Will you break off our betrothal? You don't think *that* will undermine what I'm trying to do?"

A muscle in his jaw twitched as he looked away from her. He shook his head. "I don't know." He moved toward the painting, toward the hidden corridor.

"If you walk out of this room," she said, voice shaking, "don't come back."

He looked over his shoulder at her. "Don't threaten me."

"Don't make me, then."

For a moment, it looked like he might say something more. Anything.

But he didn't.

He stepped into the shadows and closed the panel behind him.

Gwen didn't cry.

Not at first.

She just stood there, heart pounding, hands shaking, wondering how a room full of kings hadn't broken her—but *he* could.

CHAPTER TWENTY

The chapel was empty, save for the thick beeswax candles.

Their glow illuminated the small area around them, flickering off the cold stone walls near the memorial mantel. The rest of the area was cloaked in shadows. The tapestries were all hidden from view now, not that she needed to see them to know what they were. She knew every inch of them like the back of her own hand.

Gwen made her way to the mantel and lit a candle, thinking of her father. What would he think of this mess they had found themselves in? Magic. Dragons. Her relationship, or possibly lack of one, with Tyreal. She moved to a worn wooden bench halfway up the aisle, not daring to get closer to the altar where she was supposed to speak her true wedding vows in just a few short hours.

She hadn't meant to come here. Her feet had just carried her here after the argument, down the twisting hallways, past the guards who looked confused to see her walking around without Tyreal on her betrothal night. Her chambers had felt too much like a battlefield, and the war had left her standing alone in the wreckage.

She just needed to think somewhere he rarely came.

Her crown felt heavier than ever, just the idea of it pressing down on her. She wasn't sure she could carry it. At Mist Castle, standing up to the High Sister, she'd believed she was ready, that she'd grown into her title.

Now, that felt like something she'd imagined, or perhaps dreamed—a moment that never really belonged to her.

From behind the pulpit, a quiet shuffle of movement caught her attention. The Arbiter stepped into view, robed in simple slate gray, his hands folded behind his back. He didn't look surprised to see her.

"Not exactly how you envisioned the night going, I take it?" His voice was gentle, and he sat beside her, laying his wrinkled hand on top of hers.

Gwen stared ahead at the altar, trying to find words that didn't make her heart shatter anew. "We fought," she said finally, voice flat. "We both said awful things. Well, mainly I said awful things. He was... less cruel, but more..." she trailed off and shook her head. "He doesn't know if we should still be wed. I told him if he walked out of the room, he shouldn't come back."

Malcolum nodded slowly, as if she had said something as banal as the weather. "And now you wonder if you meant it."

"I don't," she whispered, voice shaky as burning started behind her eyes. She blinked rapidly, trying to hold the tears at bay. "But I might have ruined everything." The tears streamed down her cheeks then, and she leaned into his shoulder.

There was a long silence. Not the heavy kind—just quiet. That was one of her favorite things about talking to him. There was never any unneeded conversation. Just quiet reflection and guiding questions to get you where your mind needed to go.

"You know, I have been Arbiter at this castle for a very long time. I have watched the two of you grow from foolish children into the most stubborn adults I've ever counseled."

She gave a watery laugh in surprise.

"What's always been clear," he continued, "is the love you have for each other. I tried to give Tyreal an out when he was named High Captain. He could've walked away. He didn't. He stayed—chose duty—even when he thought he'd never be yours. Do you really believe he'll walk away now, with a war threatening and a chance to finally be your husband?"

Gwen stared at her hands. Her voice came out smaller than she liked.

"I didn't think so. But now… I don't know. I don't know how to hold this kingdom together, or this fragile peace, without making him feel lesser."

Malcolum nodded once. Then turned slightly to face her.

"What does he want?"

She blinked at him. "What?"

"Not what he's angry about. Not what he's afraid of. What does *Tyreal* want?"

She opened her mouth—then closed it again.

"I thought he wanted to stand beside me," she said eventually. "To protect me. To help me lead."

"And now?"

"I think he wants to be… useful. I don't think I realized how vital that is to him. Maybe because I can't understand how he doesn't see himself the way I do. He *is* vital to me. Even without magic. Even without a title. He's my—" She broke off, pressing a hand to her chest, as if it would help the ache beneath her ribs. "He's the place I go when the world is too much. The one person I don't have to perform for. I need him to take care of me when I forget how."

"And do you let him?" Malcolum asked gently. "Truly? Not just when your headaches hit. Do you let him be himself with you?"

She hesitated.

"I try."

"Trying isn't trusting," he said, voice still kind. "You love his steadiness. His sword. His honesty. But do you *welcome* it? Even when it doesn't fit the image of the court or what you think a queen should act like? Even when it isn't pretty or strategic?"

Gwen didn't answer.

"In all things," he said, "there is balance. You're careful. He's blunt. You think in steps. He moves on instinct. Sometimes you're too measured when his sharp cut is needed. Sometimes he charges when he should wait. That's the point of partnership, Gwen. You're trying to carry both halves of a whole instead of sharing the burden."

She looked down at her hands again. Her fingers were trembling.

"I don't know how to fix it." Gwen swallowed hard before continuing. "I don't even know if he'll come back, or what I'll tell everyone. You're supposed to be wedding us in the morning."

Malcolum half snorted, half chuckled. "He'll come back. He always does."

He said it with such certainty that Gwen almost believed him.

"As for what to tell everyone," he added, "there's not much to tell. Frankly, in my opinion,

I wedded you both the day we named him High Captain."

Her brows lifted.

He smiled. "Your vows need to be edited to reflect an actual marriage, and Tyreal's band will need removed and then placed back on, but..." He waved a hand, dismissive. "Those are details."

Gwen let out another laugh, surprised at how light she felt now.

Malcolum's expression softened. "Come back here in the morning. The ceremony is just the three of us. Tell anyone that asks that he is meeting you here. Sit in prayer for a while. When he finds his way back to you—which I believe he will—I'll tell the court the ceremony has been completed." He leaned closer, eyes twinkling. "No need to give the court more gossip than the dragons already have."

Tyreal walked as far from the castle as his feet would carry him without heading into the village proper. Past the stables. Past the barracks. He didn't stop until he reached the low stone cottage on the edge of the north field—where the commoners with magic had been offered space to live, to train and adjust.

The ones like him.

The ones who hadn't asked for power but had it, anyway. The ones who would never be accepted by the nobles that had sired them.

A fire's glow flickered out back, lighting the night sky with orange and gold. Tyreal circled the cottage and followed the light until the sound of rhythmic thudding met his ears. He found Mason behind the house, swinging an ax down hard on a thick log. The older man's shirt was damp with sweat, sleeves shoved to his elbows. A pile of split firewood lay at his feet, neat and tall.

Mason stopped when he saw him.

He didn't speak right away, just studied Tyreal's face like it was a page he needed to read from top to bottom. Then, with a tilt of his chin, he nodded toward the second ax stuck in a stump nearby. "Get at it."

Tyreal didn't argue. He walked over, pulled the ax free, and took up the rhythm.

They chopped in silence for a while. The swing and thud of each strike filled the air between them. The monotonous physical exertion soothed him.

When he finally stripped off his gloves, breath shallow, Mason spoke. "You look like someone who lost something."

Tyreal didn't look over. "Maybe I did."

"You'd know if you did."

Tyreal wasn't sure how to respond to that. The first initial emotion was anger. How dare this man act like Tyreal didn't know what loss was? Then, resignation. He *didn't* know what loss was, not in the way Mason did at this moment.

Mason gave a low grunt and lifted another log. "You know what my magic is?" he asked. "Not the power to control water like Princess Anya, something that could have saved my boy. Not invisibility, like Finn. I can summon light. Just plain, regular light." He shook his head. "I should have been the one with the fire power. My life is almost over. His was just beginning."

Tyreal leaned on the ax handle. "The gods do like their tricks. Mine is healing."

Mason snorted. "Bit ironic."

"Tell me about it."

Mason let the silence settle before adding, "You ever think maybe the gods gave you exactly what you needed instead of what you wanted?"

Tyreal stared into the pile of firewood. "No. I haven't thought that."

"I didn't ask if you liked the answer."

That made Tyreal huff—something close to a laugh.

They stood there a while longer, the sweat cooling into goose bumps on their skin as the chilly night air blew past them. The fire cracked and popped, and the sea waves could be heard crashing.

Finally, Mason said, "You come here looking for something?"

"Clarity."

"You expecting me to hand it to you?" Mason sat down on the stump where they'd been splitting wood and stretched his legs out with a groan.

"I was hoping to borrow some."

"Well, I'm gonna need to know what happened if you expect me to dig some up." He gave Tyreal another once-over. "By the look on your face and the fact you're down here on your betrothal night, I'd wager you had a hell of a fight with the wife."

Tyreal let out a long breath. "Something like that."

He coughed, trying to clear the tightness in his throat. He didn't know where to start—or how much was even appropriate to say. Did King Consorts typically wander out to chop wood and ask for marriage advice from men they only sort of knew from drunken nights at the tavern?

Was he even King Consort anymore?

"The meeting with the monarchs..." he started. "It showed me I don't belong. I'm no use to her in that room, and what she is doing right now is too important. Without getting all the nobles on board with peace, we are dragon fodder. I'm just a soldier."

Mason scratched at the back of his neck. "I don't think life's ever been that clean-cut." He paused, then added, "I might not be too happy with the gods these days, and I sure as hell don't understand why they let things happen the way they do. But I know love."

His voice softened. "I was with my wife for twenty-five summers. Beautiful years. Spent most of them hoping for a child. Thought it'd never happen. Then finally, it did. She was the best mother I've ever seen—better than mine, I'll tell you that."

He stared into the fire, eyes far away.

"She made everything warmer, brighter. I lived for the way she'd smile when he fell asleep on her chest. But he was only eight summers gone when she got sick. One week, and she was no longer there. I kept going for my boy. Only reason I made it through."

Another pause.

"Then he was gone too."

Tyreal said nothing. His chest ached.

"I'm lost now, if I'm honest. I don't know how to keep going without love." Mason looked over at him, gaze steady. "All that to say—*you* have love. Real love. Anyone with half a working eye can see it. You want to make things right?" He pointed at Tyreal's chest. "Stop trying to become what she doesn't need."

Tyreal frowned. "I don't understand."

"You think she needs someone polished, political, safe for the nobles to look at." Mason leaned forward. "She's already surrounded by those people. What she needs is someone who doesn't give a damn what they think. Someone who sees the fire when everyone else keeps insisting the room's just warm. Once upon a time, I would have sworn that man was you. At least, that's the captain of the guard I've always known."

Tyreal's jaw flexed. He looked away, toward the fire pit.

"She needs *you*, son, the real you. The man who I heard fought through a panicking crowd tonight and took on an untold number of men to reach her. Not the version you think fits better beside a throne." Mason stood, grabbing another log. "Now, you're welcome to stand here and chop wood with me till sunrise. But if I were you—and I've been a fool of a newlywed before—I'd go remind that girl what safety feels like."

He tossed the log into the pile. "The rest?" he said. "Just noise."

CHAPTER TWENTY-ONE

The chapel was cold this early in the morning. Servants had lit the spaced-out braziers, their iron bellies glowing with soft amber light. Gwen must have just missed them—the warmth hadn't spread yet. Her breath rose in faint puffs, and the chill raised bumps on her arms.

She shivered and pulled the heavy white velvet cloak tighter around herself as she walked slowly down the aisle toward the altar. Rose petals had been scattered across the path, and Gwen's lips tipped into a sad smile. She hadn't asked for that. Tavian weddings were simple affairs. No court. No pageantry. Just her, Tyreal, and their vows. However, some servant must've taken it upon themselves to add a bit of romance.

She wished Tyreal could see that there were plenty of people who saw things the way she did. The romantic servant clearly agreed, and they weren't alone. He belonged here. Their marriage *was* the path forward. She didn't care what the other royals thought of him being rough around the edges. That was the whole point. He was Tyreal. Her other half.

She was early—not something she was particularly known for. The moon still lingered in the sky, and only the faintest streaks of pink and violet touched the horizon. Per Tavian tradition, they were meant to be wed just after first light. A private rite before the world stirred—Malcolum officiating, and only the gods and tapestries as witnesses.

And yet, she was alone.

She hadn't slept at all. Every small sound set her heart pounding, waiting for him to appear. She wouldn't have minded if he came back angry, as long as he was there.

Andais had looked first concerned, then furious, when she left her chambers alone. He had tried to ask where Tyreal was, but she'd silenced him with a sharp shake of her head. She knew she should have lied, reassured him that Tyreal would be along shortly. The problem was, she didn't know that. Saying it aloud would make it real.

Still, Malcolum's words from the night before had stayed with her. This was Tyreal, the most steadfast, infuriatingly loyal part of her life. They'd fought badly since childhood—both of them stubborn, hot-blooded, reckless. But he *always* came back. He *always* chose her. Anything else would mean the world no longer made sense. And with everything else unraveling, she wasn't sure she could survive one more change.

Gwen sat in the front pew, folding her hands into her cloak. She looked up at her favorite tapestry—Myaessa, radiant and wild—and she prayed. Prayed for understanding. Prayed for Tyreal to walk through that door. Prayed for some kind of answer, if he didn't.

The space was still.

As always, Myaessa and the gods remained silent.

She took a deep breath. The smell of incense drifted from the braziers—sweet, floral, earthy with wood smoke. Normally, it comforted her. Today, it did little. Comfort would only find her if it came in the form of Tyreal's arms and a whispered apology from both of them.

She glanced at the altar.

On it was the golden cord to handfast them, a gold bracelet for her, a small hooked tool to remove Tyreal's before placing it back on at the same time as hers, Tyreal's diadem, and Malcolum's scrawled chicken-scratch notes of their vows. Nausea rolled over her. Panic bloomed in her chest—but she shoved it down.

He will come.He has to come.

Gwen didn't know how long she sat there before the chapel doors creaked open. She turned sharply, hair whipping over her shoulder and knocking the hood of her cloak down so that it pooled down her back. His name slipped from her lips, trailing off when she saw who it was.

Malcolum stepped in, offering her a sad, knowing smile before gently closing the heavy door behind him. He walked slowly, the stiff shuffle in his gait more noticeable in the early morning hours.

He joined her without a word. Sat beside her.

And they waited in silence.

The morning sun finally reached the stained-glass windows, some cracked now from Viamar's landing. Broken shafts of red, gold, and sapphire crept across the marble floor, crawling toward them inch by inch.

They sat without speaking. Gwen's eyes moved forward and her jaw tight. The light through the stained glass was crawling past the altar now, where it was supposed to be casting its radiance and warmth upon them and blessing their union.

Still no footsteps.

Malcolum shifted, taking pressure off his hip. She knew he was giving her space, a grace she usually appreciated. Today, the quiet wasn't sacred. It felt cruel. Every moment sitting in it felt like it might suffocate her.

Her throat burned as she stared back up at the tapestry. Now that she looked at it closer, she realized it was Viamar that Myaessa was riding. She wondered if the dragon would tell her more about the queen that had changed the world. What would Viamar have to say about Tyreal's absence? The dragon had claimed that Tyreal loved her more than he loved their country or people. That she was his mate. And yet...

She let out a sharp breath, curling her hands together so tightly that her nails bit into her palm. They were almost certainly bloody. Did she care?

Her thoughts pulled her back to the last time she had seen him. The fight. How his jaw had clenched and how damn calm his voice had been. Gods, the last thing she said—

If you walk out, don't come back.

Why had she said that? She didn't mean it. She *never* meant it. He had called her bluff on it before, but this felt so different. He had said he didn't know if he was breaking their betrothal.

Maybe this time, the cut was just too deep. Something between them actually severed.

The thought cracked something open in her chest. She clenched her teeth, forcing her breathing to stay steady, but her shoulders trembled with the effort.

The brazier closest to them let out a low *pop* of embers. The scent of rose and burnt cedar filled the air again, but thicker now. Somehow the sweetness suddenly smelled pungent, like rotting fruit. She jumped up from the pew, pacing in front of it and trying to get away from the brazier to gulp in the cool, fresh air. But her chest felt constricted, like she couldn't fully fill her lungs.

"He will come, child." Malcolum said quietly.

She thought about arguing, about letting all her fear funnel into something sharper, louder, angrier. But the Arbiter didn't deserve that. He wasn't at fault here. Instead, she resumed her place on the bench, lingering, as if too much haste might shatter something fragile in her chest.

Gwen broke the silence, perhaps moments, perhaps hours later. "I don't know what to pray for," she said, not looking at him. "I prayed for everything I can think of."

Malcolum made a quiet sound—not approval or disapproval. Just a low breath of encouragement, urging her forward.

"I used to think that I knew how the gods spoke," she said. "That if you were quiet enough, you could hear something back. Not words, exactly, but something. A presence." She paused. "Lately, though, I've started wondering if that was a child's fantasy. Not because I'm not listening, but because maybe they don't know what to say either. Maybe they are watching this mess unfold, and they are just as lost as we are."

She stood again, needing to move. Her hands brushed along the carved edge of the pew as she stepped back into the aisle. She didn't pace this time. She moved towards the altar, standing where she should have been. The colored lights moving like water over her cloak. She stared at the space beside her before finally looking up at Malcolum.

Her voice cracked when she spoke. "Can you please ask Andais to come inside?" Even to her own ears, she sounded far away. Numbness was settling where the panic had been.

He wasn't coming.

He had left her.

Malcolum opened his mouth as if to argue, perhaps to offer one last thread of hope, but the look on her face must have stilled him and he closed it. He gave her a long, sad look, but finally nodded. Without a word, he rose from the bench and walked towards the chapel doors.

It was a while before the great chapel doors opened again, reluctant on their hinges. Even though she knew it was likely Andais, her heart still leapt into her throat with hope, until another wave of disappointment crested over her as she saw her Lower Captain. He was in partial uniform, his chest plate missing, and his sword belt looking slightly askew. Had she been in this chapel so long that his night shift was over?

He stopped in the aisle, brown eyes searching the space around the altar, confusion etched across his features. "Your Majesty? You sent for me?"

Tears welled in her eyes, and she opened her mouth to speak. The words didn't come at first, but finally, she thought of everything that was at stake. She was queen. She didn't have time to break down over this.

She waved him forward. "I take it you see the problem?"

He frowned and came closer. "I know you came here alone. It looks like you are still alone. But I can't for the life of me understand why."

She closed her eyes, working up the courage to speak it into existence. "Well, I understand why, but I didn't really think it would happen. He's gone." The words felt foreign. Blunt. Like holding her drawing pencils in the wrong hand.

"What the hell do you mean, he's gone?" The shock and doubt on his face was so clear that it almost made her hope again. He didn't even apologize for cursing in her presence. Everyone believed he would be here.

"We fought. Last night. After we met with the other royals."

"And? You two fight constantly. It's practically half of your relationship."

"He believes that I can't save Valine from the dragons with him at my side because he isn't good at politics and diplomacy."

Andais' brows furrowed, and he spread his hands wide. "That's... possibly the dumbest thing I've ever heard. But that aside, he still wouldn't *leave*. Not on your wedding day. Not without talking to me first. Certainly not with Prince Grigor landing at any moment with violent intentions. No. That doesn't make sense."

She shrugged, tears spilling down her cheeks. "I told him if he walked out, not to come back. He's not here."

"You think he actually listened?" Andais shook his head again. "Absolutely not. Something is wrong."

"Maybe. Maybe not. Either way, whatever the truth is, we cannot let it leak. If the court finds out he is missing, or worse, that he broke our betrothal, they'll use it to undermine the accord. They'll say that the High Captain of the Guard lost faith in what I'm trying to build, that even *he* doesn't believe in the path forward."

Andais looked sick. "That's not what this is. You can't believe that."

"I don't know what to believe. I just know what I see and what I know. We have to control this."

He stared at her for a long moment, then gave a slow, disbelieving breath. "What do you wanna do?"

She let out a hollow laugh. "Well, I want to go bar myself in my room and cry for the rest of the day and make myself sick on Cook's cookies while I try to nurse my broken heart. However, lacking that option, we will first let people think the ceremony went well and that Tyreal and I returned to my chambers to consummate our union. Malcolum has agreed to tell everyone that it happened. Then we will need to make up some kind of excuse, something calling him away from the castle on important business."

Andais snorted. "It'll have to be pretty damn important for anyone to even remotely believe he willingly left your bed. No offense, Your Majesty."

She waved her hand dismissively. "None taken. You're right. I don't have the wits about me at this moment to come up with an excuse. I know that you've been up all night, and this is a lot to ask, but I need you to talk with Anya, Max, and Hedontas. Explain what happened and come up with something. You are acting High Captain for now."

"I'm not worried about being tired. We will figure this out, and I'll find him. In the meantime…" He trailed off, and she could see the thoughts racing through his mind as he tried to come up with a logistical plan. "We have to figure out how to get you to your chambers with no one seeing you alone."

"Go clear the hallways. Say Tyreal won't let anyone else lay eyes on me until I'm officially his. That sounds—"

"Very like him. No one will doubt it. Give me a moment and I will get you to your chambers, Your Majesty."

She nodded, and he turned to walk away from her. He paused and spoke over his shoulder. "You think he left you. I think he didn't. One of us is right."

"I hope it's you," she whispered.

Andais took a deep breath before continuing down the aisle. "If he's out there," he said, "I'll find him."

CHAPTER TWENTY-TWO

"**Y**ou can do this. You're just a happily-in-love newlywed. And it's perfectly reasonable to be sad because your husband was called away."

Gwen blew out a breath, lips pursing. She stared into the looking glass and wondered if, by repeating it enough times, she might actually believe it. She leaned forward, pressing her fingers to the swollen skin beneath her eyes. The bags were dark, red-rimmed, unmistakable. Anyone could see she'd spent the night crying, not making love to her husband.

"This will never work," she muttered to her reflection.

But it had to.

Any sign of weakness now would be blood in the water. A missing groom on your wedding day didn't exactly scream stability—especially when that groom was the High Captain and the leader of your entire military.

Andais and Hedontas had assured her everything was under control. The men didn't know Tyreal was gone—or *missing*, as they both insisted—and they remained focused on Lovell's impending arrival. So far, only her inner circle knew the truth. And every one of them had refused to believe Tyreal had left her.

She wanted to believe them. Part of her did believe them. Which brought a fresh wave of fear and anxiety. Was he hurt? Did he need her?

Then the other part, the quieter, crueler voice that surfaced when she was alone, kept replaying his strange distance over the past few days. The quiet tension. The way he'd looked at her during their last argument. The unease that shadowed him whenever the topic of magic came up.

Or that day at his mother's, when he'd vulnerably asked if she didn't want to marry him because he wasn't noble-born.

She had thought he was over that.

Maybe the pressure had been building under the surface the whole time, unspoken and unresolved.

Maybe it was just too much.

Maybe *she* was too much.

Yes, they were in love. Yes, they'd wanted each other for what felt like forever. Sometimes, though, reality wasn't as exciting as fantasy.

Needing an outlet, anything to relieve the pressure, she curled her fingers into fists and dug her nails into her palms. A scream welled in her throat, but she didn't let it out. She just felt it—burning, silent, desperate.

The logs in the hearth exploded into flame, and all the candles blazed. A roar filled the room as fire surged, snapping high up the chimney and throwing sudden heat outwards. It made her flinch. She looked down at her hands, trembling.

If she let herself feel all of it at once, she could probably burn the entire castle down. Or, if she could ever learn to control it, topple it with gale force winds.

Wouldn't that be full circle? Myaessa had formed Mist Castle and shaped it after Thorncliff in her heartbreak and rage. Gwen destroying Thorncliff in hers. Poetic, almost.

Gwen could practically hear Tyreal in her mind, so frustratingly rational when she was spiraling out. An edge of humor in his voice, but a gravely serious look on his face. *Hard to burn down stone though, sweet girl. You'll need to come up with a better plan.*

She let the fire burn for a moment unchecked, before finally extinguishing it as she stood. Her circlet rested on a pillow nearby, and she reached for it, arranging it carefully on top of her curls. She practiced smiling in the looking glass.

It didn't quite work.

She bit at her lips, hoping to plump them up enough that she looked freshly kissed. Reached up and tugged just a few curls from her pinned-up look so that it looked like wayward fingers might have slipped into them. The fatigue, she could cover. A new bride with a war looming, and a touch sad that her High Captain was called away.

The story was already writing itself. Wasn't that what Tensha had said they should do? Get ahead of the narrative?

She crossed the room toward the door. As she opened it, she forced a soft, throaty laugh. "You have to go. And so do I," she said lightly. To no one. Then, louder, just before stepping into the hall, "You do *not* need another kiss."

She shut the door firmly behind her before the guards could glance inside. One of them raised an eyebrow, and she rolled her eyes in mock exasperation with a soft smile.

He snorted, barely stifling a laugh.

Maybe she could do this.

Chairs scraped and voices died mid-sentence as Gwen entered the library. Everyone rose. She inclined her head in acknowledgment to her fellow monarchs, her steps steady as she made her way to the head of the table. Her chin was high. Her expression composed.

Just a queen. Just a newlywed.

Just a girl trying her best to hold the world together.

Her eyes scanned the room as she reached her place. One seat stood noticeably empty—the one meant for Drakon. His guard was absent as well.

She turned to Hedontas with a questioning look.

He shrugged, hands spread wide. "He left. Said he wanted no part of any alliance or the dragons. He claims his country will remain neutral, and he hopes the dragons will respect that."

Gwen winced, just slightly. Was that true? Or was he lying in wait, ready to align with Grigor the moment things turned? There was no way to be sure.

"I don't know that he's entirely wrong," King Samyad said quietly. "If there's a battle coming, it's between Tavia and Adaltus. I'm not convinced the rest of us need to be involved."

Gwen's jaw tensed. She didn't reply immediately. Instead, she rested her hands lightly along the carved edge of the table, letting the silence stretch just long enough to make everyone lean in, waiting for her reaction.

"There is no such thing as neutrality when the sky is on fire."

Several monarchs shifted in their seats.

"I can't stop you from leaving or force you to join me," Gwen said. "However, know this—Grigor *is* coming. Either alone or with the full support of his father and the Adaltan army.

And he comes with every intention of taking Tavia by whatever means necessary. We already know he believes that no one outside his family should wield magic. He won't stop with me. Do you truly believe, in your heart of hearts, that he won't wage a full-scale war before this is over and get all of us killed in the process?"

"You have no way of knowing that, dear," said King Henri, in what had to be the most patronizing tone Gwen had ever heard from him.

"Father," Anya hissed.

Gwen straightened in her chair. "Firstly—and I know you know this—I am not your dear. I am a monarch, the same as you. You are a guest in *my* country. Secondly, I do know. The High Captain's spies uncovered direct evidence of Lovell's treachery, including bribing my nobles, turning my guards, funding operations to steal food from our hearths, and conspiring to kidnap the prince in an attempt to force me to accept his proposal."

Her anger swelled even higher inside her as she listed everything out, and she thought back to Malcolum's words. How she needed Tyreal's bluntness sometimes. Maybe it wasn't completely wrong to let her temper flare. "I've seen fragments of his letters to the High Sister. I heard her tirade about their bloodline and magic, just after she killed one of my friends and tried to murder every person in that temple—including your daughter. So, if you'd like to call someone *dear*, perhaps ask Anya what she thinks of that."

She practically spat the words.

Henri paled, and Isolde sucked in a dramatic gasp. "Anya, is this true? Were you in danger?"

Anya rolled her eyes. "I told you we were attacked. What did you think that meant?"

The table went silent.

Uncomfortable silence filled the room before King Thalion cleared his throat. "Speaking of the High Captain, where is he? I would think you two would be inseparable right now."

It was like a dagger under Gwen's ribs, but she didn't react, merely frowned sadly. "I wish that was a possibility. The High Captain traveled to the southern border to make sure we are prepared for Lovell's arrival. We expect him any day now."

Max smoothly interjected right after Gwen finished, not allowing anyone time for follow-up questions. "I think we should return to the topic of the alliance," he said smoothly, hands steepled on the table. "We'd like to hear any remaining doubts you may have. What will it take to ensure every kingdom at this table feels equally secure and respected?"

The trick to staving off the cloying weight of anxiety was to simply stay too busy to think about it. Which is what Gwen immediately did as soon as she could get to her study. Piles of parchment waited for her on the long mahogany desk, important updates and issues that Hedontas hadn't felt comfortable addressing in her absence during the trek to Mist Castle. A pot of fresh ink sat ready for her, with a line of new quills in a neat row beside it.

She slipped out of the cloak she'd been wearing to fight the chill she just couldn't seem to shake, hanging it neatly on a hook. The gold of her marriage bracelet glinted as she did, its weight still unfamiliar. Her eyes lingered on it briefly before she turned to the work at hand.

She pulled the first parchment to her—a list of revised trade terms with Espera, negotiated before the magic fiasco, and a copy of the military rota from the troops along the southern coastal border. A manifest of the arriving monarchy, now already present, so now useless. She tossed it aside. A stack of complaints between various nobles in the districts of Tavia, and a winter budget that needed her attention.

Her pen hovered over it, but didn't move.

She blinked once, then forced her hand down and signed her name.

Queen Gwendolyn Thorncrest of Tavia.

Still true. Still real. Even if she doubted herself.

Half an hour passed. Maybe more. She skimmed and approved. Rejected two items. Wrote a note chastising two squabbling nobles that were acting like children. Reviewed the potential list of candidates for her new advisory council, thankfully now with some commoners on it. Her eyes burned, but she kept going.

Then something caught her attention.

It was a minor logistics summary of offloaded goods accepted into Thorncliff two days prior from the man that oversaw the trading docks, Branneth. Nothing out of the ordinary. Leather for the armory, wool for the seamstresses, dried fruit Cook had requested. Regular, everyday trade items.

However, it was the name of the trader that stood out.

Kiel Ingram. A familiar name from her security reports from Tyreal. Tyreal believed him to be pirating goods he brokered through Adaltus, though he couldn't prove it yet. There were just too many convenient disappearances and too many ties to merchant routes that coincided with attacks.

He was supposed to be under surveillance and not allowed in Tavian waters.

Yet here he was, unloading cargo in her castle. On the same day, Tyreal was nowhere to be found.

Her heart pounded in her chest. Could Ingram be connected somehow? He almost had to be. She didn't believe in those kinds of coincidences.

She pushed her chair back and opened her door, grabbing Andais' arm and pulling him into the room.

"What's wrong?" he asked, immediately on alert.

She waved the shipping manifest at him, mildly aware that she probably looked more than a little deranged. "Ingram. Kiel Ingram is here at Thorncliff."

Andais frowned. "The one Tyreal has been watching for piracy? He shouldn't be anywhere near Tavia right now at all, much less in the castle. When did he arrive?"

"Two days ago! What if he's still here? What if he *has* Tyreal? Branneth signed off on the supply run—do you think he's compromised?" The questions flew from her in a rush, each breath faster than the last. "Could Ingram have bribed him? Used him? What if—"

"I think someone certainly has Tyreal," Andais interrupted.

She blinked. "What?"

"We found Braken, still in the stable."

Gwen went completely still.

Her throat tightened. "What?" she repeated.

Andais nodded gravely. "We've moved him into the confinement stall and started a rumor he's got an infection in his hooves. Micah is keeping everyone away from him."

Her mind reeled. All thoughts of Ingram, Adaltus, even Branneth blurred into static.

Braken was still here.

Tyreal didn't go *anywhere* without Braken, ever. He'd trained the stallion from a foal. They practically moved like extensions of each other. Hell, the horse would kill on command by a whistle. They were a deadly efficient unit.

Her voice was low and shaky. "How could you not tell me this?"

"I only found out right before I came on shift," Andais said. "I was going to tell you once you'd thrown yourself into your work for a while. I know that's how you cope. But it changes nothing. We're still looking."

"It changes *everything*," she said.

"It confirms what we suspected, that he didn't leave."

Gwen stepped away from him, one hand pressed to her mouth, the other clenched tight at her side. Guilt, hot and acidic, rose in her throat. How could she have doubted him? She'd been so focused on appearances that she'd delayed searching for him immediately. If something had happened, she would be completely at fault.

The room tunneled. Her vision narrowed, and her knees threatened to give beneath her.

Andais moved fast.

He guided her gently toward the nearest chair, one hand braced lightly on her back, the other steadying her elbow. "I've been looking since you told me," he said, crouching beside her. "Tensha and Jameson have been combing Thorncliff, every corridor, every cellar, every off-duty guard house. And you were right not to alert the other monarchs."

His voice was soft, measured, meant to soothe.

Gwen shut her eyes tightly. Her breath came in uneven bursts. She *wanted* to believe him—wanted to trust that she hadn't already failed Tyreal by waiting.

She prayed he was okay so she could beg his forgiveness.

CHAPTER TWENTY-THREE

G wen rarely ate breakfast in the sunroom, but she wasn't sure she had it in her to play pretend in front of everyone. What had started as grief and betrayal simmering in her gut had hardened into fear.

She couldn't stop the questions about Tyreal's safety circling in her mind. They were eating her alive.

The anger wanted out. She wanted to rip through every hall of the castle, demanding answers. She wanted to drag nobles from their beds and set fire to everything around them until she got honesty. But she'd already told the other monarchs that Tyreal had been called away on official castle business. Going full vengeful queen now, when she had zero proof, would make her look unstable. Desperate.

So instead, she sat at a quiet table with Pip, watching him chow down on honey rolls as if someone would come and take the platter away from him.

"Do you think dragons like honey?" he asked suddenly, mouth full.

Gwen blinked, trying to catch up with the mental jumps Pip must have taken to get to that question. Had she missed part of the conversation? Her mind had been halfway through a mental list of everything that could still go wrong. "I'm not sure," she said. "I think they mostly eat meat."

Pip nodded, thoughtful. "Cook makes that honey pork that's really good. Maybe they'd like that." He kept sketching while he spoke. Sheets of parchment were spread across the table, most covered in smudged charcoal. One sketch was a dragon—too many teeth, one wing bigger than the other, but definitely a dragon. In the other hand, Pip gripped what she thought might be his third roll.

Gwen let herself smile, though she moved the platter away from him and pushed the plate full of bacon closer. "It's hard to resist Cook's food," she said, "though too many of her sweets would give even a dragon a bellyache, much less a prince. You think if we offered them dinner, the dragons might side with us?"

He looked up, grinning. "You're joking."

"A little."

Pip went back to his drawing. "All I'm saying is… has anyone tried just being nice?"

He wasn't *wrong*.

"You might be on to something, Pip. Maybe I'll ask Viamar next time I see him." She reached for her tea, trying to just let herself enjoy the quiet of a breakfast with her brother, for even a moment—when three quick sharp raps came at the door. Andais entered before she could call him in.

His face was pinched in annoyance, and though he didn't look fearful or furious, she couldn't stop her mind from jumping to the worst-case scenario.

"What is it? Did something happen?" she asked sharply, her heart in her throat.

Andais shook his head quickly, knowing where her mind had gone. "Nothing like that, Your Majesty. I don't have any news about the High Captain. We received a message that you will not like, though." He held up a folded piece of parchment. "I just received this from the west watchtower."

Pip looked up, chewing slowly. Gwen wiped her fingers on a napkin and took the note from him. It was brief, but said all it needed to.

King Damaris departed the castle at first light with only his personal guard. Tavian watch lost visual. Destination unknown.

Her brows furrowed. "He left without his wife?"

"So it seems. No official statement. No reason given. He didn't even use the main corridor." Andais crossed his arms. "Maybe he's coming back. But why dodge our guard? If he needed air and wanted to go for a ride, he could've just said that."

"How did he give the guard the slip? Presumably, I've been training them on how to catch that for the last several years," Gwen said, setting the note aside.

"As you aren't known for moving around too much at dawn, the overnight guard doesn't have the same level of experience," Andais quipped with a grin, before he grew annoyed again. "They'll be running drills for a year for this. Losing sight of a monarch on my watch? I don't think so."

"Try not to be too hard on them. I'm sure it was Damaris' guard that helped him escape. I doubt he would have been able to do it on his own." Gwen tapped a finger against her lips, thinking through the possibilities of what Damaris could be doing. Was this a sign that he was about to leave and give up on the alliance like Drakon had done? Or was there something else?

"Do you think he's meeting someone?" she asked. "Maybe a lover? Something he wouldn't want the queen to know about?"

Andais made a face. "Seems like a poor plan. She's definitely going to notice his absence. Would've been easier to just duck off into the brothel...er, I mean—" He froze, remembering that the prince was in the room.

"What's a brothel?" Pip asked, head cocked to one side like an inquisitive puppy.

Gwen didn't even flinch. "A place where men go to kiss women they're not married to. Not somewhere a young prince needs to be thinking about." She shot Andais a sharp look as she said it. He winced.

To his credit, the guard looked properly sheepish, his cheeks darkening to a deeper brown as he blushed. "Sorry, Your Majesty. I wasn't thinking."

Pip rolled his eyes like he was already used to adults being weird, then grabbed a piece of bacon and went back to chewing.

Gwen set the message down and let her fingers tap absently against the wood. Her eyes drifted toward the window again, west-facing, where the path to the outer gates wound toward the hills.

She had a feeling she was about to find out exactly why Damaris had left. And she would not like it.

Part of her wanted to grab her riding cloak, saddle Akasha, and ride until the wind stole every thought from her head. Ride until the world stopped spinning.

Maybe Drakon had the right idea.

But then Pip shifted, charcoal scratching faintly against the parchment as he resumed working on his dragon sketch, and the sound tugged her back to the present.

She wasn't Drakon. She didn't have the luxury of giving up.

She was still here. Still ruling. Still hoping Tyreal would walk through the damn doors.

And she would not run.

"Your Majesty? You need to see what's happening in the courtyard."

Gwen looked up from her parchments, startled. Cora stood in the doorway, her hands clasped tightly in front of her. Her eyes were pinched, and a rare frown marred her face.

"What is it?" Gwen asked, already rising.

"King Damaris has returned. And he isn't alone."

Gwen took a deep breath and motioned for Cora to follow her out of the room. The sound of her boots echoed on the floor, and her skirts rustled against the stones as the hallway seemed to stretch further and further in front of her, feeling longer than it should have been. Each step forward felt heavier than the last, as if her body were trying to prevent her from turning the page into the next chapter. The one that would change everything.

By the time she stepped out into the court-yard, people were already parting for her. All of them looked concerned and nervous.

Damaris was already dismounting. He didn't look at her at first, his gaze wandering to the sky and the crowd. Anywhere but her. Finally, though, he tipped his chin up defiantly and met her eyes.

There was no apology on his face.

Her gaze slid over to the man beside him.

Grigor Lovell.

Seated atop a pristine white horse, posture relaxed, like he was visiting a dear friend. He wasn't smiling, not yet, but the arrogance was still there in the slight curve at the corners of his lips and the tilt of his head. However, draped across the neck of his mount—a white sash.

The sign of the Covenant.

Her chest tightened. The Covenant was sacred, the only law the Sisters of the Mist had enacted not having to do with royal marriage and bloodlines. No sovereign could deny another a chance to speak under peaceful diplomatic request, not if the sash was worn and an Arbiter bore witness.

Seated on a mount beside Lovell, there was a young man dressed in Arbiter robes. He looked little older than Gwen.

Fury rose in Gwen's chest so hot, it made her fingers twitch. She could burn him where he sat. She *wanted* to. But if she did—if she even touched him—*she'd be the one breaking the law.*

Lovell had wrapped himself in protection and strolled into her house, daring her to swing first.

A muscle jumped in her jaw and her hands curled into fists inside her sleeves. She didn't move immediately, just looked at the trio silently.

She straightened her spine, kept her face completely neutral, and walked forward. Andais and Hedontas quickly flanked her on either side. Their body language was decidedly *not* neutral.

Lovell dismounted as she moved closer. He bowed, low and theatrical. "Queen Gwendolyn, you look radiant. Grief suits you."

"What a positively bizarre thing to say. Grief doesn't suit anyone, particularly when someone's parent is taken far too soon." She couldn't tell if the barb found its mark, if it affected him to be reminded of High Sister's role in her father's death. Unfortunately, his face also remained neutral. "It is bold of you to show your face here, considering."

"I come in peace," he said, fingering the white sash, "under the Covenant. Sanctified and witnessed by my Arbiter and a fellow monarch." He gestured towards Damaris, who shifted a little uneasily, but remained quiet.

Gwen didn't break eye contact. "You left my castle without a word," she said to Damaris, voice like ice. "And returned with a man known to be aligned with the High Sister—a woman who had a direct hand in the chaos we now find ourselves in."

Damaris didn't blink. "He invoked the Covenant. I honored the law. I'd hope you'd do the same."

"I'm not here to fight, Gwendolyn—" Grigor started.

"It's queen, or Your Majesty in my lands, *Prince* Grigor," she snapped. Her neutrality was cracking at the edges as her anger steadily grew. She could feel the palms of her hands heating as her fire licked just beneath their surface.

He gave a shallow bow, just this side of mocking. "Of course. My apologies. Your ascension happened so quickly, I must've forgotten my manners.

"I didn't come to fight, Your Majesty," he continued smoothly. "Only to clear up the unfortunate rumors and defend myself. Perhaps even seek help with this magic I've... unexpectedly inherited."

"Strange," Gwen said. "My reports suggested you weren't struggling at all. In fact, they mentioned full sails in windless waters—part of how you arrived far earlier than expected."

Grigor gave a modest shrug. "I'll admit I could piece together the basics. The High Sister provided just enough for me to make sense of it, especially once some of my relatives aboard began showing signs as well."

"And where are these relatives? Did you not bring them as part of your diplomatic party?"

"I thought it wiser to leave them aboard the ship. A show of good faith. I wanted you to see I came to talk, not posture." She noticed he didn't name *which* relatives. Surely King Zendor would have arrived with him if he'd been along for the journey.

Gwen stepped one pace closer. "Interesting, considering the *good faith* you've shown thus far. One of my nobles—bribed by you—first attempted to pressure me into accepting your proposal. When that failed, he tried to kidnap me. On your orders." She tapped the small scar at the base of her throat. "Unfortunate business."

Grigor's expression barely changed. "And your proof? The word of a traitor desperate to save himself?"

Gwen tilted her head. "The traitor who bragged about it to me and then confessed to my High Captain and Lower Captain in the dungeons." She didn't wait for him to respond. "Tell me, Prince Grigor, is that the diplomacy you plan to bring to this court? The kind that ends with people in my dungeon?" she continued, voice low.

He gave a soft, humorless chuckle. "It's a bit of a leap, don't you think? One man's actions, and suddenly I'm the villain. An entire kingdom discredited on hearsay?"

"I said that was the *first* piece of evidence," Gwen replied coolly. "Not all of it." She gave him a saccharine smile. "You aren't on trial, though I can arrange that if you'd like."

He smiled like it amused him. "If your proof is so abundant, Your Majesty, why haven't the other monarchs seen it? Surely you're not expecting this entire council to act on implication alone."

"I assure you," Gwen said, "what I present, and when, is a matter of strategy. Not supply."

Lovell brushed something off his tunic, nonplussed by their conversation. "Hmm. And here I assumed it was because your High Captain had little more than whispers from his spies."

A beat. He tilted his head, just slightly.

"Speaking of—where is the High Captain, anyway?"

Gwen's breath stayed even, but her spine stiffened. That wasn't curiosity. That was a test.

She gave no reaction. "The High Captain was called away to our southern border. I expect him back shortly."

Lovell made a thoughtful sound. "How dutiful. I imagine it must've been rather urgent to pull him from his marriage bed so soon. From the reports I heard, no one's seen him since the betrothal ball. Seems he was called away almost immediately after your vows."

Gwen's smile was sharper but no less sickly sweet. "Don't worry, Prince Grigor. The High

Captain was *more than capable* of consummating our union before his departure."

Lovell's jaw tensed, just for a second. Then the smile returned. Polished. Insincere.

"I'm relieved to hear it," he said smoothly. "Rumors spread quickly in times like these."

"Indeed, they do." She motioned her hand broadly. "Please get your horse settled and make yourself comfortable. We can meet after lunch for your Covenant-prescribed diplomatic discussion." She deliberately turned her back on him and walked back inside the castle, Andais and Hedontas quickly falling in step behind her.

As soon as they were safely in the kitchen and away from everyone but Cook, she turned to them. "I want triple guards on Pip. We know he has talked about using him to get me to fall in line in the past. Hedontas, please see to that personally."

The older man gave a sharp nod.

"Andais, please tell me we have some kind of news about Tyreal, or at the very least, something on Ingram."

"We have people trailing Ingram. He is making it a point to be seen in town, flashing lots of coin at the pub. A bit too flashy, if you ask me. Tensha found something down at the beach near the cliffs."

Gwen spun to face him more directly. "What did she find?"

"She said the trail is old, and nothing she can tell with certainty. But there are signs of a struggle. Possibly drag marks."

Gwen fought the nausea welling in her throat. "Show me."

The air grew damper and saltier as they descended old, rocky steps towards a patch of beach rarely used. It looked like nothing, just a forgotten edge of the coastline. At the bottom, there was a ledge flanked by scraggly branches and sea grass. The grass was torn in places, and Tensha stood near a large rock with what appeared to be dried blood on it.

"I also found this, Your Majesty, after I talked to the Lower Captain," Tensha said quietly. She handed Gwen a scrap of gray fabric with golden embroidery that had been ripped away. The edges were frayed, and Gwen's heart felt like it would shatter in her chest as she looked at it. A piece of Tyreal's betrothal jacket.

"He was taken," she said, voice thick with tears. "He was really taken. He didn't leave me."

"No, Your Majesty. He didn't leave."

CHAPTER TWENTY-FOUR

The worst part wasn't the stone floor beneath him or the iron cuffs biting into his wrists. It wasn't the damp, cold air that clung to his skin and sapped his strength. It wasn't the shame of being High Captain and getting caught.

No.

It was knowing Gwen probably thought he'd left her.

If you walk out that door, don't come back.

She'd said it before, usually during an argument when tempers flared and words landed harder than either of them intended. That was just the nature of their arguments sometimes. This fight had felt different, though. Sharper.

Like everything they had hoped for was slipping through their fingers, undone by expectations and misunderstandings.

He had thought he understood what she had to do to be queen. The politics. The subtle maneuvering. The way she had to play the game to keep the board in her favor. In truth, he hadn't understood at all.

He had been angry when she didn't speak up—when she let the court look down on him like he was some stray dog that had somehow wandered into the throne room. She hadn't defended him, and he'd felt the weight of her silence. Logically, he knew she couldn't risk it, but still, the sting had settled deep.

He had been angrier at himself for letting it happen. He should have said something else when Damaris and Drakon used his words as a springboard to undermine his and Gwen's relationship. Instead, he stood there trying to conform himself to what he thought a noble would do, to play nice and let Gwen handle it because she was the queen. He thought that was what was expected of him.

Better yet, he should have punched one of those pompous kings in the throat and let that be the end. He was King Consort now, wasn't he? None of them would have let that kind of disrespect happen in their castle.

Still, he hadn't left to hurt her. He'd left because he needed to think, to let some of his anger fizzle out. Her jab about him feeling emasculated had landed harder than it should have, and he hadn't wanted to say something he'd truly regret. There was likely some truth to her statement that he would need to reflect on later, not at its surface level truth, but there was something.

He'd planned to go back to the castle after his talk with Mason. Back to Gwen. To their chambers. To an actual conversation. Hell, maybe even a long talk with Malcolum. As long as he and Gwen did it together, like they'd promised. He had just needed a little more time to get together everything he wanted to say, so a walk along the beach seemed like a good idea. Couldn't risk being seen wandering on his betrothal night, so he'd chosen a mostly unused stretch of beach—where he'd come across a group of men loading up goods they clearly hadn't acquired by legal means. Including Thane, the guard that Tyreal had dismissed after the incident with the villagers.

Tyreal exhaled slowly, trying to shift to a more comfortable position, if such a thing could be had on a stone floor. The bruises along his sides protested. They hadn't gone easy on him—too many for even him to fight off. Thane had taken particular enjoyment in raining blows on his ribs. He'd dropped four of them before one of the cowardly pricks had stabbed him with something sharp and tipped in poison.

The burn of it had been instantaneous. His sword fell from his grip just as his knees buckled into the sand. After that, the world had gone watery and distant, sounds muffled like he was hearing them from the bottom of the sea.

He had woken in this gods-forsaken cavern, the walls slick with slimy moss and the scent of salt and rotting fish in the air. He doubted this would be his ultimate prison. No, this was a holding cell, likely while Ingram figured out exactly what to do with him and how to get him out to sea and to Lovell.

Because Prince Grigor had to be behind this. Probably.

There was the slight chance that this had nothing to do with court politics and every-thing to do with Tyreal screwing up Ingram's most lucrative route by barring him access to Thorncliff and placing him under surveillance. Pirates tended to get rather crabby about that.

Still. Timing was too convenient, and he'd al-ways suspected that Ingram was funneling at least some of his stolen goods through Adaltus.

Tyreal leaned his head back against the wall. The clink of his chains brought him back to the present. This wasn't the time to dwell on what he should have said or done. He was here now.

But he would not die here.

He certainly would not let Gwen believe he'd walked away for good.

He rolled his shoulder, just enough to test the bruised muscles. The shackles allowed barely two paces in either direction. Just enough to reach the bucket his captors had been kind enough to leave for his bodily needs. The shackles were forged into the rock wall, too thick to break without leverage—and Ingram had made sure he had none.

It seemed overkill to have him chained to the wall and in a rusted iron cage, in Tyreal's opinion. They were obviously concerned about his ability to escape. Probably the only smart thing they had done.

The guards changed every few hours—not in the rotation itself, but in the way they did it. Never at the same time of day, and never a real shift change. Sometimes two would come, other times only one. Once, no one had come at all.

It was about as organized as Tyreal would expect from pirates—bribed thugs with too much drink on their breath and not enough discipline. Sloppy. Which meant they were exploitable.

Eventually.

Not yet. Not until his ribs stopped feeling like shattered pottery, and the room stopped tilting every time he moved too fast. He still wasn't sure how long the poison would stay in his system. He had tried to heal himself, but the attempt had gone exactly nowhere, just like when he had tried to heal Gwen's headache. Well, not exactly the same. It had felt different. Instead of his power feeling muted, this time, he just didn't know where to send it. How to turn it inward on something he couldn't see.

So instead, he spent his time thinking about how he could escape. He had initially hoped to taunt Ingram into an altercation, but he hadn't seen Ingram since they'd dragged him here. Ingram was likely making himself very obviously seen in Thorncliff to help build an alibi, in case Tyreal's disappearance became a problem.

Unfortunately, that wasn't likely to happen. Tyreal knew Gwen wouldn't risk looking weak in front of the other monarchs, no matter what she privately thought. She would almost certainly be keeping his disappearance a secret. All he could hope for was Andais or Hedontas searching for him—not that he had any idea where the hell he *was*. He had certainly never seen this cave or any like it before, and he had covered a good amount of Thorncliff's coastline. For all he knew, he wasn't in Tavia at all. He couldn't be sure how long he'd been out of it.

He closed his eyes, trying to work it out. How many steps from where he sat until the tunnel echoed? How deep was he? Had the last guard worn keys, or was Ingram keeping them for himself?

A sound broke the silence—stone skittering. Something small, light, moving toward him.

Tyreal's eyes snapped open.

He saw the orbs first. Small and orange, glowing gently as they floated into view. They moved in unpredictable patterns, as if alive, flickering like the lights inside the fairydew tree when they'd returned to Tavia.

Then came the fox.

Her coat was deep red, fur tangled with blooming violet flowers, moss, and faintly glowing mushrooms. Bright butterflies and the orbs moved around her as though they were drawn to her. He didn't know why he thought of her as *she*. There was no real indication. But it felt right.

Perhaps the poison hadn't worked its way out of his system after all.

The fox stopped just beyond the reach of his chains and sat, tail curling neatly around her paws. She looked at him with golden eyes that burned too brightly to be natural. As if anything else was about her.

Tyreal didn't move, but his muscles tensed.

The voice spoke in his mind, just like when Viamar talked to them. It was feminine, patient, and fairly amused, like she was in on some joke that Tyreal wasn't privy to. *Still reaching for a sword,* she said, *even with no blade in hand.*

He didn't answer right away. She hadn't threatened him, and she might not be real. After a few moments of her sitting and regarding him silently, he swallowed, then gave in and spoke. "Who are you?"

You may call me Liora. I am no friend to the one who holds you.

"Then why are you here?"

She tilted her head. Her gaze sharpened. *Because your destiny is intertwined with hers and with the whole of our land.*

Tyreal went still.

"I need to get to her."

Yes. Though not entirely for the reasons you think. There is work you must do before you can be of true use.

His brow furrowed. What in the bloody crows was *that* supposed to mean? "What work? I'm chained to the wall."

If magical, possibly-not-real foxes could sigh in exasperation, this one did.

Not all work requires the use of your body. You must rectify an imbalance within you to become the mate the Fates intended for her. One with blade and balm in equal measure.

"I don't understand."

One of the glowing orbs floated toward him, hovering near his chest. It cast soft orange light over the ruined front of his tunic. He hated looking at it—what had once been cream and gold betrothal finery was now stained, shredded, and stiff with blood. He turned his eyes away and waited.

You feel at ease with your sword. That part of you has been shaped by years of pain, discipline, and your fierce instinct to protect the one you love.

But the other part? The one that heals? You fight it. You think it is soft. You think it is weak.

Tyreal said nothing, though her words landed like a blow to his gut. She wasn't wrong.

You see healer and warrior as opposite roles. But they were never meant to be. One breaks.

One restores. *Both halves should balance within you if you are to become whole.*

"What if I can't?" he whispered aloud.

Then you will remain here. Not just physically until they come to kill you, but spiritually. Trapped. Divided. Less than what you are meant to become. And we will all suffer for it.

Liora stepped closer, the orb nearest him pulsing brighter where it hovered, demanding attention.

She does not need a sword alone. She needs all of you. Where your healing tempers your warrior's instinct, you, in turn, temper her fire. You are her balance, just as she is yours.

The Thorncrests are a powerful bloodline—have been since their feet first touched this land. But there's one truth that has held across every generation: they are not meant to stand alone.

Pack creatures, one might say.

Fate has placed a heavy crown on her head. And though she bears it with strength, even strength has limits. She can carry the weight of a kingdom, but not without someone at her side who sees her fully, and stands steady when the world cracks.

Tyreal looked down, silent, the ache in his chest sharper than before. *She needs all of you.* Wasn't that basically the same thing that Mason had said?

It ate at him. Like an itch he couldn't scratch.

He'd always thought he offered Gwen all of himself. Believed himself to be a "get what you see" sort of man. He offered her his loyalty, his strength, his body, and his love. Was that all of him? Was he holding pieces back?

Maybe.

Did he know how to truly let *anyone* see all of him? He had never truly been taught how to be anything more than just a warrior. His father was a guard, and his father before him. Tyreal had decided that he would be Gwen's guard before his voice cracked or hair formed on his chest. His life and destiny had always seemed mapped out clearly ahead of him.

This new power, the revelation of his bloodline opened up the possibility that maybe he knew nothing. It had allowed him the opportunity to marry Gwen, which he would forever be grateful for, but it also meant that his role as guard and the path his life was on were wiped out in an instant, like a landslide had washed it away. He supposed there was the chance that with everything going on, he had not had a chance to truly make peace with that.

While he truly worried about the ability of the other monarchs to accept him for being common-born, there was the real possibility that his issue boiled down to being afraid to learn who he truly was. What if he didn't like that version? What if Gwen didn't?

Liora took another step closer, her tail tickling against his leg as she lightly swished it. Her golden eyes gleamed, unreadable but not unkind.

You think healing is weak because you view it as the opposite of power. But healing is a strength most cannot endure.

"Why?"

Because it requires surrender. Forgiveness. I think there are things you do not know how to forgive yourself for. Truths you have buried.

He swallowed. He had a good idea what she meant. There were parts of his past he'd never shared with Gwen. She knew the general idea of the things he had been forced to do in the name of Tavia and her crown. Not the full truth, though. Never that. The lives taken under orders. The mistakes in battle that lost him good men. Failures that often weighed heavier than victories. He could barely think of them fully himself. Could she ever possibly accept him if she knew? Or worse, the parts of him that welcomed the violence? Almost... craved it? What if she thought him a monster?

Liora turned, the orbs circling her as if preparing to retreat.

Tyreal took a sharp breath. "You're leaving?"

For now.

"I thought you were going to help me? For her sake. For... fate."

I have. Now help yourself.

Tyreal's jaw clenched. "What exactly am I supposed to do?"

She paused, her head tilting slightly again as she looked over her shoulder at him.

Find the wound beneath your rage and fear. Look without flinching. Sit in the discomfort until you recognize it and make peace with it. Healing is not gentle, and it is not clean. It is pain turned inwards to restore instead of hurt.

Do this and I will return when you are ready.

The orbs drifted away, slowly taking their light with them. The butterflies followed, vanishing into the shadows as if they had never been there at all.

The fox lingered for one heartbeat more.

She will need you soon, so I suggest you hurry. Only if you become whole will you be strong enough to stand beside her.

And then she was gone.

Tyreal sat in the dark, alone again with the cold pressing in. No spells to unlock his chains. No dramatic escape. Just a task that was as intangible as smoke and twice as hard to grasp.

Heal himself. Great.

He exhaled slowly through his nose. Fine. He could start with what he knew—focus, breath, control. He slipped into the place he went before a battle, that deep, still center.

Except now, it was different.

He could visualize it, where before it had always just been something internal. Not clearly, but enough to recognize it, like standing in a dark cellar before lighting a torch. The shape of things were there, just barely outlined in the dark, but he couldn't see them yet.

At the edge, something pulsed. Something broken. He reached for it in his mind. The golden glow he always saw when he used his powers sparked almost immediately. He poured his will into it. Not rage, not urgency, just the quiet, stubborn desire to fix what was broken.

Warmth bloomed in his chest. Slowly, the pain in his ribs dulled. The broken glass sensation receded into a deep ache. Still present, but no longer consuming.

Until now, he'd only ever healed others, and only with wounds he could see. Maybe this—this ability to reach inward and heal himself—was what Liora meant. Maybe it was the key to unlocking everything else.

Maybe it would bring her back to free him.

Tyreal cracked open one eye. Still chained. Still in a damp cave that stunk of fish rot. Still tired. Still angry.

He made a frustrated sound.

"Find the wound," he muttered under his breath. "Sit with the discomfort."

After a beat, "Fuck."

He closed his eyes again.

Fine.

He'd sit with it.

He had nothing but time.

CHAPTER TWENTY-FIVE

Gwen had stopped sitting whenever she met with the other monarchs. It was entirely too easy for them to talk over her when she did. Instead, she stood, hands casually placed on the table in front of her. Not clenched. Not too stiff. Just enough to remind them who owned the wood they sat at.

"As I said," she continued, keeping her voice level and her chin high, "with this alliance, everyone would be on the same footing. Border patrols would continue just as they always have, but information would be shared freely in the name of open communication. And every adolescent will be trained by the Sisters of the Mist when their magic manifests."

She didn't look at Grigor when she said it. She didn't have to. She could feel him smiling.

"I'm still confused," he said, "about why you think any alliance needs to provide oversight over the Sisters of the Mist. It seems they've done fine for the last five hundred summers. They trained *you.*"

He sounded curious, respectable. Like he hadn't spent the last hour subtly undermining her with veiled questions and strategic forgetfulness. Nothing outright—just a little too much need for clarification. Follow-ups that weren't asked of the kings. And when she answered with anything sharper than saccharine gentleness, he'd tilt his head like she was being emotional.

Patronizing. Placating. Until her cheeks had burned.

Gwen took a slow breath through her nose and gave him a smile with no softness in it.

"Well, yes and no," she said calmly. "I'd say the whole thing with your aunt abusing all the other sisters and unleashing magic upon an unsuspecting world sort of shows that maybe they shouldn't be completely unmonitored."

That landed.

Let them remember. His family had been part of that chaos, and Gwen had once openly accused him of playing a role in it. She let the room sit in it.

A quiet shuffle passed down the line of monarchs. No one defended him.

Grigor didn't flinch. "Of course. A tragic chapter. But isolated, surely."

"Not that isolated." Gwen's gaze didn't waver as she held eye contact with him. "The last time the ruling families had magic, they launched the continent into a war that nearly ended civilization. Magic is back now, fully. That means we either have structure—or we have another war."

Grigor leaned back, fingers clasped behind his head like he was having a relaxing conversation with friends, not like he was discussing how to prevent the dragons from burning them all to ash.

"How exactly do you feel about sovereignty?" he asked. "Because I have to admit, sometimes it sounds as though you don't actually believe in it. How can we be free to rule as ultimate authority with a council we're required to report to?"

The sunlight behind him caught his hair. She couldn't tell if it was just that greasy or if whatever oil he used was practically gleaming. Gwen wondered, briefly, if it was flammable.

"Sovereignty doesn't mean silence and isolation," she said. "We're either open to transparency and input from the people we rule, or we continue as we always have because we're afraid to imagine alternatives that might cost us power."

No one spoke. They didn't agree. But they didn't argue.

Lovell smiled. "Strong words. Some might say bold. Aspirational, even."

And there it was. Not practical. Not realistic. *Aspirational.*

The kind of word you used when you wanted to make someone sound naïve without calling them that.

"Better than the lack of ideas that *you're* proposing," Gwen said, and let the words hang. "Something tells me your version of peace comes with a footnote."

Lovell dipped his head in what might have passed for contrition—if not for the faint twitch at the corners of his mouth. "I'm simply trying to get clarification, Your Majesty. Surely you understand that changes of this magnitude need to be considered from all angles. It's easy to miss things... when you have been through as much as you have or dismissed your entire advisory council."

She saw a look pass between King Damaris and King Henri at Lovell's words and the rage threatened to bubble up within her. There was one more piece of evidence in the case he was not-so-subtly building that she was an inept, emotional woman.

She opened her mouth to say something, but King Thalion beat her to it.

"I can't help but notice," he said, voice dry, "that you are the only one asking so many questions of the queen, but not offering any input. To my understanding, she has asked us here to build an alliance, not present a finished one for your dissection."

Gwen gave him a small smile and glanced across the table. Eliana caught her eye and winked, casual and quick. The weight pressing against Gwen's chest eased—slightly.

She wasn't entirely alone.

Anya sat with her hands folded primly in her lap, but Gwen recognized the tension in her knuckles, the muscle ticking in her cheek. She was losing patience with Lovell's little performance and with her father's continued indulgence of it.

Max, seated just beside her, must have had the same observation. He turned toward his father. "I, for one, believe this is just a logical growth from the alliances we already have in place," he said. "Transparency, at the cost of not being burned to death by dragons, seems a fair trade to me?" He looked around the table with a warm smile and a chuckle, getting everyone else to relax a little. "Wouldn't you agree, father?"

King Corven tapped his fingers against the table. His tone was casual. "I have no desire to fight dragons, especially after the spectacle the other night. Espera and Tavia have always been allies."

It was careful. Just vague enough to sound agreeable. Gwen had heard enough statements like that to know what they were really meant to do—create space to backpedal later.

Across from her, Max frowned. It was quick—gone almost as soon as it appeared—but she caught it.

"Yes, close friends," he said. "Which is why, after almost being killed by the High Sister and being up close and personal with a dragon, I'm more than ready to build something that keeps that from happening again."

He looked straight at his father, refusing to back down and play the dutiful son. Instead, an heir adding in valuable input. "Alric thought the High Sister—and the people working with her—needed to be stopped. The best way to stop more good men from dying is to prevent the violence in the first place."

The silence stretched.

Corven shifted. Barely. The guilt was evident, though, in the twitch in his jaw. Long blinks followed by looking down like he'd just remembered something urgent under the table.

"Yes," he said after a second. "Of course. I want that too."

Gwen didn't speak. She was grateful for Max's input—the reminder of Espera and Tavia's shared history, that Alric had died believing the High Sister had to be stopped. That Max had nearly died at her hand. It mattered.

It should've mattered more. Corven's hesitation terrified her.

She'd come into this with the numbers. Espera. Gagerland. Obrye. Solid ground. Malticai leaned neutral, but that would work fine in a council where neutrality still meant cooperation.

Half the ruling families. She'd thought it enough to begin.

Now she wasn't so sure.

By midday, Gwen's patience was wearing thin. The distance between her and her allies seemed to grow further by the minute. Even with Max and Anya weighing in, it didn't feel like enough. The only ones who seemed actively irritated by Lovell's constant barrage were King Thalion and Queen Caliane. Even that likely had more to do with Eliana and the constant unspoken battle she fought just to be taken seriously. Gwen knew that war too well.

Then Grigor leaned back in his chair, voice light and pleasant. "Perhaps we should take a break for the day. The queen looks tired. A shame the High Captain isn't here to tend to her."

No one laughed.

That was the worst part. He'd made it sound like a teasing joke, but everyone in the room understood what it really was—a cut, clean and deliberate.

Gwen didn't flinch. Didn't blink. Didn't even look at him.

She reached for her water and took a measured sip, letting the silence stretch just long enough to let them feel it. When she set the glass down, she looked up at him with a smile. "I didn't realize my stamina was suddenly in question. I assure you, I feel just fine. If you'd like to compare our staminas, I'm agreeable to a measuring contest of sorts. Perhaps a test of our magic, or maybe something you'd be more likely to win, like arm wrestling?"

A few heads turned. King Thalion gave a quiet, choked laugh.

Grigor's smile faltered, but he recovered. "I'm simply suggesting a moment to regroup. Tempers can fray when the conversation is... ambitious."

"No one seems frayed but you." Gwen kept her tone light. "Is there something in the proposal that's confusing you?" She cocked her head to one side and blinked at him, lobbing back his fake concern.

Lovell leaned forward, threading his fingers together like he was preparing to give a sermon. "Not confusing, no. But the queen has repeatedly declined to explain why the man who commands her army—and shares her bed—has vanished during the most critical negotiations our kingdoms have faced in a generation."

That landed harder than the last.

"Once again," Thalion said, voice clipped, "you've done a masterful job of asking questions while offering absolutely nothing of your own.

Where is the man who commands *your* army? Or for that matter, where are the leaders of our armies?"

Queen Caliane nodded and spoke from beside her husband. "If your concern was genuine, you'd ask the queen directly, not perform it for the rest of us."

Grigor opened his mouth, but Caliane didn't let him speak. "You want to discuss power structure? Say so. You want to change terms? Present them. But this—" she gestured to the table "—this little theater? It's growing old."

A pause followed.

Max exhaled through his nose and glanced at Lovell, then back to the table. "If we're calling for transparency, maybe it's time we all stop pretending this is about concern."

"I'm sure I don't know what you mean, Prince Maximillen."

"I believe you do, *Prince Grigor.*"

It wasn't Max's usual tone. He was rarely so blunt and aggressive. Diplomacy seemed on pause. The words themselves were mild—the jab wasn't.

They were both princes, but only Max stood next in line for his throne. Grigor's brother would inherit Adaltus, not him. And if the rumors were true, the two barely spoke.

Across the table, Gwen saw the flicker of rage that passed over Grigor's face, clean and sharp. It stripped the charm right off him for just a second, enough to see what lived underneath.

Then it was gone. The mask returned like it had never left.

Max didn't flinch, didn't even look away. If anything, his posture shifted—just slightly—but enough to read as a challenge. Not defensive, but daring, like he was hoping Lovell would escalate. Gwen's mind flicked back to Alric's funeral pyre, to the fury Max hadn't known where to put. Maybe he'd finally found a place to burn it.

The tension in the room grew palpable.

Then the doors creaked open. One of Gwen's guards stepped inside, eyes darting from face to face like he'd walked in on something important. "Cook asked me to inform you that lunch is ready in the dining room," he said.

Gwen gave a warm smile she didn't feel. "Yes, thank you, Orlan." She turned to the room. "Your Majesties. Your Highnesses. The guards will escort you to the dining hall. I'll be along shortly." Then, with practiced ease, "Princess Anya, make sure everyone gets a chance to try Cook's cookies."

She smiled wider, with the attentive graciousness expected of a queen hosting other monarchs.

"Absolutely not," Anya replied, perky as ever. "That means less for me."

It was the role she always played—bubbly, sweet, harmless.

Gwen met her eyes and mouthed, *Later.*

Anya gave the tiniest nod, her smile never fading.

Gwen needed air after lunch. They all did, probably. Hours locked in the library, and she wasn't sure they'd gotten anywhere, just more political theater. More careful language with nothing behind it.

Luckily, she wasn't forced to be the one that suggested it. Queen Isolde had done that favor for her. Anya's mother was famous for her love of naps, so she insisted they be allowed to retreat to their rooms for midday rest or wine.

Gwen though, she needed to move.

The best thing she could do when her skin felt too tight and her jaw ached from holding it shut?

Ride. A hard, fast ride on Akasha—long enough to feel like her body belonged to her again. Maybe even to the fairydew tree. The thought made her suddenly nauseous. No, not yet. She couldn't do that. She didn't trust herself to face that place yet, not without completely shattering, it was too meaningful to her and Tyreal's relationship.

Andais had promised her that Tensha and Jameson were handling the investigation. They were tracking Ingram, preparing to apprehend him under suspicion of piracy. Andais was convinced they could get him to talk. Hedontas agreed.

Gwen wasn't so sure. She knew they were skilled with torture, but Ingram was a mercenary at the very least, a pirate at the most likely. They weren't exactly a fragile bunch. She supposed, if all else failed, she could just set him on fire until he talked. Most people were pretty willing to talk as their skin burned.

She shook her head. Magic was a poor idea when she felt this out of control. She couldn't control the other monarchs. Couldn't control Grigor. Couldn't get this godsdamn air power to listen to her. Couldn't control the dragons. Couldn't control the silence where her husband should be.

But she could control her hands. Her breath. The direction her boots were pointing.

And right now, they were guiding her toward the stables.

She passed the training ring on the way, the air smelling strongly of sweat, sun-warmed leather, and dust. The familiar sound of steel on steel rang out, and though it should have been grounding and comforting, it hit her like a wave. The grief was immediate. How many times had she stood right there, watching Tyreal lead drills and barking orders with his sleeves rolled up and dust in his hair?

The ache nearly bent her in half.

Then came the sound—*crack*. A foreign sound.

Something wrong.

Then a second sound, heavier—a body hitting the ground, hard. Followed by screaming. Gwen grabbed her skirts and ran, yelling, "Move! Out of the way!" Guards parted as she pushed through the crowd. A young man she recognized as one of the villagers with new magic was on the ground, screaming. His wrist was twisted, shattered. The angle was sickening. His whole body spasmed as he thrashed.

A guard she recognized, Merren, was already there, one hand pressed to the villager's chest, trying to hold him still. Rykan hovered nearby, desperately trying to help.

There wasn't time for questions. She dropped to her knees and placed her hand gently on his forehead. Just like the day she'd copied all the notices about magic, her instinct was guiding her.

She closed her eyes and mentally dove into where her magic was, only to find the deep well within her blunted somehow, like she could see it but not access it. The normal wall of stone she surrounded her magic with now was more like a dome.

Gwen wasn't sure what to make of that, but there wasn't time to dwell. If she couldn't access her magic, she would have to just use her mind. She had taught him how to make his shield. Surely she could get past it enough to help him.

She cast a mental net outward until she could sense his consciousness. The pain must be so overwhelming that the twisted forest of tree branches he had surrounded his magic with lay in piles on the ground, easy enough to step over.

Instead of a swirl of magic wrapped around the figure in the middle, there was a stillness inside the ring of downed branches. Just his energy, his self, writhing in pain.

She didn't speak aloud; she didn't need to. *Sleep. Relax. Sleep. Relax.* The intention pulsed through her, over and over again. It felt different. Dulled. Like she wasn't using her magic at all, just the mind control that had come with years of training.

The thrashing slowed.

Sleep. Relax.

Finally, the figure stilled. She looked around at the surrounding space, the heavy stillness. It felt wrong. She could sense something there, like a shimmery haze. But she couldn't make it out, couldn't reach out and touch it with her own magic like she could when she and Anya trained. Because she also couldn't access hers.

She needed to figure out what was going on, and quickly.

Gwen opened her eyes. Merren and Rykan stared at her, agape.

"Someone get him to Klause before this man wakes up, and someone else tell me what the hell just happened?" she snapped.

CHAPTER TWENTY-SIX

"We were running drills," Merren said. "Mathias, the one who was injured, was working on using his weather magic defensively. He wants to remain in Thorncliff and join the guard, so Andais has me training him."

"Alright, and then what happened?" Gwen tried to keep her tone level, but her focus was split in a way that was nerve-racking. As the man spoke, she reached for her fire, the most instinctive magic she had. Nothing came. Just like during the dragon attack, when she'd been unable to stop the debris from falling on the crowd. As it had done then, mild panic swept through her at the loss.

"He jumped from the fence like he's done before. Usually, he shifts his landing with a gust of wind. This time, nothing happened. He just hit the ground."

Gwen turned to Rykan. "Where were you during this?"

"I'd just walked up," he said. "I heard about the drill and wanted to watch."

Her gaze lingered on Rykan. There was something there, just on the edge of her awareness, but out of reach. Before Gwen could question him further, the sound of boots scuffed through the dirt behind them. Everyone turned as Andais stepped into view, his eyes scanning the training ring. Guards were lifting Mathias onto a makeshift stretcher to carry him to Klause, the castle healer.

"I came as soon as I heard," Andais said, frowning. "What happened?"

Merren explained again quickly. The drill. The jump. The missing wind and then the fall.

Andais pursed his lips as he listened, glancing over at Rykan and Gwen with a thoughtful expression. "That's twice now. Which isn't much—but odd that it's happened twice."

Gwen straightened. "What do you mean?"

"During the dragon attack, Rykan had just stepped outside behind you when the magic around the courtyard failed. I remember, because Tyreal and I were both relieved to see a guard that close. Tyreal was pushed away by the crowd, and he wanted me to reach the tower for a better vantage point."

"What does that have to do with anything?" Rykan asked. His voice rose slightly, defensive.

"Maybe nothing," Andais said. "But it's strange you were nearby both times."

A memory tugged at Gwen. She bit her lip, chasing it down. Then it surfaced. "The chapel," she breathed. "That night I had the horrible headache when we returned to Thorncliff. Tyreal tried to heal me but couldn't. We thought he just hadn't trained enough yet." She looked at the young guard, who was developing pink splotches on his freckled cheeks. "Rykan, you were on duty outside the door that night."

"Your Majesty, I—"

Gwen interrupted him. "Actually, I... I think there was another too. So, four times now." She glanced over at Andais, who had shifted closer to her. "When the villagers presented with magic, the day we brought them into the castle grounds, Rykan was there with the guard then."

"I thought they said their magic failed them in the cart because they were all so frightened?" Rykan questioned, clearly trying to push away any suspicion of wrongdoing.

"That isn't how it works, though," Gwen said. "Magic gets harder to control when you are emotional. It lashes out. It doesn't just vanish."

They all fell quiet, the implication heavy in the air.

"So you think I'm the cause?" Rykan asked. "I don't even know how I could be!"

"I don't know either," Gwen admitted, her voice low. "But it feels like too much of a coincidence to ignore." She studied him. He looked genuinely stunned—brow drawn, jaw tight, fear just beneath the surface. If he was hiding something, he was hiding it from himself, too.

"What if he has magic," Merren said slowly, "and his ability is to—"

"—nullify other people's powers," Andais finished.

Gwen let the thought settle. It wasn't impossible. They knew so little about the magic that had existed before Myaessa's spell. Elemental magic had always been the framework of their land, and Viamar had told them their magic came from the dragons and the land itself. Nature certainly had examples of exceptions to every rule.

"Maybe it's like how fog dampens sound," she said, "or how certain plants that change the soil so nothing else can grow nearby. It isn't intentional. Just present."

"Are you able to use your magic right now?" Andais asked.

Gwen shook her head.

"We need to go to a different location. Test if you can without Rykan, and if you can't when he's present."

"If this is true, then Rykan could be considered a weapon. No one will believe we didn't know. Drakon already accused me of stripping them of their powers before he left."

"I know. And the last thing we need is something else for them to doubt right now," Andais said quietly.

The monarchs reconvened in the library that afternoon. Gwen was seriously beginning to think this was nothing but a waste of time. Everyone talked and talked, but no progress was made. She would get something going, Grigor would undermine her again, and everything would spiral back out. Now, after Rykan had proven multiple times to nullify her magic with just his presence, Gwen was rapidly beginning to feel hopeless. Rykan, Tyreal... so many secrets forced upon her again, when everything she had done of late had been to rid herself of them.

She had a powerful urge to just kick all of them out, to build up Tavia's walls and just completely isolate from the rest of the country. Let them fight amongst themselves and the dragons burn them to ash.

She wouldn't do that, of course. Without imports, her people would suffer, not to mention the income they got from their own items, like fish and salt. There was simply not a way to live on Valine without an open trade economy.

The sound of King Damaris and Queen Isolde arguing about some minor point that nobody even cared about was a drone in the background, and Gwen could not focus on it. All she could think about was Tyreal. Did he have food?

She felt Grigor's eyes on her, and it dragged her attention back to the table. He had his fingers steepled together in the habit of his that was driving Gwen insane. She met his gaze head on, not backing down. His lips twitched into a smile as he cleared his throat.

"Forgive the interruption, Your Majesties, but I find I am just unable to remain silent any longer. I would like to address a question that I have received from several sources within Thorncliff's own walls."

Gwen rolled her eyes with a heavy sigh, no longer able to keep her actions neutral after two full days of his nonsense. "Name this supposed concern of yours so we can try to get back to work, please."

A few monarchs frowned at her rudeness, but she was well past caring.

"I understand this is a touchy and emotional subject, but I have to again ask, where is the High Captain? I have it on good authority that his horse remains in the stable, and many people have told me he doesn't go anywhere without his horse."

"I've already told you, Tyreal is on assignment. And Braken has a hoof injury he is recovering from, so he took a different horse. I worry, though, why you feel it appropriate to question my people and staff about something that does not affect you. You seem *very* interested in the movements of my guards."

Grigor shrugged. "From what I've heard, the horse shows no signs of injury. And with respect, his absence does concern me—and all of us. Every monarch present has brought their spouse or heir. Even princes and princesses like myself are here. But your husband is not."

"Your father and older brother aren't here either. You aren't even in line for the throne. Shall I question their whereabouts?" Gwen snapped back.

Lovell's smile faltered slightly, and his eyes narrowed at the jab. He didn't reply right away, instead letting the silence stretch as he put on a hurt expression and looked around the table, as if to say, *can you believe she said that?*

King Corven cleared his throat. "Let us not let personal tensions derail the talks. I believe the prince's question stems from concern, nothing more."

Concern. It was always concern. Always veiled, always polite, conveniently packaged to excuse every accusation without ever admitting it.

Max gave his father a sharp look, disbelief etched into every line of his face. But Queen

Caliane laid a hand on his arm and gave the smallest shake of her head. A silent warning, *not now*. He looked at Gwen with helpless anger burning behind his eyes.

"I don't see how his question is now suddenly a concern," Anya said, her voice simultaneously bored and annoyed. "Yesterday, we all saw it for the performance it was. The queen has answered about the High Captain's movements more than once. If it will lay this ridiculous line of conversation to rest, then fine—I witnessed him leave from the stable, dressed in official Tavian gear and with supplies for a trip."

She cocked her head, eyes narrowed on Grigor.

He was quiet. He couldn't call her a liar without suggesting he knew more about Tyreal's disappearance than he was pretending. That would unravel his carefully maintained position of plausible ignorance and *concern*.

Queen Isolde gave her daughter an admonishing glare, but Anya ignored her. She wasn't technically bound to Gagerland's court anymore, not since marrying Max, but her mother-in-law didn't look thrilled, either.

The room was still for a beat too long. The older monarchs were now watching Anya with a look they'd been giving Gwen more frequently of late. Mildly patronizing, annoyed with her youth, and concern for what they considered recklessness.

Grigor recovered quickly. "I meant no offense, of course. It's just that if the matter of the High Captain's absence is resolved, it's curious that the only confirmation we've received comes from a single source that is so... *close* to the queen. However, trusted she may be."

Anya narrowed her eyes. "Are you calling me a liar?"

Max's parents and Anya's were both looking at Lovell cooly now, and Gwen sincerely hoped he continued pushing the issue and ruined whatever ground he had gained with them.

Unfortunately, he was too smart for that.

"Not at all," he said smoothly. "Only noting that in delicate matters, those closest to the crown often carry... certain biases. It's natural to be protective. Especially when one's personal circumstances might make impartiality a challenge."

Anya stiffened, but her expression didn't change. Gwen saw it, though—the flicker in her eyes. She understood the insinuation, even if only she, Gwen, and Max did. *Personal circumstances.* A hidden accusation about her marriage being a cover. Tyreal had said that the High Sister had a file with information regarding Anya's sexuality. It wasn't surprising that she had shared that information with her nephew.

"I think you need to explain what sort of personal circumstances you are suggesting my wife has," Max said, shoulders squaring back.

"I'm sorry, I misspoke. Just that Princess Anya and the queen have been friends for such a long time. I only raise the point because transparency is essential. If people are talking to me, an outsider, I think it would help quiet speculation and unease within Tavia and other countries if someone else had also witnessed the High Captain's departure."

Eliana stood, clearing her throat. She smoothed the flowing green silk fabric that flowed and draped over her tall and lean silhouette. "Princess Anya's word should be enough. Are you looking for some sort of written testimony from several eyewitnesses? The queen and her Lower Captain have told you. The princess has confirmed it. Or does confirmation only matter when it comes from someone you personally approve of?"

Lovell looked her over with measured consideration. "I understand you are young and new to the world of politics and court gossip, particularly since Obrye is isolated. I'm just trying to be prudent."

Gwen noticed he didn't use Eliana's title or name. She suspected Thalion and Caliane noticed as well, because the queen's fingers tapped on the table beside her goblet. They looked at each other, and then back to Lovell, a clear and unspoken warning.

"Look, I know you all think I am just being an ass with questioning about the High Captain. But I really am trying to help. I know that

Princess Anya has always been a passionate advocate for Her Majesty. Passion is not the same as perspective, though, and I'm just concerned." Lovell gave his most charming smile and sincere voice.

"If my people have concerns, then I will deal with that. This is my castle and my country. You can be concerned about yours when you are a ruler." She knew she sounded bitter. She was so tired of these games.

The monarchs looked around at each other, disapproval clear over Gwen's second jab at Lovell's place in Adaltus' succession.

"Perhaps," Lovell said with a soft smile, "a short recess will give everyone a chance to collect themselves. I do not want you to get overwhelmed. I understand that all of you are young, and this is a lot to take in."

The other monarchs, all except Eliana's parents, nodded in agreement. Neither Max nor Anya's parents spoke up in their defense, and certainly no one spoke up for Gwen. The realization was sinking in that the other monarchs were threatened by their children. She remembered what Alric had said during their trip to Mist Castle, that the three of them were different. Not that their parents were bad, they simply accepted how things had always been and never challenged for something better.

Grigor gave her an overly polite smile, lines crinkled around his eyes as they twinkled. He thought he had won, and that in the monarchs' silence, they were choosing him.

Perhaps he had.

After a quick check-in with Andais to see if there was any news on the search for Tyreal, Anya had practically dragged Gwen back to her chambers for a chance to vent in private. Along the way, she had also snagged Eliana, and even made a last-minute decision to let Max join in on the impromptu girls' night.

Anya sprawled across the bed, a platter of Cook's thumbprint cookies in front of her. Eliana sat cross-legged on the floor in front of the fire-filled hearth. Max paced around the room, and Gwen sat in a chair near her window and the painting that hid the corridor to Tyreal's room.

They were quiet at first, all busy reflecting on the disastrous meeting.

Anya, in a most unladylike fashion, shoved two cookies into her mouth.

"Don't get crumbs in my bed, you animal," Gwen said with a loving, if exhausted, rebuke.

Anya rolled her eyes, making a dramatic sweeping motion with her hand to brush off any crumbs that may have fallen.

"I... I think we may have lost them. And I don't entirely understand how," Max said quietly. He sounded hollow. There was no lingering rage. He just looked lost. It was very similar to how Anya had looked at Mist Castle when she realized that the High Sister, someone she had looked up to for most of her life, wasn't what she'd thought.

"He's not trying to win by argument," Gwen said. She reached up, twisting a curl around her finger as she spoke. She had the strongest urge to cry, but it was as if her body was too tired. There was no energy for tears. "We could have beaten him easily with that. Instead, he makes one of us look emotional, young, or naïve, and then he steps in as the voice of reason. Even when they see the lie, he's just polite enough that they won't call him out. Or at least, only Eliana's parents will."

Eliana shook her head. "He's been so careful. Just shy of insulting anyone directly. My parents are annoyed by him, but even they don't seem to realize how much of a snake he truly is. If he'd just come right out and say all the horrible things I know he thinks about me, they would bury him."

Gwen nodded. Pain was building behind her eyes as her stress continued to climb. The last thing she could handle right now was one of her nasty headaches. *Please, don't do this right now.*

Quiet fell over the room again. Anya folded her arms and stared at the wall. Eliana's jaw ticked as she looked back into the fire. Max looked like he wanted to throw something.

Gwen knew she should try to say something positive, rally all of them to keep up the fight, to remember why it was so important to get everyone to agree to the alliance.

She had nothing positive to say, though.

"He's feeding into something none of them want to admit," Gwen said quietly. "They are afraid. Not nearly as much of the dragons and magic as they should be. But of us. Of change. Of what happens if the people they trained to inherit the world actually start doing it differently. That's why Eliana's parents are handling it better than anyone else. They already had to accept their fear when Eliana realized who she truly was."

"They aren't perfect, though," Eliana said with a sigh. She shook her head. "I love them, and they are good parents. But do you think they wouldn't change me if they had the opportunity? If for nothing else, but to keep me from dealing with how judgmental and mean the public can be? No, my parents would love to keep everything as it always was, if they had the chance."

"The world needs to change. I'm so tired of all these rules that prevent us from just being able to be who we are. Love who we love. They don't see the need for it because they sit in a place of privilege. They've never had to see. The way it's set up suits them just fine." Anya's voice was bitter, and it hurt Gwen to hear the tone from her normally optimistic friend.

"When we push back, though, he makes us look like children throwing tantrums," Max growled, resuming his pacing.

"No," Gwen said. "He made them *want* to see it that way."

CHAPTER TWENTY-SEVEN

He wasn't sure how long it had been since the fox had visited him.

Hell, he wasn't even sure she'd been real.

Time had collapsed in on itself inside the damp stone walls—hours, days, maybe more. All he knew for certain was that he'd been sitting so long that the dull ache in his ribs had faded beneath a sharper, more immediate pain. His hips were locked. The muscles in his lower back cramped so badly, he could barely shift his weight without feeling like something inside him might tear.

With a grimace, Tyreal pushed himself up-right. The movement came slowly, muscles screaming as the weight shifted through his body. The pain nearly dropped him, white-hot and immediate. Black spots floated at the edge of his vision. He clenched his jaw and held still, breath sharp through his teeth.

One breath. Two. Then three more.

Eventually, the muscles loosened. He stayed standing. The cavern tilted slightly around him as the vertigo clawed at his balance. That damned poison still lingered, thicker in his blood than it had any right to be.

"Bloody crows," he muttered. "How much did they dose me with?"

Fine. He'd healed himself once. He'd do it again.

He went through the steps of meditation he'd taken earlier and found the poison in his mind's eye, dark and pooling under his ribs like oil. This time, he didn't coax it out. He didn't plead with the magic to help him ease his symptoms. It differed from any time he had truly used it before.

He ordered it to burn.

The golden light responded immediately, blooming hot in his chest. Heat surged through him, hotter than any fever he could remember. His blood quickened. His skin flushed. The fire inside him climbed until he felt like he might combust.

It took everything in him not to scream.

And then, as quickly as it had come, the fever broke. His breath hitched, then came easier. The fog in his skull lifted, and the dizziness faded away as the last remnants of the poison burned to ash.

He could *think* again.

And he'd been thinking a lot. Liora was right—he had treated healing like a weakness, something passive and meant to follow pain. Now, with more clarity in his mind, a truth he hadn't considered finally worked its way out from under his insecurity and fear.

What *was* healing, really?

Repair.

Repairs weren't always gentle, though. They could be painful. Violent, even. Setting a bone. Cauterizing a wound. Sometimes healing hurt more than the injury itself.

Gwen said that his intention mattered most of all for his magic. If that was true, and intention could be shaped, then it meant healing didn't have to be passive. It could *force* change. Over-correct.

So why couldn't it be used like a weapon?

Then, as if the gods themselves were granting him a gift, he heard heavy footsteps making their way towards him. A single set, so just one guard. What a perfect opportunity to test his theory.

And possibly escape. Depending on how giving the gods felt that day.

Tyreal shifted just enough to slump back in the posture he had been in earlier. His shoulders sagged, head lowered, and breathing shallow. The look of an injured man that was close to giving up.

He listened carefully, counting steps. Five. Four. Two.

Keys jingled, and the gate scraped open. Tyreal lifted his eyes to view the guard, an older, grizzled man with a limp that screamed *old injury poorly earned*. His left eye drooped significantly, and he stunk of stale booze and sweat. He was spinning a knife lazily between his fingers.

This guard, Tyreal remembered. He was a sadistic, arrogant bastard, liked to cause pain just because he could.

"Well, look at you," the guard said. "Still breathing. Was starting to wonder if we'd overdone it on the poison. You're a big son of a bitch. We weren't sure how much we needed."

Tyreal didn't answer.

The man stepped closer, close enough that Tyreal could see the dried piss stains on his breeches. He crouched, grinning as he jabbed the point of the knife into Tyreal's bruised side—not hard enough to break skin, just enough to hurt.

Tyreal didn't flinch.

The man chuckled. "Gone soft already? Thought the queen's lapdog had more bite."

Tyreal kept his head down, but whispered, "Get closer."

The guard leaned in. "What did you say? Speak up, *boy*," he sneered.

"I said, get closer and see what happens," Tyreal said, a little louder, but not much. One, because his voice was hoarse from lack of use, but mainly to get the guard right where he wanted him.

The man snorted. "Big talk, seeing as you're injured and chained to a—"

He never finished.

Tyreal exploded upward, twisting at the waist, and slammed the top of his skull into the man's nose. The crunch was loud. The knife clattered to the stone and warm blood sprayed in an arc across Tyreal's face.

Before the guard could scream, Tyreal drove an elbow into his throat.

The man hit the ground, choking.

Tyreal didn't wait. He dropped to one knee and snatched the key ring from the guard's belt. He jammed the first key into the lock on one of his cuffs. It didn't fit. He turned the second. *Click.*

The cuff fell away, and he quickly opened the other one, letting the weight of the chains fall to the ground with a satisfying *clang*. His wrists throbbed, but with barely any extra thought, Tyreal could quickly heal the torn and raw skin. The magic was getting easier now.

He crouched and picked up the knife off the ground, plunging it into the guard's throat without ceremony. He felt no remorse. The man had kidnapped him, beat him, and taken such joy out of it that Tyreal knew he wasn't this man's first victim.

He exhaled, trying to center himself, just as he heard more men entering the cave mouth. A dark grin split his face, and he pulled the knife back out of the dead guard. The cave was no longer his prison. He was damn sure about to make them regret leaving him alive.

He had a wife to get home to.

If he had to guess, he'd say there were three, maybe four, coming. It was hard to tell over the irregular thump of boots on the damp stone. Their voices were low, so he had an inkling that they were at least suspicious that something had happened. Normally, they were sloppy and loud when they approached.

Tyreal backed into the shadow beside the cell gate, knife held low. If he was lucky, they wouldn't spot him or the dead guard right away, giving him enough time to get the drop on them.

Unfortunately, it looked like he wasn't *that* lucky.

The first figure that rounded the bend didn't hesitate. He ducked low, sword drawn, crouched and ready for action. Behind him, another guard had a crossbow aimed and loaded. They spotted the dead guard and cursed, pulling back just enough so that Tyreal couldn't make any sort of move on them without fully exposing himself. Not something he was keen to do with the crossbow in the mix. He could heal himself now, but he wasn't sure how quickly, and if the arrow would need to be removed first. *Shit*, he thought.

The middle of a fight didn't seem to be the place to further test his new abilities.

He was about to retreat deeper into the dark when a flicker of motion caught his eye—soft orange light drifting out of the deeper parts of the cave. The orbs glided towards them, and he heard the men in the cave mouth whispering about them.

Liora followed behind the orbs, padding into the open area near the cave like she owned it, fur glowing faintly beneath the moss and the mushrooms tangled in her coat. She turned her head towards him, and her golden eyes locked on his.

Behind her, something far larger moved.

A massive figure stepped from the shadows, hunching to fit beneath the low ceiling. Eight feet tall, at least. Humanoid only in the vaguest sense. Its skin was bark and lichen, limbs gnarled like ancient tree roots. Moss dripped from its shoulders, and glowing mushrooms pulsed along its body, almost as if they matched its breathing. If such a thing needed to breathe.

The resemblance to Liora was striking, in the moss and the color of the mushrooms was striking. Tyreal couldn't help but wonder if they were two sides of the same coin. Perhaps one creature split into two bodies?

He didn't have time to ponder further, because the creature opened its mouth, and the sound that came out was less a roar as it was the screaming sound of frigid winter wind whipping outside a house in the middle of a blizzard.

One guard yelled, "What the hell *is* that—"

The creature surged forward.

Tyreal pressed himself flat against the wall as the beast barreled past, one arm slamming into the edge of the cave mouth. Stone cracked, and the crossbow guard screamed as he was lifted off his feet and hurled into the wall. The man with the sword had dodged the blow and was now attempting to run.

He didn't make it far.

The creature made quick work of him and the guard Tyreal hadn't even seen. It *ruined* them. Limbs bent at wrong angles. Bones crushed beneath its dark, bark-covered fists.

And all the while, Liora stood perfectly still, her eyes never leaving Tyreal.

When the sounds of crunching bones and gurgled death rattles finally abated, the creature turned back, mushrooms heaving, glowing eyes scanning the cave for new threats.

Tyreal slid further down the cave wall away from it, keeping his movements slow. He didn't think it would attack him, since it appeared to be helping him escape. But he sure as hell would not risk angering it by moving too quickly.

"What is that thing?" he asked out loud.

He is me. I am him. We are bound to the Thorncrest line. We have been since the death of Viamar's mate. You were never meant to escape alone.

Whatever the hell that meant.

Tyreal looked past her at the ruined guards and took a deep breath. "Would have been nice if you had shown up earlier," he quipped, and then winced. Probably not a good idea to antagonize the magical creature with the terrifying bodyguard.

You were not ready earlier. She padded towards him, sitting down and rubbing one of her paws along her ear. It was a decidedly feline movement, though she was not. *You are whole enough to wield your gifts now, but there is much to do. We will clear your path and get you to the castle, but only you can face what waits ahead.*

"I figured as much."

The beast snorted, lichen fluttering with the motion. Tyreal flinched, eyeing it suspiciously. Luckily, it didn't begin pummeling him. Instead, it turned toward the now-collapsed section of tunnel that led out of the cave. With a single slam of its fists, it split the rock open. Dust and small pieces of stone rained down over it, but it didn't seem to notice. A jagged path emerged.

After you, warrior.

He wasn't particularly keen on having the creatures behind him, but it didn't appear he had much of a choice.

The new tunnel was tight, and the air was difficult to breathe, filled with dust and floating bits of moss. Tyreal pressed forward, knife ready in his hand. Behind him, he could hear the beast moving with heavy thuds. The fox danced between them, moving with a carefree grace that had no fear of anything she might come upon. And why would she? Not with that thing at her back.

They came to a fork—one path curling upward toward distant light, and the other echoing with the sound of approaching boots. He could hear his captors talking loudly about the sounds, wondering if the cave had collapsed on their friends. One of them even complained that if Tyreal was dead, they'd never hear the end from Ingram, assuming he even let them live.

Tyreal motioned for the beast to wait, and they turned toward the approaching men. Tyreal pressed himself back, trying to give the creature room to move forward and handle the guards like it had done the last batch. Instead, it just cocked its head. Liora sat down by its feet, both of them silently staring at him.

He sighed. "This one is on me, huh?"

He was met with silence, but it didn't matter. He knew the answer.

Tyreal moved forward, so that the men would spot him as soon as they turned the corner that brought them to the fork. He got only a few calming breaths in before a blade flew by his head.

He ducked on instinct, rolled, and came up swinging. The knife in his hand bit into cloth and flesh, and the guard closest to him cried out. Tyreal bent himself away from the injured man's defensive swing, but that brought him right into the heavy hilt of another man's sword, and it pummeled Tyreal's hip.

There were three men, all of them trained just enough to be dangerous.

Tyreal dodged another swing and kicked one square in the knee. Bone cracked.

Then a dagger sliced across his shoulder, severing the tendon. Tyreal roared in pain, his sword arm drooping uselessly along his side, the knife clattering to the floor. He staggered back, breathing hard, heart pounding.

Too fast. Too many. Healing himself earlier had bought him time, but this injury was fresh, and he'd barely eaten or drank anything in gods knew how long. He could feel blood pouring down his side, and he was lightheaded. At this rate, losing was less of a concern and dying was looking more likely. And where would that leave Gwen?

He pushed through the pain and drilled himself downward into the golden glow of his magic. It swelled upwards to meet him, and he mentally captured it, rolling it into a ball that he could launch. He felt his shoulder begin to heal, the pain breathtaking as the nerves and muscles repaired themselves.

He didn't stop there, though.

He directed more of it outward, shoving it at the men attacking him.

The man closest to him—a wiry bastard with a scar down his jaw—froze. His eyes widened.

Tyreal did not know what he was doing.

He just kept pushing the healing outward, directing it toward the man. Gold light filled the cave, and then the man screamed.

The man's face and hair rippled like something underneath was crawling to get out. The scar on his cheek tightened unnaturally, like a seam being pulled too tight. His skin spasmed and folded inward on itself. The man tried to scream but couldn't as it kept collapsing. It pulled away from the muscle of his jaw, revealing the wet pink flesh beneath. He fell to his knees and then onto his side on the cave floor.

The other two backed away, eyes wide with horror.

The man twitched and writhed on the ground like every nerve in his body was being lit from the inside out.

Tyreal's magic had found an old wound and set out to heal it. Only, it was too much healing. Too fast. The body couldn't take it. The magic overwhelmed, overwriting everything natural.

It was grotesque and terrible, but Tyreal couldn't, *wouldn't*, turn his eyes away. He had caused this, was making this man die in what was probably one of the worst ways imaginable. Right or wrong, Tyreal made himself bear witness.

The other two turned and bolted.

Try again, but see if you can only injure, not kill.

Tyreal glanced over at Liora, who gave a soft nod. He turned his attention back to the two fleeing men and let his magic flare. This time he sent out just a small stream, not a rushing river, like he had done to the other.

One man's leg collapsed beneath him, knee swelling outward to an impossible shape, skin splitting along its edges.

The other's arm bent backwards, new bone growth bursting outward from his forearm.

Both of them screamed in agony.

Tell your magic to stop.

Tyreal took a deep breath in, and pulled the stream back towards him, the golden light retreating and sinking into his chest.

The creature moved then, smashing both injured men simultaneously with its giant fists.

Tyreal looked at Liora with a raised eyebrow.

She gave as close to a shrug as a fox could. *I told you to not kill them. I didn't say we wouldn't.*

CHAPTER TWENTY-EIGHT

It had taken three staff members, two stable hands, and finally Cook—who only knew because Pip had sent down a request for snacks—before Gwen could track her brother down.

The rookery tower.

Of course.

She climbed the spiral stairs, the early morning wind slipping through the open slits in the stone, twisting her cloak around her legs and tugging at the edges of her braided curls. It carried the sharp tang of low tide and the distant caw of gulls flying over the sea.

Inside the heavy door, Gwen found Pippen exactly as she should have expected—holding court with crows.

A plate of cheese and nuts sat between him and three sleek birds perched boldly along the edge of the table, pecking with well-fed entitlement. A large book lay cracked open in front of him, its pages weighed down with two smooth stones. Nearby, Hedontas sat in a creaking chair, the table before him scattered with half-used parchment and three different quills intended for writing the messages the crows carried. His eyes were dark and underlined with the same exhaustion she felt down to her bones.

"Any news yet?" she asked quietly.

He shook his in response, and disappointment flooded over her.

Every guard she trusted was out searching. Andais had been working Ingram over for hours now with methods he told her she didn't need to concern herself with. If *he* hadn't broken the bastard, it meant there was nothing to break or knowledge so dangerous that even Ingram feared revealing it. Either option turned her stomach.

Pip looked up at her, eyes that mirrored her own scanning over her face. He frowned. "You look like one of the drawings in a book where everyone is about to die in battle."

Gwen managed a dry smile. "Well, that's cheerful."

He shrugged. "It hasn't been cheerful here in a while."

Her chest tightened. Gods, he was too young to sound that old.

"I know," she murmured, crossing the room to sit beside him. "I'm so sorry, Pip. This..." she motioned with her hands as she spoke, "none of this is how I wanted things to go. You should be worrying about your next riding lesson or sneaking extra dessert. Wrestling. Hunting. Getting muddy in the courtyard."

He leaned into her as she pulled him close beneath her arm. His head tucked into her shoulder like it used to when he was small—before the funeral, before the magic, before the dragons. There had been no time to properly grieve or get their bearings before the next thing happened.

She tightened her grip around him.

"I used to be able to protect you," she said, not entirely meaning to say it aloud. "I used to think I could keep everything dark away from you, because they protected *me*. Papa. Tyreal."

Now they were both gone. And all the progress she thought she had made in stepping into her own power and becoming the queen she was destined to be felt like it was slipping between her fingers like sand in an hourglass.

She took a deep breath. "I wanted to find you both because I have to leave the castle for a while." She paused. "It might be dangerous."

Hedontas sat forward, the legs of his chair scraping slightly against the stone floor. His brow knit with concern. "Where?"

Pip, still half-curled against her side, tilted his head to look at her. "Back to Mist Castle?"

"No." Gwen shook her head. "I need to find Viamar. I'm going to the cave where I first met him. If I'm lucky, he'll be there alone. I need to speak to him."

"Absolutely not," Hedontas said. The words came low and immediate, nearly a growl. "You're not going. I have to stay here and guard the prince. Andais is still working over Ingram. Every other guard we *trust* is out searching for Tyreal."

She met his eyes and gave him a small, sad smile. "I know. But I'm not asking. I'm telling you, as your queen. Stay here. Protect Pippen. I will do this alone."

His jaw tensed, and he crossed his arms tightly across his chest. He didn't respond, but the look on his face said everything it needed to. He was furious and chafing at the order, but was too loyal and well-trained to argue.

The silence between them was thick.

She stood, brushing the dust from her skirt, swallowing down the tight knot in her throat before it could rise into her voice. "Prince Grigor is winning," she said, her tone flat and tired. "The other monarchs are turning against me. I'm too young. I'm a woman. I dared to challenge everything they've always done. They haven't said it aloud yet, but I *feel* it. The next time they convene, they'll throw their lot in with Lovell's idea of unity—his version of peace. And there will be nothing I can do to stop it."

Pip looked between them both, his expression fearful.

"If Tyreal were here," Gwen continued, "if I could show them that my court is stable and in order, that he's by my side... maybe I could hold the line. Maybe they'd believe in what we're building. But every day he's gone, it makes me look weaker. They still see him as a soldier who married into a crown. A threat, not a partner."

"Leaving now gives Prince Grigor the perfect opening," Hedontas said, frustration lacing his tone. "It'll look like you ran. Like you broke."

"I know. I'm counting on timing. If I can return before they realize I'm gone, it'll be fine. Anya, Max, and Eliana are tasked with keeping their parents occupied and stalling the meeting until at least this evening." She hesitated. "If things go wrong with Viamar... if something happens to me..."

She turned to Hedontas fully. "Take Pip and leave the country."

"What?" Pip practically shouted. He jolted upright, nearly knocking the plate off the table. The startled crows shrieked and flapped away in a clatter of wings, clicking irritably as they settled on distant perches. "I'm not leaving. There must *always* be a Thorncrest in Thorncliff. That's the... the law!" His voice trailed off. "Isn't it?"

She didn't answer him right away. She was looking at Hedontas.

He said nothing, but his gaze flicked between them, clearly calculating a dozen scenarios in silence.

Gwen stepped closer to him. "You know why. If I fall, he'll come for Pip next. He'll wipe out the line completely. If that happens, the only hope this kingdom has of being reclaimed one day is if my brother lives long enough to grow into himself and take it back."

She turned to Pip then, more gently. "I don't want to leave you, but this is the only path left to me. If I can't sway the monarchs, if Lovell tightens his grip, if the dragons turn on us—then you are our last chance. You *must* survive."

Pip's face was pale now. "Then promise you'll come back." His voice cracked at the end, and she could see the shine of tears in his eyes. "You have to pinky promise again."

Gwen wondered how many times exactly someone's heart could shatter before there was nothing left.

"I can't. Because I can't break a pinky promise. That *is* a law in Tavia." She felt herself losing the battle against her tears as they spilled over her eyes. "But I promise I will do everything in my power to return to you. If I can't, Hedontas and Jameson will keep you safe. Maybe Tensha will find Tyreal and he will help too. Then one day, you will take the crown again, because Tavia will need you." She extended her pinky outwards, silently begging him to take it.

He wiped a hand across his face angrily. "No. I'm not pinky promising that. You promise to come back or just... don't talk to me at all." He sniffed loudly and stared at her. Anger, hurt, fear flickered across his small, freckled face.

Gwen took a shuddering breath. "Okay. Well, just know that I am pinky promising, even if you're mad. I love you."

She turned to look at Hedontas again. "Swear it."

A muscle ticked in his cheek and he stared her down. She thought for a moment he would refuse, but finally he gave a small nod. "If anything happens, I will take the prince far from here."

She took a deep breath and gave him a grateful, watery smile. The wind whipped through the open windows again, making her shiver. She gave Pip one last look before she turned to leave. He was stubbornly looking anywhere but her, ice spreading out from his hands on the table.

Gwen didn't look back again as she closed the door behind her.

The journey was significantly harder alone and not under dream magic. She tried at first to calm the waves with her magic, coax them into stillness to ease the rowing, but there was simply too much water, and controlling it had never been her strongest skill. Her arms burned with every pull, the oars splashing more than cutting.

Out of desperation, Gwen reached for her air power instead. If she couldn't tame the sea, maybe she could bend the wind. Not that she held much hope. It had been more accessible since magic had reawakened, but was wild and wholly unpredictable, no matter how much she tried to master it.

The wind came in sudden, sharp bursts, shoving the boat sideways and nearly toppling her. Salt spray stung her eyes as she fought to steady it, but each correction drained her further. She let out a frustrated cry, forcing all her rage and fear into the effort. She pictured the air as a blanket spread wide before her, the same way she had in the catacombs, when vengeance had given her the strength to strike at her father's murderer. With her teeth clenched and one final push, she caught hold of it, closing her fist until the wind eased and the waves stilled.

Gwen barely managed to get the boat dragged up onto the jagged rocks and frozen in place.

She collapsed at the cave mouth, her knees hitting stone hard enough to bruise. She hissed and rolled to sit on her bottom, pulling them up closer to her chest. She summoned her flames, cupping them between her palms to warm herself. It wasn't much, but it was something kind for a body that was running on stubbornness alone.

She hadn't slept in days. She had barely eaten. The worry around Tyreal's disappearance, the collapse of diplomacy, the fear for her kingdom—it had simply hollowed her out.

She couldn't even imagine what Tyreal would do to her if he saw her in this state.

Finally, with a grunt, Gwen pushed herself to her feet. She made her way through the cave tunnel, guiding her way through the darkness with a hovering orb of flame. Then a faint light showed ahead of her.

The walls opened up into the cavernous area that Viamar had created for himself.

The gods must have been in a generous mood, because Viamar was there, and he was alone.

He lay coiled in the middle, wings folded tight against his sides. Between his front claws, delicately pinned, was the blackened corpse of some large creature. It was unidentifiable now, charred beyond recognition. He peeled a strip of meat free, tossed his head back, and swallowed.

The smell hit her—half roasted meat, half rot from the piles of bones with clinging bits of meat littered around the space. Her stomach rolled.

He didn't look at her or acknowledge her right away. Not until he finished with his meal.

Hello, little Thorncrest. You do not come with good news.

"I think I'm failing." Her voice was raw and her shoulders sagged with her words. Admitting it out loud to the ancient dragon made it more real than she was ready for.

"Prince Grigor Lovell," she continued, "he's the nephew of the woman who released magic back into this world. He landed on my shores and turned the other monarchs against me. I don't… I don't think I can get them to agree with my alliance. They find me too young and idealistic, and they don't trust me. Especially with Tyreal missing." She took a shuddering breath.

"I fear that what Lovell is offering them is a lie. Once they are all aligned with his plan, he will turn on them and seize more land and control. Then we will fall into another war."

He stared at her, her mind and the cavern filled with silence. Gwen chewed the inside of her lip, trying to decide whether to keep speaking.

"Drakon of Galeigh has already walked away," she said. "He won't vote on either alliance. Said he was washing his hands of the whole thing.

That if he stays out of it, his people would be spared the fire."

She looked up at Viamar, searching his expression. "Is that true?" Her voice was hopeful. She hated it was hopeful.

The dragon flicked the tip of his tail with slow deliberation, lifting it to pick casually between two massive teeth before answering.

No.

Gwen closed her eyes. "I thought not."

She opened them again, steeling herself. "If the others side with Lovell, if they drag us into war, what will happen?"

I have already told you. If humans ignite another Great War—if they fight with their magic unchecked—we will burn you all to ash.

Gwen flinched. "Even those of us who are trying?"

When a wildfire consumes a forest, not every creature deserves to die. But they burn just the same. It is a tragedy, but also a necessity. The fire consumes what must be cleared to allow for rebirth.

He shifted slightly, and the faintest hiss of flame curled from his nostrils.

I have protected you where I could. I have driven off smaller dragons who wished to take matters into their own claws. I have spoken to the elders, pleaded for more time. Their patience is not infinite.

"How close are we to running out of time?"

Close.

He leaned forward, stretching his neck and bringing his head closer to her, so that his eyes were level. *If I cannot report soon that most of the royal houses have agreed to peace and that I can see their intentions are pure, then I can no longer hold the others back. There are larger, older dragons than I.*

The weight of the word *close* pressed down on her until she thought she might collapse again. Gwen's throat dried out, and her pulse pounded in her ears. She wasn't sure what else to say, what more to offer. The pieces she had laid on the chessboard of court politics were all she had. And Grigor had checked her queen.

She turned from him, staring back down the tunnel that led out of the cave. If she listened closely, she could hear water and the wind and the life all around her. The world sounded like it always had, and as it always would, long after she was gone.

"I don't know how to win this. I can't do it alone, and I'm out of ideas," she whispered. "Maybe this is what should happen. Maybe Myaessa did her best, but we unraveled everything we tried to build, because that is just what we do. Maybe humans really are a parasite on the land."

Viamar exhaled a low huff. The air was hot against her ankles, and it curled up her legs with just the slightest hint of steam.

Sometimes I think that.

There was no sarcasm or apology. Just brutal honesty.

Then I see the kind of love between you and your warrior. The kind I had with my mate. The kind that scorches through every part of your very existence. And I think... creatures capable of that kind of love must have something in them worth saving.

Gwen eased herself into a seated position on the floor, leaning back against the rock wall. The exhaustion was worsening now that the hopelessness was sucking her under. She wanted to think of anything else for just a moment. "Will you tell me about her?"

He stayed silent so long, she wondered if she had offended him by prying too deep. She opened her mouth to apologize, but he cut her off before she had a chance.

Her name was Sylazhar. Her scales were white as fresh snow at dawn. She was terrible in battle. Beautiful, too. Not only in the way she looked, but beautiful in her purpose. In the way she believed.

A deep sound escaped his chest, and Gwen could feel the grief radiating from him.

We ruled the skies together for centuries. She was the first to truly see your kind not as pretty or pests, but as something worthy. She was the first to befriend a human. A Thorncrest, actually. And she shared her magic with her. Convinced all of us to share.

Gwen's chest tightened.

She always pushed us, me especially, to be more. To be better. To grow. She was softer than any dragon had any right to be, but in a way that made her strong. More so than any of us gave her credit for. He waited for a beat, as if catching his breath and pushing through the pain. *When the war began, it broke her heart, but she didn't retreat. She fought harder. She believed, even then, that there was something good in humankind, and that dragons could help bring it out.*

Another long pause.

She fought so fiercely for you that I had no choice but to follow her.

He looked upwards towards the sky, and Gwen followed his eyes. His gaze wasn't focused on anything in the present. No, he was looking back into the past—at memories he carried with him.

For a heartbeat, she could almost see it too. Sylazhar, soaring above Thorncliff, wings spread wide and the white of her scales catching the sun like the iridescent shimmer of a clam's inner pearl. How brilliant would she have looked, diving through the clouds?

I didn't understand how rare she was. Not truly. Not until the day she fell.

His voice was quieter in her head now, but no less raw.

She died in battle, standing alone between Thorncliff Castle and the others who came to burn it to the ground. A set of humans had found a nest of baby dragons. Not your ancestors. I forget which ones now. It didn't matter to these dragons, though. Thorncliff was the closest, and they decided the humans within needed to pay for the crimes of their species. She held the line until she no longer could, giving the Thorncrest ruler time to get everyone to safety underground. And I—

He paused. *I wasn't there. I should have been there.*

Gwen shook her head. "Do you believe you'd have been able to save her if you had?"

Maybe. Maybe not. But at least we would have died together. He coiled his tail tightly around himself, as if protecting his heart. *Instead, I'm cursed with the worst possible future. Survival. Alone.*

Gwen felt her throat tighten, her chest constricting until she had to draw breath through her teeth.

Wasn't she doing the same thing now? Standing between two worlds—human and dragon, peace and war, tradition and change—trying to hold together something that might not last?

Trying and possibly failing.

And if she lost Tyreal...

Wouldn't she carry that same curse?

Wouldn't she be left behind, with nothing but the memory of what might have been? Or if she fell and Tyreal survived, wouldn't he?

Gwen's shoulders sagged, her arms hanging uselessly at her side. "This is hopeless," she said, her voice frayed. "Without Tyreal, without the support of the other monarchs, I'm alone. I'm trying to hold the line like she did, and I already know I'm not enough. We're just doomed to repeat the same pattern—hope followed by ruin."

Viamar went completely still for a moment, and then looked away from the sky and back at her.

No.

You are not alone.

Gwen huffed, tired and bitter, and lifted her hand in a small, sharp gesture that swept the empty cave around them. "Could have fooled me."

You forget who you are. The slits in his golden eyes narrowed further until she almost couldn't see them. *You are a Thorncrest. Your line bears the oldest of pacts. Sylazhar granted you her magic and died defending your people. That act was not forgotten. The land remembers. Magic remembers.*

He leaned in.

*When she fell, something **awoke**.*

Gwen's brow furrowed. "What do you mean? What awoke?"

Guardians of the purpose Sylazhar saw in your kind. If Myaessa had waited, if she had listened to more than just her grief, perhaps things would have turned out differently. But she did not. She acted too soon. And so, the guardians slept, just as we did.

"Guardians?" Gwen asked. "Who are they?"

Liora and the Wildguard. The Wildguard is of the land. Root, bark, and stone. Brute strength born from nature's will. It does not speak. It does not reason. It exists to restore balance when your line tilts too far in any direction.

"And Liora?"

She is nature's voice. Nature's mind. A creature of fate's many threads. She sees what could be and what must be pruned.

Gwen shivered slightly. "They are there to protect us?"

No. The word came firm.

They protect the balance. If you protect the land, they will stand with you. But if you stray too far, they will correct you instead.

A pause.

She will walk beside a Thorncrest, but never in front. Liora cannot force the line forward. She can only guide it—if you choose to move.

Gwen leaned down slightly, setting her chin on her knees and wrapping her arms around them. "How do I contact them? Get them to help me restore balance?"

You don't seek them out. They find you.

He stilled and stared past her. Past the rock walls. Past everything.

And it appears they have. Or one of you, anyway.

Gwen looked at him, confused. "What do you mean?"

Tyreal.

She bolted upright. "What about Tyreal? Where is he? Have they found him?"

Yes.

"Can you take me to him?"

The dragon lowered his neck all the way to the ground.

Climb, little Thorncrest. It appears your story is not done yet.

The sky stretched wide and bright above them as Viamar's wings beat in heavy, steady flaps. They sailed and carved currents through the clouds, and Gwen was fascinated by how the puffy clouds were as intangible as fog. She clung to spikes along the back of his neck, settled in a flat spot between his shoulders. She had formed a rope made of fire, both of them immune to the heat, and lassoed it around their bodies to help hold her in place.

The coastline passed beneath them in a blur of craggy cliffs and curling waves. Every time Gwen leaned forward and glanced down, the sheer scale of the world below left her breathless. It was terrifying.

And exhilarating.

She didn't think she would find anything in this life or the next that quite compared.

It seemed like no time before Viamar descended. She wasn't sure exactly how far they had traveled; it was impossible to tell at those speeds. She shielded her eyes with her hand, squinting and searching to find what he had seen to make him stop.

Below, there was a thin strip of sand between two massive cliffs leading out to an empty small beach, a small boat tied to a stake in the ground bobbing on the water. And then, she spotted a shape near the waterline, headed towards the boat. As they moved closer, she could begin to make out stained and ripped rags, a beard, an exhausted face.

Tyreal.

Her heart leapt. Her eyes burned as they descended.

Viamar touched down with a thunderous beat of his wings, sand billowing in waves around them. Gwen barely waited for him to lower his shoulders. She scrambled down, boots hitting the wet ground with a slap.

"Tyreal!"

He was already making his way towards her, having turned as soon as he spotted the dragon. "Gwen!" His formerly cream tunic was covered in dried blood stains and hung off him in torn strips. His hair was matted and his beard was unruly. He looked like he'd been through Ganderly and back.

But he was alive.

They ran to each other. She closed the distance as fast as her legs would carry her, and when she reached him, she flung her body at him so hard they nearly toppled over.

He caught her. Grunted softly as they collided, and his arms wrapped around her. Tightly. Desperately.

For a moment, neither of them spoke.

Then she pulled back enough to look at him, her hands framing her face.

"I'm sorry," they spoke in unison.

Tears welled in her eyes. "I thought you left me."

He shook his head. "No. Was on my way back when they got the drop on me. You won't get rid of me that easily."

"Took you long enough to get free. Getting rusty in your old age?"

He laughed, hoarse and low. "I had to get lost first. Apparently, that was part of fate's plan. Something about making peace with myself and becoming whole, or so the magical fox and her terrifying bodyguard tell me."

He motioned with his thumb back at the creatures standing on the beach near Viamar. She blinked for a moment, overwhelmed with what she was seeing, but decided she couldn't divide her attention and focus on them too closely.

Instead, she turned back to her husband and kissed him. Hard. Felt the warmth and realness of him against her.

"You owe me a wedding, you know."

"Yes. I do. Let's rid our castle of the vermin, and then we will lock ourselves in our chambers for a year."

She took a deep, shuddering breath. "It's all gone to shit. I'm losing everything. Grigor turned them..."

Tyreal pulled back enough to look her in the eyes. "Lovell is at Thorncliff? That's why Ingram kidnapped me?"

She nodded.

Tyreal smiled wickedly. "Well then, let's go home and I can show him my neat new trick."

CHAPTER TWENTY-NINE

Of all the ways Tyreal thought this day might go, waking up chained inside a cave, practically turning a man inside out with his magic, and riding a dragon would not have been a guess. The best he had hoped for was maybe Liora setting him free and him figuring out both where he was and how to get home.

He certainly hadn't expected to be held to said dragon by a thin rope of water as his only protection if Viamar banked too hard. Gwen wasn't exactly a master of water magic, so it did little to make him feel protected. She had said that she couldn't risk burning him if she used the fire rope again.

Still, he had to admit, pressing his face against the warm skin between his wife's throat and shoulder, breathing in the scent of her soap and hair oil—it beat rotting fish and moss by a mile. No matter the ride.

"I think we should land near the fairydew tree," Gwen called over the wind. "Liora and the Wildguard can hide there if needed. We can walk to the castle."

Tyreal shook his head. "No. We need to make a show of this. You're returning on dragon back, with the husband you rescued, like the terrifying queen I always knew you would be."

She shook her head, and he knew she was trying not to laugh. "You rescued yourself."

"Sort of. The scary beast behind us did a solid portion of it." He nodded back at Viamar's rear, where Liora and the Wildguard rode somehow without falling. Liora, curled up with her tail tucked over her nose, was already asleep.

"Can you land on the wall on the edge of the cliff and give us enough room to dismount?" Tyreal didn't bother trying to yell the words. He was fairly certain he didn't even need to speak them aloud for Viamar to hear.

Yes, warrior. I already planned on it. You are right to play on their fear of me. It will make her look like a female they shouldn't underestimate or cross. Sometimes, fear is the only language humans respond to.

Tyreal glanced back again at the magical creatures who'd freed him. Gwen had said that

Viamar seemed surprised that Liora was helping him, like he respected her and gave her actions a certain weight. If Liora, the embodiment of nature's mind and a creature of balance, had taken Gwen's side, surely that was all the proof the dragons needed.

Ask your question, warrior. Perhaps I'll answer.

Instead of asking aloud, Tyreal thought his question. "There was never really a threat from the dragons if Gwen failed to form the alliance, was there?"

Dragons are always a threat.

"I think you know what I mean."

It took a while for Viamar to respond. Only the sound of his wings slowly flapping filled the air.

The danger is real. With magic's return, I know too well that you humans' thirst for power will as well. Too many dragons see you as parasites. I feared how quickly it could rise, and I was right to. The attack from the small blue dragon is proof of that. You and Gwen needed to be tempered before that day came. The land itself demanded it. Perhaps it was Liora's hand guiding you both, I can't speak of her plans. I stressed urgency to prevent complacency, but I did not lie.

"She won't take kindly to being manipulated. And I'm certainly not going to keep it from her."

A sound almost like a chuckle echoed in Tyreal's mind. *I had a mate. I know your fear well. Do not lie to her. She can be angry with me all she wants.*

Tyreal wasn't sure how he felt about being manipulated, either. Though, he had to admit—he felt lighter than he had in weeks, now that he had made peace with who he was, the darkness inside him and the healing power he had viewed as a weakness. Maybe he wouldn't have faced any of it without the cave or his fight with Gwen.

Still, he was too tired to dwell on the games that gods, magic, and dragons liked to play. So he let it go, leaned forward, and rested his forehead against the back of Gwen's neck, eyes falling closed, once again filling his nose with her scent.

Then Gwen shifted sharply.

The rope of water cinched tight against his side, and his instincts screamed- *falling*—his eyes snapped open, heart pounding. He squeezed his arms around her, and she wiggled uncomfortably. It was then he realized she was just trying to get a better view of something below on the water.

Tyreal exhaled slowly with a long-suffering sigh, rubbing a hand down his face.

"Thank you for that heart attack. What are you looking at?"

She pointed. "Look over there, by the southern inlet. Is that ship flying the Adaltus royal flag?"

He followed her finger, squinting. At first, he couldn't see much other than a dark smudge over the glimmer of the waves. Then the winds shifted, and the clouds parted, revealing a ship flying a large white flag with a blue X and a golden sun above it.

The Adaltus flag with the royal crest.

"That's not the ship Grigor arrived on," Gwen said. "Why would they be here? Do you think it's the king? Do you think this means they are preparing to invade?"

"Not with only one ship," Tyreal responded. "It's definitely someone from the royal family, though."

She wrinkled her nose, thinking. "The brother?"

"Could be. He's no fan of Grigor. That much we know." He could tell she wasn't satisfied with that answer. Her body was tense, as if she was already preparing for a battle. "All we can do is wait," he added gently. "Focus on the problem in front of us for now."

The castle loomed ahead, the high outer walls carved from the very rock of the cliff they were built on. As Viamar descended, Tyreal could see the chaos the dragon's appearance was causing below. His men rushed to the walls, some with spears, some with bows, none of which would matter against a dragon, but he was glad to see them determined to protect the castle any way they could.

More worrisome were the ones that stood hesitating, eyes wide and mouths agape. He noted them. He'd have to talk to Andais about further training.

Viamar banked sharply, and the men below spotted Gwen and Tyreal on the dragon's back. He heard shouts announcing their arrival, and everyone lowered their weapons. With a huge flare of his wings, Viamar hovered, shaking some of the loose clay tiles off the watchtower roof. Then he landed, balancing easily on the thick edge of the cliff wall, with his massive talons curling into the rock.

He tucked his wings in close and descended his neck, lining it up with the staircase leading to the watchtower.

Gwen released the watery tether around them and slid off the dragon as easily as if she was dismounting Akasha. She landed on the steps with a hop, brushing the windswept curls that had escaped her braids out of her face and dusting off her cloak.

Tyreal swung his leg over and dropped, not bothering to make any attempts to make himself look presentable. He'd spent nearly four days beaten and locked in a cave. There was no hope for him until he located the nearest hot bath.

People were spilling into the courtyard down below, staring up at the dragon and their queen. She turned to look over her shoulder at him and extended her hand. "Ready to face our people, King Consort?"

He thought it might be the first time she'd ever said those words and he hadn't immediately felt a pit of fear open up inside his belly.

"Yes, my queen."

She pushed open the door leading from the watchtower stairs into the courtyard.

The noise hit her first—people yelling and fighting for a better viewing spot in the crowd. She scanned the sea of faces, hoping to spot Pip. She wasn't surprised to not find him. Hedontas likely hadn't let him outside with Viamar perched on the wall, like a nightmarish bird. Still, she was eager for him to see that she had returned after all, and to apologize for frightening him.

Unfortunately, she *did* spot Grigor.

He was shoving his way through the press of bodies, cloak tangled around one arm, circlet tilted like he'd thrown it on mid-run. His tunic wasn't fully tied, either. He looked—rumpled, and for once, gloriously unprepared.

His expression kept shifting, as if he couldn't decide between fury or a satisfied smugness, as if he thought her stunt might further his narrative.

Until he saw Tyreal.

The change was immediate. Color drained from his face, and his steps faltered. Gwen caught the twitch of his hand, casting something. To attack? To protect himself?

There was no way to be certain, because nothing happened.

His eyes widened, pure panic causing his mouth to fall agape and his body to freeze.

Gwen hid her smile, looking just past Lovell at Andais and Rykan, who were standing casually against the wall near Cook's garden. Her eyes met Andais' and she tilted her head subtly toward the kitchen door, then to Rykan. He nodded—message received. If things turned ugly, Rykan would be taken inside, where Gwen and Tyreal could fight unrestrained.

Tyreal leaned in close and whispered in her ear, "Oh, he's pissed."

Gwen didn't respond. She simply stepped outward onto the courtyard stone, Tyreal's hand in hers.

They must've made quite the sight. Her in a riding cloak, dismounting from a dragon like it was a commonplace occurrence, and Tyreal in the ripped and bloodied tatters of what they would all recognize as the remains of his betrothal outfit.

She could hear the whispers.

Is that the High Captain?

I thought he was at the border.

What happened to his clothes?

He looks awful.

She let them continue talking, let the confusion spread as she approached the gathering group of monarchs that now half-circled the Adaltan prince.

Grigor stood waiting—until she got too close.

Then he stepped back.

Just a half step.

But the other monarchs saw it.

And *he* knew they saw it.

He straightened immediately, trying to look composed, but the damage was already done.

"Your Majesty," Grigor said, trying for a breezy tone, "I certainly don't mean to question how you conduct affairs in your own kingdom, but this is a bit... dramatic, don't you think? Arriving on the very beast you claim will destroy us? And—" his eyes flicked to Tyreal's ruined clothes "—what happened to your High Captain? I thought you said he was on assignment?"

"I lied," Gwen said flatly.

The crowd gasped.

Grigor blinked. "I—what?"

"I lied," she repeated. "I knew if I made Tyreal's kidnapping public, *you* would use it to paint me as weak. If I pretended he was away on a mission, you couldn't press too hard without exposing yourself."

Grigor scoffed. "Another of your baseless accusations? I thought we were past that. I think the bigger issue here is that you felt so comfortable lying to people you claim you want as allies."

"If the High Captain was indeed kidnapped," King Thalion said, "she was right to do so."

Several of the other monarchs nodded in agreement.

"I think my appearance makes it clear I didn't leave of my own free will," Tyreal said. "I was attacked on the beach by men working for Kiel Ingram. Who, in turn, was working for *you*."

"You're lying," Grigor snapped, eyes darting around the courtyard. "That's not true."

"Only if Ingram's lying too," Andais spoke up casually, arms crossed across his chest. "He's in our dungeon and has been spending some quality time with me. Sang like a bird."

Gwen didn't know if this was true. Last she'd heard, Ingram hadn't confessed to anything. Maybe something had changed. Or maybe Andais was bluffing to rattle the prince. Either way, it was working.

"Is this true, Prince Grigor? You've certainly been pushing hard about the High Captain's absence," King Damaris said. "Frankly, many of us found your persistence unsettling."

Gwen almost rolled her eyes. *Now* Damaris wanted to play concerned ally? He'd welcomed Lovell under the guise of diplomacy. He'd echoed his doubts in the library when they met. Now that the tide was turning, he was jumping ship.

Typical.

Grigor's mouth opened and closed silently. He was unraveling, and everyone could see it now. All of his earlier confidence, the slick, polished performance, had thinned into tight, dry lips and nervous eyes.

Tyreal took a step forward. "Your move, Prince Grigor. If you've got another sneaky defense tucked into your cloak, this would be the time to use it."

Grigor let out a short, breathless laugh. "You're accusing me with no evidence, just like you did after the High Sister's treachery."

Tyreal made a dramatized look of confusion. "Who said I didn't have any evidence of that? The queen may not have known the exact location and couldn't produce it in my absence. But I assure you, I have plenty of evidence. And even if I didn't, everyone here can see the truth. You flinched the second you saw me, because you didn't expect me to come back."

Lovell looked around at the crowd, face pleading with the other monarchs. "You are really all going to stand here and take their word for it?" he demanded. "She lied. She admitted it in front of you. Lied to your faces and misled this court, just like she did about having magic and this nonsense about a new world with a bastard commoner."

"Excuse you, I'm not a bastard," Tyreal quipped.

"Enough," Grigor snapped. "This is ridiculous! The queen brings home her betrothed in tatters, riding a dragon, surrounded by whatever the hell *those* are." He motioned up towards where Liora and the Wildguard stood watching silently on the guard tower. "And suddenly I'm the villain?"

"Pretty much," Andais said.

A few people chuckled around the courtyard. Grigor's face turned an ugly, splotchy red and purple color. He opened his mouth, and Gwen knew whatever he was going to say would be vicious and would likely spark the battle that was brewing.

But he never got a chance.

"Your Majesty!" the town crier rushed into the courtyard. "Crown Prince Caldrin from Adaltus is at the front gate and requesting entry."

Lovell went very, very still.

Tyreal grinned and looked back over at him. "Looks like big brother is here. Wonder which version of the truth he will agree with?"

CHAPTER THIRTY

The gates creaked open, and a small entourage rode into the courtyard. At its center, unmistakable even at a glance, was the prince. He wore a deep blue tunic trimmed with gold filigree, the designs curling along the high collar and trailing down his chest like vines. Draped over his shoulders was a crimson cloak lined with black fur, the same intricate gold pattern stitched into the fabric. His beard was full and well-kept, his thick, dark hair long enough to brush the fur at his neck.

Gwen had to admit—he was outrageously handsome.

He sat the saddle with the same self-assured arrogance as his younger brother, but where

Grigor's bravado had always felt like a performance, this had weight behind it, confidence without bluster. Her papa used to say it wasn't arrogance if you could prove it.

She studied him longer than she meant to. There was something about him that drew attention and held it. His body language almost reminded her of Tyreal, like a man that was accustomed to keeping dangerous company and trusting very few fully. She wondered if that was learned—or earned.

She searched her memory, trying to place him. Had they ever met before? Maybe once, when she was small, at a royal banquet or a summer festival. He'd been a lanky boy back then, about Pip's age, all awkward limbs and sharp elbows. She'd been too busy chasing after Tyreal for him to make much of an impression.

But now, he was impossible to ignore. Good thing she was a married woman.

Well, she would be as soon as she and Tyreal could get alone in the chapel with Malcolum in the morning.

Beside him rode someone even harder to miss—a woman in a guard's uniform. Gwen blinked. A *female guard* here, riding beside the Crown Prince of Adaltus? That matched nothing she'd been told. Tyreal's informants had painted the Adaltan court as more traditional than any other kingdom, and yet here was this woman, front and center, not hidden at all, and looking very comfortable with her place at his side.

And if Caldrin was striking, he paled beside the woman at his left.

She had long dark hair pulled back in a braid that only sharpened the delicate lines of her oval-shaped face. Full lips, dark eyes. She wore the same white tunic embroidered with the Lovell crest as the other guards, but over it was a leather harness strapped crisscrossed and framing her breasts. The straps were functional—but they definitely drew the eye. Not a coincidence, Gwen suspected. The woman knew how she looked, and didn't seem bothered by the attention.

Daggers rested in small sheaths along the straps. A curved sword hung at her hip—shorter than Tyreal's, but no doubt just as lethal. Something told Gwen that was true of the woman as a whole, not just her sword.

If Caldrin reminded her of Tyreal, then this woman reminded her of Tensha. A warrior underestimated not just because of her gender, but also because she was apt to watch everything and rarely blink. Gwen would wager that not much got by her.

Bodyguard? Lover? Gwen couldn't quite pin what the two were to each other.

"Well," Gwen murmured, leaning closer to Tyreal, "they make a rather dashing pair. I thought you said Adaltus was backward when it came to women. Why does she look like a guard?"

"I said their father was," Tyreal replied with a shrug. "Or that's what my spies said. Grigor certainly acts like he inherited the same views. I guess I assumed Caldrin did, too."

Gwen stepped forward. "Welcome, Prince Caldrin. I was unaware you were traveling to us, or I would have had a welcoming party ready at the docks for you."

"Yes," Caldrin replied. "I didn't send notice. I've been sailing for some time, and once the magic broke loose, I had my hands full, as you can imagine. From there, it was mostly just conversing with my father via crow." As he spoke, he dismounted with ease. Though his words were directed at Gwen, his eyes were locked on his brother.

"You must have made incredible time," Tyreal said.

Caldrin turned to him, brow lifting as he took in Tyreal's stained and jagged rags. "I apologize if I should know already. But who are you, and what happened to you?"

"Tyreal Blackbane—Tyreal Thorncrest now," he replied, stepping forward with casual pride. "King Consort and High Captain of the Tavian Guard." He slid his hand into Gwen's. "And as far as what happened to me, we were actually just discussing that. Your brother paid a pirate to kidnap me and hold me hostage the last few days. I escaped with the help of our new friends." He motioned upwards at the stairs of the guard tower.

To his credit, Caldrin absorbed the accusation without a visible reaction. The only tell Gwen could get on his thoughts was a nervous flick of his eyes up at Viamar. Liora and the Wildguard were no longer anywhere to be seen.

"Yes," he said slowly, "that's part of why I'm here. It seems my brother has been acting under the Adaltan crest and flag without our sanction."

Grigor flinched as every head turned toward him.

"I... I think that's somewhat oversimplified," he said, voice shaking.

Caldrin tilted his head. "Oh? What's missing?"

"There's context. Nuance. Things you don't—"

"Facts don't require nuance, Grigor," Caldrin said coldly. For the first time, Gwen could see the emotions on the crown prince's face. He was furious. "You wouldn't accept King Lorne's refusal of your marriage proposal—a proposal you made without our knowledge. You diverted royal funds to bribe Tavian guards and stir unrest. And now Father found out you worked with our dear aunt to help unlock this wild magic. He found your stack of letters. Let me know if I've misstated anything."

Grigor's face flushed a furious red.

Caldrin turned back to Gwen and Tyreal, his tone polite once more. "I'd like to offer a formal apology on behalf of the Lovell family and the kingdom of Adaltus. None of Grigor's actions were sanctioned. Though you are within your rights to administer justice here in Tavia, my father has requested that you permit me to bring him home to face his punishment."

"No!" Grigor's voice cracked as he stepped forward, face contorted with rage. "You will not take this from me too!" His sword was suddenly in his hand, drawn with a trembling fury. "I was supposed to be a king!" he shouted. "You already ruined my chance of ruling Adaltus just by being born sooner, and now here—Tavia! You think she deserves this? A whore who spreads her legs for a commoner has no place on a throne!"

Gwen's breath caught.

He charged toward her, sword raised.

Caldrin winced and let out a tired sigh. "Well. I suppose that answers that question."

Even before the crown prince had finished speaking, Tyreal and Andais had already moved. A ring of guards closed in on Grigor, and he swung his sword wildly in a circle, trying to hold them back.

"Andais," Tyreal growled, hand outstretched, "give me a gods-damned sword. The pirate bastards took mine."

Andais began to unsheathe his sword.

"Wait!" Gwen commanded loudly. "Disarm him, but do not harm him. Not yet." She looked at Caldrin. "You agree I am within my rights to administer punishment and I am no longer bound by the Covenant?"

Caldrin's expression barely shifted. "Seeing as my brother was here with no official authority, he wasn't acting as a monarch. The Covenant was never enacted." His tone was dry, matter-of-fact. "So yes. You are. My father's feeling sentimental toward his youngest child, but I made peace with who Grigor is long ago. Do as you will."

Gwen nodded once, slowly, her voice steady. "Seeing as Grigor stands no chance against any of my guards, *especially* my husband with a blade, and considering he helped unlock this magic he was so desperate for, no matter the cost…"

She looked to Tyreal. "Let us have a duel. Though since there is no way he could ever beat him, I suppose it will have to be with magic."

Grigor laughed bitterly. "A duel? That's rich. Whatever trick you pulled to shut down our magic must still be in place. Unless you want to watch me blow my breath, this little challenge of yours won't go far." He sneered. "Lucky break for your husband, really. Healing doesn't get you far in an actual fight."

Tyreal grinned, slow and dangerous. "Tough talk for a man I could strangle to death without breaking a sweat."

Grigor's grip on his sword tightened.

"I never said you'd be dueling the High Captain. And I'm not sure what you mean," Gwen said coolly, seeing Rykan no longer standing by the wall. She extended a hand, conjuring a fireball the size of a melon, the heat rippling off her palm in visible waves. "My magic is working just fine."

Anya raised one arm and summoned a column of water that danced around her in a spiraling ribbon. "So is mine," she said sweetly.

"Mine too," Eliana said, stepping forward. With a flourish, she waved her hand over her body. Her form shimmered and collapsed into a new one, matching the woman that had ridden in with the prince.

Anya whistled softly. "Show-off."

The woman in question dismounted and cocked her head to one side, assessing Eliana's likeness of her. "Does my harness really make my breasts look like that?"

"Yes," Caldrin and some of the other men who had ridden in with him said in unison.

"Hmmm. Well, you are all welcome. But I think I'd prefer to be the only person wearing this face, if you don't mind."

Eliana nodded and changed back to herself.

Gwen's attention flicked briefly to Anya—just in time to catch her staring at the woman. Her brow was lightly furrowed, nose just slightly scrunched and lips parted, almost like she had forgotten where she was. She caught herself when the woman looked directly at Anya, and Anya's eyes immediately dropped to the ground, then up again with a practiced neutrality that didn't quite hide the blush at the tips of her ears.

Gwen hid her smile. She couldn't blame her friend. It was a tad hard not to stare. She glanced back at the woman, who also seemed to fight a smile as she continued looking at Anya.

Caldrin caught Gwen looking at his companion. "Her name is Sera Vale. She's our half-sister. My father cast out her mother before she was born, one of the lesser scandals of the time. Sera was raised by mercenaries near the coast, came back with her own sword and her own name." He glanced at his brother, who was still gripping his sword like it was the only hope he had. "They all hate her, which is why I trust her. She is loyal to me, not the crown."

"Enough! Gods, it's so unfair that you three even have magic," Grigor snarled. He tossed down his sword and began swirling air around him—picking up dust, leaves, and small rocks, making him difficult to see. "A whore. A queer. And a man who thinks he's a woman and convinced everyone to go along with a lie. I'll kill you all!"

Tyreal shook his head. "Bloody crows, you talk too fucking much."

He flicked his hand, and Grigor hit the ground screaming, all the things that had been swirling around him dropping beside him. Blood spread outward in delicate patterns across his tunic, every old wound splitting open at once—scratches, nicks from blades, bruises made physical again.

Tyreal stood over him, eyes narrowed.

"Anyone with a weak stomach," he said calmly, "might want to look away."

Grigor screamed again, blood beginning to bubble and pour from the corners of his mouth. He kicked his legs out, almost like a child throwing a tantrum.

Several people turned away as warned, nauseated by the blood. Others were looking at Tyreal with a newfound fear and respect.

Gwen looked at Caldrin and Sera. Sera watched with a passive interest, arms crossed and weight evenly balanced, like she was observing a game of chess rather than a man screaming on the ground. It didn't appear there was any love lost for her other half-brother. Caldrin, despite saying he had made peace with it, was clearly wrestling with something. There was a quiver to his bottom lip, barely visible unless you were looking for it. His jaw clenched, and fists squeezed tight.

He doesn't want to watch this, but he's not stopping it, she thought.

Gwen's eyes drifted upward toward the high spire, where Pip's chambers were. She pictured him there, likely watching from the window, gangly arms wrapped around his knees as he pouted about not being able to get a closer view of the dragon. She wondered if he was still angry at her.

And then she imagined him down here, bloodied and shrieking like Grigor. Her heart clenched so tightly she had to swallow.

Could she do it? Could she stand there and watch while someone else unmade her brother right before her eyes? No matter what he had done?

She didn't know.

Gods, she was so sick of death.

Gwen thought of Viamar, who had since flown off and left the humans to their petty squabbles. The pain she had felt from him when he had described Sylazhar's death. She'd been killed defending the humans, Gwen's ancestors. Had the other dragon that killed her believed he was righteous in the act? Had he thought her a traitor against dragons? He certainly hadn't given a thought to what her death would do to her mate.

Creatures capable of that kind of love must have something in them worth saving.

That was what Viamar had said.

Was family love any different? Didn't love and mercy go hand in hand?

"Tyreal, that's enough," she commanded.

He looked over his shoulder at her with a raised eyebrow, but he lowered his hand. The bleeding stopped, though he made no move to heal Grigor.

Gwen looked at Caldrin. "Give me a blood oath right now in front of all our kingdoms that he will be punished in Adaltus and will no longer serve as a threat to anyone."

Caldrin stared at Gwen, then flicked his eyes over at his bleeding brother. A muscle jumped in his cheek. "Give me a blade," he said to Sera quietly. She handed him one from her harness, and he made a quick slice across his palm. He made a move to slice Gwen's.

"Anything more than a shallow cut, and you'll be on the ground bleeding beside your brother," Tyreal warned.

The crown prince widened his eyes and gave a chuckle. He turned the blade carefully, so the handle pointed outward towards Gwen. "Perhaps you should make your own slice. Your husband seems twitchy."

"He's paranoid and dramatic sometimes, but he's all mine," Gwen said with an indulgent smile. She took the blade and sliced her palm as well, before holding it outward for Sera.

Sera took it and wiped it clean on her breeches before sliding it back into its sheath. She tucked her arms back behind her back, and the quickest sideways glance caught Anya gaping again. Gwen needed to have a talk with Anya about subtlety, apparently.

Caldrin extended his hand and grasped Gwen's. "I solemnly give a blood oath that Grigor will face punishment for his crimes at home and will serve as no threat to any other kingdom, even if it means I have to kill him myself." He stared into her eyes as he said it.

Golden light flared around their joined palms, and Caldrin jumped in surprise.

The air around them shimmered for a moment, and suddenly, Liora was beside them, appearing out of thin air. She sat and cocked her head to the side, watching them unblinking.

Caldrin's mouth dropped open as he stared at the glowing fox covered in moss and mushrooms. The small orange orbs that floated around her made their way over towards the pair of them, gently swirling around their heads.

As quickly as Liora had appeared, the Wildguard followed. Everyone in the courtyard recoiled backwards from the beast. It made no movement though, just stood behind the fox.

"It seems blood oaths have a bit more bite with magic's return," Gwen said, lifting her voice for the crowd to hear. "I wouldn't advise testing it."

"No," Caldrin said. "I don't imagine *whatever that is* would allow it."

He gave a final, wary glance at the creatures before looking back at Gwen and clearing his throat. "My father will appreciate what you've done today. Adaltus is in your debt. Now, I believe I heard something about an alliance of some sort and restructuring the Sisters of the Mist? Shall we go inside, and you can fill me in?"

Gwen started to respond, but Tyreal moved forward and took her elbow.

"The queen and I will join the rest of you in the library for further discussion after dinner. Right now, I would very much appreciate a bath and some alone time with my wife. Oh, and a tray of food sent up to my chambers, if Cook is agreeable?" The last part he said with a hopeful tilt to his voice, giving her his best sad eyes.

Cook shook her head and tried to hide her smile. "I suppose I can't deny the King Consort, can I? Especially when he looks like something one of my mousers dragged in."

Caldrin nodded. "Of course. I would want the same." His eyes swept over Gwen briefly and then met Tyreal's. "You're a lucky man. The original plan was for me to wed Lorne's daughter until she was born first. Two heirs can't wed, so here we are."

"Here we are," Tyreal said cooly. "I know how fortunate I am. Not sure why the gods favored me on this one, but grateful they did."

CHAPTER THIRTY-ONE

Tyreal watched as Gwen accepted the tray of food from one of the kitchen girls, murmured a soft thanks, then nudged the chamber door shut with her foot. It closed with a soft *click*.

She crossed the room, set the tray on the small table, and moved toward the bath. With a swirl of her finger through the surface, the water rippled—steam rising gently a moment later.

"I tried not to make it too hot, since you are such a baby," she said with a grin.

"Not everyone wants to boil their skin off," Tyreal muttered, wiping dried blood from his chest with a damp rag. He stood near the bath, undressed and very ready to get clean. "Figured I'd get the worst of it off before I soak in it. No point stewing in my own filth."

Gwen's eyes dropped to the ruined pile of his formal attire at his feet.

"That was a beautiful outfit," she sighed. "You looked devastatingly handsome in it."

"As handsome as yonder prince?" he said, one brow lifting. "Don't act like I didn't catch you looking."

"I mean…" She dragged the word out playfully. "You're alright, I guess." A beat. "But I doubt I was looking any harder than anyone else. And you're one to talk—don't tell me *you* didn't notice how stunning his half-sister is."

"Not nearly as much as Anya did."

Gwen laughed, a low, throaty sound that hit him right in the chest. *Gods*, he'd wondered if he'd ever hear that again, lying half-conscious in that cave, listening to nothing but dripping stone.

"Noticed that too, huh?"

She stepped in closer, slipping the rag from his hand without a word. Gently, she began scrubbing at a spot on his back.

"I missed you," she said, barely more than a whisper.

Tyreal looked over his shoulder. "I missed you too, sweet girl."

Then he turned, catching her wrist, the rag falling from her fingers and landing with a soft splash against the stone. His eyes didn't leave hers as his hands moved to the ties on her dress, undoing them one by one until the fabric puddled at her feet.

"You're getting in this bath with me," he said, voice low but firm. "You need to relax just as much as I do."

She opened her mouth to protest, but he cut her off.

"Have you been sleeping? Eating?"

The flicker of guilt in her eyes was answer enough.

He narrowed his eyes and frowned at her. "That's what I thought. They'll be lucky if I even let you go back down there after dinner." He leaned in, softly kissing a freckle on her shoulder. "You have to take care of yourself, Gwen." He trailed the tips of his fingers along her collarbone and down over her arm, lightly grazing the side of her breast.

She inhaled sharply, but her voice stayed low. "I spent the first day and a half thinking you'd left me."

His hands stilled.

"I only stopped sobbing when I had to pretend everything was fine. Smile. Reassure. Watch Grigor try to dismantle my court from within, all while under the threat of dragon fire."

Tyreal grimaced and cleared his throat. "I don't know if that threat is quite as imminent as Viamar made it seem."

She pulled back slightly, brows pulling together. "What?"

He nodded, dragging a hand through his hair, and then wrinkling his nose from the feel of it. He moved to the tub and gently eased himself into the water. "It's real. He wasn't lying. Something about tempering us and avoiding complacency. Whatever the hell that means."

She just stared at him.

"I don't think there is a specific timeline or anything. They could still roast us tomorrow," he added, throwing up his hands. "I *told* Viamar you'd be pissed when you found out. The gods and their games."

Gwen rubbed at her temples with her fingers, muttering something under her breath that sounded suspiciously like a curse.

"Well," she said finally, "I guess we'd better stay prepared."

"There are still dragons who'd happily hunt a human or twenty. The little blue bastard at our betrothal ball showed us that," Tyreal said

He paused, thoughtful.

"I *am* curious about the other magical creatures, though. The ones who are stirring. The sprites in the fairydew tree. Liora. The Wildguard. The way magic's waking everything up."

Gwen nodded slowly, her hands falling away from her temples. "We're not just leading a kingdom anymore, are we?"

"No," Tyreal said, pulling her gently into the bath. "We're part of something bigger now. We just haven't seen the whole shape of it yet."

She settled into the bath beside him, the water lapping gently at her skin. For a while, they just sat in silence—his arm behind her, her cheek resting against his shoulder. The heat was soothing, but it didn't erase everything that had happened.

She reached for a bar of soap and began rubbing it into a rag. Suds bubbled up around her fingers as she worked the lather, then began wiping him down with slow, careful strokes. Gwen was focused on the task, and he knew she was processing everything in her mind. She'd speak when she was ready.

"I'm sorry I doubted you," she said quietly. "I shouldn't have. It's just... I knew I had let you down by not sticking up for you to the other monarchs. I knew you were struggling with your magic and your place in the court. That all of this," she gestured vaguely around the room, "was too much."

"I understand why you thought that," he said softly. "The timing couldn't have been worse. And I'd be lying if I said it didn't cross my mind to walk away. Not because of you. Just... the weight of it all." He exhaled. "But I talked with Mason. After everything he's lost, it really put things into perspective. I realized I couldn't walk away. Not really. I was on my way back to you when they captured me. I swear that."

She nodded. "I'm also sorry I got mean. About you feeling emasculated."

He smirked faintly. "That was pretty bitchy."

She flicked water at his face, and he grinned for a moment before his expression sobered.

"I don't think you were entirely off the mark. Only, not in the way you meant it." He shifted in the bath slightly to face her better. "I'm not threatened by you being queen. That part I'm proud of. Proud of *you*."

Her hand paused, resting on his chest, and he covered it with his own. "I think what I was struggling with," he went on, "was who I am now, as a man. I was frightened by the magic. Embarrassed, honestly. It's not a warrior's power. Well, I didn't think it was. I didn't think it was something I could use to defend you or anyone else."

She didn't interrupt. She just listened.

"Learning I was descended from royalty didn't sit right with me either. It felt like it came with expectations—expectations I never asked for. It didn't match who I thought I was."

"You're still you," she said gently.

"I know," he said. "I just needed to sit with and really face it all. And..." he swallowed, taking a deep breath before laying his final card on the metaphorical table, "I was scared that if I didn't know who I was, then it would be impossible to truly hide the parts of myself that I didn't want you to see."

She frowned. "I want to see all of you. I *love* you."

"Yeah, well," he said, smiling without humor. "I think everyone's afraid of that on some level.

That the person they love couldn't possibly love the worst parts of themselves." He paused for a moment, gathering his words. "I'm not sure that I *am* a good person, Gwen. Not down at my core. I've done things—ugly things—in the name of keeping you and this kingdom safe. And I'd be lying if I said that all of them were necessary. Or if I said that I didn't *enjoy* some of it."

Her expression didn't change, and she didn't flinch, so he kept going. "What you did today, showing Grigor mercy?" He shook his head. "I wouldn't have done it. I wasn't even sure it was a *good* idea until the magic flared around the blood oath. I wanted him dead. I still want him dead. For what he had said to you. For what he did to us. Hell, just for the fact he wanted what I consider mine."

The last word hit the air with more heat than he had intended, roughly possessive.

She cupped his cheeks in her hands. "Did you really think I didn't know all of that?"

He blinked, holding his breath and waiting for her next words.

"My father used to say men like you were vital to a country. You're ones who carry the weight others won't. Who step into the dark when the rest of us can't bear to look." Her voice softened but held no less conviction. "It takes a certain darkness to be *able* to do it. I won't pretend otherwise. The difference between you and someone evil, though, is you don't kill for the fun of it alone. You act when you have to—and I've seen you try to end things without violence, like when those men were holding Max hostage. I've watched you defend the innocent and helpless, time and time again."

She leaned in, her forehead touching his. "You don't have to prove you're good, Tyreal. You already are. Because you *choose* to be, even when it's hard. Especially then." She peppered kisses along his jawline, and whispered, "And if you want to know my dark secret... sometimes I really, *really* like watching you give in to your violent side."

He captured her lips with his. The kiss was loving in a brutal way. Aching. Recapturing. Needy. The kind of kiss that came from absence, fear, and then the sudden miracle of getting something back that you thought you'd lost.

He moved quickly in the water, causing water to splash lightly over the edge of the tub. His hands dropped to her sides, pulling her against him. She came willingly, straddling his hips, never breaking contact with his mouth.

His hands threaded up into her hair, untangling the braid and letting it loose around her shoulders. He gripped the tresses, firmly but gently, and tugged just enough that she tilted her head back and gave him access to her throat. Only then did he move his lips from hers, so he could kiss and suck his way along her skin, tasting the water and the flavor that was all Gwen.

"You're so fucking perfect. Do you know that? I could never walk away from this." He growled the words into her neck, biting gently on her earlobe.

She reached between them, gripping his cock in her hand, and he hissed in appreciation. There was no need for foreplay, not now. Too much had happened. There was too much desperation to reconnect. She lifted her hips up and lined him with her opening, before sinking herself fully onto him.

They both moaned.

This was always the best and worst moment for him. When he first slipped inside her. The glide into her wet, tight heat always nearly did him in, and it took everything not to just immediately spill inside her. She always needed a moment to adjust to his size, so he distracted himself by cupping her breasts.

His thumbs brushed gently over the tips of her nipples, testing. Some days she loved having them played with, others he was lucky to look at them. It all depended on where she was in her cycle. This time she moaned, and a wicked grin split his face. He captured them between his thumb and forefinger, rolling and tugging gently.

She cried out and moved on him, and Tyreal replaced one hand with his mouth so he could cup her ass and help her ride him. He bit and sucked, rocking her and lifting his hips to meet her thrusts.

"Yes, baby, ride me. Take what you need. You're mine and I'm yours and *nothing* will ever split us apart again," he whispered hotly against her skin.

She whimpered and rode him, but the angle in the cramped tub wasn't quite right. He could see her getting frustrated as she kept chasing her release. "I know what I need," she pouted and then bit her lip shyly. "But I'm nervous to ask for it."

That certainly caught his attention. He stopped moving, gripping the curve of her ass and holding her in place so she was forced to focus on what she was saying instead of chasing her release. "What do you mean?"

"I... I want to let it all go. I want you to restrain me, like you tried the other night. To take complete control."

He placed a fingertip against her lips, dragging it at a maddeningly slow pace downward over her throat, collarbone, and between her breasts. "Are you sure? You can always change your mind, and use your words, but still, I need to know you're doing this for you and not because it is something you think I want."

She nodded. "Yes. I think I was holding myself back. Ashamed of what I wanted. Unwilling to share the darkest parts of myself with you. Now though, I want to be dark *together*."

"Your wish is my command, *Your Majesty*." Tyreal said it so that her title was just shy of mocking. He wanted her to feel small and needy. Like everything in existence had suddenly shrunk to just him and the way he made her feel. Because he certainly felt that way about her.

He grabbed her hips and lifted her off him, scooping her into his arms and out of the tub in one fluid movement. He carried her to the wall where he had tried restraining her previously, not giving a damn how much water was splashing and dripping all over the floor.

"Use those fancy new air powers, Gwennic. Restrain yourself. Show me how much you want to be my dirty girl that likes to be tied up and hurt. Keep it nice and tight and I'll hurt you oh so good, baby. Let it slip and, well..." He dragged the word out. "Let's just say you won't enjoy the punishment that comes after."

He watched her bite her bottom lip, embarrassment staining her skin as she pushed through the emotions that came with accepting what she wanted. Being forced to restrain herself only added an extra layer of complexity to it. It didn't allow her to hide behind any idea of him *making* her do anything. They were stripped bare to each other now and only complete and raw honesty would do.

Slowly, the water covering their bodies cooled as air flowed around them, and he watched as her wrists came together, the skin indenting as invisible ropes tightened and tied them to the sconces on the wall.

Tyreal was sure that the grin that spread across his face could only be described as predatory. By the gods, she was beautiful. Seeing her give in to the darkest parts of her desires had to be the most stunning thing he had ever witnessed. He had shown her the worst parts of himself and not only had she accepted him, but here she was only moments later, offering herself to him in the greatest act of trust one could hope for.

Everything after that was a blur of fingers, lips, teeth and tongue. He bit, licked, teased and touched every inch of her until time lost all meaning. Her eyes glazed over, as if she was drunk on sweet wine. Over and over, he took her to the very edge of release, and then backed her away from it, switching to a different method of torture until the pain and pleasure blended, and she wouldn't be able to tell where one started and one ended.

He checked in with her frequently, making sure she still said gallop, though as time went on he could see the words were getting harder and harder to find as everything melted around her. Soon the only word he could truly get out of her was some form of please, and he couldn't tell if she was begging or giving in to him completely.

Finally, unable to restrain himself any longer, he growled, "enough," and gripped her legs, pulling them up around his hips as he pressed her body back firmly against the wall.

He slammed into her without notice, not that there was any doubt she was ready for him. Her thighs were sticky with need. Gwen cried out, tightening her grip around him.

The pace was relentless, his fingers digging into her hips until he knew there would be fingerprint shaped bruises marring the smooth perfection of her skin.

"Do you know how glad I am that you're finally mine in a way I can show the entire world, Gwennie? To know that almost every man in any room envies me because I get to do *this*." He thrust hard on the last word to accentuate it.

She made tiny keening sounds, meeting his thrusts as much as she could in this position.

"Keep your legs where they are," he commanded hotly against her lips, taking one of his hands off so he could slip it between their bodies. She nodded eagerly, and scrunched her nose as she focused on keeping her weight distributed so nothing would change in their rhythm. She looked so glad to have a task and to not just be receiving everything he was dishing out that it made his lips twitch upward into a soft smile. No matter how lost to his darkness he was, she was still adorable, and he was enchanted by her. His fingers slipped to where he knew she wanted them, pressing and stroking with just the right pressure as he kept pounding into her.

"One day soon, when you tell me you are ready, I'm going to quit the barrenflour root."

He reached his other hand down and nestled it between her thighs, his fingers finding her clit. He stroked it, making gentle circles as he kept pounding into her. "And I am going to fucking *love* watching your body swell and change with our child. To show the entire world that you. Are. Mine."

She screamed, and he felt her release, her walls tightening around his cock.

He talked her through it. "That's right, Gwennie. Let go. Let it all go."

She sobbed as the waves kept crashing over her, and it pushed him over the edge with her. The fire and the candles around the room roared to life as her control of her power slipped. He briefly considered covering her mouth, but fuck it. Let them hear what he did to her. She was his now, and nothing could ever change that. He growled hotly in her ear, filling her.

They stood there for several moments, panting against each other, until Gwen's legs grew wobbly and slipped from him. The air ropes released and she wrapped her arms around his neck. Tyreal eased her down, giving her legs a chance to acclimate before carrying her to the bed and gently laying her on it.

"You did so fucking good, sweet girl." He brushed her hair off her forehead and cupped her cheek. "That was beautiful. Are you okay? Did I hurt you?" He suddenly felt nervous. What if he had gone too far and she never wanted to do that again?

"It's good. It's so, so good," she said, smiling blissfully up at him as she cupped his cheek in return. "I feel empty. No anxiety. No fear. Just bliss."

He leaned into her hand, closing his eyes for a beat and allowing himself to soak in the moment. "Let me go get something to clean you up. Then I'm going to hold you for a while. I know we have to go downstairs eventually, but we are going to cuddle until you tell me you're ready."

She nodded. "Get me a glass of water too. My throat is parched from screaming."

He laughed. "Your wish is my command, wife."

CHAPTER THIRTY-TWO

Cora had been far too pleased by Tyreal's safe return to be properly annoyed about having to redo Gwen's hair—which had become a wild, frizzed halo after Gwen tried to magically dry it following their bath and their romp afterwards.

"If it weren't for the fact you've always had a gift for this, I might suspect you've got royal blood," Gwen said with a laugh, watching in the looking glass as Cora tamed another stubborn curl into place. "What you do with my hair is nothing short of magical."

"Well, you *do* give me plenty of practice," Cora replied, twisting the final braid into place. "And judging by the state of it just now, I'd wager

I'll be getting even more. *Someone* clearly can't keep his hands out of it." She cut a sly look over her shoulder at Tyreal, who sat nearby, fully dressed now but relaxed and picking idly at a thread on his sleeve.

"I'm not even sorry," he said with zero shame.

Cora rolled her eyes and tossed the brush at him. "Of course you're not."

Then she turned back to Gwen, her tone softening. "There, now you look like a proper queen again. I think this meeting will go differently. The whole mood of the castle's changed since the events of this morning."

Gwen met her gaze in the glass, Cora's face half-reflected beside hers.

"Let's hope it stays that way," she said with a smile. Then she rose, smoothed the front of her dress, and reached for Tyreal's hand. "Come on," she said. "Time to make history."

Cora was correct. The entire mood of the castle was different, and the library was no exception. It had never felt so alive.

The long table was full of monarchs, as it had been for days, but now other corners of the room teemed with courtiers, scholars, and nobles from across Tavia. A low current of excitement buzzed beneath the surface—hope, maybe, or at least curiosity.

The scribe from Mist Castle held a place of honor, quill at the ready, as she prepared to hopefully record an important moment in Valine's history.

Gwen paused in the doorway, Tyreal beside her, and the hum of polite conversation briefly dipped into silence as everyone noted their arrival. She took a deep breath. The sudden weight of so many eyes sent a ripple of nervous heat through her belly.

What if nothing had really changed? What if the others still saw her as a naïve girl who'd inherited a crown too big for her head? Would arriving on dragon back and showing mercy to Grigor be remembered as power... or weakness?

"You're overthinking again," Tyreal whispered. "You know this is a good plan. They'll see it now."

She gave him a small, grateful smile and forced her spine a little straighter. They stepped inside together and made their way to the center of the table, where two chairs stood waiting for them.

They hadn't quite reached them when a swirl of silk and perfume intercepted their path. Queen Isolde, Anya's mother, grasped Gwen's hand with a dramatic flourish. Per usual, she was a vision of impractical excess. She stood barely five feet tall, but made up for her size with her exuberant wardrobe. Her gown was a cascade of lavender and cream lace, with sleeves that draped around her like wings when she moved. Her powdered hair was piled into a grand tower of curls adorned with pearls, tiny paper roses, and a miniature silver swan perched like a crown. A gilded fan snapped open and closed in the hand not holding Gwen's.

"Your Majesty," she said with enthusiasm. "High Captain. I am so pleased to finally offer my congratulations on your betrothal, and my sincerest thanks for making this historic gathering possible. I know the last few days have been stressful for all of us."

"King Consort," Tyreal corrected, his tone pleasant but firm.

Isolde turned to him, her finely arched brows high on her face in surprise, fan fluttering to a pause. "Oh?"

"Technically," he said with a smile, "King Consort outranks High Captain. I still wear both titles, of course, but protocol matters, doesn't it?"

"Ah! Of course it does," she said, recovering with a dazzling smile. "How delightfully official." She gave his hand a pat that was almost approving, then leaned back toward Gwen. "Do excuse my manners. You look radiant, dear, positively regal. Nothing like my daughter's outfits of late."

Gwen smiled back at the older woman. Isolde was a handful, and she drove her children crazy, but Gwen always had an odd fondness for her. Even after the last few days, which Gwen chalked up more to fear than an actual desire to turn on their alliance, she still liked the queen.

"Mother, please leave them alone. And there is nothing wrong with what I'm wearing," Anya stated, moving closer to the group.

Gwen had to admit, Anya's dress was extremely flattering on her friend. It was the color of dark merlot—rich, with hints of garnet in the right light. The bodice fit close to her frame, low enough to be sensual, but not enough to be flaunting. Her shoulders were bare, the sleeves falling in a gauzy material that hinted at the skin underneath.

Yet again, it was a look that was uniquely hers, not matching the fashion of any one particular court.

Her pale blonde hair was swept back in loose twists and pinned with small, gleaming onyx combs that made her light coloring even more striking. She had smudged just enough kohl along her lash line that her blue eyes seemed an impossible shade.

"Well," Isolde managed after a pause, blinking at her daughter's gown, "a matter of opinion, I suppose. Not sure what court is influencing you to change like this."

Anya didn't flinch, just smiled sweetly. "Perhaps all of them. You raised me to be adaptable."

"I raised you to not slouch and be sweet," her mother sniffed.

"Which I'm doing—just in a better dress."

Several nearby nobles smothered their laughter behind their hands and raised goblets. Even Tyreal gave a quiet snort.

Isolde frowned and narrowed her eyes at her daughter, before turning tightly on her heel and marching off, her fan fluttering indignantly.

Gwen leaned in and hugged her friend with a smile. "You look breathtaking."

Anya gave her a half-smile. "Thanks. I figured if we're rewriting the world, I might as well look like someone who belongs in it on her own terms."

Before Gwen could respond, Max and his parents approached from the other side of the library. Max smiled broadly and leaned in to kiss Anya's cheek. "You look as stunning as ever, wife."

She grinned affectionately at him, but Gwen didn't miss the way her demeanor changed the moment her gaze flicked to King Corven and Queen Solena. The light inside her dimmed and her smile cooled into something more practiced and neutral.

Gwen resisted the urge to sigh. She recognized that shift all too well.

Clearly Grigor's words from earlier about Anya's preferred sexual partners, vile as they were, had taken root. While everyone in the courtyard seemed to have dismissed the man's tantrum as pathetic, that kind of accusation had a way of burrowing in, especially among older monarchs who prized bloodlines, heirs, and reputation above all else.

And now, Gwen wondered, would Max and Anya be forced to explain the nature of their marriage? Would they be expected to justify what went on behind their chamber doors—just to satisfy appearances?

They shouldn't have to. It wasn't anyone's business.

However, if the king and queen became suspicious enough to track Anya's movements, believing she was disloyal to their son, it could get complicated quickly. In their court, a perceived betrayal of one's spouse—especially a royal one—wasn't just scandalous. It was treason.

That was the last thing Anya *or* Max needed.

Max must have noticed Anya's shift as well, or at the very least picked up on the tension coming from his parents, because he moved even closer to his wife and slid his arm around her hip. He tilted his chin up slightly and locked eyes with his father. The message was quite clear, even if it wasn't spoken aloud. They were partners, no matter what or who they were facing.

Gwen cleared her throat to break the tension. "Well, I suppose it's time for us to get to our seats and call this meeting to order. If you'll excuse us," she said with a polite and graceful smile. Tyreal followed her, the pressure of his hand on the small of her back a quiet anchor point. Her nervousness had faded with the interactions between Anya and Max's parents. These were all normal people, just like her. She could face them, just as she'd been trained to do her entire life.

Tyreal pulled out the chair for her, but Gwen remained standing before it, facing the gathered monarchs and dignitaries with her hands folded calmly before her. "Thank you all for coming—*again*," she said, allowing a wry smile to soften her words. There was no sense in pretending everything was completely normal. "I know the last few days have been volatile. We have all been forced to reassess our allegiances, our assumptions, and our fears."

A few chuckles from around the room, and a few glances towards Caldrin, but there was no tension. She was grateful for that.

She stepped out from behind the chair, her voice clear. "The threats we face now are not the kind that respect borders. Magic, dragons, and all sorts of magical creatures have returned to our world. And as we've seen, ambition that hungers for land, control, and unchecked power is still very much alive."

She let her gaze lock with each monarch for a moment, holding their attention, to drive home the importance of her words. "We can no longer afford to face these challenges as isolated kingdoms. Not when one bad actor can destabilize the peace of an entire continent. In the alliance I propose, we will not be reactive, but *proactive*.

We will all commit to preserving peace before war ever has a chance to begin."

A hush fell over the room as they listened intently, so Gwen pressed on. "This will include a deeper and more transparent sharing of intelligence, cooperative patrols of borders and trade routes, and—perhaps most importantly—a rotating oversight council for the Sisters of the Mist. This council will include monarchs, nobles, and commoners alike."

A few brows rose at that, but Gwen didn't flinch.

"Magic affects every person in Valine, whether they wield it or not. So, *every* voice deserves to be heard in how we monitor and guide its use."

She let the words settle before continuing, now more passionate.

"In every kingdom, a new chapter of the Sisters of the Mist will be founded, tasked with identifying and supporting any child who presents with magic—regardless of their family name or social standing. Every child will travel to Mist Castle during the summers to train alongside their peers from across the continent. They will learn control, discipline, and *most importantly*, friendships and alliances. This happened at Mist Castle already with those of us that had the embers of magic and were lucky enough to attend. Now it will be available to all children who present."

A murmur of agreement stirred at the edges of the room.

"Tithes will continue to be paid by each realm to Mist Castle to fund this endeavor, and the Sisters will continue their sacred duty of preserving our histories and keeping our records intact—unbiased and unaltered."

She took a deep breath and stood even taller, happy with what she had laid out, no matter what happened from here. She hoped that somewhere in the Everafter, her parents were watching and were proud.

"This is the foundation of the alliance I now formally offer. It is built from the conversations we've had and the future we can still shape together."

She paused, gaze sweeping across the room one last time. Anya, Max, Eliana, and even Caldrin gave her smiles of encouragement.

"Are there any questions?"

There was quiet for a few moments, just long enough for Gwen to become concerned they were all about to reject her.

Finally, though, King Thalion tapped his fingers on the table and cleared his throat. He glanced over at his daughter, and then back to Gwen. "My concerns were always based on logistics. I think this covers the majority of it. I have some further clarification details I would like discussed, since mine is an island nation and doesn't share any borders, but I am satisfied enough to sign."

Apparently, all it took was for someone to break the silence. One by one, each country agreed.

Queen Isolde fluttered her fan, dramatically dabbing at her eye with a handkerchief. "I never thought I'd see the day I was signing a treaty written by a woman not even thirty summers gone. What a new world, indeed." She looked over at Anya with something a lot like pride, despite her earlier complaints regarding her daughter.

The smile that broke across Gwen's face no longer felt forced. She turned to the scribe. "Can you please read aloud the formal agreement?"

The scribe stood, parchment in hand, and read:

We, the undersigned sovereign rulers of Valine, hereby declare we willingly enter the United Alliance of Valine to foster peace, cooperation, and shared stewardship of magical training across the nations. We agree to the oversight and expansion of the Sisters of the Mist to include the training of magical youth in shared summers of learning, and the creation of an open council representing all walks of life. We pledge to preserve history, prevent armed conflict—be it weapons or magic—and uphold the dignity of all peoples. This accord shall remain open to the thrones of Ravendell and Galeigh, should they wish to join in peace.

The scribe stepped back, laying the parchment on the table beside a deep inkwell and a ceremonial quill with a gleaming gold tip. She offered Gwen a respectful nod and a small smile.

"Your Majesty," she said, "it seems only right that you do the honors."

Gwen approached the table and picked up the ceremonial quill, with its tip of gold, took a deep breath and wrote:

Gwendolyn Thorncrest
Queen of Tavia

She turned, meeting Tyreal's eyes as she offered him the quill. He raised a brow, caught slightly off guard—but then his lips tugged into a proud smile. He squared his shoulders, accepted the quill, and signed just beneath hers:

Tyreal Thorncrest
King Consort of Tavia, High Captain of the Tavian Guard

One by one, the other monarchs followed.

When the last signature dried, no one spoke. They all stood still for a beat, glancing at one another, the magnitude of the moment clear.

The world had just changed.

It wouldn't be perfect. There would be rivalries, disputes, and flare-ups of anger, because humans were messy and proud and flawed. But never in the long, blood-streaked history of Valine had so many sovereigns willingly signed a common accord.

Never before had there been a plan, a real, tangible plan, for shared magical training across borders for all genders. One that would foster friendship and understanding.

For the first time in generations, there was a plan for change.

And if they could hold to it—if they could wrestle chaos together, side by side—then maybe, just maybe…

…this time, the future would be different.

THE END

EPILOGUE

Gwen opened the door of her chambers to step out into the hall. Jameson bowed his head and gave her a salute. "Good morning, Your Majesty. Are you ready to get this wedding ceremony finally done for real?"

"Why yes, captain, I believe I am," she responded with her own matching grin.

They walked past Tyreal's door as they headed out of the wing with the royal suites and made their way to the chapel. She'd made him sleep in his own chamber the night before, which he had been *very* upset about. Not that she listened or cared. She wanted one normal traditional thing, and that was to see his face when she entered and walked down the aisle to him in her ceremonial gown.

They reached the heavy doors to the chapel, and Gwen took a deep breath before smiling at

Jameson one more time. She removed the heavy fur cloak and handed it to him, lifting the hood of her bridal cape. She had to be extra careful, so the delicate white lace didn't snag on the golden leaves and ruby rose of her crown.

She had opted to wear her mother's crown again, the same one she had worn at Tyreal's swearing-in ceremony. It had been their first marriage ceremony of sorts, and it felt wrong to wear anything else, even if it was too large to go with her hood.

She was surprised to see Pip and Hedontas waiting on the other side of the door as it opened. "What are you doing here? The ceremony is supposed to just be the three of us," she asked, confused.

Pip shrugged. "Tyreal thinks that you broke so many rules with your marriage that one more wouldn't hurt."

"Well," Hedontas said with an amused lilt to his voice. "He was a bit more succinct with it than that. I believe he said that he knew you would want the people you cared about most at your side, and that perhaps this was another new tradition you could start."

"What's the difference?" Pip asked, scrunching his nose before yawning.

Gwen laughed and put an elbow out for him.

Hedontas put his hand over hers for a moment, tears shining in the corner of his eyes. "Lorne would be so proud of you, Your Majesty. He always was, but what you've done these last few weeks… It is everything he hoped you would be as a queen."

Gwen's breath caught in her throat, and she felt tears beginning to fill her own eyes. "Thank you, Hedontas. For everything. I know this advisor role is more hands-on than you wanted, but we would have been lost without you."

He glanced at Pip. "Well, it wasn't as bad as I feared. I find the prince has grown on me. I'll still let Jameson handle the day to day, but…"

"He isn't nearly as cranky with me now," Pip finished.

Hedontas chuckled and stepped aside.

Her eyes traveled down the aisle, to where Tyreal stood at the altar with Malcolum, dressed in the formal gold armor her father had made for his swearing-in ceremony. Seemed she wasn't the only one that felt the callback to that day was necessary.

She was surprised to see Max and Andais standing at his side, though. And Anya and Eliana were waiting on hers.

On the nearest benches sat Cook, Tensha, and Cora. And even more of a surprise, Marie. Gwen wasn't sure when or how his mother had arrived, so quickly, but there she sat.

It wasn't how things were normally done. And she could see a moment of nervousness cross Tyreal's face. He knew she had been looking forward to a traditional ceremony.

She grinned broadly at him. This change, surrounding them with the family that had helped them on this path to their intertwined fate, was a welcome one.

His shoulders relaxed at her smile, and he met it with one of his own. She could see a light sheen of tears in his eyes, and they roved over her gown. The bodice was the same delicate lace as the hooded cape, with visible corset boning and tiny pearls intricately stitched in. The waistline went into a deep V over the full white silk underskirt. She had taken a page out of Anya's book and designed a dress that was uniquely for her. She wore no jewels other than her crown, and the whole thing was exactly as she wanted.

Delicate. Graceful. Hers.

Pip walked her down the aisle, and she was thrilled to find new rose petals again lining the walkway from whoever the romantic servant was. She really needed to find out who that was and thank them.

They reached the end, and Pip stood on tiptoe to kiss her cheek, though not nearly as much as he used to have to. He very seriously took her hand and placed it into Tyreal's before returning to his seat.

The dawning sunlight cast through the stained-glass windows and settled over them. Tyreal leaned his head and murmured, "There are not words for how beautiful you look right now, Gwennie. I am the luckiest man alive."

The scene was so drastically different from when she had stood in that spot just a few days prior, that it was hard to find words to respond just then. All she could do was beam and press her forehead to his for a moment.

Malcolum cleared his throat, pulling their attention, but the smile he wore when they both looked at him sheepishly was an affectionate one.

"Well now, I think it is time to finally get you two where you've always been meant to be. The gods and fate certainly took you on an adventure first, but anything less wouldn't have been worthy of your love story."

He handed Tyreal the tool to remove his golden bracelet. "Normally I'd do this myself, but growing older is not kind to the body."

Tyreal made quick work of it, frowning as the band slipped away before handing it to Malcolum. He rubbed a thumb over his bare wrist. "Feels strange without it."

"It will be returned to its proper place soon enough. Now both of you, extend your left hands."

They did as they were told, and Gwen could feel her heart pounding. She glanced around at their loved ones as Malcolum tied the golden cord around their wrists. Everyone looked so happy for them. In fact, Cook looked like her face might break if she smiled any wider. The whole chapel was filled with love.

For a moment, she was struck with sadness, how she wished her parents could be there as well. Then, the sunlight spread across the lace sleeve of her dress, lighting it in brilliant shades of red and gold, and she could practically feel their presence. She knew they were with her, watching from the Everafter.

"Recite your vows in unison," Malcolum instructed.

Tyreal gave her a tiny nod to signal when to start so they'd match up, and she began to speak. "Blood of my blood, flesh of my flesh, I swear to protect you, serve you, guide you, and listen to you. Our union is the will of the Gods, and we will honor them in all we do, in this life and any the gods may grant us from the Everafter."

Malcolum spread their hands just enough to reach in and slice both of their palms with the dagger. Gwen winced. "I seem to be making blood oaths rather frequently. Good thing I know an excellent healer."

Tyreal chuckled. "I promise, I'll kiss it and make it better in just a moment."

They clasped their palms together tightly, letting their blood intermingle. As it had done the day before when Gwen had made the oath with Caldrin, golden light flared around them.

Malcolum made an appreciative sound low in his throat, clearly pleased. He placed their bands on their wrists and stepped back. "By the power given to me by our gods in this temple at their altar, I name you truly, blood of each other's blood and flesh of each other's flesh. What the gods have joined together, may no man tear apart." He stepped back, addressing everyone else in a louder voice. "And now, as the great father and great mother were joined for a year alone in the center of the world as the whole of creation grew around them, so you will be here in our place of worship. I will return in one hour and remove the cord."

Gwen murmured her thanks, but she couldn't tear her eyes away from Tyreal's. Everyone walked by them and whispered congratulations before they left the chapel.

The sound of the door closing behind the last one out echoed through the space. Using their conjoined wrists, Tyreal tugged her even closer, so her body was pressed to his.

"Now then, *wife*... how do you think we should spend an hour?"

Afterword

I hope you enjoyed "Flames of Change"! Tyreal and Gwen's story might be technically concluded, but you haven't seen the last of them. Anya and Max will be up next in book three, and we will travel to Espera. In the meantime, if you'd like to stay in Tavia a little longer, you can get a free short story about Myaessa and Mist Castle by signing up for my newsletter at my website, https://www.daniloughary.com

THANKS

In many ways, your second book is harder to write than your first. You no longer have that "Can I publish a book?" drive. Add in making it a sequel that needs multiple storylines wrapped up, and it gets even more complicated. So, I owe many people a thank you for helping to keep me motivated and on track.

To Katie, Cassie, and Brittany—my incredible beta readers. You were with me on Embers and have pushed me to improve as a writer with every unhinged comment, criticism of my millennial ellipses, and more. I'm sorry I stressed everyone out with Tyreal's disappearance. I hope you all stick with me for every book I ever write.

To Aarika and Emily, for never doubting me. Ever.

To Ryan, for asking me if I was supposed to be writing. A million times.

My amazing editor, Ana. There's something magical when you find someone whose work style fits with your own like a puzzle piece. The perfect balance of praise mixed in with the "hear me out" comments that gently read me for filth. I think you love my characters almost as much as I do, and I cannot thank you enough for it.

For my TMHTTP girlies... no one would have ever guessed we'd still be here five years later. Thank you for always cheering me on.

And lastly, my husband, as always, for everything. In particular lending Tyreal your voice and his trademark "you talk too fucking much". I will love you in this life and the next.

ABOUT THE AUTHOR

Dani is an indie author that made her debut on the romantasy scene with Embers of Fate in February 2025.

Ever since she got pulled into the principal's office for writing stories instead of doing math, she's been obsessed with writing about love and magic.

She lives in Missouri with her husband, two teenagers, and far too many animals. She works a day job in the non-profit sector. Otherwise, you can usually find her with her nose in a book, on social media, or playing The Sims 4 on her overpowered gaming computer.

www.ingramcontent.com/pod-product-compliance
Lightning Source LLC
Chambersburg PA
CBHW022256310726

48973CB00001B/87